SPLINTERED MAGIC OMNIBUS

BOOKS 1-3

JILLEEN DOLBEARE

ICE RAVEN
PUBLICATIONS

Splintered Magic Omnibus
Books 1-3
Jilleen Dolbeare

ICE RAVEN
PUBLICATIONS

Copyright © 2023
Editor: Cissell Ink
Cover Designer: Crimson Phoenix Creations
Interior Art: Rose Rasmussen

JILLEEN DOLBEARE

SPLINTER CAT

Splintercat
Jilleen Dolbeare

ICE RAVEN
PUBLICATIONS

Copyright © 2023
Editor: Cissell Ink
Cover Designer: Crimson Phoenix Creations
Interior Art: Rose Rasmussen

To my very own Mr. Mittens—Gus. Thanks for being an inspiration, and a good boy!

CHAPTER
ONE

I bounced along the rutted drive, going as slow as possible, my nerves jangling. This was a bad idea. Of course, it was a bad idea! Who was I kidding? I tried to take a calming sip of coffee, but it splashed out of the little hole at top and splattered on my favorite blouse. The universe was trying to speak to me. To warn me away.

I clenched my teeth. The universe could go screw itself—where was the universe when I married Evan? There should have been a thunderstorm on our wedding day, or an earthquake, or some other suitable portent to warn me about the cataclysmic mistake I was about to make.

I put the coffee back in the cupholder. I didn't want to drink the lukewarm crap, anyway. Maybe this was a bad idea. Did I really want to take this step? Move out of my comfort zone? Like, really far out of it? Evan had said he'd take me back if I dropped my demands. For the millionth time, my resolution wavered. Evan was all I knew; he was the *easy* choice. But every fiber of my stubborn being knew he wasn't the *right* choice.

Thinking of Evan was a habit, a bad one I needed to break. I couldn't go back to him, couldn't trust him. Besides, *I'd* be the home-wrecker now. He'd gotten the skank pregnant. She'd carried the baby I never could. *Don't be bitter, Brigid, don't be bitter. She* wasn't even pretty. She had youth on her side while mine was fleeing me like a rat from a sinking ship.

The house loomed out of the misty rain, and my breath caught. Grey, decrepit, and depressing. But something in me sang. Oh, the potential! If I squinted, I could see what this place could be. For the first time in I-don't-know-how-long, hope and excitement buzzed in my chest. This could be the start of something special, something amazing, just for me. Screw Evan. *Don't think about Evan, dammit!*

Brush blocked the driveway as it curved around to the back of the house. I would need to hire someone to clear that out so the workers could get in to restore this beast. If it was even possible. The house looked ready to collapse, but even so, the old building *spoke* to me.

I parked next to the realtor's jaunty red hybrid and stepped out. The misty rain decided at that moment to change into a downpour, and I had to run to the sagging porch. Luckily, the old cobbled walkway up to the front of the house was still solid, so I avoided the worst of the mud. I stepped up the old rock stairs and onto the wooden porch. It squeaked under me and had far too much bounce. I frowned at it. Would it hold my weight?

I pushed back my long, damp hair and scanned the porch and the roof above me. Nothing was in good shape. Was it even safe to enter? I blew out a breath. Maybe my optimism a moment ago was delusional. I frowned doubtfully at the building around me. Before I could second guess myself yet again, the front door swung open with a loud squeak. For a moment, I thought it had opened by itself, but then the realtor beamed at me in her dark red power suit and helmet hair. I couldn't judge her. I was rumpled, crumpled, and covered in coffee stains. I summoned my best social smile and continued into my old home.

"Hi, I'm Karen Trask. I talked to you on the phone." She stuck a hand out.

"Brigid Coleman, nice to finally meet you." I stumbled slightly over my last name. I was stuck with it until the divorce was final and I could go back to Donovan, my maiden name. I shook her hand and stepped over the threshold.

It had been twenty-three years since I'd set foot in this house. And the years hadn't been kind to it. You could still see its beautiful bones if you knew how to look, but they were covered by grime and disrepair. The vaulted ceilings, the floors, and crown moldings were exquisite, but they needed sanding, painting, and repair. That's what I saw every-where—repair needed. The realtor used her hands to express her excitement over the "solid structure" and "diamond in the rough."

I smiled wanly. "I grew up here. I lived here the first eighteen years of my life."

I'd told her this on the phone when I'd made the appointment, but she acted as though it were exciting new news.

"Really? That's marvelous!" Then she returned to her spiel.

She was going to give the hard sell to get rid of this slumbering beast and didn't want to be distracted from any of her prepared selling points. I rolled my eyes behind her back. It didn't matter what I said; she had a speech and was on a roll.

We walked up the central staircase. I remembered it as grand and sweeping, and it was, but the carpet that had been a little threadbare in my day was now ripped, stained, and smelled awful. I wrinkled my nose. Maybe renovating this house would be biting off more than I could chew, but something about it called to me and had since the moment this mad idea had popped into my head.

She took us to the third floor. I remembered this climb. I'd loved playing on the massive staircase, pretending I was a princess in a grand castle. Surprisingly, the staircase felt solid under my feet and didn't even squeak. That was a good sign. Relief swept through me; it wasn't total shit.

"The house was built in the 1880s. This town had only been founded in the 1850s, so it was still building into what it is today," Karen droned. "The original owners must have valued their privacy. You've driven the long drive up and know the house is completely hidden from the highway and any neighbors by acres of old growth forest…"

The realtor continued her speech about the house's construction and history. I knew it, so I tuned her out.

Those original owners were my family. The house was a Victorian in the Queen Anne style—she hadn't mentioned that. I snorted a little, then looked up at her, she hadn't noticed.

"...Three stories with a huge turret that stretches the entire height, three grand fireplaces, three original bathrooms, and many rooms." I caught the tail end of her speech.

As we trailed through the third story, Karen opened door after door into empty rooms full of dust and grime and memories. I sneezed. A lot. Suddenly, she froze. I stopped just in time to keep from running into her.

"Sorry," she said with a little breathless laugh. "I can't remember where this door goes." She stared at the door oddly.

I shrugged. "It's the attic."

"Attic?" She had a strange tone in her voice, and she hurriedly swiped through the phone in her hand. "I don't remember there being an attic. It's not listed in the paperwork." She scrolled hurriedly but finally looked up. "Umm, sorry. Just an extra feature left off the listing. It happens occasionally."

I nodded. It seemed like a strange thing to leave off, but I didn't know. I was in computers, not real estate. Evan had handled all our properties. I stopped that thought. No. I didn't need him. Mustn't think of him. I could handle it all myself.

"It doesn't matter," I said kindly. "These things happen."

We continued the tour, and no more mistakes were noted. The house did have good bones. There was potential if you knew where to look. Several walls were full of holes, and the carpets were ripped up in most rooms. It was hard to overlook the mess this place had become. It looked as though the place had been vandalized.

"How long has it been empty?" I asked after another room with holes and ripped-up rugs.

"Just slightly over a year," she answered, obviously uncomfortable.

"How much land is still with the house?" I asked. When we'd moved out, there were only two hundred acres left. My family had sold six hundred acres off to a logging company. I'd been investigating, and the land was back on the market, unlogged. Premium untouched, primordial timber. Almost unheard of. If I bought back the original land, my investment into that would pay for itself *and* the house.

"There are two hundred acres listed with the house," she replied after checking her notes.

What had the previous owners done? It seemed like nothing but an attempted bad remodel and then abandonment. I shook my head.

Before we finished the tour, a driving compulsion almost staggered me. An urgency, a *need*. This place had to be mine. "I want it. I'll b-buy it."

I had the down payment, even without the divorce settlement. We'd done well at our business—very well. I was due half of the business, and although Evan was fighting me, I was going to get my share. The money I had in my accounts would cover this and the lawyer, but if the divorce settlement didn't go through, I'd be dead broke. Saying I'd buy it was a huge risk.

She stopped, surprised. "You will?" She blinked, catching herself. "I mean, great! You will. Fantastic. OK. Umm, we can sign the paperwork at the office."

"Sure." I took one last look around and followed her out to the cars. We drove convoy-style to the office, and I signed the offer papers before I had the chance to change my mind.

Signing the papers felt life changing—like a choir of angels should be singing, complete with a sunbeam shining down on me. I looked up. Nothing. It was mildly disappointing.

I returned to my dingy hotel and parked in the dubious lot. I was staying in a small dive hotel because they took cash. Evan monitored my spending, and every time I used a joint credit card, he'd cancel it. So, I'd applied for all new ones in just my name, but I hadn't yet received any of the new ones in the mail. We were wealthy. *I, not we. I* was unbelievably wealthy, especially once I received what I was due from Evan. The money I spent was miniscule, but still he tried to control it and keep it from me. I was the reason the business had even been successful. Me, not him!

My heart beat hard, and my breath rasped. Great, I was about to give myself another panic attack. I leaned back in the driver's seat and worked to calm down. *Deep breaths, Brigid, you're fine. You can do this. This isn't a terrible mistake. Please* don't let this be a terrible mistake.

Once my breathing was controlled, and my heart had stopped beating out of my chest, I stepped out, locked the doors, and walked into my hotel room. I'd checked in earlier, after I'd arrived and before I'd met Karen at the house. It was old and worn, but clean. The bed was a little saggy in the middle, but if I didn't have to sleep in it for very long, it would be comfortable enough. I hoped the soft mattress wouldn't cause my back pain to flare up. It'd been a fourteen-hour drive to get here from Utah, and my back was tight. I was staying for a week. Hopefully that would be enough time to get the down payment money transferred and to investigate the local restoration companies. I was a woman with a plan.

I threw my bag down and stepped into the bathroom to take off my makeup and change into my pajamas. I was going to lie in bed and watch something trashy on tv—if the tv worked. Just as I was pulling the covers back, someone knocked on my door. Fear washed over me. Had Evan sent someone here to harass me? I wouldn't put it past the bastard.

I swallowed hard and creeped forward, looking cautiously through the peephole. It was blocked. Shit.

CHAPTER

TWO

My heart hammered harder. No one knew I was here besides my best friend Megan, and she wouldn't tell a soul. I clenched my teeth and put my sweaty hand on the doorknob. I twisted, but nothing happened. A spike of fear grabbed me. Then, I realized I'd forgotten to unlock the deadbolt. I flicked it and twisted the knob.

A pizza delivery guy stood outside my door—an older teenager with bad skin, skinny jeans, and a frown. He thrust a red bag at me with the Velcro flap open.

"That's twenty-eight bucks plus tip," he said.

I blinked. "Um, I didn't order a pizza."

"You're Brigid at..." He checked the number on my door and looked at his phone. "Two twenty-three."

I couldn't argue. My name was Brigid, and my room was two twenty-three. I pulled some cash from my bag, paid him, and took the pizza. I was seriously confused. Who'd sent me a pizza?

I relocked the door, a shiver running over me. I set the pizza down on the hotel desk and pulled out my phone.

I opened my text app. "Meg, did you order a pizza and send it to my room?"

"No, why would I? That's weird," she texted back.

"Yeah, that's what I thought."

"Don't eat it. It could be poisoned!"

"Nah, it came from the local pizza joint." I reviewed everything in my mind. The pizza guy had a shirt and hat from the pizza place. I'd followed him out to check that the car had the little placard on top. While he'd slumped down the stairs, I'd checked over the balcony.

"You trust it?"

"The pizza?"

"Yeah, duh."

"Yeah, I just don't know who'd send it."

"Could be a local joke, send pizza to a random place," Megan texted.

"True, but the delivery guy knew my name."

I waited for a moment for the next text.

"Freaky."

"Yeah."

"Watch your back."

"I will. Thanks, night."

Now I was nervous about eating the pizza. I threw open the lid. It looked like a regular old pepperoni pizza. I sniffed it. Smelled normal. I took a piece and ate a tiny bite. It tasted good, so I let it sit in my mouth before I chewed and swallowed. Nothing strange. I waited fifteen minutes. Everything seemed fine, so I ate two slices.

Maybe the realtor had sent it over. But after what she was making on this deal, she should have paid for it. I wonder if she did, and that pizza boy had just double dipped. Probably. I shrugged, turned on the tv, and vegged for the rest of the night—weird pizza experience forgotten.

* * *

MY OFFER WAS ACCEPTED, SO THE NEXT DAY I HAD TO FINISH UP paperwork with the bank and wire over the rest of the offer money. Once that was done, the realtor handed me the keys—relief on her face. She was probably worried she would be stuck with that listing for a long time. Since it was only on the market a few days, she must be dancing in her practical kitten heels. I would have to give the keys back until we closed forty-five days from now, but the sellers had agreed to allow me access for a few days since I was from out of state and needed access for restoration bids. The realtor's office didn't have anyone available to help me in the timeframe I needed—small town issues.

I had one stop, and then I wanted to go back and really look at the house without any interference. I had a couple more days to spend here, and I wanted to see if I could find any keepsakes left in the house —even if it was a long shot.

I pulled up to Whelan Restoration. A pretty blonde girl with bright green eyes sat behind the desk.

"Hi, I'm Madison Whelan. How can I help you?" she asked politely.

"I'm Brigid Coleman. I talked to Craig," I said uncertainly.

"Yes. Craig is the owner."

"Oh, well, I just bought the old Victorian off 101 south of town. The old Donovan place."

She nodded.

"I didn't really have time to talk to him about it much, but I wanted to engage your company to do a full restoration."

"Oh," she said.

"He said someone would be by to look at it."

Madison nodded.

"I have the keys, so…"

"I have you on the calendar. My brother, Luke, will come out and take all the notes and talk to you about timelines and bids." She looked at her notes. "He's scheduled to be out there at three."

"Oh, good! Do I need to fill anything out?"

"Yes." She handed me a packet of paper.

I sat in a comfortable chair and filled out the paperwork. When I handed it back, I asked her, "Do you know when they can start?"

Madison shook her head. "No. It depends on several things. We're also booked out a year, so it could be awhile. But I don't make those decisions. I'll have my dad, Craig, call you."

I nodded and gave her a smile, but my heart sank. A year? I wanted to move in, so I could get out of Utah where my current wreck of a life was and start my new one. I turned and walked out, trying to control the tears that threatened to overwhelm me.

Truth was, I wanted to start my new life now. I guess I needed more time. The divorce wasn't final, the money stuff hadn't been finalized, so I tried to convince myself a year wasn't that big of a deal. I took a calming breath and swallowed back the tears. I was on my own, but I could do it.

I climbed in the car. Time to go look at the property without interference.

It was raining, as was common on the Oregon coast. I drove south out of my hometown of Kilchis and pulled onto Highway 101—the Pacific Coast Highway. The old driveway was really hard to see, and I almost drove past it. Luckily, when I slammed on my brakes, no one rear-ended me.

The house didn't look any better today under the droopy grey sky. I shuddered. Did I want to do this? I gathered my courage and nodded. Yes. It was mine—back in the family after twenty-three years. We should never have gotten rid of it—although I didn't really blame my mom. She'd lost her mother-in-law and her husband, and with no income, a teenager, and a huge house, she probably didn't feel she had a choice. I turned off the car, gathered the new keys, and walked up to the porch.

Before I turned the key, something brushed against my leg. I jumped. Then, I saw what had startled me and relaxed. Just a cat. I did a doubletake. He looked identical to my childhood cat. It couldn't be! I shook my head, no. No cat lived that long; it must be a descendent of my childhood cat from long ago. The cat was looking up at me, waiting. I reached out and petted its head; it leaned into me.

"You're gorgeous," I said. It was a huge long-haired cat with blue-grey points, front white mittens, and large, luminous, periwinkle blue eyes. "Well, come on inside outta the rain," I said, inviting it in. The cat followed me in.

It was gloomier inside today than the day before. But when I flicked the switch, the lights came on and with them, the warm and welcome feeling I remembered from this house filled me. Calm washed through me, and I sighed in relief. I wandered through the first floor as I pictured what I wanted to do with the house.

The large entrance soared up to the top of the third floor, all open. On each side was a room. On the right was a spacious room along with a turret, and on the left was another nice sized room. It would have been used as the parlor or a library in the days of my great-grandmother. The entry took up most of the main floor space. Behind the grand staircase was the pantry and a spacious kitchen. I wanted to turn the turret room into a main bedroom suite, the pantry into a main floor laundry, and redo the kitchen. Maybe I could convince the new restoration team to complete that first, then I could move in while they finished the rest.

The cat kept pace and followed me. I kept looking at it oddly. Its fur seemed strangely luminescent, almost glowing. I blinked. That was stupid. It probably just had a healthy coat. It marched alongside me, more like a dog than a stray cat. Every once in a while, I'd bend and give it a pat, enjoying its company.

We climbed to the second floor. This was where my family had our bedrooms growing up. My parents had the larger room in the turret. That would have been the master bedroom when the house was built, and it had remained so. It had a grand fireplace to match the one below and the best view.

The bathroom for this floor was in between my room and my parent's old room. I planned to add more baths and combine some rooms to make fewer rooms that would be more spacious and useful than now. Again, I noted the destruction to the walls and carpets. The realtor had said that the past owners had started a renovation, but this looked more like vandalism. I shrugged it off. It didn't matter now. I'd have to replace all the wiring and plumbing to bring the place into the twenty-first century, so all the walls would likely be stripped, anyway.

The cat meowed at me, and I looked at it, startled. "What, boy?" I asked, then I felt stupid. As dog-like as the cat had acted, it wasn't *Lassie*. I didn't know what sex it was, but it felt male. I figured I'd just think of it that way.

Then, I heard the knock. I looked back at the cat; it had obviously heard a car or someone approaching. I glanced at my phone. Crap, it was already three, and one of the Whelans was meeting me. I gave the cat a pat and went downstairs to let them in.

I opened the door, and a handsome if rugged looking man stood there. He was dressed casually in jeans, a t-shirt, and a baseball cap.

"Hi, I'm Luke. My sister told you I was coming out to have a look."

I nodded and waved him in. "I'm Brigid. Thanks for coming over. I just bought it, and I want it fully restored. I have ideas for changes as well."

He took off his cap and smoothed his honey blonde hair. He nodded, looking around. "It's in rough shape, but the structure appears sound. I won't know for sure until the engineer looks at it."

We walked through, and I explained what I wanted. He took a lot of notes and measurements, told me he'd have to have a whole slew of others come in and do the same, and then he'd get me an estimate. I nodded, told him I'd drop off a set of keys to the office, and he left.

A few moments after the door shut behind him, there was another knock. Thinking it was Luke returning to grab something he forgot, I opened it with a smile. It wasn't Luke. Standing in front of me was the woman who had finished off my marriage—Vanessa.

CHAPTER
THREE

I was stunned into silence. What was she doing here? My mouth was open, so I closed it with a click of my teeth.

She was humming, and a shiver followed by goosebumps washed over me.

"What do you want?" I asked, coldly, hand still on the door. Only burning curiosity kept me from slamming it in her homely face.

She smiled. Her bright red lipstick emphasized her sneer. I'd never found her attractive, but something about her had men panting, including my soon-to-be-ex-husband. She had a heart-shaped face, mousy brown hair, hazel eyes, and a mouth that was too wide for her narrow chin. Her eyes were wide and large. Maybe that was the draw. She could do "helpless fawn" effortlessly. She did have a great figure, and her belly had snapped right back to flat after she had Evan's baby. She knew how to dress herself as well. Tight, low cut, lycra dresses that hugged her tiny waist and focused the eyes on her impressive cleavage. I hoped her thong chafed.

Really, I should thank her. I'd been in an emotionally abusive relationship for so long, I'd become a timid shadow of myself. I should be grateful Evan slipped and his penis fell into her. Because finding out about his skanky, pregnant, secretary sidepiece was the final straw that not only broke the camel's back but gave me the push I needed to get out.

I plastered on a fake smile to match hers. I raised my eyebrows when it took her a moment to answer.

"Stay away from Evan," she hissed. Then, she went back to humming her song. Frankly, she couldn't carry a tune. Her song was flat.

I was confused. I *was* staying away. The divorce was in the final stages, and I'd just bought a house two states away. Not my fault Evan had tried to get me to come back.

"What?"

"Stay away, or I'll make you pay."

I laughed. "Are you nuts on top of being a home-wrecking whore?" I might have said that out loud, but I *for sure* thought it.

Her expression didn't change, so I probably just thought it.

"You're safe. You can have him," I said and went to shut the door.

She sneered and shoved the door open. I had two inches and twenty pounds on her, and she moved me with the door. I gasped in shock.

She hummed a few more notes. It was weird.

"You aren't listening. You stay away from him, you stay away from his business, and his money," she spat out.

That was too far. She could have Evan—he was no prize—but I'd built that business, and half of everything was mine. Both legally and ethically. Frankly, more than half was mine, since my money had been invested to start it, and my ideas had been the start of everything.

I wedged my foot behind the door so she couldn't push it open further. "I'll take what's mine. You can have the rest with my blessing," I said magnanimously with a sweep of my arm. "Now, get off my porch, or I'm calling the cops. I'll have them charge you with trespassing and harassment."

I pulled out my phone, swiped it open, and punched in 911. She backed up, frowning. She actually looked a little confused. I slammed the door. Good riddance. I couldn't believe she'd followed me out of state for this stupid spat. How insecure must she be? Plus, how had she found me? I just barely signed the papers. I doubted the paperwork had even been filed yet. Knowing Evan, he probably had a tracking device on my car. I heard her wheels kick up gravel as she raced down the driveway. I shook my head and tucked my phone back into the pocket of my jeans.

When I turned, the cat was waiting, a look of concern on his grumpy face. I patted him again. I'd have to get some cat food if he was going to hang around. Once I was sure Vanessa was off the driveway and gone, I let the cat out, locked up, and headed back to my hotel.

* * *

I LOCKED MY HOTEL ROOM DOOR BEHIND ME. BUT WHEN I TURNED around, I gasped. My room had been tossed. I mean thoroughly gone through, and everything was in shambles. My suitcase was emptied and clothes thrown everywhere. My bed had been flipped, and both mattresses were lying on the floor. My makeup bag was emptied in the sink, and my toothpaste had even been opened, and the contents emptied—all over my makeup. Red spray paint spelling out "bitch," among other lovely words, was all over the room, the mirror, the shower.

My heart raced. It had to be Vanessa. Who else would do this? She'd used the pizza guy to verify I was in this room. The crazy bitch! Plus, I don't know how else she'd have found out where my house was. My copy of the paperwork was strewn all over the room. It was malicious. I didn't have anything to steal. She'd done this out of spite and to find my new house.

I called the hotel management. They were very kind and set me up in a new room. They called the cops since the room had also been vandalized.

By the time I'd met with the cops and picked up anything that wasn't damaged, my shakes had stopped, and my heart had finally gone back to its normal beat. I called Megan, my best friend, and told her what had happened.

"That homewrecking ho," she said.

I giggled a little because that was exactly what I thought of Vanessa. And because my nervous energy was still hanging on.

"Boy, do those two deserve each other," she finished.

I sighed.

"Sorry, Bridge. But you know Evan isn't worth any of this hassle. He's despicable and proved it by hooking up with that...that...floozy!"

"Floozy?" I laughed for real this time. "Where did you get that old word from?"

"Pssh. I'm a wordsmith." I could picture her brushing me away with her hand.

"Since when?"

We both laughed. I knew she just couldn't think of a word bad enough for Vanessa and plucked something obscure from her memory. She did like to read, but we both knew no one considered her a "wordsmith."

The laughter died down, and we were quiet a moment.

"What are you going to do?" she asked.

"I already talked to the cops, and they are reviewing the camera footage from the hotel. Unfortunately, they just have one exterior camera, and it only films the view by the office entrance. I told them about Vanessa threatening me, and they said they'd look into it, but I don't have much hope that she'll get in any trouble."

"Aren't there laws against stalking?" Megan asked.

"I'm sure there are, but I doubt one confrontation equals stalking to the law."

"Well, I'm gonna research it. I'll let you know."

I smiled. She was the kind of ride or die friend everyone should have. She'd look it up, and if the cops weren't doing their part, she'd harass them until they did.

"Thanks, Megan. I feel better."

"Love you."

"Love you, too!"

She was still working at my ex-business for my soon-to-be-ex-husband, and he wasn't making it easy for her. He wanted to force her to quit to hurt me because he couldn't find any good reason to fire her, so he'd just been making her life miserable instead. As soon as I got this place together, I'd beg her to come to Oregon with me.

I was tired, so I ordered some food and climbed into bed. I'd already gathered up my things and tossed them into my suitcase. I hoped Vanessa's little fit had satisfied her need to hurt me.

CHAPTER
FOUR

I had extra keys made to give to the Whelans and dropped them off. Once the restoration began, the doors and locks would be changed, or at least re-finished, but until then, I needed the doors kept locked to keep out vandals and treasure hunters since the house had been empty for over a year. Actually, looking at it, I had a hard time believing anyone had lived here since we'd left, but that's what the realtor had told me. I shrugged; it didn't matter.

Since the realtor hadn't shown me the attic, and I hadn't had a chance to look at it when Luke was here—I'd stayed out of his way—I decided to go have a look. The door stuck some, and I had to yank it open. The interior stairs were clogged with cobwebs and dust. Hadn't the last owners ever come up here? There was a single bulb, and it didn't give much light, but the view that I did have showed the attic was full and looked the same as the last time I'd seen it right before we'd moved. I shook my head. I didn't know what to do with all this dusty stuff, so I walked back out, chagrined. Why hadn't they sold all this stuff off? A mystery.

I didn't have much left to do here and only one more day left in my stay, but the house was so welcoming, and I yearned to be living here already. It was hard to make myself leave. While I fantasized about what the place would be like after the restoration, I heard a meow and looked down. The cat was back. I frowned. I hadn't let him in. Was there a hole somewhere? A broken window?

I remembered that I'd picked up a couple of cans of cheap cat food.

"Come on kitty. I have a treat for you."

He cocked his head at me, looking for all the world as though he listened and understood. He followed me into the kitchen. I took the tins out of my bag, and opened one for him, and placed it on the dusty floor. He gave me a decidedly disgusted look, sniffed at it, and batted the tin with his paw. He kept glancing at me as though I was going to pull a full turkey dinner out of my bag, and when I didn't, he gave up and ate the offered food.

"Picky, aren't you?" I asked, but why a stray would be picky was beyond me. He probably ate well in the woods. Lots of wildlife. He was fancy for an outdoor cat though. It would be difficult for a long-haired cat in the wild. He must struggle to keep his cream-colored fur pristine. I took a picture of him and googled other cats like him. It didn't take long.

"Huh, you are a blue-mitted Ragdoll, a popular and expensive breed," I told him. He made a noise that sounded for all the world like a human, "Hmpf."

I laughed and gave him a few ear scratches. He flopped over onto his back, and I also gave him a good belly rub. Weird cat. You'd think he'd be feral. That made me think. Had he been dumped? Was he a housecat someone got tired of caring for? I'd petted him all over, and his body felt firm and muscular, not skinny or underfed. Maybe he had wandered over from the neighbors a few miles away. I should see if someone was missing a very fancy, expensive cat. I'd look when I got back to my computer at the hotel.

"I'm going to take a walk, cat. I'll see you later."

I exited through the back kitchen entrance and observed the over-grown parking area. It wouldn't be hard to restore, although, it needed the brush knocked back and to be paved or re-graveled. I quickly found the old trail to the waterfall—my favorite place to go when I was a girl.

It was my secret haven. It was a bit of a walk, although I'd skipped or run there in my youth, so it couldn't have been too far.

I was wrong. It was a hike. To my surprise, the cat followed me, so I greeted him and continued on my way. I passed the spring, ran my finger through it in delight, and took a long drink of the sweet, pure water. When I turned the corner on the trail and saw the waterfall, it took my breath away.

Surrounded by rhododendrons and ferns, the small pool at the bottom glowed in a beam of sunlight. Moss and grass softened the banks, and a few large boulders rimmed it. I sat on my favorite boulder. I used to come here and write and draw as a kid. In fact, my cat would sit on the other boulder just like this one was doing. I sighed and got caught up in my memories.

I'd had a wonderful boyfriend before we moved, one I thought I'd share my life with. But he'd left for medical school, and I'd moved away, and we lost track of each other. My life would have been a whole lot happier if I'd gone that path. Oh well. I guess that was the pang of nostalgia—a loss and a promise that was never fulfilled.

I gazed at the gently rippling water that gathered in a pond below the falls. My face reflected back at me. Still pretty for forty. My eyes were a deep blue, my hair, which I considered my best feature, was still long and lustrous. It blazed red in the sun, although it looked closer to auburn indoors. I pushed it back and braided it out of my way. It wouldn't stay that way for long without a hair tie, but it was curly enough to stick in the braid for a time.

The sun warmed me, and the scent of water and greenery filled the air. This place filled my batteries. I'd forgotten how much I loved it here. I leaned back on my elbows and watched the sun glint off the water and the spray from the falls. Little rainbows coalesced in places. I smiled.

You shouldn't come here without my protection. A growly deep voice rattled through my thoughts.

"What?" I sat up straight. I must have been dreaming or drifting off. No one was around.

I looked at the cat. He blinked at me, his luminous eyes serious.

"Was that you?" I teased.

Yes.

This time, I shot up off the rock and faced the cat. "No. That isn't possible. You aren't speaking to me."

I am. We don't have much time, so listen, the cat said.

"No, no. This is nuts. I'm going back."

I turned to leave, but he stopped me.

You won't be able to hear me once we leave this place, he said. *So please stay and listen.*

I paused. He was a cat. Just a fluffy housecat that talked. *Talked.* I was crazy. Evan and his side piece had finally pushed me over the edge. What did it matter if I stayed and listened? It was all in my head, anyway.

I'm not a voice in your head. I'm a Splintercat. Your protector, sent here to protect your great-grandmother, your grandmother, your father, and now you. You are in great danger.

Danger? From what? A pissed-off secretary? A restoration? I could handle those. Well, the police and I could.

"What could I possibly be in danger from?" I finally responded to the cat.

That woman that came to the house yesterday is a Siren, he said.

"A Siren? Like from the *Odyssey*?"

He blinked at me. Right, cat. He didn't read. Or did he? He talked? But he didn't answer, so I tried another tact. "Umm, like a mermaid that lures men in with her voice and drowns them?"

I don't know about merpeople, but Sirens are sentient creatures that can shift into a human form. They are large and birdlike and use their voice to control humans. Males of your species are particularly favorite targets for Sirens. They are nasty business and usually use up their chosen mates before moving on. But they are extremely possessive until then. This one appears to have fixated on you. It won't stop until you are dead.

Man, this hallucination was getting complex. I must have been really disturbed by Vanessa's crazy act yesterday.

"So, she's going to try to kill me?" I asked.

Will you give her all that you own and stay away from her mate?

"I'm not giving her shit. I earned half of everything, more than half, and I'm taking it back," I replied stubbornly, but in reality, it all depended on the court and who had the better lawyer.

Then, yes. She will try to kill you. You only have access to your magic in this place, unless you can find and reintegrate it soon. This is the place of your power, where your land is linked to the land of Faerie, and the magic flows between worlds.

Ok, this was a really complicated hallucination. Go, subconscious! No way could magic be real. Thinking about the possibility made my heart flutter alarmingly, and my hands sweat. Magic just wasn't real. No way. That meant I was asleep, hallucinating, or crazy. Could someone be all three? I shook my head.

"So, what should I do? I can't hang by the waterfall; I'm going back to Utah tomorrow."

He cocked his head, thinking. *You must defeat her here. On this land. Take her magic so she can't defeat you. Kill her if you can.*

"Kill her?" I scrambled down off the boulder. Brushing off my jeans and backing away from the cat. "I'm not a murderer! I'd go to jail. That's enough, subconscious, I'm waking up." I waved dismissively at the cat.

He blinked again, confused. *I am right here. You are not asleep. Listen.*

"Nope. I've had enough."

I turned and headed back to the house. The cat made an exasperated noise, but he dutifully followed.

CHAPTER
FIVE

T alking cats, Siren mistresses. My subconscious really was working on me. I couldn't believe I fell asleep and had such a weird dream at the waterfall—that was the only explanation I could come up with—I'd fallen asleep. Which was dumb. The woods were all around, and I knew we had dangerous animals that lived there —bears, cougars, wolves. Okay, I wasn't sure about wolves in coastal Oregon, but there could be. Anyway, it was a stupid dream. Telepathic cats. I had no idea how I came up with that.

I was still berating myself when I walked off the trail and into my backyard. A truck was parked in the back, in what was the parking area. I stopped in surprise. The brush had choked off the access around the house, but when I looked, it was gone. I hurried up to the truck, to see what was going on. It was a white work truck with "Whelan Restoration" stamped on the side along with their logo. It looked like some kind of stylized animal, maybe a wolf?

Luke was sitting on the back stairs, a pile of brush neatly stacked in an open area.

"You didn't have to do that!" I exclaimed, surprised.

He shrugged. "It's no big deal. Several people are coming through here in the next week or two to assess the house, and there's no parking. This was an easy fix."

"Goodness," I said embarrassed. "Let me pay you. I was going to have someone come clear this and improve the driveway before you started."

He waved me away. "We'll add it to the bill."

"Does that mean you're going to start soon?" I asked.

"I don't decide that, but the people coming will work up the bids, and that will help my dad decide on a starting date." He stood and brushed off his jeans. "I couldn't get you on the phone, but I wanted to let you know before I left."

"Thanks!" I didn't know what else to say. He gave a quick wave and climbed back into his truck.

So far, I'd been impressed with the Whelans. They were really on top of stuff. I did feel bad that Luke had to clean up my driveway, but it gave me the impetus to call people to improve the drive and parking area. The workers needed to be able to get here and park safely. I needed to return to the hotel and start working.

Before I did that, I decided to take another run through the house. I wanted to relish a moment of pleasure knowing it was mine and would soon be magnificent again. Surprisingly, the cat followed me closely. My stupid daydream may have been because he'd attached himself to me in a short amount of time. I made a mental note to check the local vet and newspapers to locate his owners. A cat like this had to belong to somebody.

I took my last look and went to lock up. Since I'd parked out front, I locked the back door first. Looking through the dirty window, I thought I saw a car and wondered if Luke had come back for something. I opened the door right as Vanessa barreled up the stairs and shoved me into the kitchen. I tripped over the cat, backing up, and landed painfully on my rump.

"Ow!" I yelled, as pain shot up my spine and blinded me for an instant. "What the hell!"

Vanessa stood over me, a creepy smile on her too-wide mouth. Then she opened it and started to sing.

The sound wasn't pleasant. It was screeching, fingernails on the chalkboard and grinding metal all at the same time, and I flinched. The sound seemed to rattle my bones. It pierced my skull and caused stabbing pain. I tried to stand and found I couldn't move. Worse, my legs had pinned the cat, and he struggled to get free. I felt terrible. I could have crushed him when I fell. I'd probably injured him. He was a fraction of my size. My legs were immobile though, and the cat wasn't making much progress. All I could do was follow Vanessa with my eyes.

She came in and shut the kitchen door. Her song didn't stop. I wondered what would happen when she took a breath. Would it free me? Was my dream not a dream? Was this…magic? My head was swimming, mostly from the horrible song, but I was also scared. Vanessa had crazy shining out of her eyes, and no matter what was holding me down, I was at her mercy. I had no doubt she wanted me dead.

I tried to speak. "S..s..stop," I managed to mumble. I guess I could move a little, at least my mouth.

She sang louder, and my mouth clamped shut. Dammit. She was controlling me. I focused my will, and this time I got more out. "You can't hurt me. I already called the police after you destroyed my hotel room."

Her eyes blazed, and she leaned over me and slapped me across the face. My eyes watered with pain, and my face burned. The cat kept squiggling around under my legs. I could feel it pulling itself a centimeter at a time out from under me. I had no doubt a housecat could eat a dead human, but I had no idea what even a large housecat could do to a fully functional one. I concentrated on lifting one of my legs. At least one of us should be able to escape.

My toes wiggled. Vanessa took her bag off her shoulder and started rifling through it, continuing her song and throwing glances my way. She pulled things out and placed them on the old oak table that had been there for as long as I could remember. Apparently, the last owners hadn't wanted to take it with them. It was too massive and heavy.

Once she'd taken out what she wanted, she turned her attention back to me. With surprising strength, she grabbed me under the arms and hefted me into a sitting position. The movement finally freed the cat, who leapt away. She repositioned and dragged me up onto the table. I was limp, unmoving.

"Run, cat," I screamed, since it was all I could do. Plus, I remembered him speaking to me at the waterfall. Maybe he could do something since he'd claimed to be my protector. He could find help.

Instead, he stomped into the now open space next to the table, and right before our eyes, he transformed into a gigantic monster. Vanessa took one look at him and backed away. Her song stopped, and I sat up.

The cat was probably more than four hundred pounds. He was tawny with spots like a jaguar. His head was massive and round, and his mouth was full of long fangs that hung below his jaw like a saber-toothed tiger. Only he didn't look like he came from this planet. His back sloped like a hyena, and his claws looked like razors. He roared at Vanessa, and she ran out of the kitchen and through the back door. She screamed a sound at the cat, and when he attempted to bound after her, he slammed into a solid wall and fell to his side. I got up, slid off the table, and backed away.

I tried to sneak out of the kitchen in the other direction, but when the cat couldn't get out, his head swung to me. I threw up my hands and kept backing up.

"Stop!" I yelled, like that would help.

The cat stopped.

Huh. "What are you?" I mumbled, not expecting an answer.

I'm a Splintercat. I told you. I'm your protector.

I tend to babble when I'm terrified, so I kept talking. "I thought you couldn't speak to me away from the waterfall?"

Only in this form, and only on this land. If you regain your magic, we'll be able to speak in any form at any time.

"Oh." I stopped backing up. "What's a Splintercat?"

There was a crash of glass from the front of the house.

Hmpf. I will explain after we defeat the Siren that is trying to kill you.

"Right, that's a good idea." I'd worry about my mind and its

32

colorful hallucinations later. Maybe this was a dream or a nightmare, but until it was over, and Vanessa defeated, I'd go with it.

"What do we do? I don't have any magic. Do you?"

He blinked at me—the same periwinkle gaze he had in his smaller form. *This is the extent of my magic. I transform, I'm resistant to most magic, I heal quickly.*

"What can Sirens do?"

I'm not sure about the full extent, but depending on their strength, anything. As long as they can make a sound, they control a wide range of powers.

"So, if she comes back, we need to shut her up?"

Yes.

I looked around. There wasn't anything in this house but dust, destruction, and cobwebs. I looked at the table. Vanessa's bag and the things she'd laid out were still there. She'd put out a series of knives. Knives! Was she planning to slit my throat? I froze, staring.

This was getting too real. I swallowed. How did I stop a creature with infinite magic with only a cat? He was an impressive cat, but still. She'd stopped him easily enough. I hoped I woke up from this nightmare before I died in my sleep. Did that happen, or was it an old wives' tale? Who knew, but I still didn't want to die no matter if this was real or not. Solid plan. Don't die.

I picked up a knife. I didn't know what to do with it, but its solidity felt comforting in my hand. I had something to fight back with. Now, how did I keep her quiet? A gag? Did I have anything to use as a gag? I looked around, nothing. Did gags really shut people up? Not really. She'd still be able to make sound. I'd have to knock her out or shove something so far down her throat she'd choke. Could I kill someone? I didn't think so. I mean maybe—she was trying to kill me, but that wasn't really something I'd ever thought I'd have to do. I doubted I could go through with it.

The front door rattled, and another windowpane crashed to the floor. She was either throwing a fit or trying to lead off the cat.

So, I'd hit her over the head. With what? There were a lot of loose house pieces around. Maybe there was a board. I started searching for something large enough I could clunk her over the head with it.

"I'm gonna find a board," I told the cat. He either ignored me or was busy with his own planning because he was stalking through the house, going window to window—trying to track her passage as she broke windows and scratched and pounded on the exterior walls.

I shoved the knife carefully in the back of my pants and ran upstairs—where I remembered the biggest mess was—and started sorting through debris. I picked up a good-sized board. Maybe three feet long, solid. I hefted it. *Yep. This works*.

I flew down the stairs. Three steps from the bottom, the front door blew open, and Vanessa floated in. She had transformed. Still vaguely humanoid, she had narrow bright peacock blue wings, her face was still hers, but more *bird*. She was still wide-eyed, but her nose was more beakish than human. Feathers framed her face and formed her hair. Her blouse was torn, and her breasts were bared, but a light blue down dusted her skin, lightening to the middle of her chest, which was white. Was this her Siren form? She was hideous.

She opened her mouth, and the awful sound poured forth. My body froze on the stairs, but my momentum didn't. Because I was partway down them, I over-balanced and tumbled the last steps to the bottom.

CHAPTER
SIX

I landed on the hard floor, the breath knocked out of me. I gasped, unable to get my breath, and pain shot through me. I'd have doubled over, only I couldn't, which made getting air into my lungs harder. After what seemed like several moments, I finally gasped. Cool air filled my lungs, and I sobbed with joy.

Where was the cat? I could still move my eyes, so I scanned around me. There wasn't a lot I could see, so he could be anywhere. He seemed intelligent. Maybe he was smart enough to hide. Cats were ambush hunters, right? I sure hoped so.

The Siren beat her wings and lifted into the space in the grand foyer. I wished the space in the entrance were smaller right now, because even though she still wore her skinny jeans, where her shoes should have been were enormous bird talons. And I don't mean little songbird talons. Nope, more like an eagle or other bird of prey. I guess she no longer needed knives.

She was scanning the space. Ah, worried about the cat. I used her distraction to try to move my limbs. The cat had told me I had magic. I didn't know what he meant about reintegrating it, but I'd worry about that later. Right now, I had to get free. I concentrated on moving my hand. If I could reach the knife, maybe I could do something. I was lucky that while falling down the stairs, I hadn't stabbed myself since I'd shoved the knife into the back of my pants like a dumbass. Who knew—maybe I did cut myself. I was in pain. I assumed it was from falling.

Not important. I was still breathing, so I wasn't dead. Injuries would heal. *Move hand!* I shouted in my mind. A streak moved in the corner of my eye. The cat? Vanessa's voice stuttered. Using that instant to move, I sat up and grabbed the knife before she could trap me in the spell again.

My movement caught her eye, and with a single note, she froze me again. I wanted to scream in frustration. If I was magical, as the cat claimed, why couldn't I break free?

A tawny streak flashed by my gaze. The Siren screamed, and another window shattered. I flinched. I was free again. I jumped up and ran for the space behind the stairs. I needed to be out of her vision, her reach. I heard snarls, and discordant music but nothing was aimed at me. The cat had her full attention.

I peered around the stairs. The Siren had her talons sunk into the cat's back. Blood gushed down his sides, and he screamed. My heart pounded. I didn't want him hurt defending me. The Siren beat her wings, attempting to lift the cat in the high-ceilinged foyer. He was large and densely muscled, but he might have been heavier than she'd anticipated because she only lifted him a couple of feet off the ground before he tore free. Then with a bound, he leapt up and snagged Vanessa out of the air. They rolled around the floor, slashing and biting.

My adrenaline was off the charts—my heart beat so hard I was afraid it would explode out of my chest. My head swam. I needed to do something. I ran out and slashed at her wing. I hit meat, because blood sprayed, and she screamed a paralyzing note that caused my right eardrum to rupture. It felt like a spike had been driven through my head, and warm sticky blood poured out and down my neck. She thrashed harder, drawing more blood from the cat, but he had a solid grip on her arm with his teeth, and he kept pulling her off balance. I stumbled away.

He pulled her down to her knees. Once she was down, he released her for a better hold, but she anticipated and shot back, her powerful hind legs throwing her six feet away. He growled, and pounced, but she rolled. She desperately looked for an escape. The front door or the back door were her two choices, but the front door was a lot closer.

If I wanted this to end, I needed to help. I saw what she was going to do. She'd never been the brightest of Evan's secretaries. She was going to lurch left to draw the cat away, and then shoot to the door. I needed to be there to stop her, so the cat could finish her off.

She moved to the left, and I rushed to the door, right past Vanessa and the cat. Just as I passed her, she lunged for the door. I was there first. Standing in front of it, I stabbed out with the knife. I struck something. I felt solid flesh give. Then a wing clipped me and sent me sprawling. But I'd slowed her down and prevented her from disappearing out the door. Most importantly, it gave the cat time to snag a better hold.

"Don't kill her!" I yelled at the cat, impulsively.

He hesitated, but they continued to roll across the floor, spitting, and screeching.

I should want her dead, but she had a new baby—no baby should have to grow up without a mama. And while there was no way in hell I'd take the lying, cheating, no-good bastard back, Evan had been my husband for eighteen years. I didn't want to be the cause of him losing his baby mama—even if I hated her and she was trying to kill me.

That was a good point. She was literally a monster. Huh, I should rethink my priorities. I thought for one second. Damn. I still didn't want to kill her—crazy as she was. Now to convince her to leave. The cat was doing his best, but she was tough. She dripped blood, as was the cat, but her fury was out of control. I looked around for the board I'd brought down the stairs. It was still where I'd dropped it when I fell. That meant I had to slip around the savage fight, snag the board, and clunk the right creature in the head. Since the fight was so brutal, and the combatants were rolling around, I didn't know what my chances were, but I'd worry about it after I got the board.

I moved when they moved. If the fight went left, I went right. It took a few rounds, but I finally made the stairs and rushed up the three steps to the board. I grasped it and clambered back down. Vanessa was on top this time. She had the cat by the throat with her hand, one set of talons securely on the ground, the other set around the cat's belly. I swallowed, one move, and she'd rip his guts out.

I screamed and swung with all my might at the back of her head. I connected, the board striking her head making a hollow sound. She dropped like a stone. I fell to my knees, panting. The cat rolled out from under her and licked his wounds. I watched them heal before my eyes. That was a nifty trick.

In her sleep, the Siren reverted back to her human form. It must be a defense mechanism to keep them undetected.

I checked her pulse. It was strong and steady. I breathed a sigh of relief that I hadn't brained her. Either she was particularly hard-headed, or Sirens were extremely tough. I didn't have anything to tie her up with, so I used the knife to cut free the cords on the window blinds and bound her hands and feet as tightly as I could. I was starting to come down off the adrenaline, and by the time I was done, I was sweating and shaking uncontrollably.

The cat lay on his side, panting. He was a mess of cuts and blood-soaked fur.

"Cat, are you OK?" I asked.

I am healing. Her wings had razor edges, he said.

"They did?"

She'd caught me with a wing. I looked down. She'd slashed me from shoulder to hip. Blood flowed. It'd already soaked through my clothes. How had I missed that? I blinked at it, confused. How hadn't I felt a wound this size? I put my hands to the slice. Damn. She'd cut right through my best bra. That was expensive. I blinked again; I was looking at the ceiling. It was really far up there. How was I going to change the bulbs in the chandelier? How did I get on the floor?

Brigid? I heard a small voice in my mind. *Stay with me!*

And that was all.

CHAPTER
SEVEN

I think I remember seeing trees. Just trees, swaying in a gentle summer breeze, their tops alight in the sun. Then, I heard water flowing. It was so peaceful. This had to be heaven. Did I deserve to go to heaven? I didn't know. I wasn't particularly religious. What was heaven? Why could I only hear water from one ear? My eyes snapped shut.

When my eyes opened again, I could see flowers. I must be in heaven. It smelled lovely, the sky was so blue, the trees and flowers so well, heavenly. Yes. I had died, and I was in a better place.

Then, I remembered. I'd been bleeding—a lot. I looked down. My clothes were split open, and I was drenched in blood. A wave of nausea overwhelmed me. I rolled to my side in time to vomit on the ground. It wasn't much, thankfully.

I struggled to push myself up to a sitting position. It hurt. The muscles of my stomach must have been sliced because moving was like pouring lava down my guts. I panted, and my heart labored to pump what blood I had left to the rest of my body.

My hair was out of its braid. It fell over my face and tangled around my arms. I'd gotten vomit in it. Joy. Once I was steady, I brushed it back and twisted it into a knot. It was dirty and tangled enough it stayed. I looked around. I was at the waterfall. How did I get here?

Don't move. You'll start bleeding again.

The voice startled me, and I whipped my head around. That's right. The cat. He could talk into my mind.

"Cat!" I said, too loudly, even for my one ear. I swayed. I balanced myself with my hands, and even though it hurt with the movement, I scooted so my back was resting against my favorite boulder.

"How did I get here?" It was a dumb question if I thought about it. I obviously hadn't walked. "Did you carry me?" That was another dumb one. He didn't have arms.

I dragged you here.

"Dragged me?" I was really out of it. I couldn't think clearly or say what I really wanted. That was over a mile long hike. He must be really strong.

The cat sighed. I didn't even know cats could do that. Of course, he wasn't a normal cat. He only looked like one. Huh. He'd changed back to his fluffy size. "Weren't you bigger?" I said, confused. Blood loss was a bitch.

I've called for help. You need to be still; I don't know how much blood you can afford to lose. If you move, you could die before help gets here.

"Who did you call? Do you have a phone?" I giggled. Even that hurt my stomach muscles, so I stopped abruptly.

The cat's face grew grumpier. *I do not need a phone. I have an artifact.*

"Where, in your pockets?" I didn't know why silly things kept tumbling out of my mouth.

He sighed again. *No. It is here, at the waterfall. If you remember, this is the strongest magical place in this land.*

I vaguely remember him saying something about that.

"How is help going to find us here?" I imagined the paramedics dragging a stretcher up that steep, narrow, and winding trail.

Rest Brigid. You are bleeding again. The cat's voice was worried, and it scared me.

I looked down, and the wound was oozing blood again. I took shallow breaths and tried to be utterly still. I didn't want to die.

We sat silent, barely breathing, until the bleeding stopped again.

"What did you do with the Siren?" I asked.

Nothing. She is tied up in the house. When we left, she was still out cold.

That was good at least. I hope she stayed that way until the police could pick her up. The cat came over to me and laid down next to my leg. He was warm, and his firm presence was comforting. He purred.

"How long until help arrives?" I asked, as the pain flared, and I sagged from exhaustion.

I do not know. Soon. I said it was urgent.

"Who is coming?" I couldn't imagine who the cat would call. Local services? Supernatural paramedics? What? Who could a cat call?

He gave me a sad, large-eyed stare. *I called the best healer I know, but I do not know for sure who will come.*

That made me concerned. He didn't know? How did he call? Who answered? I opened my mouth to ask just as a bright flash of light blinded me. I felt the cat stand.

"How dare you summon me!" an imperious voice rang out. Black eyes drifted over me briefly, and then to the cat. "What is the matter, Xrsrphn?"

I had no choice, Dana. My charge has been grievously wounded. She needs a healer, and you are the only one I could think to contact.

I didn't have the energy to react, but the thing in front of me was terrifying and strange. She had pale green skin, and luxurious, long wavy green hair. But her face? Her eyes were solid black with no white sclera. She had a faint muzzle, not doglike, more horsey, as were her ears—small, flexible, and standing straight up on top of her head. Her feet, since I was closer to them, were hooved, and I think I saw the swish of a horse tail under her cream colored, silky robe. Her arms were folded, and I could see her extra-long, extra-jointed, six-fingered hands, with evil-looking, sharp, and curved talons at the ends. This was a nightmare made flesh.

I could only stare. Even my heart didn't have the energy to speed up, although it did skip a few beats. I gasped. Then, because I didn't have the core strength, and my arm gave out, I slipped to the side, and I was laying down again.

The horse thing stared at me, unblinking. "It's not very impressive."

The cat snorted. *Yet, it is mine. I must protect it. My lord says so. So, please help. It is his will.*

The green creature gave a little anxious whicker and bent down to look at my wound. She pushed my shoulder until I was lying on my back. She peeled the ruined shirt away and prodded the wound with a long talon.

"The cut is deep, but it isn't into the body cavity. Only meat." She bent near and sniffed, then stepped back. "The wound is unclean."

Poison? The cat asked.

She bent closer and sniffed again. "No, a toxin of some sort. Designed to keep the wound from closing. Before I can heal her, we'll need to cleanse the wound."

The cat nodded. *The water here is pure and infused with magic from the Fae realm.*

I blinked. The green horse woman made a small gesture with one of her hands, and a thin, golden stream of water snaked towards me. It undulated, reflecting and refracting the sunlight as it moved. If I hadn't been so weak and in pain, I'd have found it wondrous. It seemed to take forever to get to me, but when it did, the water drove into the wound.

I screamed.

The water didn't stop, but continued to drive through the wound, reopening it, and causing the blood to flow again. The cold was excruciating, and ironically, it burned like acid as she washed my wound. I felt that with every new heartbeat, my heart grew slower, and my pain lessened as I began to drift away.

After what felt like hours, she bent and sniffed the wound again. "It is clean," she pronounced. Then she knelt beside me and placed her hands a few inches above the bottom of my ribs and closed her eyes. A golden light surged out of her hands and blazed into me with what felt like the force of a million suns. After the chill of the icy water, the heat was unbearable. I took a breath to let out another scream, but I didn't have the strength. I passed out.

When I came to, both the green woman and the cat were staring at each other, deep in conversation, I assumed. My hands automatically drifted to the wound and felt...clear, unbroken flesh. I scrambled up to a sitting position and looked down. Nothing. Not even a scar.

"How?" I mumbled. I wasn't sure if I should be confused, relieved, terrified, or committed. I just stared. At the wound, at my companions, at the proof evidenced by my blood-soaked clothing. It was real. Everything was real. My breath accelerated.

Meanwhile, as my world crashed around me, they ignored me, intent on whatever they were talking silently about. I slowly stood, turning first to my knees, and then helping myself up by grasping the boulder. When I was done, I leaned on it, gasping. That finally got their attention.

"Thank you for healing me," I said because I could be polite. My mother had raised me that way.

She inclined her head to me. "The master will be pleased that you are well."

"The master?" I parroted, confused.

She ignored me and turned to the cat. "I must return." She stood, but the cat wasn't done with her.

Wait, Dana. I need a favor. This time for me, not the master.

She hesitated. "Go on."

The girl isn't ready. Her magic is lost, and she is not going to be here for some time. I think you should erase her memory, and that of the creature that attacked us.

Dana cocked her head. "Intriguing. You should kill the creature that attacked you. Convince me. Why should I erase their memories?" After a momentary pause, she said, "I'm not sure the master would enjoy me messing with the head of his progeny."

I didn't hear the cat's reply. Either he'd switched his telepathy to privacy mode, or I just didn't have the energy to listen in. Regardless, it seemed like I blinked, and the scene changed.

Dana was nodding. "Sufficient. I will grant you the boon in return for a future favor within the terms provided."

She vanished in a flash of light.

"What was that all about?" I asked.

Bargains are the way of the Fae, he answered simply. Of course, that hadn't answered my question.

"She was Fae?" I asked confused. I thought Fae were little winged creatures that caused mischief, or elves like in Lord of the Rings.

No, she is half Fae, half Kelpie, he replied.

That explained the horse-like features. "Is she a friend of yours?" I asked curiously since I didn't know why he'd called her.

No. She is your great-grandfather's mistress of magic.

I had a great-grandfather who was still alive? I staggered a bit and leaned heavily against my boulder. "My great-grandfather is alive?"

Yes. His tone was confused, but I didn't know why he would be. My great-grandfather had been a full-grown man in the 1880s. He'd be well over a hundred and forty-years old. He shouldn't be alive.

"What did you ask her to do? I didn't get that part of the conversation."

I asked her to clear your memory and that of the Siren, so she'd leave you alone, he answered, simply.

"Oh. What if I don't want my memory cleared?" I demanded.

Before he could answer, another bright flash of light appeared, and Dana stood there in her green glory.

She reached out a hand to me. "The golden ball will erase what happened here from your memory. Anything magical will be gone. The silver ball is for your enemy. She will forget any bad thoughts she has for you and will stop seeking vengeance and your material goods. You will both have to swallow a ball."

Before I could do anything but grasp the balls in my hand, she turned and vanished in a flash of light.

"I guess that answered my question," I said.

Indeed. We should hurry back if you are up for it. We need to get back before the Siren awakens or breaks free.

I agreed. My legs were shaky, but I could feel the magic strengthening me as we walked.

It took twice as long as I remembered to get back to the house. I was drenched with sweat. Luckily, my bag was in the car. I grabbed non-bloody clothes and changed at the car. No one could see me but the cat, and he was a cat, so I didn't care. I gathered up my destroyed clothing and threw them on the ground next to the trash can. I'd look for a trash bag inside the house.

When I was ready, I followed the cat inside. Vanessa was still trussed up on the floor, but she was awake and seething mad.

"How do we get this silver ball in her?" I asked the cat.

He blinked at me.

"That's right you can't talk to me in that form. Sorry."

He answered by morphing into his Splintercat form. *I can hold her down, or you can bash her on the head again if you don't want to get bitten,* he answered his large eyes glowing.

"I'm not sure about bashing her in the head too many times. I might do permanent damage."

Sirens are extremely tough. Plus, they aren't that intelligent, so bashing won't damage her, he replied, smugly.

"Huh." And since I couldn't damage her, and I owed her one, I bashed her in the head with my board. I stood back and surveyed my handiwork. "That works for me," I said and dropped the board.

Then, I reached into my pocket and drew out the silver orb. I pried open her teeth with my abandoned knife and pushed it as far down her throat as I could. Then, I massaged her throat until she swallowed. I stood and wiped my hands on my jeans.

"That should do it."

Yes. She will remember, but all avarice and desire to harm you should be gone. Let's get her out of here.

Together, we dragged her out, untied her, and stuffed her into her car.

We waited quietly out of sight until she woke up and drove off. I breathed a sigh of relief. "Well, that seemed to work."

Yes.

We stood silent until we heard the car turn off the gravel drive.

What will you do, Brigid?

I'd done nothing but think about it since Dana had presented me with the golden orb. Magic was real. I had a great-grandfather that was not only alive but wasn't human. I wasn't sure I could deal with that knowledge on top of a talking horse and a talking cat. Add in a home-wrecking ho in the form of a Siren—it was a lot. Maybe too much.

I still had to go back, finish the divorce—including our upcoming court appearances—and pack. I had this house to think of now. It would be a year before I was ready to move here if the restoration company could get started soon. Officially, I didn't even own it for forty-five more days.

The truth was...I wasn't ready for a world of magic to be real. I could feel the pull of this big world that was my far past and my future, but I wasn't ready for it to be my present.

I took a deep breath. "I don't think I'm ready yet. Maybe when I live here and am away from the world I live in now, I'll give it another shot, if you'll help me?"

Yes. I will always be here for you.

"Thanks, Mr. Mittens."

His eyes flew open wide. You remembered my name?

"I think I remembered from the start; I just wasn't sure you were my cat. I've *never* forgotten you."

I'll never forget you, he replied softly, love glowing in his eyes.

"I'll see you again, soon," I said, a lump growing in my throat. I did want this world when it was the right time. I scratched him behind the ears one last time and blinked the tears from my eyes. Taking a deep breath, I popped the golden orb in my mouth and swallowed.

The end.

JILLEEN DOLBEARE

Splintered Magic

Splinter Magic
Jilleen Dolbeare

ICE RAVEN
PUBLICATIONS

Copyright © 2023
Editor: Cissell Ink
Cover Designer: Crimson Phoenix Creations
Interior Art: Rose Rasmussen

I dedicate this book to the people that have supported and encouraged me along the way. To my mom, who taught me to love sci-fi and fantasy. I wouldn't be anything without you! To my husband for not getting upset when I'm busy with the books. To my Mastermind Group, thanks so much! To my niece, Baylee Rose who read everything, kept me focused, made suggestions, and for her brilliant art. And to all my alpha and beta and ARC readers. Thank you all!

CHAPTER

ONE

The rain pounded down so hard I could barely see the turnoff. The tension in my shoulders after my long drive fueled a pounding headache. I rubbed my right shoulder with my left hand and almost missed the turn into the long winding driveway to the house. I slammed on the brakes and turned sharply. The trailer swayed behind me, causing the car to slide on the wet road. I gasped in fear. I turned the steering wheel to compensate and made the hard turn onto the gravel road. My heart pounded.

I stopped the car once I'd pulled fully off the highway. The long gravel drive stretched in front of me. I turned off the car and panted. I wiped the sweat that had formed at my hairline with a napkin that was sitting in the passenger seat and waited until my heart slowed down and the adrenaline shakes calmed. It was late afternoon, but the heavy grey sky and rain hid everything but the dark expense of woods ahead. I shivered. Anticipation and fear grasped my throat and choked me. This was a huge moment. The biggest thing I'd ever done on my own.

I took a deep breath, stretched my neck, and started the car back up. The road was narrow, and though the gravel had been laid recently, it was intimidating with the trailer behind me. Regardless, the excitement boiled up. I hadn't seen the old house in person since the renovation had begun. It had been my favorite place, full of happy memories with my parents and grandmother. Although they weren't there anymore, I finally felt like I was coming home.

The drive up was only a couple of miles from the highway, but the anticipation made it drag on. When I finally cleared the trees and the house loomed in front of me, I gasped. Instead of a lovely home, it was a freaking haunted house. The paint was mostly gone—what was left was peeling and ugly. Only the weathered grey siding in need of repair greeted me. Patches of old paint here and there that had been protected by the eaves showed the original color like glimpses of happiness through a good, solid cry. A wave of disappointment washed over me. This wasn't what I'd been expecting. I guess I'd thought the restoration would be further along.

The restoration company had informed me that the roof was done, and the important parts were ready. I had a working kitchen, one bathroom, and a finished bedroom. While the rest was being done, I'd be marginally warm and comfortable. I sighed. It was a going to be a long haul.

The rain had slackened off to a drizzle, so after I pulled in front of the house, I got out and soaked in the rich smells of home—evergreens, like Christmas, and the wet clean rain. I walked up the front steps to the porch—areas patched with new wood—and smiled. It would be the glorious Victorian it was meant to be, and I was responsible for that. My heart swelled. I found the correct key on the ring sent by the restoration company and turned it in the front door lock.

I took in the construction mess as I walked in and smelled fresh sawdust. The grand foyer was full of sawhorses, equipment I couldn't name, boards, and tools. I moved quickly between the kitchen, bedroom, and bathroom. Whelan Restoration had delivered as promised.

Luckily, my bed had been delivered and the frame and mattresses had been assembled for me. One of the workers must be a gem. In the kitchen, the old country table was still there from my childhood, so the previous owners must have left it. I hoped some of the old furniture was still in the attic, but I had no idea what the previous owners had done or sold off when they ran out of funds and abandoned the house to the bank. I'd investigate later.

I went back out, brought in my suitcases, and started to haul in the items from my trailer. There weren't many. Mostly treasures from my childhood—photos, and basic items like towels, bedding, plates, and cookware. That took a couple of hours, and when I was done, I was muddy, soaked, and exhausted. I'd used my adrenaline from seeing the house to finish those tasks, and now the travel and the moving hit me.

As I dragged in the last box, I spotted a cat sitting by the door. He was a beautiful tom, huge, pushing twenty pounds or more, with light creamy fur, and blue-grey points. He turned his head to gaze at me, and I was struck with the brightest periwinkle eyes I'd ever seen. He blinked slowly at me. For the life of me, he looked identical to the cat we had when I lived here as a child, down to the two white mitted feet on his front paws. Our old cat must have gotten around.

"Hello there, pretty kitty. Do you live close by?" I asked as I pushed open the front door and set my box down. The cat meowed at me and rubbed on my legs. I bent down to stroke his long, silky fur. "You are a beauty."

It would be odd if the cat did have a family close by. This house was in the middle of about six hundred acres, mostly forest, and an additional two hundred that had once been a dairy farm. The people who'd bought the house from my mom, and the two hundred acres that were left at that time, had intended to log the trees, but they'd never got around to it. They'd owned it for nearly twenty years before they quit making mortgage payments and abandoned the property. I purchased it for a good price from the bank, then bought back the rest of the property surrounding it, including the old dairy.

My divorce had been difficult, and my husband had attempted to deny me half of our marital assets, although I'd worked as hard as he to build them. After a long fight, I walked away with a nice settlement, although not as much as I should have received. I'd be more than comfortable for a long time, even with the cost of the property and restoration. It was worth giving up something to finally be free.

The cat looked around the house and followed me as I walked back to the bedroom. I wanted a nice hot soak in the beautiful claw-footed soaker tub in the main bath, and then I'd find the bedding, make up the bed, and collapse. I should find a grocery store first, but I didn't know if I cared enough. If I was hungry after my bath, I'd order a pizza. That'd work for breakfast too.

In the middle of my musings, the doorbell rang. I started in surprise, shocked that anyone would come out here in the dark when the house had been unoccupied for so long. I looked around for a weapon but couldn't find anything but a sawhorse supporting some kind of saw. Since I didn't know what to do with that, I opened the door anyway.

An older couple stood there with a plant and a bag. The man cleared his throat. "Hi, you must be Brigid?"

"Yes," I answered, still confused.

"I'm Craig Whelan, and this is my wife, Anna."

"Hi, Brigid," she said with a tiny wave.

I smiled warmly. "Oh, hi! I'm so glad to meet you! I love what you've done so far. Come in!" I waved the couple in and took them to the kitchen where the only furniture was. Craig Whelan ran Whelan Restoration; he was in charge of restoring my house.

We stood around the old table. The cat had followed and was rubbing hard against my legs. Craig leaned down, and gave the cat an ear scratch, then the cat came back to me and leaned hard against my leg again.

"Do you want me to let you out, buddy?" I asked the cat, but he gave me a grumpy look, and I swear the look conveyed a perfect, "Are you kidding? It's raining" vibe. I laughed.

"We stopped by to bring you a little housewarming gift after your journey," Anna said. She handed me the plant.

"It's lovely, thanks!" I placed it in what would be a sunny kitchen window in the daylight.

"And this." Craig handed me the bag. It had a supply of goodies, including a couple of cans of cat food for the cat, some light packaged snacks, and a bottle of wine. Craig looked abashed when I pulled out the cat food.

"Is the cat yours?" I asked, confused.

"He showed up when we started working and hasn't left. Someone might have dumped him. He was begging food from the workers, so I started bringing food. Figured I'd see if you wanted him before I took him to the shelter," Craig explained.

I looked at the cat. He was beautiful, and I was alone. Plus, something about those large eyes drew me in. If he wanted to stay, I was good with it. "I think I'll keep him. It's very thoughtful of you to bring this by," I said, truly overjoyed that someone would think of me and make the effort to reach out to a stranger.

Craig and Anna only stayed a few minutes; they could probably see the exhaustion in my eyes. I showed them out.

It was just me and the cat again. I put the wine in the fridge and the snacks away. It was kind of them, but nothing looked appetizing. I petted the cat for a few seconds. I wandered back to my bathroom; the cat followed. I was worried about leaving him in the house, since I didn't know if he was house trained, but I figured the cat wouldn't pee anywhere in the hour I needed to soak the aches out of my body in the tub. So, I started the hot water. I found my Epsom salts, underwear, sleep shirt, and started stripping. I kicked my filthy clothes into the corner and stepped into the hot bath.

The cat checked on me a couple of times, shoving the closed door open with a bang, to make sure I hadn't drowned. Water, you know, the enemy of cats everywhere. I was too lazy and relaxed to get up and shut the door, so I left it open, even though a cold breeze raised goosebumps on the skin not submerged in water. After the fourth time he checked on me, I realized he was hungry and hoping I'd get out and feed him. Luckily, the Whelans had brought cat food since I had nothing else in the house. I sighed and unplugged the tub. I turned on to my knees, and shampooed and conditioned my long, thick hair and rinsed it with the hand sprayer. Then I toweled off and wrapped my hair up in a separate towel. I put on my underwear and sleepshirt, found my robe and slippers, and went into the kitchen to feed the cat.

Luckily, the food had a pop top, because I had no idea what box contained the can opener. I popped the lid and put the food on the floor.

The cat gave me a decidedly disgusted look. Realizing there were no other choices, he dug in. I patted him again and went back to the bedroom. Quickly, I found the bedding, made the bed, and slipped into the sheets, then I fell asleep with my hair still in the towel, cat forgotten.

The next morning, I woke up, the sun streaming directly into my face. It was pleasant until I realized a cat was lying on my full bladder, and I was hearing the muted sound of strange voices. I shot out of bed. The cat mewed his disapproval and threw me a grumpy look. There weren't any curtains or blinds, and I was only wearing panties with a very ragged oversized t-shirt. Hurriedly I grabbed some clean clothes from my open suitcase, lunged into the bathroom, dressed quickly, brushed my teeth, and looked up at my reflection. My auburn-colored hair was a tangled mess. I attempted to brush it, but it took a long time before I got the knots out. Even then, there was no saving it, so I twisted it up into a messy bun.

I looked around for the cat as I wandered out to meet my construction crew. Craig was directing workers when I stepped outside. I smiled at him.

"Hi, Craig!" I said brightly.

"Hello, Brigid," he answered. His eyes twinkling.

"I didn't get time to tell you much last night, but I do love what you've done so far."

"Why thanks. I've wanted to restore this house for thirty years."

"Thirty? So, you knew my folks?"

"I did. I remember you too."

I looked at him more closely, trying to recognize his face. "I'm sorry, I don't remember you."

"Don't worry about it. I wouldn't expect a kid to remember all the adults she came into contact with." He looked around. "Let me introduce you to the crew. On the ladder is my and Anna's oldest, Noah." He shouted up, "Noah, this is Brigid, the owner."

Noah waved down. I waved up at him.

"Carrying the paint can is my second, Lucas."

I also waved at him. I'd met Luke before when I'd first met with the company.

"The youngest boy went to get coffee; he should be back soon. His name is Michael. My daughter, Isabella, will help with the interior design, and she'll meet with you in a few days. She's working on another project right now."

"Four, and they all work with you?" I asked.

"Five actually, I have another daughter, but she does her own thing. She didn't want to go into the family business, although she'll help out if we get in a bind. Her name is Madison."

I'd actually met Madison. She'd been at the front desk the first time I'd gone into the office. "That's cool." I thanked him again for the house-warming gift. The conversation sort of died after that, and I figured I'd leave them alone to do their jobs. I had to go to the store and return my trailer. So, I went back inside to get my bag. The cat was waiting for me. He meowed for his breakfast, and since there was only one more can of cat food, I opened it for him and sat it on the floor. Again, the disgusted look, but he ate it. I looked around for a garbage bag to throw the old can in. I opened all the lower cabinets, starting with the one under the sink.

The new cabinets were beautiful, an all-white kitchen with marble, a lovely island, and cabinets that reached to the vaulted ceiling crowned with gorgeous molding. They'd really done a lovely job restoring and updating the room.

I opened the gigantic commercial refrigerator. The only thing in it was the wine from last night, someone's lunch bag, and a carton of coffee creamer. I had a lot of grocery shopping to do. I figured since I needed to go to town to shop, I should probably check out the attic and see what else I'd need, furniture wise. I climbed the stairs to the old attic and opened the door. It was stiff and stuck a bit. I had to shove my shoulder into it. But once it opened, I saw it looked the same as the last time I'd been in it. Nothing had been moved or taken.

I entered and looked through years of my family's treasures with wonder. Several old trunks were here among the furniture. I felt drawn to the trunk on the left. I looked at it for a moment, then opened the lid.

Reaching my hand in, I pulled out a silver charm bracelet. It had little animals all around it, charming and detailed. It called to me. Without thinking, I put it on my wrist. It sparkled in front of me like it had its own light, then with a flash, it disappeared into my skin. I gasped. A warm pulse raced through me. A wave of dizziness overcame me, and I almost fainted. I leaned over the trunk, resting on it with both hands until I could stand again. It passed quickly.

After that, I left the attic and shut the door, determined that I had imagined it. I hadn't eaten in almost thirty hours after all; I was just experiencing a visual hallucination from severely low blood sugar. I shook my head at my foolishness and picked up my bag from the kitchen table where I'd left it. The cat was sitting next to it, grooming his face. I stroked his head, and he leaned into me.

"I'm going to the store buddy; I'll pick you up some food there."

Please, no more cat *food.* He tilted his lovely face and blue eyes at me. *I prefer premium cuts of chicken, fish, and beef. Oh, and make sure you get some cream,* the cat said.

I stopped and stared at him. "I really need to eat; I'm losing it."

The cat stared back at me.

I shook my head; I hadn't heard the cat. "I'm imagining things."

No, you are not. You are finally listening.

"No, this is nuts." I backed away from the cat, my heart pounding. After all, I'd been through, this is what was going to put me in the funny farm. I walked out and got in the car.

CHAPTER
TWO

I called my bestie on the way into town. Megan answered brightly, and I filled her in on my travels and the state of the house. I didn't tell her about hearing the cat speak since I didn't want to worry her. She was at work, and Evan, my ex and her boss, kept an eye on her out of spite, so we talked fast and hung up.

I dropped off the trailer, and too hungry to do much else, went to a drive through for a breakfast sandwich and some juice. I wolfed it down without tasting it, the warmth of the food filling the empty space in my stomach. Better fortified, I faced the shopping. That done, I made a special stop at the pet store. I knew nothing about having a pet, but I figured they were the experts.

I found a bored teenager manning the front.

"Hi, what kind of food should I buy for a long-haired adult cat?"

"The cat food is in the corner," was the snotty reply. I didn't even get a pointed finger to indicate which corner.

I almost let it go. I'd spent years modulating my responses and walking on eggshells to mollify my controlling ex. Twenty years of not being able to speak my mind had trained me to not respond. But now? I didn't have to. I was a grown ass woman in control of my own destiny.

I straightened my spine and responded firmly, but pleasantly, "Where's your manager?"

The pouty teen called for the manager, and a frazzled, if kindly looking woman hurried up to the front.

"May I help you?" she asked.

"Yes, thanks. I've recently moved here and inherited a cat. I don't know what the best food is to buy, or what I need for him. Can you help me?"

She smiled, relieved I wasn't complaining about something. "Let's grab you a cart."

I went back up front and grabbed a cart and hurried after her to the far back corner. She chatted about food and litter and raw diet versus processed. I'm sure I didn't retain much. But the hallucination about cuts of chicken, fish, and beef kept coming back to me. So, I loaded up with premium raw cat food, bought a litter box, litter, treats, catnip, toys, and left with a cart full of items for the first pet I'd owned since I was a child.

I loved animals. My ex hadn't let me have any. I realized that the stupid cat was filling a void I didn't know about, and he'd been around me for less than a day. The thing had just cost me a small fortune too, and I didn't even know if he'd hang around.

The manager also suggested that I make him a vet appointment. He'd need shots, flea treatment, deworming, and an exam. I added a pet carrier. She gave me the vet's number. I thanked her. It seemed like owning a pet was a bigger responsibility than I thought. I hoped the cat stuck around.

When I returned home, several packages sat on the wide front porch. The construction workers were kind enough to help me haul everything into the house, and I spent several hours putting things away and assembling the delivered items. Once that work was done, I turned my attention to the cat problem.

I hadn't seen the cat when I came in. He must be wandering the grounds or hunting. But once I started worrying about him, he showed up.

"Hi there, lovely," I greeted him as he rubbed on my legs. "If you're going to stick around, I suppose you should have a name." I sat down on the porch stairs, and the cat laid next to me, so I could stroke it.

"How about, Gus? You look like a Gus to me." I scratched Gus's ears.

I already have a name. The cat's voice filled my mind.

I jumped back, away from the cat. His bright periwinkle eyes gazed straight into mine.

"What?" I gasped.

I have a name. The cat's voice drawled in my mind as it casually licked a paw.

"I'm going nuts." I stood up. My phone was in my back pocket, so I plucked it out and opened Google. I searched for local doctors. There had to be something wrong with me.

The cat stretched, front paws extended, ears back, bum in the air. *You aren't crazy. Now that you can hear me, you are finally listening.*

"No, cat, I'm losing it. Cats don't talk."

You are speaking to me. I most certainly do talk. And I'm not just a cat.

I looked around. No one was paying me any mind. They were doing their tasks, rebuilding my family home, and I was quietly going bonkers.

"What are you then?" I was already talking to my hallucination, might as well go all the way.

The cat sat back down and peered up at me proudly. *I am a Splintercat.*

"OK. Since this is all in my head anyway, I'll bite. What's a Splintercat?" I asked out loud, not sure if the cat read my thoughts or just spoke into my mind.

The cat yawned and moved over a small bit, so it was more fully in a sunbeam. *This is a long story. Are you ready for it?*

"No, I need to call the doctor first. Come inside. I got you some things."

The cat followed me in, and when I pulled out his new food and dishes, he rubbed on my legs so hard he almost pushed me down.

Hmmm, not what I requested, but much better than that slop you fed me this morning.

I sighed. Opening my phone again, I searched for doctors.

I found a clinic and called for an appointment. The receptionist answered, took my information, and put me down for the next day at ten. That done, I called the vet and made an appointment for the cat as well. By then, the cat had wandered off, so my hallucination would have to wait for his long story.

Afterwards, I went back to the attic. I wanted to find something to use as a nightstand for my room, and maybe a chair and table to use as a reading nook. I didn't have much else to do in the evenings. I could spend the days cleaning, but it would be nice to have a reading space and somewhere to sit.

A search led me to a lovely set of mission style nightstands. I pulled them out and set them by the door. Next, I searched for a chair. I vaguely remembered that Grandma had a leather chair that I'd loved as a child. I hoped it was still here somewhere.

Beyond where the nightstands had been, the attic was dark. When I tried the switch, the lights didn't work. There was light filtering in from the stained-glass windows, but it was difficult to see much. I decided to go look for a flashlight. I could use the one on my phone, but it didn't pierce the gloom well enough. Maybe Craig had a decent flashlight. I headed down to find him.

He was leaning against his truck, studying a plan. He caught my approach from the corner of his eye and looked up as I drew near.

"Brigid," he greeted me warmly. "We are almost done with the structural issues and will be starting on the interior soon. The exterior is almost ready for paint."

"Oh, that's nice!" The house was really coming together. "Do you happen to have a flashlight I could borrow?" I asked.

He wrinkled his brow. "Sure," he said in a confused tone. "Is something wrong? Do we need to check something?"

Craig was really a sweet man. He looked truly concerned that they hadn't done something right. "No, no, don't worry. I was looking for something in the attic, but the lights aren't working. It's no big deal."

"The attic?"

This time, I was confused. "Yes?"

"I'm sorry, we've been all over this house and haven't found an attic access. We could tell the space was there, but someone had long ago plastered over the entrance or never put one in. I was going to ask you if you wanted me to add an access door."

"I don't know what you mean. The door to the attic stairs is at the end of the third story hall. It's been there since I was a child."

This really cemented that I was going to need that doctor's appointment. "Come with me, I'll show you." I needed to know I wasn't hallucinating that I'd spent the morning in the attic. I was beginning to doubt myself. My palms started to sweat.

Craig followed me dutifully into the house and up to the third-floor landing. "See, the door is right there." I pointed.

Craig shook his head and looked back at me strangely. "I just see a wall."

Panic filled me. My heart raced, and I fully doubted my sanity. Was I really here? Was this happening? I wiped my palms down my jeans. This was crazy. I was perfectly sane. I had to be. Straightening my spine, I marched down the hall and tugged on the door. It opened with a squeak.

Craig gasped behind me. "There's a door," he said weakly.

"Yes, that's what I said."

He looked at me for a moment.

Uncomfortable at his scrutiny, I said, "For a moment, I thought I was losing it."

"You seem perfectly normal." He smiled, then seeing something in my face, he reached out and gave me a quick fatherly side hug.

It should have felt strange or uncomfortable; we were veritable strangers after all, but instead it felt warm and sincere. A wave of loss for my father swept over me. I pushed that feeling away, and Craig followed me into the attic and up the stairs.

He looked around in amazement. "I can't believe this is all here."

63

"Yeah, everything looks the same from when I was a kid," I said.

"This is wonderful!" he exclaimed. "I'll get someone up here to work on the lights. The electrical here hasn't been updated, so it'll need some work."

He handed me the flashlight he'd brought. I shone it toward the back and saw the chair. It had another chair stacked on it.

"There it is!" I said and tried to pull off the chair stacked on top.

"Let me do that," Craig said. "If you point out what items you want, I'll have the guys come get them."

"Thanks so much. I don't know what the deal is with the door. I'll leave it open."

He looked at me strangely and opened his mouth to speak. A large crash came from outside, so he excused himself and hurried down the stairs.

Why was the door only visible to me? Why was the cat talking to me? What was going on? I leaned against an old steamer trunk, the curved top banded with wood.

Under me, the old, hammered tin trunk was cool to the touch. I brushed a hand lovingly over it. This trunk used to sit in the library and held blankets and pillows, so you could grab one and snuggle up with a book. As my hand passed over it, a soft glow started along the seam where the top joined the bottom. I jumped up. Either these things were really happening, or my mental state was quickly deteriorating. But then again, the attic door was real and solid, and Craig had seen it.

I popped the lid open. Inside, lying on the old quilts, was a seashell necklace. It was made of silver, like the bracelet had been, with tiny, scalloped shells separated by pearls. It was exquisite. I picked it up and admired it. Then I felt compelled to slip it over my head. It was warm around my neck. Then in a flash of light, just like the bracelet, it vanished and instead of a burst of warmth, a cool wet feeling splashed through me like sea spray. I shivered. Then, the strangeness of it all overwhelmed me, and I ran out of the room, down the stairs, and into the kitchen.

I drank a glass of water and put some on to boil for some cocoa.

This was all too weird. I needed to talk to someone. I couldn't wait for my appointment tomorrow. I opened my phone to check the clinic I'd called earlier. It had an urgent care associated with it. Yes. I turned off the teapot, grabbed my bag and keys, and headed out.

CHAPTER

THREE

The waiting room was full of coughing kids, stressed out mothers, and grumpy medical staff. I checked in on the computer and gave the front desk my insurance information. They asked what I needed to be seen for. Too embarrassed to answer honestly, I said stomach distress.

I sat down to wait.

Luckily, I had a book on my phone, because it was forty-five minutes before I was called in. They took me back and weighed me. I was concerned to see I'd lost ten more pounds. All the stress from the divorce had caused me to lose nearly forty pounds. I had been slightly overweight, but I was concerned now that I was starting to look gaunt. Gaunt didn't look good on anyone over forty. It made us look *old*.

Since I felt less old and more like I was hitting my prime, I vowed to do better and eat more consistently. The MA took me back and did the usual blood pressure, temperature, etc. I passed. She asked me again about the reason for the visit. Since it was just her and I, I told her about having some hallucinations. She typed it dutifully into the computer. Then she finally left with, "the doctor will be in soon."

I sat uncomfortably on the exam table. Fifteen minutes later, I contemplated getting up and retrieving my phone. I was bored and my back ached. Just as I jumped up, the door opened, and a tall man dressed in a white coat strolled in.

"Gabe?" I checked his name tag and stared. Could it be?

Gabriel Ambrose had been my last high school boyfriend before we moved away. He was a handsome kid, nice, and I had thought myself in love. Maybe I had been. I wasn't sure what love was anymore.

He looked up from his laptop and stopped.

"Brigid?" We both gaped at each other.

I smiled, genuinely happy to see him. His warm brown hair had a little grey at the temples, but I'd have recognized him anywhere. He was still tall and lean. His hazel eyes were full of mischief. His jaw was a little more chiseled, and he had laugh lines around his mouth and the tiniest trace of crow's feet at the corners of his eyes.

"You still look the same," he exclaimed.

I shook my head. "Hardly, but it's kind of you to say."

I was proud that my best feature, my auburn hair, was still thick, long, and shiny. However, it was in a messy bun on my head, I wasn't wearing makeup, and I had on a dirty t-shirt and old ragged jeans. I blushed, suddenly horrified. Plus, I had to tell him about my mental breakdown.

"I probably should get someone else to see you considering our history," he said with a tiny frown.

I was kind of wishing the same but seeing him stirred up all kinds of emotions. Nostalgia being the greatest, I think. I was suddenly overcome with grief and loss. I hadn't allowed myself to deal with it before, and I burst into tears. Not the pretty kind either, but the full range of ugly crying, snot included. The embarrassment I felt over that just made it worse.

He set his laptop down, seemingly unsure what to do for a minute, but then he wrapped me in a hug. Twenty-four years fell away, and we were eighteen again and desperate for each other. My body melted into his, and he placed a tender kiss on the top of my head. There were a couple of chairs in the room, and after I'd sobbed myself out, he sat me down and joined me.

"What's going on, Bridge?" The old nickname fell off his tongue easily.

I didn't feel like this was the place for the whole enchilada, so I told him about being exhausted, hungry, and having weird hallucinations about glowing jewelry and a talking cat.

Gabe listened politely. "Tell me about the hallucinations."

"What do you mean? I think I told you everything?"

"How were you feeling? What sensations did you have, if you had any at the time? What was your frame of mind?"

"Oh." I thought back. "Well, when I put on the bracelet, warmth rushed through me, and I felt dizzy and faint and had to brace myself for a moment. When I put on the necklace, the feeling of a cold ocean wave washed over me, but I didn't feel faint. When the cat spoke, I heard it in my mind, not out loud. In fact, I checked to make sure if anyone else could hear him. They didn't react. I guess my frame of mind, at first, was calm, but as each strange thing occurred, I became more and more freaked out."

He stared at me a moment, and then stood up and paced the room.

Having made some kind of decision, he said, "Brigid, you aren't having hallucinations."

"I'm not?"

He sighed, then sat back down. "Do you believe in magic?"

"What are you talking about? Magic? You believe magic is real?"

"This is gonna take a while. How about you come over for dinner tonight, and we'll talk?"

My heart raced. I wasn't sure if he was putting me on. But this was Gabe. One of the few people in the world I trusted. In high school, he'd been there for me when I needed him after my dad died. He was either delusional, or he was telling the truth. My heart said he was telling the truth.

I made the decision. "What time?"

He gave me his address and phone number. We hugged again, and I left.

When I saw myself in the car's rear-view mirror, I wanted to cry again. I was a disaster. This wouldn't do. I'd have to get seriously dolled up to wipe this memory out of his mind. On the way home, I picked up something to eat. I'd gone from stress starving to stress eating in a single day. If I had any natural hormones left, I'd be breaking out in acne tomorrow since my meal was nothing but grease with a side of chocolate milkshake. This was a dairy town after all.

I shoved everything into my face on the drive home and was finishing my shake when I pulled up to the house. The graying wood siding sported a new coat of primer, and a little flutter of joy filled my heart. I couldn't wait to see it finished in the traditional dark green, brick red, and tan I'd chosen.

I walked in, and the cat greeted me at the door. He gave me a distinct, "Meow." I looked at him oddly. He had been speaking to me in my mind. I knew he had. Having Gabe tell me I wasn't hallucinating, gave me a feeling of confidence. Did magic exist? It would explain this and some other strange things I remembered from childhood.

"You told me you already had a name. I forgot to ask what it is," I said to the cat, feeling a tiny bit foolish.

You don't remember my name? the cat asked.

"Why would I?" I asked.

Because you grew up with me, he said.

"No way. You'd be over forty years old!"

Hmpf. I'm over two hundred years old.

"What?"

I'm a Splintercat. I only appear to be a Ragdoll.

"So, you *are* Mr. Mittens?"

Yes. He looked smug.

I started to laugh. Here was a two-hundred-year-old magical cat, and he went by Mr. Mittens. Everything was too ridiculous. Everything. Pretty soon, I was snorting, and I couldn't breathe. The cat looked at me, turned in a huff, and sashayed into my room. He jumped up on the bed, turned around a few times, and plopped in the middle with his back to me. Someone was touchy.

If this magic thing was just a hallucination after all, I was going to be upset. That interaction seemed so real.

I couldn't keep my mind off what Gabe had said, and what he was going to reveal to me. Since my "magical" misadventures had started in the attic, I figured I'd go up there and try to figure things out for myself. I had at least three hours before I needed to be presentable. I climbed the stairs. The door was still open, and the nightstands were still stacked by the door, so Craig hadn't had the guys come move stuff for me yet. No big deal, they were busy.

I went to the first trunk where I had found the bracelet and lifted the lid. It was packed with an assortment of things I hadn't really noticed the first time—old photos, books, and some clothing. I started to pull items out when I realized these were my grandmother's things. Her vanity set, a silver-plated mirror, brush, and tray were in there. I remembered those. I used to sit at her vanity and brush my hair. My mind was flooded with good memories. I set the tray with its brush and mirror aside. I'd put them in my bathroom on the new vanity. I kept digging. I grabbed a couple of photo albums to peruse later.

In about the middle of the trunk were a set of three journals. Maybe what I wanted would be in there. I stacked them with the photo albums. Nothing else really interested me, so I put everything back neatly and closed the lid. I set the books and vanity set by the stairs, so I'd remember to take them down with me when I was done.

Next, I went to the trunk that had held the seashell necklace and opened it. There weren't any books in this one, but among the blankets and pillows were things I vaguely recognized as my grandmother's. My dad must have placed all of this in the attic when she'd died, and my mother must not have checked the attic after he died. Or, like Craig, she couldn't access the attic.

Maybe you had to be a blood relative? Who knew? I closed it and checked another trunk. This trunk was full of clothing. Beautiful pieces from the 20s and 30s. If my grandmother had worn these clothes that were obviously made for an adult, that meant she would have been in her late nineties when she died. I didn't know how old she was. Everyone seemed old when I was young. If she hadn't fallen, I wondered how long she might have lived. I sighed and replaced the items. I don't know what I was looking for. More magical jewelry?

I closed the lid and began searching for more furniture. I needed a dresser. When I turned around from the trunk, I was surprised to see a dresser in front of me. It was a simple thing, rectangular with a slight curve at the bottom just above the feet. It had simple black pulls but was a gorgeous rich wood I'd have to look at when I got it out. The mirror was sitting next to it. I realized they were mission style as well and would match the nightstands. I'd have to let the guys know so they could bring this down as well. I clapped my hands together; this would be beautiful once I cleaned it up.

I searched a bit longer, getting dustier and collecting cobwebs. There were years of beautiful and unique things up here, and I couldn't wait until the house was done so I could display them properly. However, nothing else "magical" revealed itself, and I again wondered if I had imagined the bracelet and necklace that had disappeared into my body.

I checked the time on my phone and realized that I had to go get ready. I grabbed my books and the vanity set and headed downstairs.

Since I didn't have a dresser in my room yet, I rifled through the things in my suitcase that I hadn't hung up, found my underwear, and went into the bathroom to shower and make myself presentable for my dinner date.

CHAPTER
FOUR

After the shower, I sat at my vanity and admired my grandmother's brush set. The boar bristle brush slid through my hair with ease and left it shiny. I smiled. Even though I was young when she died, I had loved her. I could remember her brushing my hair, making snickerdoodles just for me, and her warm hugs. The brush made me feel close to her.

I put on my makeup and dressed. Since this wasn't an official *date* I knew of, I wore jeans, a fluttery blue top that enhanced my eyes, and crocs. Crocs are great for Oregon coast weather. They weren't the kind with all the holes, but little, short boots that kept out the wet.

I drove to Gabe's and pulled up to an old split-level farmhouse. It wasn't very big. It was right off the highway, so I had to pull around back to park. In the back was a large shop or barn, and a paddock. A horse trailer was parked in back along with a full-sized truck and an SUV. I parked alongside the other vehicles, opened the gate, and approached the back door. He hadn't specified which door to come too, but this one made sense. So, I knocked timidly. After a few moments, Gabe opened the door. I was grateful because it was starting to drizzle, and my hair was looking good. I didn't need it to curl up into a bunch of frizz.

The door opened into a combination mudroom and laundry and then another door led to the kitchen. I kicked off my muddy boots in the mud room, and Gabe was kind enough to take my rain jacket. I followed him into the house. Glorious smells greeted me, and my stomach rumbled in anticipation. Gabe gave a little laugh. I blushed.

"Sorry, I guess I'm hungry," I said.

"It'll be ready soon, so we'll take care of that."

He took me through the kitchen and into his warm, cozy living room; a fire blazed in a wood-burning stove. Soft music played in the background. I took a seat on his leather sofa while he went back into the kitchen to finish supper. I looked around the room. No sign of a wife or girlfriend, although it would be odd for him to invite me to his place if he had either of those.

His house was kind of bare. He had furniture, but no pictures, art, or any other decorations. I wondered if he had just moved in. Just as I was about to go back into the kitchen and ask, he came in and told me dinner was ready.

I sat at his dinner table and admired the spread. He'd made a roast with carrots and potatoes. He served me, and I thanked him. The whole time I was anticipating what he was going to tell me about magic. I couldn't imagine what he would know that I didn't. The objects had come from my house, my grandmother's past if the trunks they came out of had any say in the matter.

I was hungry, so I ate, and waited for him to bring it up. There was a stretch of awkward silence.

"So, Gabe, did you just move in? Your house is sort of bare." Then, I blushed. That sounded sort of rude.

He chuckled. "Yeah, I just moved back here a couple of months ago."

"Oh! Where did you move from?" I asked.

His face darkened slightly, and he frowned. "Back East," he answered. And since his answer was vague and literally everywhere in the country was east of us with the exception of Alaska and Hawaii, that left quite a lot of story to fill in. He obviously didn't want to talk about it.

"That's cool," I said quietly, reading the room. "Did you just start your practice here?" It was a dumb question, but I had to say something.

"Yeah, the last doctor retired and left an opening here, which was convenient timing for me."

I smiled. Another awkward silence stretched, and we both ate to cover it. I was dying to ask about magic, and frankly I was deeply curious about what had transpired "back East" that caused him to avoid talking about it.

"So, did you ever get married?" I asked. I figured that was a common question between high school friends.

"Yes, I was married for about seven years. It didn't work out."

"Any children?"

"No."

"Oh. Me either."

That had been one of my greatest disappointments. I'd wanted children so much and tried for so long and so hard. At forty-two, I knew my chance was gone. Not only was I older, I'd had all the equipment removed. It was something I still mourned. My ex basically threw me away after all of that. He found himself a young thing, and she was pregnant almost as soon as he started the affair. Either that, or he lied about when he'd started seeing her. I wondered how Gabe felt about not having children. That was a little too personal for a first date though—if this was a date.

"Magic," Gabe started.

I looked up from my food to him. He was leaning back in his chair, looking away towards the living room.

"Yeah?" I prompted.

"I come from a line of magical healers." He pushed his plate back. "It seemed to skip my parents' generation and my brother, but I got it all. I found out when I was still a preteen."

I looked at him with amazement. We'd dated and been very close, and he'd never told me any of this.

He must have read the chagrin on my face because he said, "We don't talk to non-magic users about it. Sort of an unwritten rule in the different magical communities."

I nodded.

"The problem with being a healer is that all the various magical beings want to control you. Healing is a rare gift, and it can help magic users with not only health, but corrections to their magic. Human magic has a tendency to change, to break people down more quickly, and a healer, well a healer prevents that." He picked up the dishes to put them away. I stood and began to help him.

"So, what did you do?"

He cleared his throat. I got the feeling this was hard for him to talk about.

"After you left, the pressure began to build with the local witches' coven. They wanted me to join and become their healer. I was eighteen. I wasn't ready to make any commitments. I wanted to see the world. When I refused, they got ugly about it. It started small with threats but quickly escalated. Pretty soon my family was being plagued with magical curses. My parents packed us up, and we fled town in the middle of the night. After that, I swore to keep my talent to myself. I went to medical school, and here I am."

"Wow, that's terrible!" I exclaimed. "Not the medical school, but the rest. Has the same coven bugged you since you've been back?"

He was quiet a moment, thinking or wondering what to tell me.

"They have asked me to be their healer, but that's as far as it has gone."

"What are you gonna do?"

He took a sip of water. "I've told them I'll treat them if they come to the clinic, but I won't be joining the coven."

"How did they take it?"

"So far, it's been quiet, but I'll wait and see. My experience with witches has been...poor."

I nodded. I realized I'd accepted his story as true. Magic was real. Just having him give me the benefit of the doubt helped. I'd been told so many times I was crazy or put down for expressing my ideas, that his simple assurance that magic was real calmed me and let me see that what I had experienced wasn't a hallucination. That meant that the Splintercat was really talking to me. Huh.

"Have you ever heard of a Splintercat?" I asked.

There was a long pause while he considered. "I don't know. I know there is a Splintercat Creek in the Cascades. It's a popular place to hike."

"Oh. OK."

"Why do you ask?"

"Well, that's what my talking cat says he is. I wondered if you knew anything about them because to me, a talking cat seems magical."

He laughed. "Yeah, I'd think so too. There are many types of magical beings besides healers and witches. There are shape changers, fae, lots of magical beasts, and in this town there's a nice sized werewolf pack."

"Werewolves are real?" I choked out.

"Yeah, they're pretty outstanding members of the community here. The pack leader owns a big business, he does construction or something." He waved his hand to indicate the something.

"What's his name?" I had a sudden wave of vertigo.

"Craig Whelan, he's pretty well known in these parts."

I coughed. *Craig*? Craig was a werewolf and the pack leader? That explained the look on his face when he realized only I could see the attic door. He'd been about to tell me something when he was called away. Maybe it was to tell me about magic.

"Is he dangerous?" I managed to say through my shock.

"I imagine he can be. But he's a super nice guy. I've met him a couple of times, and when I was in school, he was the assistant football coach. He was great."

I'd forgotten that Gabe had played football, it was so long ago in a different life.

"He's the one restoring my house."

"Oh? Really? I've heard he's really good. He's hard to get; his company is usually booked up."

I nodded again. That was true. I'd booked him and was told it could be a long time before he got to the house. I was lucky he'd wanted to restore the old thing and pushed some other projects back.

"So, you said something about magical artifacts?" I took the conversation back.

"Oh, yes, you were talking about a bracelet and a necklace? I couldn't understand all of what you said."

I blushed. I had been a soggy mess. Of course, he couldn't understand me.

"Umm, yeah, so I pulled the bracelet out of my grandmother's trunk. I put it on, and there was a flash and it disappeared into my arm. Then again with the necklace. Both times I felt compelled to put the jewelry on and then a flash, and they disappeared."

I stopped and took a breath, then I figured I'd better tell him about the disappearing door and proceeded to do so.

"It sounds like you have objects that might be tuned to either your direct heritage, or to you specifically. The door only appeared when you were there, and the bracelet and necklace responded once you touched them."

"I guess. But how?"

"I think that maybe one of your parents, or your grandmother were magical."

I didn't remember any time I'd seen magic used growing up. I'd never heard them speak about magic or magical artifacts. It was shocking and irritating all at once to have been lied to my whole life.

"What do you think the point of the magical jewelry is?" I asked.

"I really don't know. I'm not familiar with that type of magic."

I thought for a moment. Trying to figure out how I could find out. "Do you think the local coven might know?"

He shrugged. "They might."

"Do you trust them, after…?" I asked.

"The people who pursued me are no longer leading the coven. I'm wary, but the coven leader went to school with us. She has been fair with me so far," he answered.

A wave of relief washed over me. "I'll give her a try. Who is it? Do you have her number?"

"Yeah, if you are determined." He dug through a drawer in the kitchen and handed me a business card.

I glanced down at it. Sofia Kettle. I looked up at him. "Is this Sofia Bergman from school?" I asked on a whim.

He nodded.

"Wow, she's the head witch. Really not a stretch." Sofia had been the head cheerleader my last year in school. She was popular, aloof, and a little bitchy. She hadn't been anything to me, I was bookish and didn't run in the same circles, so I'd been beneath her notice.

Gabe laughed. "She's not like that anymore. She's pretty nice."

I gave him a look from under my lashes. Had he dated her? That was one of those leading lines that hinted to me that maybe he had.

We reminisced awhile; everything was easy with Gabe. I felt eighteen again, and I forgot magic, my divorce, and all my other problems. He walked me out to my car after that and he leaned in and left me with a gentle kiss—the kind that makes you feel treasured and wanting more. I pulled away, not knowing what else to do. My hands were sweaty, and I didn't know what to do with them. I wiped them on my pants. Then, because he was standing close and my date protocol notebook was empty on ideas, I thanked him for a great evening and thrust my hand out to shake. On the inside I was berating myself for my awkward and embarrassing moves. He chuckled, shook my hand, and let me go.

My insides weren't obeying me on the drive home. They were twisted with butterflies and other fluttering creatures. I don't think I'd ever gotten over Gabriel Ambrose, and I had a serious crush blossoming.

CHAPTER

FIVE

T he next day, I wanted to start off with a bang. So, firmly sure of my sanity, I called the head witch. She'd been the queen bee, everyone in school knew her, but I doubted she knew my name. So, I was temporarily shocked when she remembered me. It wasn't a big town, we'd had a few classes together, but I really hadn't interacted with her during school at all. She seemed upbeat and sweet, so I invited her over for lunch.

I jotted down all my questions, made sure the kitchen was clean, and prepared lunch. The rest of the house really was in a state of disrepair, and there wasn't another room I'd take a guest to. According to Craig, the last owners had started a remodel which explained the beat-up nature of the house replete with torn up walls and floor in various places. After the Whelans completed the outside, they were moving in to do the interior. I couldn't wait to have a finished house.

Sofia was prompt. I had to give her that. She knocked on the front door precisely at eleven. I opened it to a lovely forty-two-year-old woman who was meticulous in every part of her person. I don't know what I was expecting. She'd been a good dresser and always made up in school. I was in jeans, a nice long-sleeved t-shirt, and had my hair in a French braid. She was dressed in a business suit, pumps, and a tight chignon. I wore mascara, she had a full face of make-up on. I'd be lying if I said that didn't throw me off balance a little.

I invited her in and almost giggled. The lore that you shouldn't invite a vampire in ran through my mind. Since she was a witch, it was probably OK to invite her in. I guess I was still a bit punchy about being thrust into a world of magic.

"I've always loved this house," Sofia said once she stood in the foyer with all the construction equipment lying around. "I'm so glad you're restoring it."

"Thanks, that's sweet. I didn't know you'd ever seen the house?" I asked. She'd never come here when I lived here as a child. Not even for a birthday party.

"Oh, yes. When it went back on the market, I considered buying it, but it sold too fast. I guess it's a good thing it went back to its original owners." Her voice didn't sound glad, but if she'd wanted to buy it, she must be feeling a little bitter. That was natural.

"I'd show it to you, but it's currently a disaster zone. That's why we're going to hang out in the kitchen. The Whelans restored that and my suite first, so I would have somewhere to live."

She nodded. "That would be lovely. I'd like to see what they did." Her reply was much more friendly this time.

I smiled and led her to the kitchen at the back of the house.

"Wow," she said as she looked around.

The kitchen was a gorgeous mix of the original charm with a modern upgrade. I had commercial grade appliances, marble counter-tops, and beautiful cabinets—all glowing with their newness. The original oak floors had been repaired and redone, so that feel of the old remained. The Whelans had done a spectacular job, and I was proud to show it off.

"This is lovely."

I glowed with pride.

"An old farmhouse table and the original floors!" She looked around in wonder. "Who did the cabinets?"

"Craig had those built locally. I'd have to ask him."

She waved that away as rhetorical. "It's really a wonderful kitchen."

"Thanks."

I seated her at the table. The food was already there and just needed to be uncovered. I'd made salad with a large selection of toppings.

She picked and chose through the options without complaint, although I noticed she didn't select meat, cheese, eggs, or bread. I wondered if she was vegan or something. Was that a requirement of being a witch?

"I'm sorry, are you a vegetarian?" I asked politely.

"Not really, just watching my figure," she answered.

So not a witch thing.

"Oh, I hope you don't think I was being nosey; I just didn't know what the dietary requirements were for witches." I blushed.

She laughed. "There aren't any diet requirements."

"I'm sorry. I wasn't trying to offend you." I was horrified. I was already blowing my interview into the magical community.

"I'm not offended. Please don't worry. The only requirement to be in the coven is to have been born a witch. The rest is just business, you know, membership requirements and paying your yearly dues."

"Oh. I don't know anything. I'm new to all of this," I said and took a drink of my ice water. "I don't even know what I am, really. Just weird things have been happening, and my cat talks to me."

"That is interesting."

"Do you think I could be a witch?" I asked.

She shook her head. "I don't know. Did anyone in your family have witch blood?"

"I'm sorry, I don't know. My grandmother died when I was five, and this seems to be related to her somehow. My dad died when we still lived here, and none of them mentioned anything to me."

She frowned. "When did you start noticing things?"

I told her about the bracelet and the necklace.

"So, they both flashed, disappeared, and then you had different sensations, and things started to get weird?

"That's about it."

"Did the jewelry have any strange markings or symbols?"

I was about to answer no, but then I remembered the appearance of the links of each item.

"The silver necklace was interlocking seashells with pearls. The bracelet had little charms of different animals."

She looked thoughtful. "What happened after the bracelet?"

"The cat started to talk to me. He said he always had, but I was finally listening."

"And the necklace?"

"I'm not sure yet. I haven't put anything directly together with it."

"I don't have much to go on, but what you're describing doesn't sound like witch magic," she said.

My heart sank. How was I going to figure this out without guidance?

"It could be some type of elemental magic." She chewed thoughtfully. She even grabbed a hard roll and tore off a piece. "The charms could be representative of earth, the seashells of water." She looked up at me. "But I'm just guessing. You'd have to experiment to see if that was true."

"How do I do that?" I asked. My heart raced.

"Well, you already said you can talk to and hear your cat. That's an earth element skill. You could try to exert your will over water. Then you'd know that's what the necklace gave you."

I looked at my water glass. "How do I try that?"

"I can tell you how a witch would try, but your magic may be different."

"That's OK, I have to start somewhere."

She nodded. "Witch magic is will driven. We focus on what we want and then use the force of our will to cause the outcome. We use objects, spells, chants, etc. to help pinpoint and focus that will to our desires."

"So, I focus on what I want and then it happens?"

"You must believe that it will happen, and you must command it to happen through your will."

I wasn't really getting it, and that fact must have shown on my face.

"I'll demonstrate. First, witches have little elemental control, and we are usually better at one element than all of them. Our magic lies elsewhere, but I can do something small."

She looked at her water glass. She was still a moment, then she said, "Swirl."

The water in her glass started to rotate, and soon, a small whirlpool appeared and faded.

"Wow."

She smiled briefly. "Could you feel the magic?"

I shook my head. I thought for a second I'd felt a tingle, but it hadn't lasted. "I'm sorry. I couldn't feel anything."

She shrugged. "I didn't think you were a witch, that just proves it. It doesn't matter. Just try it. Concentrate on your water, focus your will, believe and tell it what you want."

"OK, I'll try." My hands were sweating. I don't know why. This felt important, at least it was important to me, and I didn't want to fail.

I stared at my glass, then focused on making it swirl, like I'd seen Sofia's water. I said, "Swirl." I felt something like a connection to the water. The water swirled, then it raged, then it exploded out of my glass shattering it, and splashing us with water. I sat there like a dork with my mouth open.

I looked at Sofia. She stood up, brushed the water off her suit and blinked at me. Then, she started to laugh. Her mascara was dripping, I'm sure mine was too. Pretty soon we were both howling.

"I'm sorry!" I choked out after a few moments.

"That was great," she replied. "You are the best student I've ever had."

The laughter continued.

Finally, I cleared away the sodden food, and I showed her to my bathroom so she could clean herself up. When she came out, I apologized again.

"Don't worry about it. I think you've got it. You also have a definite affinity to elemental water magic!"

I smiled back. "Thanks so much, between you and Gabe, I'm feeling a lot better about myself. I thought I was going crazy there for a minute."

"No problem, I'm glad I could help. We should do this again sometime, this time my treat."

"I'd really love that."

"I'll call you."

"Thanks so much for everything, again. I had a good time." I walked her to her car.

She nodded, smiled, and got in. As she backed out and turned the car around, I smiled to myself. Maybe Gabe was wrong to be wary. This new generation of witch was different. Regardless, I knew one thing for sure, I had a new friend. Things were going great.

CHAPTER
SIX

After she left, I realized I had forgotten to ask her what the other elements were. I gathered that earth and water were some, so I opened my phone browser and started Googling, "what are the elements?"

The first thing to come up was the periodic table. I ignored that. The next thing was a Wiki list. "What are the seven elements of earth?" That looked helpful, but when I opened it, it was things like plants, soil, etc. and that didn't feel right. The next list was, "What are the five elements of nature?" The list was earth, air, fire, water, and space. I wasn't sure about that one. The next was, "What are the twelve elements of nature?" The list was similar, just expanded. It included earth, air, fire, water, thunder, ice, force, time, flower, shadow, light, and moon. The google lists went on with all kinds of different things. The only four that kept coming up were earth, air, fire, and water. I figured if there was more to my elemental magic, I'd figure it out later. I could probably expect fire and air artifacts. I should be good with earth and water. I put the phone away. After I cleaned myself up, I swore I'd practice outside next time.

Next on my list for the day was a vet appointment for Mr. Mittens. I didn't know how things would go for a magical cat, but he should still be checked out. My family hadn't lived here for twenty-four years, and that seemed like a long time without a doctor's appointment. I looked around for him. He didn't seem to be in the house. I got the carrier ready and set it by the back door.

"Mr. Mittens! Where are you?" I said aloud.

He walked around the corner and looked at me.

"Hi, how are things going with you today?" I asked.

He meowed for all the world like any other house cat. *I've killed three threats today*, he said into my mind. There went that fantasy.

"Threats?" I queried and then imagined fanged super mice. I shook my head. He'd probably killed a few rodents around the house. "We're going into town today, would you get into the carrier for me, please?"

He sat down and folded his tail gracefully around his body and over his front feet.

You do know I am not a pet, he growled.

"Yeah, of course." I was trying to mollify him.

I'm a powerful protector, but I'm limited off this land. I can't assume my true form or use more than a few of my innate abilities, he said gruffly.

"I think we'll be safe for an hour," I replied.

He didn't look amused, but then his face had a slightly angry expression all the time, so I might be reading something into it.

I do not travel in plastic boxes.

"You like boxes, I saw you jumping in and out of them when I was unpacking."

He turned away, looking abashed, if that was possible. He may have mumbled something in cat sounds.

"What was that?" I asked, amused.

But he just gave me a disgusted look, strolled up to the carrier, sniffed around it, then strolled in like it was his idea to begin with.

I'm glad you sprung for the elite package, he grumbled.

I hadn't bought the memory foam pad, since they'd been out of the size needed for this carrier, so I'd tucked in a fuzzy blanket to pad the hard plastic.

"We'll be back in no time. You'll be fine." I shut the wire gate and pinched the device that engaged the latch.

Hmpf. He was quiet while I loaded him in the car, put the seatbelt around the carrier, and got in. I started the car.

Where are we going? he asked.

Not my fault he hadn't asked sooner. "The vet." Best to just get that out there upfront.

The vet? Whatever for? He sounded truly confused.

"I'm getting you fixed."

What?! That got his attention.

I laughed. "Don't worry, you're getting your shots, an exam, and dewormed."

I'm a Splintercat. I do not need to be dewormed.

"You do if I'm to have you properly licensed." That wasn't true, he just needed a rabies shot. I figured if you eat even one mouse, you stood a chance of worms. So, dewormed he was going to get.

He hissed, turned his back to me, and was quiet the rest of the ride. I caught the tip of his tail twitching, the only sign of his displeasure. I wondered how hard he was going to fight the vet.

I lugged his cage inside and signed in. We didn't have to wait long, so that was a blessing, because the silence coming from his cage was weighted. Once we were alone inside, I opened his door and asked him to come out onto the stainless-steel exam table.

This place smells like disinfectant and despair, he mumbled, but he dutifully walked out. I placed the carrier on the floor.

"Remember you're a Ragdoll. Don't embarrass me," I said.

You would do well to remember I am not *a Ragdoll.* He plopped down and splooted on the steel table, front and back legs straight out taking up the full length of the table.

I ran my hand over his silky coat, scratching behind his ears and under his chin.

Maybe I'll forgive you, he purred.

The vet walked in. I felt Mr. Mittens tense, but then he forced himself to relax. His tail swished, but he stayed splooted and stretched the entire length of the table.

"Wow, that's a big boy," The vet said. "I'm Dr. Adams."

"I'm Brigid, and this is Mr. Mittens."

We shook hands, and he asked me what we were in for.

"Well, I just moved in, and Mr. Mittens was on the property. Since he wants to stay, I figured I'd better get him checked out and all of his shots and deworming done."

"Sounds like a plan." He smiled and forgot me as he pulled his stethoscope around and plugged it into his ears. He poked and prodded, took Mr. Mittens temperature—I got a severely dirty look at that one—and took blood. The vet left the room for a while.

That was uncalled for, Mr. Mittens said after the vet left the room.

"I didn't know he'd do that, sorry." I truly was, I wouldn't want to have anyone watch while a doctor stuck a thermometer up my rear either.

You will pay for that.

"Can I pay with premium cuts of chicken, fish, or beef?"

If you add in cream. That would be acceptable.

"Deal. We'll go to the store…"

The vet walked in. "Well, everything looks fine. The blood work is good. The tech will bring in the shots, and we'll see you in a year."

"Thanks," I replied, and he walked out. The tech came in and finished up, then we left with rabies tags and an appointment reminder for the following year.

I stopped at the creamery and picked up fresh cream for Mr. Mittens as well as cheese curds and ice cream for myself. Then I stopped at the butcher and bought him fresh chicken and beef—then to the waterfront for fresh king salmon. With my cat master appeased, we finally went home.

After his belly was hard and full, I got a terse, *You are forgiven.* Then he wandered off to nap.

I was pretty tired after my day, but I'd intended to do some work in the attic, cataloging and sorting things I wanted to use when the rest of the interior was done. I was meeting with the Whelans' interior designer on Monday and wanted her to incorporate the original furniture where possible.

I also wanted to see if the other artifacts representing fire and air were up there as well. I kept forgetting to ask Mr. Mittens what he knew about them. He usually had his own agenda, so it was hard to impose on him.

I climbed the stairs. The nightstands and chair were gone, so the Whelans must have taken them downstairs. I was excited. The door was still open, so they could see that it was there. I could hear voices, and I was confused until I remembered Craig was having the wiring updated. Once I entered the attic proper, I could see a few guys working on the wiring. Since I didn't want them to think I was there to supervise, I waved and left. It would be nice to be able to see up there, so I was glad. Since that project was off my list, I decided to go outside and practice my new power.

In the far corner of my property, deep in the woods, was a small waterfall. I'd spent time there as a child in the company of my cat. Now I knew the cat had been watching over me, I felt a warmth in my heart for him. I changed into hiking boots and grabbed a jacket. I didn't want to bother Mr. Mittens since he was sleeping off shots and a premium meal, so I took my phone and left out the back door.

The sun was shining, and the workers were painting the exterior. A flood of joy filled me at the dark green color, and I couldn't wait to see it finished. I waved at the crew and headed to the trail. It was a little overgrown, but still visible. It appeared the local wildlife used the trail as well which helped keep it preserved. The path was mossy, and it muffled my steps and lent the path a feeling of softness.

It was a bit of a hike and walking it made me feel better about myself since I was moving and doing something constructive. The path wove through the old-growth trees and wild flora. I vowed to get a book that would tell me what everything I saw was, particularly the wildflowers and trees. Up ahead, I could see a small rock pond that someone had made to collect the water of a small spring. I stopped and drank the crystal-clear water and marveled at its sweetness.

It was a good thirty-minute leisurely hike to the waterfall. I sat on a large boulder like I used too and soaked in the peace of the place. I wasn't sure what to do to practice my magic. I thought about the swirling and the water explosion. I should probably start small. A ripple? I'd try it. The pool under the falls wasn't large, it was on a hill after all, and the stream mainly sluiced away most of the water. I concentrated on the pool, gathered my will, and said, "Ripple."

I felt stupid. The water was already churned up, and I couldn't tell if anything happened. I thought about what would show. I did it again and said, "Wave."

This time, I was lucky I was far enough away and sitting up on the boulder, because I emptied the pool. The splash still hit my boots. I stood on top of the boulder. What was I doing wrong? This was much more than I pictured in my mind. Either I had zero control, or my power was really strong.

Once the pool refilled, I tried again. This time, I concentrated hard on a small effect. A two-inch wave. That's all I wanted. It worked, sort of. I didn't empty the pool, but the wave was three feet high. I let everything calm again.

At about my twentieth or thirtieth try, I finally got a small wave. Good enough, I thought and decided to stop. I was tired. Not physically tired, but mentally tired. In reality, my body felt a little amped, like using the magic invigorated me. I wondered if that was normal. I shook my head, climbed down from my boulder and stretched my back. It was a little sore from sitting still for so long without support. I must have really been concentrating. I hadn't noticed it until now.

I shuffled a few steps until it loosened up, then started back down the trail. It was growing dark. I had stayed much longer than I thought. If I didn't hurry, I'd be stuck with only the flashlight on my phone to guide me back.

The light under the tree cover was sparse, and I was struggling to see the trail by about the halfway point. I wasn't that concerned, but I could hear Mr. Mittens chastising me for not waking him up before I headed out alone. What kind of person worried about what her cat thought of her? I put other crazy cat ladies to shame.

I was smiling until the bear lumbered onto the trail about a hundred feet ahead. I stopped cold. It was a black bear. It wasn't that large, but it was a *bear*. I tried to remember what you did if you ran into a bear. Did you yell? Run? Throw things at it? Play dead? Shit.

I stopped cold. The bear looked at me then turned and faced me. That's when two cubs joined her. Double shit. I froze with fear. The bear huffed and clacked her teeth at me. That didn't seem good. I didn't have bear spray, a weapon, or even a stick. I had an angry mama bear and…nothing else.

I took a deep shuddering breath. The bear stomped her feet at me, then charged about thirty feet. My heart nearly stopped. She never quit watching me. I started to back up slowly. When I moved, she clacked her teeth at me again.

My heart pounded, and I couldn't catch my breath. She was going to charge again; I could feel it like a pressure in my chest. Like magic. Magic? I had magic! Something Sofia said, raced through my mind. Earth magic meant I could communicate with animals. Hopefully, just like I did with my cat. I had to try something fast. She was stomping her feet again. I knew better than to run, no way I could outrun a bear. I was slow as tar. I couldn't outrun an evil tortoise. I pretended she was Mr. Mittens.

"I won't hurt your babies," I said. I didn't know if I had to use my will for this although I was positive I couldn't concentrate on it in my current state of terror. The bear looked over her shoulder. Her cubs were wrestling in the path.

She looked back at me and huffed. So that didn't work. I had to pull myself together and concentrate. I tried again. "Go away."

The bear stopped. Her lips trembled like she was confused. I calmed down slightly and found my will. "Go away!" This time I shouted.

The bear flinched and shook her head. I had to have gotten through. Would she understand my commands? Did she speak English? Maybe it was all about the feeling. I needed her to feel safe and calm. I gathered my will and concentrated on those feelings. "Calm," I said. The bear visibly relaxed. She turned towards the cubs and walked back a dozen steps. Then she looked back at me like she didn't know why she was leaving. That was enough for her, she broke into a run and bellowed at her cubs, then faded back into the trees.

I fought the urge to run. I wanted out of here as soon as possible, but I knew it was the wrong thing to do. There was no telling how far away the bear had run or if she was still watching me. I was panting, the adrenaline spike hitting me hard. My hands shook, and my legs turned to jelly. I stumbled down the trail for several yards barely hanging on to my reason.

Just as I was about to stop and collapse, I saw Mr. Mittens racing towards me. I don't know why a twenty-five-pound house cat made me feel safe, but he did. He scanned the area as he ran, his speed pressing his floof against his body. His blue eyes blazed.

You left me, he accused. *I am your protector. If you are on this land, I must accompany you.*

I should have been ashamed at the scolding, but I was just relieved. "Believe me, I won't go without you again." I didn't know what a housecat could do, no matter his aspirations of grandeur, but his presence was comforting.

He stopped cold and looked up at my eyes. *What happened?*

"A mama bear and her cubs."

That is not good.

"No." I looked around. "I don't want to do that again."

How did you get away safely?

"Magic?"

Is that a question or a sarcastic remark?

"No, I used magic. But I'm not sure if I did it right. She left though."

Hmmm, he said. *You should practice.*

"I was." I frowned down at him. "That's why I went to the waterfall, to practice my water magic."

You were at the waterfall? There was a hitch in his mental voice.

For some reason, a wave of fear passed over me.

"Yes, why?"

Since you returned, there have been several incursions by magical entities. They are drawn by your magic. On your native land, the magic calls to them. Not all are benign. Some wish to steal your magic.

I gulped and shivered. "Is it possible to steal someone's magic?" I stuttered out.

It is not easy, but it is possible. This is why I was made the protector of your family.

"Well, shit."

Indeed.

He turned and walked back towards the house, I followed. *I will insist, once again, that you do not leave the house without having someone with you. It would be best if that were me. I am your protector and have the power to do so.*

I still wasn't sure, besides having better senses than I, what he could do, but I didn't like him upset at me. "OK."

He nodded.

Mr. Mittens's fur glowed slightly in the darkening forest, enough I didn't need my phone flashlight. I wondered if that was normal for him or part of his mystical powers. I didn't ask. He was too mad at me, and I was too upset at my stupidity to bother. We were silent the rest of the way home.

CHAPTER

SEVEN

It took two days to wire the attic. They told me it wasn't a big deal, it had been previously wired, so the holes and things in the rafters they needed were already there. They just had to run updated wire and put in a new electrical box. The existing light fixtures were there, so they changed them out and put in lighted ceiling fans. Now the attic would be comfortable and well lit. The air flow would help with the buildup of humidity and keep the mold down.

When I entered it and flipped the switches, I was amazed at how well I could see each piece. I clapped my hands with delight. My cat must have been curious why I kept going up there because he followed me this time.

"So, Mr. Mittens, any idea where to look for the rest of my magic?"

No, not really.

"Do you know anything about it? I keep forgetting to ask you."

He licked a hair that had strayed out of place on his shoulder. *I know that the magical artifacts were created from your magic.*

I looked at him, "My magic? I had magic once?"

Yes. It is quite common for the fae that live in this realm to bind their children's magic until they are old enough to be responsible and not give themselves away.

I sat heavily in the dust, shellshocked. I squeaked out, "I'm Fae?"

Your great-grandfather is a Fae lord. Your great-grandmother was a witch.

Maybe Sofia was wrong; I did have witch blood. I think. I wasn't sure how supernatural genetics worked. Even that thought blew my mind. It was like living in some strange TV series like a Telenovela or something. I'd never actually seen one of those, I was just having a hard time dealing.

My next thought was how did I get power and why was it taken from me. "My father?" I asked.

He was part witch, part Fae, and half human.

"What about my mother?"

She was human.

"So, who bound my power?"

I got a mental shrug. *I assume your father and grandmother did. I wasn't there when they did it.*

"That would have been nice to know earlier."

Would you have believed?

I hated when my cat made sense. "No."

Did my mom know?

Another mental shrug.

Cats were terrible sources of information. I tried to settle this new knowledge in my head and sort it into my new reality. I wasn't sure it was working, but all I could do was keep asking questions until it made sense.

"You keep saying 'the Fae' like you aren't one of them," I said.

I'm not from this realm or the Fae realm.

"Where are you from?"

He jumped up onto one of the trunks. *I am from a realm that does not have a name in your language. I used to travel the realms. I incurred a debt with your great-grandfather. The geas upon me is to watch over this land and his progeny until they are no more. Until then, I'm bound here.*

"I wasn't able to have children," I said, watching him for signs of relief. There wasn't a reaction.

Yes, but you could live a very long time.

I scoffed. "Yeah, if I'm lucky I'll get fifty more years give or take."

You are a Fae creature; you could live for millennia.

"What?" I was starting to take the bombshells in stride. Or I was saving them for a mental breakdown later, I wasn't sure yet.

Even though you have human blood, you inherited strong Fae magic. Use of that magic will increase your lifespan. If your parents had not died, you would have received the magic at a much younger age and stopped aging then. You still appear to be in your prime for a halfling.

"Thanks, I think."

I don't pay much mind to humans.

And that was the end of the compliments.

I opened my mouth to tell him he had insulted me when a huge crash came from outside. I would have ignored it, but it was followed by shouting. I looked at the cat, both of our eyes wide, and flew down the stairs and out the back to see what was wrong.

I dialed 911 before I even knew what had happened. I had a very bad feeling that something was horribly wrong.

Once at the scaffolding, I ran toward the gathering of workers. Craig Whelan lay on the ground. He was pale and broken. His sons were by him. They begged him to shift. Craig wasn't responding.

"What happened!" I yelled into the crowd.

Someone answered. "He fell from up there."

I looked at where the man was pointing. It was near the top of the third floor. I shuddered. There was no way he could survive that fall. I realized that everyone around me must be part of the pack.

"What can I do?" I asked. "I called for an ambulance."

"If he can't shift, I don't know what will save him," someone mumbled. I'm not sure if they intended for me to hear.

Below Craig's body, a pool of blood was forming. I was sick. He couldn't die, not because of me. The pack surrounded him, their hands on his body, begging him to shift. I could feel the tendrils of magic leaking off them. They must be using some type of inherent magic to force him to shift.

It was working. Fur sprouted as his body changed. Then it stopped, and he reverted to his human form. The pack stepped away.

"Something is stopping his shift," a pack member commented.

They looked scared now, scared, and worried.

I sobbed. I could hear the ambulance in the distance. I must have given them my address and location, but I couldn't remember what I'd said. I looked over towards the house to see if I could spot the ambulance coming up the drive. Mr. Mittens sat on the porch rail, his head hanging down. I think he had more compassion for humans than he let on.

Finally, the ambulance came into view. Some men guided it back behind the house and soon enough, they had Craig loaded up and racing to the hospital. I prayed in my heart that he would make it. I sent everyone home, they were distraught, and it felt like the right thing since I was ill with worry and grief myself.

A sudden idea occurred to me. Maybe Gabe with his magical healing ability could save him. I fumbled with my phone, looking for his number. It seemed to take forever to locate it. It rang and rang, no pickup. Damn, he must be at work. I texted, "Craig Whelan fell from the top of my house, not sure he's going to make it. Can you meet us at the hospital?" Then I grabbed my bag and followed the ambulance to the hospital.

I hoped the ambulance would make it in time. I was behind several trucks since Craig's family and pack were also following the ambulance. I wondered if they would even welcome my presence, but I felt I had to be there. After several days of having them around, I felt like we were friendly if not friends by now. We'd joked around, eaten, and drank buckets of coffee together. Still, I was nervous following them into the emergency waiting room.

The air was filled with tension. I happened to sit next to Luke Whelan. He gave me a tight smile, laced with fear and grief.

"Are you OK?" I asked. I didn't know what else to say.

He gave me a terse nod.

"Do werewolves heal fast?"

He gave me a double take.

"I didn't know you knew," he said quietly.

"I know. But you all seemed so surprised that he wasn't getting up. Do werewolves heal quickly?"

"Yes, if we shift, we can heal instantly. But Dad didn't shift. Something's seriously wrong. I think he might be cursed."

"Cursed?" I felt my eyebrows lift in surprise. "How does that happen?"

"There have been some strange things happening around the house."

I looked at him with alarm. "Why didn't you tell me?"

"They were minor, and it seemed too small to worry about."

"What's been happening?"

He looked abashed. "Well, it started with small things missing. Like I'd lay down a hammer and it would turn up ten feet away, or inside the truck or something. Things like that. Immediately you think you just mislaid it. But it kept happening, so we started experimenting. Sure enough we weren't mislaying things."

"Why do you think it's a curse?"

"My sister Isabella has a witch friend. She asked her friend, and she said it's a hindrance curse."

"Hindrance? What else does that kind of curse do? Could it have caused your dad's fall?" I leaned in closer, so no one else could overhear.

"According to Isabella's friend, no. They are mischief curses, designed mostly to annoy." He shivered suddenly and wrapped his arms around himself.

"That sounds mean, but not dangerous." I frowned.

"Yeah, that's what I thought. But dad fell because brand new scaffolding, that I installed *correctly*, broke. That's hard to believe, plus, he started to shift, we gave him all our pack magic, and something broke the magic and undid his shift."

"So, that wasn't normal?"

He shook his head.

"Do you have any witch enemies?"

He shrugged. "Not that I know of. We've had run-ins with the local coven, but we aren't at war or unfriendly."

"Huh."

"Maybe they were intended to harm you?" he asked.

"I don't know anybody," I replied, surprised. The thought hadn't entered my head. I barely knew anyone in town, and when I left as a teen, I didn't have any enemies.

"Maybe it's about the house," he remarked. "It's been around a long time. Maybe someone wants it gone?"

"I don't know. It sat here untouched for twenty years. You'd think if someone wanted it gone, they would have set it on fire."

"Yeah, I guess. It's all so strange."

I nodded.

We sat in silence for a long while. I kept checking my phone, but there was no response from Gabe. His phone was probably off. Good practice for a doctor.

Just as I was about to despair, the handsome form of Gabriel Ambrose breezed through the doorway. The family looked up with hope. He was coming from the hospital side, so he must have already been here, or got my text and made it to the hospital before us.

He located Noah, the eldest son, who was sitting next to his mother Anna. Of course, Gabe would know who they were. Luke and the rest of the family stood up to listen to what he had to say.

His face was very solemn, and my heart sank. "I'm so sorry. He's gone."

The family looked shocked.

"What?" Noah managed to choke out.

"I tried my best to heal him, but his body wouldn't respond. I've never seen anything like it before."

Luke sent a quick desperate glance at me. "Cursed." I almost heard him say.

Then the family was weeping and comforting each other. Gabe drifted away when they had no more questions. His part was done. He'd tried.

I walked over and caught his arm. "Thanks. Thank you so much for coming and trying."

His eyes were red as though he shared their grief. He probably did.

"Thank you," he said gruffly.

"I'm gonna go. This isn't my place. They need to be with their family and friends right now. Just know, I'm grateful."

He nodded, gave me a brief hug, and walked back into the emergency room.

I saw Luke, squeezed his shoulder, gave Anna my condolences, and left them to their grief.

I broke down in the car. I couldn't believe that someone had died working for me, helping me out. Someone as warm and friendly as Craig Whelan. One of the nicest men I'd ever met. I could barely see through my tears. I almost didn't want to go back to the house. He'd been hurt there. Before I could leave the parking lot, I called my best friend, Megan. Her warmth and concern helped, and I was able to make myself go home.

When I pulled up to the house and walked in, the same loving, warm feeling that always greeted me filled my heart. No. No one was chasing me out of my house. Especially a witch. How dare they? How dare a witch curse my friend, my home? My grief turned to rage. I had a witch to find and punish.

CHAPTER

EIGHT

"Mr. Mittens!" I yelled. I had to do something, but I didn't know where to start. He wandered into the foyer. Tail aloft, blue eyes pinned on me.

Yes?

"There you are." Then I proceeded to dump everything that had happened on him. I ended with, "What do I do now?"

I sat down heavily in the middle of the construction mess in my foyer. Mr. Mittens came and plopped on my lap. He proceeded to take a bath like my entire reason for living was to be his cat bed.

You said they believe there is a witch's curse?

"That's what Luke was saying."

Hmmm.

I waited a moment, since the "hmmm" usually indicated that he was thinking. I stroked his fur and scratched his chin—his eyes half closed with pleasure.

I believe that you may have the power to detect a curse. At least your grandmother could. He paused for a moment and looked up at me. *I don't know if that will require another artifact, or if it's an inherent power to your being.*

I scratched behind his ear. "How do I find out?"

105

You try to detect the curse.

I sighed. "How do I do that?"

I don't know. I'm not Fae, or a witch, and my power does not work like yours.

"Should I call my new witch friend?"

Mr. Mittens stood up. *How do you know she didn't place the curse in the first place?*

"What?" I said, startled. "Why would she?" That was a real stretch. She'd been warm and friendly, and I'd gone to school with her. The old witches were the ones Gabe had problems with, and he had basically said she wasn't an issue. No. This had to be another witch. Someone the Whelans had issues with.

I don't know her. Mr. Mittens said. *But she has been on this property more than once. She is a witch. This is a witch's curse, according to the werewolf. It makes sense that she is a suspect.*

"No, that's impossible. I just met her. Why would she want to hurt me, the house, or the crew? It doesn't make sense."

You asked my opinion. I may be wrong about her, but I'd try to locate the curse yourself before you involve any more witches.

That made sense to me. "Ok, I can do that. Or at least I can try."

Mr. Mittens meowed his agreement and wandered off to do whatever he did.

"Thanks," I yelled after him. I got a brief tail swish in reply, and he disappeared.

I went outside. I didn't know what to do to detect a curse, but I figured that like the water and the bear, it would involve concentration and will. I looked at the broken scaffolding and the blood where Craig had lain. Tears began to fall again. I rubbed my eyes. No, I was going to do this. I was not going to wallow. I'd think about the fall and Craig's death tomorrow. Today, I was going to find out if there was a curse.

I sat on the porch and tried to concentrate on the curse. It was so esoteric; I was having a hard time. Was I looking for an object? A glowing field around the house? What? I shook my head.

So, I concentrated on the word, curse, and spoke out loud. "Find curse." I looked around. Nothing. I didn't see or feel anything. Maybe I was too close to the house. I walked out further into the driveway. Once the whole house was in my field of vision, I tried again. "Find curse." This time, I didn't limit myself to a tiny bit of power, I let it go like the first time with the glass of water.

Something happened. I wasn't sure what, but I felt a pull. I let it guide me. It tugged me to the side of the house closest to the woods. I followed. When it stopped tugging, I stopped moving. I looked all around even though I didn't know what for. My magic still tugged at me, but not like before, not in a direction. I must be wherever the curse was. I searched more diligently. Finally, I spotted…something. A small bag poked up from the rose bushes that lined this side of the house. I got closer. Yes, it was a small purple velvet bag, like jewelry came in. I reached for it. When my hand was maybe an inch from the bag, I got an electric shock like touching metal after you dragged your stocking feet over carpet. I yelped. Determined, I reached through the shock and grabbed the bag.

It had something inside. I took it in the house and emptied it on the table. I bellowed for my cat again. I had no idea what this was, but he might. He appeared. I started to wonder if he could teleport, since he always appeared when I wanted him. I shook my head, I'd ask later.

"I think I found the source of the curse," I said.

He jumped up on the kitchen table. The items from the bag were laying there. All strange to me. There were some leaves, some tiny bones, a piece of wood, and some hair. Mr. Mittens sniffed it. He lurched back.

"What's wrong?"

It stung my nose, he said incredulously.

"It zapped me the first time I tried to touch it."

Hmmm.

He stepped in and sniffed it more cautiously. *I smell wolfsbane, mouse, and dog.*

"What do you think these items do?"

I can only guess.

"Well, that's better than me. I have no guesses. Let me have it."

He sat and stared at the items for a moment. *From what little I know, a lot of witch magic is representational.*

"OK, what does that mean?"

When they focus their will to achieve a spell, they use representations of what their purpose is to focus the spell or keep it running.

I must have had a blank look, because my cat sighed, then said, *For example, if I wanted a spell to keep snails out of the garden, but I didn't want to have to spend every moment in the garden concentrating on an anti-snail spell, I'd make one of these gris-gris to run the spell. Inside, I'd use something that represents the idea of 'no snails' so maybe I'd place an old snail shell with salt in the bag.*

I nodded. "OK."

That's what we are looking at. The wolfsbane and dog hair are indicating a werewolf go away spell.

"What about the mouse bones?"

He looked down at them. *Do you see that they are broken?*

I hadn't, so I peered down on them. "No."

It could indicate that the curse meant harm or broken bones. Although it is very hard to harm a werewolf.

"Could it be directed at me?"

I don't think so, it's definitely directed at the werewolves.

"Huh."

It made me feel slightly better knowing that it wasn't because of me the wolves were targeted. They must have an enemy they didn't know about.

"Thanks, Mr. Mittens. Do you think the curse is broken now that I found the bag?"

Yes, although there may be another. The accident and the inability of the wolf to shift indicates a more directed or active spell than this one.

My heart fell. "This is the only one I felt."

Since the spell was strong enough to overcome the pack magic you described, it's quite possible that the witch was here when it happened.

"What? I didn't see anyone!" I thought for a moment. "Can witches turn invisible?"

I do not know. There would be no need for it though, this place is surrounded by forest. It would be easy enough to hide without wasting energy on an invisibility spell.

"Unless witches fly on brooms, they'd have to have left a car somewhere. We are several miles from town."

I will search the grounds for any unwelcome tracks.

"Thank you, Mr. Mittens."

It is my job to keep you safe.

He jumped down. I stared at the gruesome contents of the bag, shuddered, put all the pieces in a Ziplock, shoved it to the back of the junk drawer, and disinfected the tabletop.

I didn't have much to do but brood over the events and grieve for Craig Whelan while I waited for Mr. Mittens to find more evidence. So, I plugged in my earbuds, blasted some rock music so I couldn't think, and cleaned the dresser and two end tables that the kindly wolves had brought down for me. That wasn't distracting me enough, so when I finished that, I cleaned the house.

A few hours later, I heard the ancient doorbell. I don't know how, since I had the music loud, but it managed to break through the guitar and drums. I turned off the music and went to the door.

Gabe stood there. He looked as haggard as I felt.

"Hey, I was worried about you," he said.

I felt a little flutter in my stomach.

"I'm alright," I said. "Just sad."

"Yeah, same." He scuffed his foot over the boards of the porch. "Do you mind if I come in?"

"Of course, sorry. I was cleaning. Come in." I led him into the kitchen, not really having anywhere else to see company.

"Sorry, only this room and my suite are finished. The rest is torn up."

"Don't worry about it, I can see you're remodeling." He smiled.

"Can I get you something to drink? I can make tea, coffee, or I have Coke in the fridge?"

"I'll take a Coke, thank you."

I got up and grabbed two Cokes from the fridge and handed one to him. "Ice?"

"No, the can is fine, thanks."

We used the drinks to navigate any awkwardness. "A witch put a curse on the werewolves," I said.

He choked a little on his Coke. "What?"

"I found this little velvet bag with strange items in it. My cat, you know, the Splintercat?"

He nodded.

"He said they represent harm against the werewolves."

"Why would it be here?" he asked.

I frowned. That was a very good question. Why here? If they wanted to hurt Craig, it would make more sense to put the curse on his truck or his home.

"I don't know. Because they're working here?"

He shrugged. "Maybe…"

We had no answers.

"Did he suffer?" I asked.

He shook his head. "He never woke up."

Grief overwhelmed me again, and I turned my head away until I could push it back down.

"You know some of the coven members, do you know anyone who'd do this?"

He shook his head again. "I would like to think that no one would do this, but there are a few bitter witches. Some even have a ridiculous prejudice against the wolves, but if this hadn't happened, I'd say none would go this far."

I nodded, but it didn't help me pinpoint the culprit. Just as I was about to ask more questions, Mr. Mittens came strolling in. His fur was lightly damp; it must be raining again. He shook it out.

I found tracks.

I turned back to Gabe. "He says he found tracks."

Gabe lifted his eyebrows. "This is the Splintercat?"

"Yes, his name is Mr. Mittens. This is his disguise for this realm. He's a Ragdoll."

Gabe faced Mr. Mittens. "I'm very pleased to meet you."

Likewise, my cat replied.

"He returns the greeting," I said.

"Let's go see what he found," Gabe said.

We both stood. I grabbed my rain jacket. Gabe's was on the back of the chair, so he also put it on, and we followed my cat outside.

We followed the cat deep into the woods on the same side of the house where I'd found the gris-gris bag. He stopped where the tracks began. There was a road into my woods. Granted, I had recently bought back this stretch, but still, I didn't know a road led to my house from this side. I was going to have to put up a gate to close it off as soon as possible. It creeped me out that someone could spy on me without my knowledge.

Besides the tire tracks, there were human tracks that led to the edge of the woods, where I assumed the witch had done her dirty work. It was a woman's foot, about the same size as mine—which wasn't much of a stretch, I wore the most average shoe size there was. It looked like an athletic shoe track. It seemed pretty official now. Craig had been murdered by a witch. Why though? He was the nicest man.

Gabe's jaw tightened, and his countenance darkened as we reviewed the evidence that someone had been watching the house and had killed Craig on purpose.

"You probably shouldn't stay out here alone," he said.

I shivered. I hadn't felt unsafe here. Well, until today anyway. "I'll be fine. I have Mr. Mittens."

"He's a housecat."

Mr. Mittens growled at him. *I'm most certainly not a housecat.*

"He disagrees."

"Regardless, he is one cat. Can he stop a witch's curse?"

I looked down at him. "Can you?"

Well, I can stop a witch if I see one.

"No," I answered Gabe. "But between him and my magic, I think we'll be fine. The curse was aimed at the werewolves, not me."

"Are you sure the curse wasn't designed to scare the werewolves away from you?"

I felt a chill race down my spine, but I brushed it away. "No. That's a stretch. I don't know anyone but you, the Whelans, and now Sofia. Why would anyone want to curse me? I'm sure I'm fine here."

He looked unconvinced, but what could he do? He'd warned me.

"Promise, you'll call if you have any problems at all?"

I promised. We walked back to the house and after making me promise again, he left.

It was too late to call any fencing people to block off the road, but I mentally added it to my list for first thing in the morning. For the first time since I'd moved back, I locked all the doors, promising myself I'd get new locks installed just in case. I made some food, although I didn't feel much like eating, and soaked in my tub. I'd never be able to look at this beautiful bathroom again without thinking about Craig. It broke my heart.

CHAPTER
NINE

The following week, the fencing guys met me to install the new locked gate to prevent entry by vehicle. I had already had the locks redone. After I left them to do their work and was heading back to the house, I got a call from Luke Whelan. They'd had the funeral and were working on the business concerns. Luke called to thank me for the flowers I'd sent, and to let me know they wouldn't be able to finish the restoration. It made me sad, but I understood. They were cutting back, and this was where their father had been murdered. It made sense.

"I found a gris-gris bag," I said to Luke. "You were right. There was a curse."

Luke was quiet for a beat or two.

I continued, filling the air since I knew he was struggling. "It had items in it specific to harming werewolves."

A strangled cry came from his end of the phone.

I waited a moment. "I'm going to find the witch. Do you want me to keep you in the loop?" I asked, uncertain how he'd feel about it.

A rough growl, brief but terrifying, answered me. When Luke was able to speak again, he said, "I can't answer for the pack, I'm not the leader. I'll talk to Noah, but regardless of what he says, yes, I want to know."

I thanked him and his family for their beautiful work and told him to send me the final bill. That concluded, as far as I knew, the Whelans —except for Luke—were done with me. Although it was selfish, I was feeling disgruntled about the state of the house. It was a wreck. Half painted on the outside, and barely started on the inside. I didn't know what to do. There was only one company like Craig's in town. Everyone I'd called before Craig had long wait lists. I'd be living in this mess for a year or longer before I could find someone else. I sighed and got on my computer. At least the internet had been installed.

By noon, I'd been turned down by seven companies. The project was too big, they couldn't get to it until next year.

I even asked Gabe if he knew anyone. He didn't. I called Sofia since she was the only other person I knew in town, but she didn't answer so I left her a message. I was feeling discouraged.

As I hit end on my last call, I heard a car crunching on the gravel of the drive. I walked out the back door to see who it was. It was a small stylish white Range Rover. Isabella Whelan waved to me then climbed out. She was a leggy blonde with green eyes. She dressed stylishly and was one of those effortless beauties.

"Hi, what can I do for you?" I asked, confused. I assumed I'd never see another Whelan, some workers from the company had picked up their equipment earlier in the day.

"My brother sent me with the bill." She handed me an envelope. "But that's not the reason I'm here. I have the plans I drew up for the house. Since you've already paid for them, I thought I'd go over them with you and see if you want any final changes?"

"Oh. I'd like that, thanks!"

Isabella followed me into the kitchen and spread out the plans for the interior of my house on the kitchen table.

After she showed me the plans and explained everything, I could picture how magnificent this house was going to be if I could find someone to do the work. I thanked her, wrote a check for the bill, and waved goodbye as she left.

Since I'd turned the sound off on my phone while Isabella explained her plans, I'd missed a return call from Sofia. I listened to my voicemail.

"Hi, Brigid. It's Sofia. I might know someone who could help you out. My cousin is just starting a restoration business, and he's still building clientele. If you don't mind someone new to the biz, I'll give you his number. Call me back!"

I called.

"Hello?"

"Hi, Sofia, it's Brigid. Yes, I want your cousin's number. I've called seven different places and they're all booked up. I don't mind trying someone new, especially if he's good. Is he good?"

She laughed. "I really don't know if he's good, but he's gotten calls back, and he's relatively cheap for now."

"Sounds great."

"Hey, do you want to have dinner or something soon?" she asked.

"Yes, that would be nice."

"Great! I'll text you my cousin's number. How about we meet tomorrow at O'Malley's?"

"I'm free, sounds like fun."

"See you then! Bye."

"Bye."

The day was looking up. Someone to fix the house, and a friend to commiserate with. Now if only Gabe wanted to do something with me, my day would be complete.

Once Sofia sent her cousin's number, I called it immediately.

"Scott Harris Construction and Restoration," a deep male voice answered.

"Hi, my name is Brigid Donovan. Your cousin, Sofia, gave me your number. I have an old Victorian house I'm restoring. My current restoration company just quit on me, and I'm living in a partially finished house. I was hoping I could get a bid on finishing. Do you think you could look at it?"

"Sure, hold on, I'm checking my calendar." I could hear construction noise in the background.

"Uh, I could come by tomorrow about midday. If you like the bid, we'll be done with our current job midweek next week if that's OK."

Was that, OK? I almost danced a jig.

"That sounds wonderful." I gave him my address, and we hung up. I immediately texted Sofia with a thanks and a bunch of happy emojis.

* * *

THE NEXT DAY, I WAITED WITH ANTICIPATION AND HOPE THAT SCOTT Harris Construction would take my job. Finally, a large white truck pulled up to the front of the house. A tall blond man stepped out and looked around the outside. After a few minutes, he came up and rang the bell. I didn't want him to think I'd been watching him, so I waited a little while to answer the door.

"Hi, mam, I'm Scott Harris?"

Mam? He looked like we were about the same age. He was probably just being polite, but I cringed just a little on the inside.

"Yes, I'm Brigid." I looked up into the most brilliant blue eyes I'd ever seen. He was one of those white blond, blonds. It may have been that he was sporting a dark tan from being outside, and his hair was probably sun-bleached. He had it cut high and tight as though he'd been in the military at some time. He had a flat carpenter's pencil behind an ear, and I realized he was holding a baseball cap in his hand. He must have had it on before he rang the door. I smiled to myself at his old-fashioned manners.

"Come on in. I'll show you the inside, then we can go look at the rest that needs to be finished on the outside."

I took him up to the third floor. He looked around at the beat-up walls, the holes everywhere, the doors lying in the halls, and the severely outdated bathrooms. It wasn't much better on the other two floors either. At least the electric and the HVAC had already been replaced. Then we went outside, although he'd already looked.

After we came into the kitchen, I showed him Isabella's plans. His eyes lit up.

"Wow, this could be a real show piece," he said after he'd looked over everything.

"Could you, do it? I mean can you fit me in?" I asked, nervously.

"I'd love to do it. I'll work up the bid tonight. Do you mind if I borrow these plans? It'll help."

"No, no, please if you can take the job, sure!" I rolled them up and shoved them into the cardboard tube. He laughed and tucked them under his arm.

"OK, I'll email you the bid?"

"Sure." I found a scrap of paper and jotted my email down.

He waved as he drove off. I felt so relieved I had to sit down. I wasn't going to be stuck in this decaying husk for another year.

I could hardly wait to tell Sofia. I'd wait until our dinner plans tonight though. I was excited at making a new friend as well. This was the first time we'd done anything since our lunch date where I'd soaked her with water.

I hadn't been to O'Malley's since high school. I remembered it was a nicer steak house. The place you take a date for a school dance. I dressed up some. Nice jeans, an expensive top, makeup, and heels. Something I would have worn if my ex took me to a nicer, casual restaurant.

I pulled up to the restaurant. I'd made the right call. People were mainly dressed as I was, nicer jeans or slacks, collared shirts, some dresses, even a few ties here or there. Good. I walked inside. Sofia was in the waiting area.

"Hi!" I said.

"I've got us on the list, shouldn't be too long."

"Cool." I sat next to her. "Your cousin came by."

She raised her eyebrows.

"He's sending me a bid tomorrow. He said he can start next week. Isn't that great?"

She smiled. "It is! I'm happy for you!"

"Thank you so much. I was about to pack up and forget about it. I was so upset! You saved me."

I thought I caught a brief frown on her face, but it was probably directed at the couple being seated before us. "Anytime. Happy I could help."

Finally, the hostess took us back. We got our drinks, and the waitress took our orders.

"I have so much to tell you," I said, starting the conversation once the waitress left.

"Oh? What's up? I heard Craig Whelan died because of a fall at your house. How awful!"

"Yeah. It was terrible. They tried to get him to shift, but even though he partially shifted, they couldn't get him to complete one." I took a drink of my Coke, my mouth dry from discussing the tragedy. "He was cursed."

Sofia's eyes flew open wide. "Cursed?"

"Yeah, I found a gris-gris bag on my property. When we opened it, it had items that looked specific to werewolves. Then, we found out that someone has been spying on the house from the woods. A woman."

"You must be so scared," she remarked.

"I'm OK. Since you showed me how to use my magic, I've been practicing. I even saved myself from a bear."

"Wow, you are a quick learner."

I smiled at that, proud of myself. "Thanks."

"So, a gris-gris bag wouldn't be strong enough to kill a werewolf, what do you think really happened?" she asked.

"Well, Gabe helped me out some. After we found the tracks in the woods, he suggested that a witch would have to be actively working a spell to keep him from shifting, and probably to knock him off the scaffolding as well." I don't know why I didn't mention my cat to her. Maybe I thought it all would sound silly to tell her my cat was helping solve the mystery.

She looked at me as though she were mulling it over. "Probably true. That would take a powerful spell. Werewolves are tough."

"Do you think someone in your coven could be responsible?" I hadn't wanted to ask; I was afraid of offending her since we were new friends.

She frowned and tilted her head to the side in thought. After a few seconds she answered, "I want to say no. I don't want to believe anyone in the coven would take a life. But I don't know everyone very well. I'm new at the leader business. We sort of trade off among the senior members on a yearly basis. So, I can't answer. I can try to find out quietly, if possible."

The waitress brought out our food and deposited the plates in front of us. I had a steak, it was a steakhouse after all, but Sofia had the vegetable plate and a baked potato. Why did she bring me to a steakhouse to eat rabbit food? I shrugged inwardly. She was a little odd.

"So, have you found any more magical artifacts?" She was frowning at her plate; probably sad she didn't have a steak.

"No, I haven't really looked very hard. I've had too many things going on." I chewed thoughtfully and swallowed. "Oh, I almost forgot to ask. You said I had elemental magic. Besides the four obvious, Earth, Water, Air, and Fire, what else is there? The internet gave me a million different answers."

She looked at me oddly. "It depends on your magic."

"Oh," my mind was racing. What the hell did that mean? "I'm not sure I know what you mean."

"If you were a witch, those would be the main four elements. Like I said, elemental magic isn't really a strong witch thing. Your magic isn't witch magic, so it could be a whole list of elements, it just depends on you."

I sighed in defeat. That wasn't a help. There could be a dozen more artifacts out there bearing my magic, and I had no idea what they were or where they were.

"Thanks, I appreciate the answer, it just doesn't help me." I smiled at her apologetically.

She shook her head; she really couldn't help me anymore.

After that, we ate and chatted amicably about our lives and what had happened from high school until now. She was also divorced, no children, so that added more that we had in common. It sounded like her marriage had also been a disaster. She said she was happy that I'd reconnected with Gabe. She'd thought we'd been cute together in high school. Since I seriously thought she didn't know I'd existed in high school, I felt flattered. I did have to tell her nothing was going on. He'd helped me out a couple of times but hadn't asked me out or pursued me. It made me sad. But he probably just wasn't interested any more.

Overall, our dinner was a success. I felt I really did have a friend after all. I hoped she felt the same. I went home happy for once. Between Mr. Mittens, Gabe, and Sofia, I was building a new life with new people in my soon to be finished new home. Romance—well, I'd enjoy it, but I could live without for a while. I just wouldn't worry about Gabe and how he felt about me. I was fine.

Mr. Mittens was waiting when I returned home. At first, I thought something must be wrong, but after a strong and bossy meow, I realized he was hungry. I had to remember I had a pet now. I was responsible for his happiness.

I prepared his food and put it on the table in his dish. He purred as he ate. I stroked his fur and told him about my day. That was nice.

Be careful around witches, he said finally, after he'd polished his bowl.

"Sofia is nice."

You can't trust them. They only want two things. Power and more power.

"You can't say that about all witches. There have to be good people in all the supernatural arenas."

He looked up at me, his periwinkle eyes glowing. *You don't know who killed Mr. Whelan. But you do know it was a witch. It could be your witch friend. You don't know. I wouldn't trust any of them until you do.*

"No, Sofia is my friend. I knew her in high school. She didn't run in the same crowds, but she was nice enough." I looked at him, thinking, "Why are you so distrustful of witches? What happened to you?"

He cleaned his face daintily with one paw. Making sure all the food was removed from his whiskers. *Witches are responsible for the deaths of your grandmother and father.*

"What!"

As far as I knew, my father had died in a freak accident and my grandmother in a fall. I said that to my witch hating cat.

Those are what their deaths appeared to be. I know better, I was there when your grandmother died. He stopped his bath and sat there calmly; blue eyes focused on me in perfect seriousness.

"Why haven't you told me this before?" I asked him.

I'm a Splintercat. We live in the moment. I did not think of it until you told me of your witch.

"Why do you think a witch killed grandma? She fell in this house?" I thought for a moment, trying to remember. "She was over ninety years old. She had to have been frail and shouldn't have been on the stairs, anyway."

She was half Fae. Not as powerful as you, but young by Fae standards. For a human, she was as spry as you are and appeared about the same age. She wasn't frail. She was cursed.

"You told me only active magic could cause the death of a powerful being. If she was powerful, how did the witch kill her?" I asked, petulantly trying to show him he was wrong.

Witches want power. Your father and grandmother had just bound your power into the artifacts. The witches coveted it. They could sense it, you see. As long as one with Fae blood is near, the artifacts draw other magical beings. That's why I'm so busy patrolling. Your grandmother and father stood in their way. So, they removed her, by surprise. A witch befriended your grandmother much like Sofia has done with you. Then when your grandmother was distracted, the witch caused the fall and blocked your grandmother's power so she could not save herself.

"And my father?" I was beginning to see why Mr. Mittens hated witches if any of his accusations were true. I had to know if something similar had befallen my dad. My mother had told me he'd died in a shooting accident. "Was it an accident?"

Perhaps. But he was shot from a stray bullet, miles from any known hunting activity in the woods. You'd assume any stray bullet would hit a tree from that distance long before a human. It seemed fishy.

"So, you assumed it was magic?"

He gave me a disdainful look. *It was.*

"How do you know this?"

I overheard the police when they came to inform your mother. They were baffled.

My poor mom. She must have been so confused on top of her grief.

"This makes no sense. If they were after the artifacts that hold my power, they've had twenty-plus years to find them. Two that I know of were in this house which had been abandoned for years."

No one of Fae blood was here. Those holes in the walls weren't from a previous attempt at remodeling. This house has been searched. The artifacts only respond to your blood. Now that you are back, they can be found and your magic stolen.

"Do you know how many artifacts there are?"

Numbers mean nothing to me. I know there are more. I don't know where they are except it makes sense they are here in this house. Your grandmother would have wanted them close so she could give them back when it was time.

That was the only thing that made sense. Two artifacts in the shape of silver jewelry. If it were me, I'd put them in my jewelry box. That would both camouflage them and make them seem ordinary. Silver was pretty, but it wasn't that expensive. A thief might overlook them for gold or jewels. I needed to search all the trunks and see if my grandmother had a jewelry box. Then again, the necklace and bracelet were separate and in random trunks.

"Do you think any have been taken?"

I got the kitty equivalent of a mental shrug. *I do not know. To me, the artifacts appear to be only shiny metal.*

"So, don't trust witches, witches are evil. Find artifacts before witches do?"

He gave me a disdainful look. *You can ignore my warnings, but it would be foolish.*

"I'm not making fun. Sorry. I'll think about what you said."

Fine. I must patrol. There have been several more incursions.

"Off with you then my great protector."

That got me an annoyed tail swish. After he left, I trudged up to the attic. With my new lights, I could now work there at night. I flipped them on and proceeded to open the first trunk I hadn't already searched. Nothing. The next, nothing.

Four more to go. The next one was a beautiful steamer trunk. I thought it would look nice in my room with quilts in it. I decided to see if I could find someone, maybe my new crew, to bring it down. I opened it. Jackpot. Grandma's furs and a jewelry box.

I reached in to pull it out. My fingers tingled. It was a beautiful wooden box with an inlay of various woods and something shiny. I lifted the lid. Wow. Grandma had some nice stuff.

I had no way to know if anything was an artifact. The others that I'd found had images that sort of represented what they did—the seashells, the intricately carved animals. Nothing looked like that in here. I pulled out a stunning sapphire necklace and matching earrings and bracelet. It made me wish I could dress up and have somewhere to go. I put them back. Next was a diamond ring. It looked like a wedding set. Had she put it away after grandpa had died? I didn't know or remember seeing it before. Towards the bottom was a fire opal set in a silver ring. The desire to put it on filled my mind.

This time I studied the piece before I put it on. It was the most brilliant opal I'd ever seen, the fire blazed in it, and I wondered if this was the representation of elemental fire. It made sense. The silver was covered with intricate filigree. As I studied it, I realized it was in the shape of flames. My heart raced, and I took a deep breath. Then I slid it onto my finger.

A flash of light, then the hot flash from hell. Sweat poured off me, and I couldn't catch my breath. Molten lava blazed through me and if I could've gotten enough air, I would've screamed. Luckily it only lasted a few moments. I think I enjoyed water much more than fire.

After I cooled down, I searched the jewelry for more items. Nothing pulled at me or caught my eye—nothing representing air.

There were beautiful things, some looked quite valuable. Someday I might have a place to wear them to, but for now, I'd take the box and add it to my vanity. I could look at the pretty things at least.

I searched the final three trunks, but nothing stood out. I closed them, brushed the dust off my jeans, took my jewelry box, and went back down. I was tired and grubby. But before I washed up and went to bed, I wanted to try my new power out.

I went into the kitchen. I put a paper towel in the sink and concentrated on it. I said, "Fire." Probably not the brightest thing I'd done in my life. It flashed so hot and bright; I fell backwards on my butt. It hurt, but I leapt up and turned the water on as fast as possible. Flames were shooting out of my sink completely out of proportion to the small amount of flammable material.

I forgot I needed to control my output, dammit. I put the fire out. I'd had enough. I decided to work on it tomorrow.

CHAPTER
TEN

I woke up excited. Today was the day they were going to work on my house. The bid I'd accepted was fair and less than the Whelans' had been. I jumped out of bed and hurriedly got ready. A box of pastries I'd picked up last night sat waiting in the fridge. I pulled them out and took one for myself, put it on a plate, and shoved it in the microwave. The coffee started to fill the room with its fragrance. Everything should be ready for my new crew to arrive. Mr. Mittens strolled in for his breakfast, and I fed him. He "m'rowed" when I reminded him, they were coming today. I guess that was cat for "OK."

I think he was glad the last crew had left. He wasn't fond of all the noise and confusion, and he wasn't sure who was friend or foe. Scott knew about the supernatural world, but I had no idea about his crew. So that left poor Mr. Mittens tiptoeing around in his Ragdoll shape, rather than feeling free to be himself, whatever that entailed. It made him grumpy. *Pets*. I shook my head.

Finally, trucks started pulling up behind the house. I might have squeed a little in delight. I might have even clapped my hands—I will deny this though. I walked out the back, and Scott strolled up to me. He handed me a cup of coffee.

"Thanks! Umm, you didn't have to get me coffee, I have some brewing inside for everyone—and pastries."

"I figured I'd get on the boss lady's good side," he said and then smiled.

His smile almost knocked me over; it was so breathtaking. He was seriously gorgeous. I didn't usually go for blonds, but I'd definitely make an exception for a handsome, charming one that brought me gifts and made my house better.

"I'll let the boys know they're welcome to go in and help themselves," he continued.

"Yes, please do."

He looked around. "We're gonna get the painting done today and tomorrow, then we'll start on the inside."

"Sounds wonderful."

"Once we start on the inside, we'll have to do the rough plumbing first, and we'll have to turn off the water. There may be a couple of days where you'll be better off out of the house."

"That's fine, I can stay in town." I had already been through this with the Whelans.

He nodded, flashed me another smile, then went to talk to the crew.

I'd had a flash of brilliance the other day. At least, I thought it was brilliant. A new idea for a business similar to what I'd created with my ex. If it worked out, I could convince Megan to come work for me. I was eager to do some research on feasibility. Even though I didn't really need to work, I enjoyed it so much and frankly, my days were boring. I grabbed my coffee and settled down at the kitchen table to do my research.

I thought that the noise outside would distract me, but it didn't. The clanking as scaffolding went up, the voices, and the hubbub brought me calm. Before the workers called it a day, I'd finished a lot. In fact, I was shocked to look up and see them leaving. Scott came in and told me they'd be back at eight the next morning. I waited until he left to run outside and look at what they'd accomplished. The main color was done, and that left just the porches and the trim. My eyes watered. This old place *was* gonna be a showstopper. I wiped my eyes and chastised myself for being a baby about a stupid house. Then, I took a deep breath and went back in to finish up.

A wolf stood in the middle of my kitchen. I gasped and backed up slowly. Then, I opened the door and ran out yelling for Mr. Mittens. I hoped he wasn't in the house. The wolf would eat him. My cat appeared right next to me. He looked up and meowed.

"Thank God you're alright!" I said.

Why wouldn't I be?

"There's a wolf in the kitchen."

Impossible.

I shuddered and shook my head. I knew what I'd seen.

He walked to the door. He was going to go in there!

"No, he'll eat you!" I yelled.

The cat scoffed at me. Then in a flash, he changed, and a gigantic bobcat looking creature took his place. It was the size of a tiger, but sort of built like a hyena. The head was heavy, and he had long fangs like a saber-toothed tiger.

I gasped. "Mr. Mittens?"

He turned his head and the same periwinkle blue eyes blazed at me.

Yes, his mental voice said with a little sarcasm attached.

"Wow."

This is my true form.

"I'm impressed. I'll stop thinking of you as a housecat," I promised.

Hmpf, it's about time.

He slunk into the house through the door I'd left open.

A few minutes later he came out.

There is nothing in there.

"What?"

He started to repeat his statement, but I shushed him. "That can't be. I know what I saw."

He morphed back into his ragdoll form. *No wolves.*

I walked cautiously back into the house. Sure enough, nothing was there. Had I imagined it? Now that I knew about magic, I wasn't as willing to think I was going over the edge.

"Mr. Mittens, what do werewolves look like when they shift?"

I'm sorry, what do you mean? He blinked.

"You know, do they change into literal wolves, are they half man half wolf, or something else?"

He looked at me strangely. *They change into wolves.*

I thought for a moment. "Do you believe in ghosts?"

No, I do not believe in them. I know they exist.

I looked down at him. "They really do exist?"

Of course. Do you think that was a ghost wolf?

"I don't know. But Craig died here. He was a werewolf. Do you think it could have been him?"

He shook his head. *I don't know.*

"If it was him, why would he appear as a wolf? Are ghosts *mean*?"

The ghosts I've run across were just like their human selves unless they were angry. But there's no reason Craig would be angry with you.

"No? He died because of me. Because he was working on my house."

Mr. Mittens shook his head. *No, he died because a witch wanted him dead. It had nothing to do with you.*

"Yeah? But does he know that?"

Mr. Mittens stretched and promised to check the house. I waited in the kitchen, thinking. I didn't know that the wolf I'd seen was Craig, it was just an intuitive leap. I knew nothing about ghosts either. Since I was researching anyway, I figured I'd look into ghosts on the internet.

First thing I discovered was that there were tons of books on ghosts. In a way, that made me feel better. Lots of people had seen ghosts or believed in them. It made me feel less nuts. Next, there were different types of ghosts. That was interesting. The first was what I thought I was seeing—the spirit of a deceased person. Usually, they appear to offer comfort or complete some business they'd left behind. The other ghosts were less appealing. Poltergeists and cold spots. Let's hope it was just the ghost of Craig trying to deliver a message. I closed my browser and went back to work on my new project. No sense getting worked up over one sighting of an apparition. If he showed up again, I'd figure it out.

The next morning, Scott showed up with coffee for me again. I didn't know what to think about that.

"Wow, you'd better stop doing this or your workers will talk," I said when he handed it to me.

"Not if they want to get paid."

"Funny. I wanted to tell you how good that paint looks."

"Thank you. My guys are good."

"I'm so glad Sofia gave me your number."

"Me too." His gaze made me think he had other motives besides a job. I blushed.

I hadn't felt the attention of a man in a long time. The divorce had left me disinterested and emotionally drained for so long, I hadn't even put myself out there. Now, I was in a new town; was it time to start? I was interested in seeing how it would go with Gabe, but he hadn't shown any real interest. He could be busy, but I'd been out of the dating scene for so long, I didn't trust my instincts. Scott was interested, but he worked for me. Would this ruin what I had going? I needed the house done a lot more than I needed romance. I didn't push it.

His smile faded. He must have felt me pull back. He looked away at the workers getting their tools and preparing for the day.

"Hey, I know this probably isn't appropriate, and I barely know you. But I'm very attracted to you. Could I take you out to dinner sometime?" he asked, nervously. When I didn't answer immediately, he continued. "Believe me, I've never acted this way with a client. I just can't get you out of my mind."

My mind raced. I was flattered, nervous, flattered, terrified, flattered, and completely staggered on top of it. I stumbled around for an answer, fully intending to say no. "Sure I'd like that." Well, blow me down.

He hit me with one of his blazing smiles. "Great, I'll plan something and get back with you."

I smiled back and realized I was really happy about this. He was gorgeous, I could feel the chemistry blazing between us, and frankly, I liked male attention. I was pleased. No, I was happy. I watched him head out to work. He wore snug jeans that hugged his tight ass, and I watched in appreciation as he walked away. He was broad shouldered and where his t-shirt stretched across them, I could see the muscles ripple underneath. That may have led to me picturing him naked.

I let out a breath I didn't know I was holding and went inside. Maybe it was time for a cold shower.

* * *

THE NEXT DAY STARTED THE WEEKEND. SCOTT SAID HE USUALLY GAVE his guys Sunday off, but since they had fit me in, they hadn't planned on working the weekend at all. So, I slept in, and since I had time, I finally pulled out the books I'd taken from the attic. They consisted of photo albums and three journals. I'd flipped through them but hadn't taken the time to actually read them. The leather chair was sitting in the rounded part that looked like a turret from the outside. Inside, it formed the perfect reading nook. The chair and a small end table with a drawer made up my nook. It would be perfect once I got a lamp. I set the journals on the table and curled up in the chair. I found the earliest journal and sat down to read.

It was dated 1908. My grams would have been thirteenish then. It was pretty typical stuff. Crushes, friend problems, how much she loved her cat. I guess she was the one that named him Mr. Mittens. I smiled. I'd have to tell him about being in her journals.

I had intended to only search for passages that talked about my powers, but I found myself engrossed in her childish view of the world. She talked about her parents. I was surprised to find that my great-grandmother had been active in the local coven. My great-grandfather was of course a high-born Fae lord. He hadn't been able to stay in this realm very long—only a few weeks here and there. So, Fae gold had bought the untouched land with the primeval forest—to help him feel at home when he visited—and the house had been built in the 1880s. At around the time of my grandmother's birth, her father gifted her Mr.

Mittens as a protector, since her father wasn't able to visit his family very often. My grams, Lucy Rose, had spent time in the Fae realm as a child, but her mother was unhappy there, finding it as foreign and alien as her husband found Earth. Lucy Rose missed her friends. So, they came back.

It must have been hard on both of my great-grandparents to be separated. But what can you do if you're from completely different realms? I sighed thinking of the sacrifices they'd made that eventually brought me into the world. The only mention of magic in this journal was that she was excited to get her magic back when she turned eighteen. Then she'd be able to travel the realms and see her father more often. Huh, I wondered if I could travel between realms?

I grabbed the next one and skimmed the first half, more of the same —musings of a young teen in the early part of the twentieth century. It was interesting, because she was my grandmother, but nothing grabbed me. I did learn that she'd met my grandfather when she was fourteen. She didn't know it of course, but I found it amusing that she hated him at first sight.

I continued flipping. Finally, she was talking about getting her magic back. Here we go. Her dad had stored her magic in jewelry as well. On her eighteenth birthday they had presented the items to her. There were thirteen items—necklaces, bracelets, and rings. Just like mine. I felt excitement grow in my guts. Thirteen? Did I have thirteen as well?

I read the powers as she described the items. Water, a seashell necklace. The excitement built. Earth, a charm bracelet with little animals. Yes, this was just like mine so far. Fire, a fire opal pendant on a silver chain. I swallowed. They were similar, but not exact. Mine had been a fire opal ring. That's all I'd seen of my magic. I eagerly continued.

Air, a necklace with little swirl decorations. Okay, those were the elements I knew of. Spirit, a turquoise ring. Mind, a moonstone ring. Aether, a necklace of clear quartz stones. Shadow, an onyx bracelet. Light, a silver necklace made of small suns. Lightning, a diamond line bracelet. Ice, a diamond necklace. Time, a watch. The last one was reality, this one was smeared, so I wasn't sure what the item was. Damn. I could guess the powers behind some of the elements, the four basic ones were obvious, earth, water, fire, air. Since I had gained three of those, I could guess that air had to do with literally manipulating air. Spirit, mind, ice, lightning, light, and shadow were also easy to guess. I assumed that spirit meant I could see and control the spirit world, and mind probably that I could either control things with my mind or read minds or something. But what the hell did Aether do? Reality? I really didn't have a clue about those. I had only found three. I was seriously behind if there were thirteen elements. Also, some could have been stolen from me.

I sighed. At least I had an idea of what I was looking for if my magic was similar to my grandmother's. Mr. Mittens had said I was stronger, but I didn't know if that meant in ability or that I had more elements to call on. I finished skimming the journals, looking for...I don't know what. A clue on who could have caused her death? But I didn't see anything that really stood out. The journals ended when she was a young adult, right before she married my grandfather at the age of twenty. So more than seventy years of her life were not recorded, or I hadn't found the rest of the journals. I tossed the last one down on the floor, and then kicked them under my bed.

I'd thought the journals would give me more than information. In truth, I was looking for some hope, or direction on how to find my lost and splintered magic, but I was nearly at the same spot I'd been before I read the stupid things. I sighed, heaved myself out of the chair, and went to the kitchen to grab a bite and work on my new business idea.

CHAPTER

ELEVEN

The next morning, I woke up early, anticipation burning in my abdomen. I was going to see Scott, and somehow, I felt like a teenager again. I frowned. I was an idiot. I liked two different men, who did that? If Gabe showed up and threw himself at me, I'd take him in a minute. Was that fair to Scott? Was I that fickle? I needed to cool my jets. This was all because I hadn't had attention paid to me in years. That was all. I needed to be calm and rational and think all of this out before I acted. Plan firmly in hand, I got ready for the day and made myself dress and act casually.

That all went out the window when Scott handed me that glorious cup of Joe and smiled his blazing smile at me. I think I may have orgasmed on the spot. I was seriously not going to be rational about him. Dammit.

I might have snuck peaks of him throughout the day, particularly when it got warm, and he took off his shirt. Nope. I did not do that, I either had it bad for this guy, or I had gone too long without a man.

The construction team had been delayed a day on the paint, when they'd discovered an area on the porch that needed to be repaired before the painting could be finished. He apologized that he hadn't found it before the bid, and it would cost extra. I reassured him it was fine all the while watching his mouth and wondering if he would kiss me. Seriously, this was not like me. I wasn't the kind of girl to be oogling strangers and hoping they'd rip my clothes off. Plus, there was always Gabe in the back of my mind.

This continued throughout the week. I couldn't stop my body from reacting to Scott. He continued to bring me coffee every day and charm me thoroughly for a few minutes before work, then I'd spend my day working on my business plan and proposal while watching him, my libido humming along painfully.

Friday, he finally made good on his promise to take me out. He had some kind of function that was supposed to help his business, and he wanted me to accompany him. Not my idea of a fun or sexy first date, but my heart fluttered in my chest, and that slow ache started in my loins. I had it bad.

I hadn't brought many of my old clothes from my old life to this one. But I'd kept some of my favorite pieces. One of them was a gorgeous cocktail dress. It was sapphire blue, clung to my curves, and brought out my eyes. I blew out and curled my hair and then brushed it until it was a burnished dark copper. It almost glowed against the blue. I finished it off with some of my grandmother's jewelry. She had jewelry crammed with gemstones that her father must have given her because they were so unique in design they couldn't have come from Earth. I took out her sapphires. The necklace was so laden with stones, it was almost too heavy to wear. I slipped it on over my head, and it rested across my chest.

I didn't bother with earrings since my hair was down, but I wore the matching bracelet and rings. Even Mr. Mittens was impressed. He batted at the bracelet as I put it on.

"For a powerful Splintercat, you sure act like a normal house cat," I said.

That made him sputter before he answered. *I do not.*

"Well, you just batted at my bracelet, you keep leaving me goodies on the back porch, you demand your food at set times of the day, you rub on my legs, and I caught you in that box tweaking on catnip the other day. Oh, and you're a bed hog. I've read that's what normal pet cats do."

I am not a normal cat.

"You keep saying that, but…" I gave him a significant look.

He hmpfed at me. *If anything, you are my pet.*

"Oh? How do you figure?" I asked dismissively.

Well, I protect you, I'm older and more experienced, and I bring you food daily.

"Is that what we're calling your offerings on the back porch? My daily meals?"

He answered by flicking his tail at me.

"And the box? I noticed you don't have an explanation for that."

All felines love boxes. You should know that.

"What about your catnip…problem?"

Do you not imbibe with a glass of wine on occasion?

"Fine, I'll drop that one, but what about the fact I wake up and you're in the middle of the bed, and I'm hugging the edge?"

I watch over you at night.

"For a watcher, you sure snore loudly."

I do not snore.

"What do you call it then?"

A purr?

I laughed. "I'm just teasing you. I'm proud to be your pet."

As you should. He smoothed a hair that was out of place with his tongue and jumped down from my vanity. This time, he jumped up in the window to watch me.

"I'm still not sure what you're doing on your patrols though. I think it's just an excuse to disappear and ignore me all day and night."

He stared at me, periwinkle eyes blazing. *I keep all the interlopers at bay.*

"I've never seen a single interloper besides the witch that killed Mr. Whelan."

He picked up a paw as though he were going to wash it and then put it down. *I'm very sorry I missed that witch. I'm only one protector.*

I kill several dangerous invaders daily. I'm so sorry I missed that one. Your werewolf friend was very kind to me.

I walked over and stroked his head. "I didn't mean to imply you weren't doing your job, sorry." He bowed his head, and I scratched his ears. "I'm sure you kill all the other nasties."

I do. But I'm not unkind about it. I make it quick, and if something isn't seeking to kill you, I let it stay on the grounds, to help balance your magic.

"What does that mean? Balance my magic?"

Your magic screams out to magical beings. They are attracted to this land to partake of the magic that is free and raging around here. Their presence helps to soak up the extra and keep the land balanced.

Another tidbit I didn't know. I sighed.

"Will I ever know anything about magic?"

It would take lifetimes to learn. There is so much magic, so many types, so many creatures and magic users, there is no way to know it all. Perhaps someday, you will travel to your great-grandfather's realm and learn of your magic.

That reminded me. "Oh, I learned something today!"

Yes?

"My grandmother, when she got her magic on her eighteenth birthday, had thirteen elements. Water, earth, fire, air, spirit, mind, aether, shadow, light, lightning, ice, time, and reality. I don't know what they all mean, but maybe that will help you remember if you've seen any of the artifacts around."

I will continue to look on my patrols.

"What kind of supernatural creatures are roaming around here? Unicorns? Are there unicorns?"

I would never suffer a unicorn to live here. They are nasty creatures.

All my hopes were smashed. "Really? Then what about all the wonderful stories about them helping young maidens and healing things with their horns?"

Propaganda.

"Unicorns put out propaganda?"

136

Yes, how else do you think they can continue to kidnap young maidens?

"Huh." I thought for a moment. "What about dragons?"

He gave me a strange look. *Dragons don't put out propaganda. They are large, scaly, flying lizards that horde treasure, and like to burn things. You should know that even if you weren't supernatural.*

I laughed. But he wasn't teasing. "Damn, you're destroying all my fun. So, what harmless supernatural critters are now crawling around my woods?"

I did not say they were harmless. I just make sure they aren't here to harm you.

"Oh."

There are many. However, I make sure that they appear in normal earth forms if there are humans around. It is one of the stipulations if they wish to stay alive.

"OK. So, if they knew I was around, they wouldn't appear in their natural forms?"

Exactly.

"So, I could have seen one already?"

Possible.

"Was that bear I scared away one of these creatures?"

No. That was a bear.

For a moment I felt faint. I think I was hoping that although I'd scared it away, it hadn't been a true threat. "Oh."

You still need to be careful in the woods. There are many things here naturally that are dangerous.

I finished up my makeup and straightened my dress. "How do I look?" I asked my cat.

Human.

"That good, huh?"

Yes, to other humans.

That was probably the best compliment I was going to get from my cat. "I tell you you're beautiful all the time," I replied.

It's true.

"Ugh."

He jumped out of the window gracefully and strolled out of the bathroom, tail straight up and all his floof gracefully swaying in the breeze of his passage. "Show off," I called after him as he disappeared out the door.

I gave my hair one last pat and went into the kitchen to wait for Scott. I figured he'd pick me up at the back door since that's where he came for work, so I was surprised when he knocked on the front door.

I hurried back up front, and opened the door, ready with my wrap and bag to walk out. He looked surprised.

"I've never picked up a date that was ready on time," he remarked.

I blushed. Had I done something wrong? My ex hated anyone who wasn't on time, and I'd adjusted my whole life to always be ten minutes earlier than expected.

"It's refreshing," he finished up.

I smiled. "Sorry, I thought I'd already blown the date. I haven't done this in a long time."

He laughed. "You are perfect and stunning."

"Thank you," I replied politely, blushing fiercely.

The function turned out to be the annual mayor's ball in Lincoln City about forty-five minutes away from my small town of Kilchis. I didn't know anyone, not that I expected too, but all the local power players were there, apparently. It was pleasant, if a little boring—the typical speeches and other stuff that didn't interest me at all. But the food, music, and dancing were fantastic. I got a lot of compliments on my dress and jewelry, which made me feel good and not as dumpy as I felt. Scott turned out to be a great dancer, and I enjoyed being held in his arms and whirled around as though I were made of air.

I was sad when the party was over. I hadn't had that good of a time in a long time, and I didn't want it to end. Scott drove me home and parked at his usual spot in the back. I was growing nervous because I didn't know what I was supposed to do. This was a first date, and I felt like a kiss would be too forward. But I was so attracted to him, I didn't trust myself. I was trying to decide how to escape with my virtue intact. I seemed to fluctuate wildly between wanting to jump his bones and wondering why I was reacting that way.

"I had a great time," he said.

I must have been quiet too long. "Me too," I said and looked over at him.

He leaned in, and my heart began to beat wildly. He wanted to kiss me. I still wasn't sure what to do, but my desire for him was running rampant. I leaned into the kiss. It was soft and gentle. His hand reached up under my hair and cupped my head. My arms reached around his shoulders, and my hand raked through his short hair.

We both deepened the kiss. Thoughts of having wild, unhinged sex with this man raged through my mind. I didn't know what was wrong with me. I liked sex as much as the next woman, but I wasn't a raging nympho on a first date. Right now, if he suggested anything, I was going to rip my clothes off and take him here. Somehow, I was already in his lap, and I was grinding on him like a horny teenager. Once I realized that, I pulled myself back, scooted over to my side of the truck and mumbled an apology. Then I opened the door and ran inside, utterly humiliated.

I locked the door. I could hear his truck start up and the crunch of gravel as he drove off, probably completely confused. One minute, I was an average date, having a good time, then a lunatic who attacked him in his truck, then a complete idiot running inside without any explanation. I stumbled to my bathroom and stripped off my clothes and jewelry, kicking them into a heap in the corner. Disgusted at myself, I crouched down in the shower and let the hot water cascade over me. I wanted to cry at my stupidity, but part of me knew this wasn't me. Could my magic be screwing around with my emotions?

Even when I *was* a horny teenager, I hadn't done anything like that. I was a forty-two-year-old woman who had to wear hormone patches —they kept me very well-regulated by the way—and no way was I awash in hormones. Something was throwing me off my game. I wish my magic came with a manual. I doubted my cat would know or care to know anything about my love life so I couldn't ask him. I'd rather die than talk about it with Sofia, my only girlfriend that understood magic, since she was Scott's cousin. I couldn't even talk to my doctor about it, since he was the man I really wanted to be with.

I stood up in shock. I wanted to be with Gabe. Why was I even seeing Scott? This was crazy. Sure, he was attractive and there was some crazy chemistry, but I'd always been a one-man woman. I fell back into my foggy self-loathing. I couldn't even blame drinking. I rarely drank and had only had ice water at the event.

I got out once the water turned cold and got ready for bed. Mr. Mittens showed up right on time to hog the bed laying in the middle while having a bath.

"Scoot over, please," I asked before I climbed in.

He moved over a foot.

I sighed.

He looked over at me. *Is something wrong?*

"No. Yes. I don't know?"

That answer just got me a long curious stare.

"Can magic mess with your...desires?"

In what way? he asked and cocked his head at me.

"Could my magic make me desire something or someone I wasn't interested in?"

He looked thoughtful or grumpy. Hard to tell.

Your personal magic shouldn't affect you at all. It is yours after all. As part of you as your blood, bones, and flesh.

I swallowed. That wasn't what I wanted to hear. If it wasn't my magic, then it was me. I was messed up. My thoughts went round and round, but then I realized something.

"You said my magic won't affect me. Could someone else's magic do this to me?"

His tail flicked in irritation. I hoped it wasn't aimed at me.

Yes. Has that witch come back?

So, he wasn't upset at me, but at the witch he'd missed.

"I don't know. Something happened tonight," I hedged. I didn't know how to explain this to my cat, and frankly I didn't want too either. It was too embarrassing. But if someone was trying to make me hot for Scott, I needed to know. It wasn't fair to him to lead him on, or to me to feel this way only when I was near him. I needed to figure it out.

I assume it has something to do with humans and procreating? he asked, sounding as if the entire subject was distasteful.

"Uh, sort of. When I'm around Scott, I'm nearly irresistibly drawn to him. I basically attacked him tonight. But when he's gone, I'm back to liking and wanting to be with Gabe. It's not like me, and it's making me feel—off balance. Odd."

It sounds like the effects of a love potion.

"Those are real?"

Yes, and extremely dangerous.

"How so?"

He circled a new spot and plopped down against my pillow. *Well, forcing someone to love someone they do not can cause a dissonance in the person that if continued too long will eventually lead to their mind splitting apart, resulting in madness.*

"Wonderful." I stretched out and yawned. "How could someone have slipped me a love potion? I make my own meals and drinks?" Of course, my kitchen was open to the workers, and they used the fridge for their lunches and drinks.

I don't know. Have you accepted any food or drink from anyone else in the last few days?

I started to say no, but I remembered that Scott brought me a coffee every day. Could that be it? Did he want me to fall in love with him? Why? He hardly knew me.

"Just the coffee Scott brings me."

Stop drinking it. See if the problem stops.

"So, the love potion isn't permanent?"

No, it has to be administered daily.

"How do you know so much? I mean, you're a cat. It's not like you're brewing your own potions."

He looked at me with his grumpy face. *I've been around a lot of magic users that have used potions.*

"Sorry, I didn't mean to offend you." I stroked his head, and he leaned into it. "I won't drink the coffee."

He nodded, slowly blinked at me, and settled into my pillow. I sighed and got comfortable on the edge of the bed. Freaking cats.

CHAPTER
TWELVE

I just couldn't face Scott. So, on Saturday morning, I got up, put on coffee for the workers, left a note on the door, and told my cat I was going on patrol with him. He frowned at me. Yes, cats frown, apparently. At least, he managed to look slightly grumpier than before.

We stayed close to the house for a little while. Once they finished the touch ups on the outside, they were moving in to start on the interior. I saw Scott go up to the back door, and then walk away from the sign. I felt bad, but not bad enough to face him.

I wandered around the forest with Mr. Mittens. Once we were completely lost in the dense woods, he shifted to his natural form. Now instead of a fluffy Ragdoll, his fierceness was up to my waist and a little bit scary.

The land was mostly flat, although it did have rolling hills, and one rocky cliff where the waterfall was.

"How do you know where to go?" I asked him.

I've done this for over a hundred years.

"Yeah, I guess so," I said absently. Not really listening, but not wanting to walk in silence.

"Are you drawn to the bad things? Is that part of your magic?"

Yes.

Wow, this was going to be a boring conversation if he only answered in short words and phrases.

"Not very talkative today, are you?"

I am on patrol. I must stay focused.

Great, alone with my thoughts. Just what I wanted after I'd made a grand fool of myself and then ran away.

I looked around trying to occupy my mind. Trees, brush, some wildflowers, trees, a rock. I should have brought a book. I opened my mouth to talk to my cat, but just as I did, he bounded off.

"Mr. Mittens!" I yelled after him. No answer.

I followed the best I could, but he was super-fast. I could see his passage for a short while, then I just kept going. I could hear crashing and growling. What did he catch? I secretly hoped it was a unicorn, but not if it would hurt him. Finally, I broke through the brush and trees into a small clearing. Mr. Mittens was wrestling with something. A large screech rang out and nearly broke my eardrums. I clutched my hands tightly to my ears. I could see grey feathers now. Some kind of large bird? The head came into view. Yes, it looked like a large bird. The head had tufts that stood up like a horned owl. But the face was more eagle than owl. A large, hooked beak stuck out and then opened, and another horrid shriek shook the air. The scuffle came back my way. The creature had two powerful hind legs, but instead of feathers, they were furred, and it had paws like a great cat. This thing wasn't a bird, it was a griffin. I gasped.

I yelled out, "Stop!" I don't know why, but I didn't want Mr. Mittens to get hurt, and I wanted to see the griffin.

Both animals froze in their tracks. Damn, I forgot to modulate myself, and I must have reached out with my magic. I reached inside and drew out my magic slowly. When I said, "release," both creatures turned and looked at me. Mr. Mittens with fury in his eyes, the griffin with a little fear.

"What's going on?" I asked.

I expected Mr. Mittens to give me grief, but instead, the griffin answered in a pleasant female sounding voice in my head.

I've come to ask for sanctuary on your land, she said.

"Sanctuary?" I questioned, looking at my cat.

Yes, as the Fae lord of this land, you can grant sanctuary to those you find worthy.

"I'm a Fae lord?"

Technically. This land is owned by a Fae. It reacts as though it were on the Fae plane, so yes. You own it, you are the lord, er, lady of the land.

"Shit."

I had no idea what to do. So, I asked the griffin. "Why do you require sanctuary?"

The griffin bowed its head at me. I cringed. I wasn't a lord or much of a lady.

I am escaping a troubled marriage, she replied.

That sounded harmless. I looked at my cat. "Is that an acceptable reason?"

I do not know. I suppose it is as long as the husband doesn't come around to make trouble. He turned to the Griffin. *Do you plan to harm anyone on this property?*

No. The Griffin answered.

I looked down at him. "Is that all you need to ask?"

Yes.

"You have my permission to stay," I said.

The griffin bowed her head. *Thank you, my lady.*

I flinched. "You don't have to call me that. I'm Brigid."

Thank you…Brigid. She hesitated over my name. *And thank you for the gift of your name. I'm Brightfeather.*

"Pleased to meet you."

Mr. Mittens gave me a thunderous look. *Remember, no human can see you in your griffin form. Other than Brigid,* Mr. Mittens addressed Brightfeather.

I can appear as an eagle or a lion.

"I'd keep it to an eagle. There aren't many lions in this part of the country," I said.

Yes, my lady.

I waved goodbye to Brightfeather and continued the patrol with my cat. "Don't you think you should talk to the creatures that come here before you attack them? Brightfeather was quite pleasant."

He scoffed. *No. Griffins are extremely dangerous. She could have been an assassin.*

"But you wouldn't know unless you asked her."

Hmpf. An assassin wouldn't tell me, now, would she?

"I don't know. I guess not. That means she could still be an assassin."

No, she did not lie.

"How do you know?"

I can sense a lie.

I sighed. "Your logic doesn't ring true. Then you could ask them, and you'd know if they were lying."

My cat was annoyed. *I have a process.*

"Uh huh. Attack first, ask questions later?"

Yes.

At that, he got quiet again. We walked along in silence for a time.

You should never give out your true name, he said after a while. That was probably why he'd given me the dirty look when I was talking to Brightfeather.

"Why not?"

It gives magical creatures power over you.

"Well, shit."

Yes indeed.

I didn't know what to say about that. I mean, everyone knew my name. The government especially, probably why they took everyone's name—to have more control over them. Dammit. Nothing I could do about it now. I changed the subject.

"If Scott is giving me a love potion, how many days before it wears off?" I asked.

I don't know. I would assume a few days.

"Huh."

I wouldn't drink the coffee Scott brought me the next couple of days. If I could secretly get rid of it on Monday, I might be able to tell if I was being slipped something or not. This sucked. If he was giving me something, that made it the equivalent of a date rape drug. That made me extremely uncomfortable. But I needed him to finish the house. I didn't know what to do. If it wasn't the coffee, then it was either me, or someone else was coming into the house and putting the potion in my food or drink. But who? It was driving me crazy!

The thing was, Scott was a nice guy. Or appeared to be a nice guy. He was good at his job too. I didn't see any reason why he'd have to drug a girl to have her like him. He was handsome and built. He had a good job. What else could a girl want? Nothing added up.

"I'm gonna head back," I announced to my cat. "I gotta face the music sometime."

He hmpfed at me and led me back to the house. Once he was close enough, he morphed back to his Ragdoll shape and walked back to the house with me. The workers were on their lunch break, and several trucks were gone. I'm sure others were in the house using the kitchen, but some sat on the porch eating sandwiches. I entered my kitchen. The ubiquitous cup of coffee sat on the counter; my name scrawled on the cardboard. I shivered. I grabbed the cup, dumped the contents, and threw it away. Three men were in line to use the microwave, and rather than bother them, I grabbed my purse and my keys. I'd just go grab something in town.

I opened the door, and Scott was standing there, filling the doorway. Shit. I almost made it.

"Hi," he said. Looking a little uncomfortable. "Are you avoiding me?"

I was about to lie and say no, but it was time to pretend to be the adult I appeared. "Yeah, maybe. I'm pretty embarrassed about my actions last night."

"Why?" He looked around. "Let's walk over there." He pointed to a spot that was out of ear shot of his workers. I nodded.

Once we were safely away, I answered. "I was not myself."

"I enjoyed it. I enjoyed you, and our entire evening." He reached out and with a finger lifted my chin gently, so I was looking at him. "There is no reason to be embarrassed."

The same overwhelming desire flooded through me again. I wanted to throw him down in the dirt and ride him until we both screamed in pleasure. It wasn't normal. I took a step back and shook my head.

"I'm sorry. I can't. This is too fast for me."

"No, don't worry. I don't want to pressure you. We'll take it slow. How about, I take you to lunch next week? That's a full seven days away, and you can think about it. I'll leave you alone until then." He flashed me one of his panty-dropping smiles and my breath caught.

"OK, thanks," I stammered out and backed away. He frowned a little as I climbed into my car and started it up. Was he disappointed his prey had escaped? Or was he sad? I couldn't tell.

I drove to town and didn't go back until after they'd left for the day.

CHAPTER
THIRTEEN

I dumped out the coffee for the entire week. By the time the lunch date I'd promised Scott came around, I was sure I could handle it rationally. I got in the truck. We drove to town. Since it was a date, I was expecting him to take me to a sit-down restaurant, but he took me to a drive-through. I laughed.

"This is good," I said. "Non-pretentious."

"That's my goal, to make you laugh and be non-pretentious."

I laughed a little more. We gave our orders to the sign and drove up to the window. We got our food, and Scott drove over to the city park. We sat comfortably in his truck and munched our food. I felt normal, no overwhelming urges to jump him for now. It was nice, and we had a good time.

Before we left to head back, he asked if he could kiss me. Since we already had kissed before on the fateful night, and I needed to see how I would respond, I agreed and scooted across the bench seat to lean into it. His lips touched mine. They were soft and yielding, and the second we touched, my entire body lit up. Before I could lose control, I threw myself back away from him.

He looked confused. I felt bad for him. I was the worst tease ever. I apologized.

"I'm so sorry. I'm just struggling," I said abashedly.

"It's OK," he said. "I remember I said we'd go slow." He started the truck and threw me a smile.

"I do appreciate lunch," I began. "It was fun."

"I'm glad."

The workers had started on the inside of the house. The third floor had been demolished and all the wreckage was hauled out. They were working on demoing the second floor. Since they were still at work, I wandered up to the second floor to check it out. They had kept some things to be reinstalled or refurbished. Pieces of crown molding were stacked neatly in the halls along with the original doors. They were solid hardwood and only required sanding and repainting. I checked the rooms. The plaster had been stripped, and the lathe was in the process of being removed. They were going to sheetrock after updating the insulation. Rough wiring had already been done by the Whelans. I wandered from room to room, imagining the finished product as based on the plans done by Isabella. As I entered the second floor sitting room, I felt a familiar pull. I reached toward the far wall and knocked out some pieces of lathe until my hand grasped a cloth bag. I pulled it out.

Why would my grandmother or father hide my magic in a wall? Wouldn't they keep the artifacts close so they could give them to me when I reached adulthood? What had happened? Did they suspect a witch was after them? I opened the bag and dumped the contents into my hand. It was a set of three rings. The first was a turquoise ring. The next was moonstone, and the last one, diamond. This time, before I put them on, I took close-up pictures with my phone. Then, because I didn't know what else to do, I put them on one at a time. The turquoise ring gave a flash and a light touch like a feather raced through me. That wasn't too bad. The moonstone flashed, and also, a light touch. The diamond ring was harder though. An icy wind passed through me and left me shivering. I tried to recall which stone represented which element. I think the turquoise was spirit. I'd have to go back and recheck my grandmother's journals.

I had regained five of hopefully thirteen pieces of my splintered magic. I pumped my fist. This was cool. Maybe the rest were in this house. I wondered if the crew had found anything on the third floor when they tore up the walls. I ran upstairs to see if I felt any pull. I wandered room to room but felt nothing. I went down to the main floor where I lived and did the same. I checked the dumpster where they put the debris. Nothing. Oh well, I'd found three more. I should count that as good.

Wondering about searching for my magic was a good way to keep my mind off Scott and Gabe. I was still disturbed about the reactions I had to Scott but having avoided the coffee for over a week left me feeling better about him. He wasn't the one dosing me. However, it was coming from somewhere. Should I look for another charmed bag? I thought for a moment. No, my cat said it had to be a potion, potions were liquid, and my assumption was it had to be consumed. I wondered if I needed to put all my food in my bedroom and lock it up. Or buy everything pre-packaged. Something else to think about.

Then there was Gabe. He was the one I was truly attracted to. I liked Scott, and knowing he was innocent made me like him more. Plus, he'd shown interest, where Gabe had not. Maybe it was time to let those hopes go. I didn't know. It was probably time to see how things went with Scott, if I could keep my love potion fueled libido under wraps. If anything happened between us, I wanted to know it was my choice. Again, I wondered why anyone would do this to me. It didn't make sense.

My business ideas were coming along, and I was shopping it out to see if there would be interest. So, I checked my email. Too soon, I told myself. I was right, there wasn't anything. I downloaded a couple of new books to my tablet and went into my room to read. I needed something else to do. My days were falling into a boring routine: getting up, checking out the house, doing chores, working on the business, reading, then staring at the walls. It was starting to wear on me. I should get involved with something in the community.

Maybe I could volunteer at the library. I promised myself I'd go to town tomorrow and check what they needed. That decided, I went back to work on my new business.

As I sat down at the table, the phone rang. It was Gabe. My heart beat faster, and my palms grew sweaty.

"Hi," I answered.

"Hey. I was calling to check on you."

"Oh, thanks. I'm good. You?"

"Same." He paused a moment. "That wasn't the only reason. I wanted to ask you out. I'm sorry I haven't before now, I've been really busy."

"Oh. Yeah, I'd like that." I did too. I wouldn't have ever said yes to Scott if I knew Gabe was interested. I guess it was time to cut it off with Scott. I just hoped it wouldn't ruin my chances at getting the house finished. But then again, I wasn't exclusive with anyone.

"How about this weekend?" he said.

"Sure." Butterflies filled my stomach.

"Saturday? We can go to the movies."

"I'd love that!" I would too. I hadn't seen a movie in ages.

He hung up after setting a time. There was only one movie theater in town, and I had no idea what was playing. I had a feeling he didn't either. It was an adventure. Just thinking about hanging out with Gabe gave me a warm feeling inside—all tingles and anticipation. I hadn't felt that with Scott. With him it was physical and sort of disturbing like Mr. Mittens had said—a dissonance.

I shook myself out of it. My goal wasn't romance, it was to get this house finished, find all my magic and learn to use it, and get my new business up and running. There was too much going on around me I had no control over. Those things I could control.

I decided I would spend time each day practicing my magic. Also, planning how to fill the house with furniture. The house was huge. The main floor consisted of the grand foyer, main bedroom and bath, the kitchen, a reception room, a library, a powder room, a dining room, and the laundry. The second floor originally had five bedrooms and two baths. The renovation consisted of changing it into three large bedrooms with ensuite baths, so that was a huge project. It also had a smaller living room area at the top of the stairs, and a sitting room in the turret. The third floor was smaller because of the attic access, and I could see why it drove the Whelans crazy since they knew the space was there but had no access. It had four bedrooms and one bath along with a turret sitting/sunroom. This conversion was changing it into two bedrooms with private baths. That way every room had its own bathroom. I made sure each floor had one larger bedroom with a full bath like mine complete with double sinks, a vanity, a shower, and a soaking tub. Someday, I'd be turning my home into a bed-and-breakfast. This way, it would be ready for guests to have their own private room and bath. To this end, I was also installing an elevator.

I wanted to use the original furniture as much as I could. I obviously would have to purchase new beds and mattresses for each room, but there was a lot of furniture in the attic. I should add an inventory to my list of things to do. Also, the workers would need some area cleared out to put the elevator hardware. So, as they got closer to that day, I'd need to move some things out. I guess if there was enough furniture left over, I could stage an estate sale. There were some beautiful antique pieces up there.

Maybe I didn't have as much free time as I'd guessed. I was just not organizing myself well enough. I sat down to make a plan for my week. First, magic. I still needed to learn control, so I didn't start a forest fire or drown my friends. Plus, I had no idea what the turquoise, moonstone, and diamond rings did. While I was thinking about it, I dug my gram's notebooks out from under my bed. I flipped to the pages describing her magical artifacts. Turquoise was for spirit; I'd remembered that one. Moonstone was for mind, cool. The only unclear one was diamond because she had a diamond line bracelet for lightning and a diamond necklace for ice. My magic could be for either. I didn't know how I'd practice lightning, so maybe I'd try ice and see if it worked first.

I called Mr. Mittens. He'd told me not to wander in the woods without his protection, so that's what I did. As usual, he strolled up a moment after I called him, and I wondered again if he could teleport.

"How do you always show up when I want you?" I asked, curiously.

Your magic calls me.

I looked at him. "What does that mean?"

You call with your magic, and the thing you want must appear.

I thought for a moment. "So, if I want a cheeseburger, it will appear?"

Probably, if it is close enough. However, you have to realize it must exist before you call. So, if you call it, you may be taking it from someone's hands. You will want to be careful.

I shivered. Yep, that would freak someone out, or expose magic. I needed to be careful with everything I did now that I was magical.

"Yes, that wouldn't be good."

Hmpf. His usual answer. *What do you require?*

"I want to go into the woods to practice my magic, and you told me not to go without you, so…"

Understood. Where do you wish to go?

"The waterfall? I need to practice water, fire, maybe lightning or ice, spirit, and mind, of which I don't even know what they mean."

Lightning? His eyes opened wide.

"Yeah, it worries me too. Figured better do that one near water. I don't want to burn down the forest."

That would be one way to cut down on magical incursions, he said drily.

"Let's still try to avoid burning anything down."

I do not have the means to douse fire, so do be careful, he replied.

I sighed. I wished I had someone to teach me. I was terrified I'd burn something down or worse. "OK. Let's go."

I followed my cat out and onto the trail that I was starting to grow accustomed to. We walked briskly, the warm sun beating on our backs. The birds were singing, so I assumed no threats were nearby, but as usual, Mr. Mittens remained on high alert. When we reached the waterfall, I found my boulder and settled onto it. I sighed at the peace and beauty of the place and took a moment to soak it in. Besides the woods and the stones surrounding the waterfall, plants I'd adored since childhood abounded. Ferns grew rampant near damp places, and sometimes an overgrown skunk cabbage peaked through. Some Salal with its shiny leaves, rhododendrons with their large, beautiful flowers, and my favorite, purply blue delphiniums all made this spot into a wild garden. Moment over, I concentrated on my task.

Since I was terrified to call lightning, I told myself that the ring was for ice. I concentrated on freezing the small pond under the falls. I gathered my will and said, "Freeze." I felt the power escape me, but nothing happened. Damn. Not ice.

I concentrated again; this time I kept the output tightly controlled; I only allowed a tiny bit of power out. I concentrated on the pond again. Not knowing a verb for lightning, I said simply, "Flash." The power left me. A bolt of lightning zapped down. The air was full of static, and the ozone smell of electricity permeated the air. The bolt struck the pond with such heat and force, the water flew up. Most of it vaporized into steam, but a cascade of water fell, drenching me and Mr. Mittens.

A startled m'row escaped my cat. He gave me an extra grumpy look. He shook himself, and then he leapt up onto a larger rock, turned his back to me, and started to groom the water away.

"Do you want me to try and dry you?" I asked, feeling guilty.

Have you found your air power?

"No, I thought I'd apply heat."

I am fine. I do not wish to become a flaming Splintercat.

"Coward."

He threw a disgusted look at me over his shoulder and continued to groom.

No, just not foolish.

"You don't trust me?" I laughed. I didn't trust me either.

No.

"Thanks for the support."

He looked up at me, shook his head, and returned to grooming.

This time, I said, "Hmpf." I shook off the water I could, but I was drenched. Luckily, it was warm and sunny, a rare thing for this part of the world. For a moment, I wondered if I could simply tell the water to leave my clothing. I thought better of it as I pictured my mummified corpse, missing all moisture, sitting by this pond forever. I shuddered and let the sun do its job.

My magic was amazing, but my control was iffy at best. I figured practicing lightning wasn't the wisest thing to do, even out in the wild. What if I hadn't hit the water, but Mr. Mittens? I'd be devastated if anything happened to him.

I still wasn't sure what the element of mind did, and I was only guessing at spirit. So, I asked my cat. He also wasn't sure. We both decided that mind had to be some kind of mind control. Since he was unwilling to let me practice controlling him, I'd have to wait until I had a willing participant. Spirit, we guessed, had something to do with ghosts, but we weren't positive. We might be able to figure it out if the wolf ghost showed up again.

I practiced my water and fire magic. With a strong hold on my power output, I could make the water do anything I wanted. It would swirl, wave, twist into a mini waterspout, and fall neatly back into the small pool. I was getting better at fire as well. I didn't burn anything I didn't intend too, and I could extinguish it with a thought. Mr. Mittens also directed me to do some things with my earth magic, notably, move earth and make plants grow. That was cool. I'd never been someone with a green thumb. Maybe I'd actually be able to keep some plants alive now or plant a garden that would thrive. Of course, we were at the end of the summer, so it'd have to wait until next year unless I had a greenhouse constructed. I smiled. Finally, a practical use for my magic.

I decided I'd research greenhouses and see if it was a viable option. It would be nice to have fresh veggies. Of course, my cat wasn't as enthused.

"I could make you a nice grassy spot to relax in the sun," I offered.

Could be nice.

"How about a nice patch of catnip?" I watched him under my lashes.

He perked up but didn't say anything.

I shrugged. You can't please everybody all the time. I practiced a little longer, then had Mr. Mittens escort me home. I felt like I had a handle on my magic, at least as long as I had time to concentrate on small bits. If I got excited, or my concentration lapsed, I tended to get large results when I wanted small ones. Mr. Mittens assured me it was simply time and practice. I guess magic was like everything else. You have to practice it correctly to do it well. I had the time now, so I guess I'd be getting really good at it.

About halfway back to the house, Mr. Mittens stopped suddenly. I almost ran him over since he was in his smaller Ragdoll shape. He sniffed around the area I'd had my bear encounter before.

"What's wrong?" I asked.

Someone's been out here, he said.

"What do you mean by 'someone'?"

A human.

"So? A worker probably took a walk during his lunch break."

No, this trail is hidden to non-magical eyes.

"It is? Why?" I thought a moment. "How?"

Yes, it is. Your grandmother hid it years ago to keep people away from the waterfall. Too dangerous.

"So, the person who came out here is magical?"

Yes.

"Can you tell who it is?"

He looked at me, I could feel his concern. It was odd. I'd never felt his emotions before. Mind magic? Maybe.

Yes. I've smelled this scent around the house.

"Could it be one of the construction workers?"

He sent a mental shrug. *The interloper is a magic user of some kind.* He sniffed around a little more. *Probably a witch.* He added with disdain. *This is a disturbing find.*

"Why? Maybe he was just hiking." It seemed innocent, but I felt an icy grip of concern squeeze my heart. Yet, nothing out here was important. It was just forest and a waterfall.

He is snooping around your territory. Males only act this way when they are planning to steal your territory.

"What? *Nooo.* He's not a male cat. He can't 'steal my territory' anyway. I own it free and clear. The laws of this land say it is so."

He cocked his head at me as though considering. *You are wrong. Whoever this is wants something from you or from the land, and he's planning to take it. Be careful, pet.*

He was calling *me* pet, now? Well, I had agreed that I liked being his pet so I couldn't really complain. I sighed. Could the interloper be Scott? Was he up to something? It made sense he could be magical. Sofia had said "witch blood," which seemed to prove that magic ran in families. It had to be innocent, no matter who had been up here. I'd proven Scott wasn't dosing me with the coffee. But, if this was a worker, maybe he was sneaking the love potion to me. I should get some kind of camera in the kitchen to check up on who was tampering with my food or drink. I could do that. I'd just have to make sure no one noticed it. Huh. I pulled out my phone to see if anyone in town sold surveillance equipment. Nothing popped up close by. I found some small cameras online and ordered them for two-day delivery. I should have thought of this before. I shrugged.

* * *

TWO DAYS LATER, MY CAMERAS ARRIVED. I TOOK THEM IN AND decided I'd wait until evening to put them up. I didn't want any witnesses. I needed to take my love potion person by surprise. So that night, after everyone was gone, I found clever spots in the kitchen to hide my little cameras and hooked up the feeds to my laptop wirelessly. After I checked the feeds to make sure there weren't blind spots and adjusted the cameras, I breathed a sigh of relief that I'd finally get to the bottom of my problem. I was still avoiding Scott as much as I could because my body's response to him was disturbing me. He continued to bring me coffee, which I'd graciously accept then dump the instant he was out of view. But I was still having effects, so I knew it wasn't the coffee.

My date with Gabe was approaching quickly, and I didn't know how I was going to juggle two guys. I wasn't that girl. In reality, I wasn't exclusive with either, but I didn't want to hurt Scott's feelings. I needed my house done. I had to let Scott know I wasn't interested soon. I was just caught in a web of fear and indecision.

I figured I'd know for sure how I felt about Gabe after our date, although I still had a suspicion that I was truly into him. The stuff with

Scott was just throwing me off. I didn't know if I could trust my emotions or my decisions.

Since I needed to take my mind off it, I completed my inventory and had some of the workers haul out items that I needed to get rid of. Once they were gone, we were able to move things out of the way for the elevator to be cut into the floor. I also made room for the elevator mechanism to go in the attic.

I put the furniture and other pieces in the receiving room on the main floor and cleaned them up. I think I half expected to find more magical artifacts, but I was disappointed. Maybe there weren't any more in the attic. I took pictures of the furniture I wasn't going to use and put them online. Someone would want these lovely things.

Next, I practiced my magic. Still wasn't going to use lightning. That scared me. Mr. Mittens refused to let me practice mind magic on him, so I had to find someone who would.

I was arguing, silently, with Mr. Mittens when Scott wandered up to where we were on the porch. Embarrassing, I know. I was totally turning into a crazy cat lady.

"Hey," he said flirtatiously, and threw in a little wink.

"Hi," I answered stiffly. I smiled though, and he warmed to it. "Everything seems to be coming together nicely." I didn't know what else to say. I was very conflicted.

He eased closer to me, and leaned against the railing next to me, our shoulders brushing. My body lit up, and I stiffened and leaned down to escape the contact. I petted Mr. Mittens, who was glaring at Scott, I could hear his growl.

Scott backed away from the twenty-five-pound feline. With all Mr. Mitten's floof, he looked pretty intimidating for a housecat. Of course, his beauty made it harder to believe he'd claw your eyes out. I knew the truth. He could eat Scott in one meal. I guess Scott sensed that.

"Sorry, he's territorial." It was a lame comment, but Scott kept his eyes on the cat.

"I'm not much of a cat guy," he responded.

I shrugged. "He's usually a sweetheart." I got an angry tail swish at that. Both Mr. Mittens and I knew he was a cold-blooded killer.

"I just wanted to let you know the plumber will be here to replace the plumbing soon, and the water will be shut off for two to three days."

I nodded; I was expecting it to happen sometime. I thanked him.

Mr. Mittens watched him walk away with cool disdain. Although that was a typical cat pose, I asked him what was wrong once we were alone, anyway.

I don't like him.

I frowned at my cat. He was starting to irritate me with his anti-witch sentiment. We didn't even know for sure if Scott was a witch. I'd already proven he wasn't dosing me, and he'd never done anything shady. "Why not? He's nice, he likes me, and he's doing good work on the house?"

He doesn't feel right.

"You still think he's a witch?"

I got his mental shrug.

"You still think he's dosing me."

Don't you? he answered.

I shrugged. "I don't know. I quit drinking the coffee, but I haven't recovered. I think I'm getting it from something else. So, no. I don't think it's him."

Hmpf, he responded. His usual dismissal.

"What feels off?"

I'm not sure. I can't pinpoint it.

"I'm keeping my distance. I don't like being influenced against my will whether it's being done by him or someone else. Regardless, he's doing great on the house, so I'm gonna try to keep him happy."

He swished his tail in agitation but didn't answer. He strolled off in a cat huff.

Now that I had a date to be out of the house, I spent some time making arrangements at a local hotel. Once that was done, I finished a few projects on the computer and made supper. By then, the workers were gone, and I breathed a sigh of relief. So far, besides the love potion, there hadn't been anything odd going on from the witch that had killed Craig. Mr. Mittens hadn't seen anything on his patrols either, witch wise. The now gated-off road hadn't been used last time I'd checked. I decided I'd walk out there before full dark and see if I could use my earth power to cause the road to regrow plants and trees. That would be a better deterrent than just a gate with a chain and padlock. Even I could figure out a way to get around that.

I put on my croc boots, and a rain jacket, since it had begun to sprinkle, and headed out the door. I walked around the back of the house and found the trail that led to the road. It wasn't too muddy; it had been sunny for a couple of days. It was a pleasant walk, and I was lost in my thoughts when I saw the strange grey eagle watching me. I looked at it oddly because it pinged my memory somehow. Suddenly it spread its huge wings and alighted before me in full griffin shape. I stopped, surprised.

"Brightfeather!" I exclaimed. I was not only startled, but a little bit terrified. The creature, though gracious the first time while I was under the protection of my Splintercat, was still an unknown.

She bowed her head slightly. *Lady Brigid, I come to bring you news.*

I tilted my head in contemplation. "Sure, that is very nice of you. I didn't grant you asylum to require anything of you."

I am full of appreciation for your kindness. She looked around the area. *I've been noticing strange humans that have been watching you from this road.*

"You have?" I was aghast. I thought the gate would keep people out. But that was foolish. It might prevent vehicles, but anyone could easily climb over or through the gate.

"Could you describe them?"

There has been a female that I have not seen you with. And a male that I have seen you with at your nest.

My heart sank a bit. Why would a nonhuman creature be able to describe a human? They weren't used to human appearances. If I saw a raccoon, I'd probably say hey, I saw a racoon. It was grey with a striped tail. I probably couldn't even tell if it was male or female at a glance. At least the griffin could tell that difference.

"I'm very grateful that you have been looking out for me. Thank you," I said and bowed my head as she had done earlier. She leapt into the air and returned to her eagle shape and flew deeper into my woods. I sighed.

So, the witch was still hanging around. Damn. And someone, possibly Scott or one of his workers, was in on it with her. What could I do? What did they want? I guess that Craig's death was not the point of their incursion. Were they trying to scare me off? The only thing I had that they could possibly get to, was my missing magic. I guess that would be worth it, although I had no idea how they could locate it since I was struggling to do so. Maybe that's what they were up to, trying to scare me away so they could do a better search. However, I had to be here for the magic to be active enough to be found, so that didn't make sense. I wish I had someone to help me. Someone besides a cat with his own agenda.

I stumbled from the trail and out onto the road. I found a tree stump and sat down. Pulling my shattered concentration back together, I commanded the road to regrow. Plants erupted from the ground. The stump I'd been sitting on expelled me with force as the tree regrew, and I fell to the ground. "Dammit!" I followed through with a bunch more colorful words and phrases that would have embarrassed my mother if she'd still been around.

I stood up on lush moss and grass and brushed off my clothes. I was suddenly back in the woods, the road gone. I grimaced. I hadn't been careful. What if I'd caused the highway beyond my property to regrow as well? I ran out to the gate. It was twisted and halfway up a tree. I ran out onto the road and breathed a sigh of relief. The affected area ended about ten feet back from the highway. I had to remember to be careful. I was too strong, and not focused enough. I looked back the way I'd come and realized I didn't know where the trail was now—if it still existed.

I had two choices. I could walk along the edge of the highway to where my long driveway began, and return home that way, or call my cat to lead me home. If I called my cat, he'd be upset I hadn't taken him with me on my adventure, and I'd get lectured. If I walked, well,

I'd be walking a few miles, and it was almost dark. I was such an idiot. I started walking.

Walking along Highway 101 was not a smart thing to do. It was a narrow road near my house with almost no shoulder, and several blind twists and turns. I wasn't wearing bright reflective clothing either. And to add insult to injury, the rain started to pour. I flicked the hood of my jacket up over my hair and zipped it up. A passing semi zoomed by, and a sheet of muddy water drenched me from head to toe. I cursed. Next time I did something stupid, I'd take the lecture and call my cat.

A car went by and honked at me. Why? What was I gonna do, speed up? I pushed further away from the road as far onto the shoulder as I could get. More vehicles passed. I was getting chilled. I hadn't even brought my phone, so I couldn't call a friend or a cab. Walking around was a lot further than I thought it was.

Another car horn beeped at me, and I rolled my eyes, but then I heard gravel crunch as someone pulled off the road behind me. I whirled around. A head popped out of the driver's side window.

"Brigid, want a ride?"

It was Sofia. I breathed a quiet sigh of relief and waved. I looked and made sure the road was clear, then hurried over and slipped into the passenger seat.

"Thanks so much! I hope you don't mind, I'm wet."

"No, I have a towel in the back, we'll just wipe down the leather after we get to your house. What are you doing out on the highway?"

I leaned my head back on her nice leather seats, then realized what I'd done and leaned forward.

"I went on a walk and got lost in my own woods, like an idiot," I replied. I don't know why I didn't tell her the truth. Maybe Mr. Mitten's comments were starting to bore a hole that was slowly filling with suspicion.

"You should have called a cab, it's dangerous on this road at night."

"Yeah, only I left my phone at home."

"Oh."

"Yep, I said I was an idiot."

We both started to laugh.

"So, besides rescuing me, what are you up to?" I asked.

"Funny you should ask." She gave me a sidelong look. "I was coming to see you."

"Yeah?" I looked at her. Other than Megan, who was almost a sister, I hadn't had another girlfriend in years. Usually, my ex discouraged them. Part of his control issues, I guess. I couldn't remember if it was normal for a friend to just turn up. I wasn't sure how to respond.

"Yeah, I was bored. I figured you had to be after the workers left for the day."

She was right, I spent a lot of time bored, and too much time talking to my cat. I did need a friend.

"It's true. I talk to my cat a lot, which probably isn't that healthy. I read. But it's much better to have living company." I wasn't the best at social graces, and I suddenly got the thought that she might have other reasons for visiting. Maybe *she* needed a friend. "Is everything OK with you?"

She flashed a smile at me. "Yeah, everything is fine." I got the distinct feeling that it wasn't, but who was I to call her a liar.

"Cool."

She pulled into my drive and started up the long road. The new gravel bed was nice and helped control the mud. I still wanted it paved, but with construction and construction vehicles, it was best to wait until everything was done. She pulled along to the back, and we both got out of her car and walked in. I stripped off my jacket and boots and left them by the back door. I'd deal with them later. I put on a kettle to boil and excused myself to go change out of my wet and muddy clothes.

After I returned, I said, "Sorry about that. I was soaked."

"I get it. No problem."

We sat silent a moment, then the kettle whistled.

"I have tea or cocoa?"

"Tea, please."

I got her tea preference ready and set it in front of her with milk and sugar. She used neither. I should have guessed. I had cocoa with whipped cream. She looked at it hungrily.

164

"I don't want to offend you because we are new friends, but why don't you eat anything? Are you well?"

She looked down at her tea, and I wondered if she would answer. "I'm fine, just have to be careful of my weight."

"You're tiny. You shouldn't have to be that careful," I blurted out without thinking. I immediately wanted to take it back because I'm sure it was none of my business.

"Thanks, it's only because I don't let myself eat carbs very often."

"So, no food allergies or anything?"

"No, just unhappy food choices." She smiled up at me.

"Sorry. I should probably be better about it. I just like my comforts too much," I replied.

She chuckled. "It isn't hurting you with the men. Scott says you went out?"

So that's why she came. A little gossip or to feel me out about her cousin.

"Yeah, he took me to a political thing a while back," I said.

"How was it?" She clasped her tea mug and sipped it daintily.

"The event was a little boring, frankly, but I had fun dancing after." I kept my response vague, but positive.

"Nice. You like to dance?" she asked, politely. Although I'm sure that wasn't what she wanted to know.

"Oh yes. I love it. I've been dancing since I was three."

A little interest lit up in her eyes—like she was doing her duty before, but now had common ground to talk about.

"Me too!" She smiled. "I took jazz, ballet, and tap."

"I did as well, but then I concentrated on ballet. I wanted to make it my career, but although I was competent, I wasn't that talented."

"Well, I'm sure you were good," she responded.

She was being polite. I was good, but just like good athletes in all areas, only the best of the best made it professionally. I'm sure there were great college football players that never made it into the NFL. That was me. I maybe could make it into the chorus of some backwater company, but I wasn't dancing as the prima in the New York Ballet. That was fine. I had other talents.

"Thanks, I was OK." I smiled.

"So did you and Scott hit it off?"

I felt like I was in junior high. Did we ever really grow out of these games?

Since I was still unsure of my true feelings, I wanted to keep it vague, but friendly. "Yes, we had a good time on the date."

"Yeah? That's good. Are you going to go out with him again?"

I shrugged noncommittally. "I don't want to hurt our working relationship. I probably should wait until after our business is done," I replied.

"Oh," she paused. She obviously had an agenda but didn't want to give it away. I didn't blame her; Scott probably had asked her to feel me out. "That's probably a smart move," she added. There really wasn't much more she could say without giving herself away.

"Yeah. I've been so busy with everything here, and my goal wasn't to date, but to finish this house. So, I'm trying to concentrate on that first. After? Who knows?" I wanted to end on a hopeful note, since I didn't want to alienate either of my new friends. I didn't bring up the date with Gabe.

That seemed to satisfy her. Hopefully, it satisfied Scott and didn't hurt his feelings. I didn't want to do that. If he was behind the love potion, I'd punish him later. If he was innocent, I didn't want to hurt him. He'd treated me well, was doing a fantastic job, and I liked him, frankly. That *like* was bound up in all the nonsense the potion was producing, but I think I liked him before I'd been dosed. I needed time to tell. I knew I liked Gabe, but I was old enough to know I should keep my options open. Who knew what could turn up or if things would work out?

We chatted a while longer, then she left. It was clear her agenda was just to find out how I felt about Scott. It made me a little mystified, and a tad suspicious. What was going on with these two?

CHAPTER

FOURTEEN

On Thursday, Scott informed me I needed to be out of the house for the weekend. They were doing the plumbing then instead of next week. It made me suspicious. What plumber worked on the weekend without charging double time? None. Plus, I'd been hoping that the dosing I was receiving would get some time off. Mr. Mittens had said it would fade after a couple of days, and I was planning to add that couple of days to the weekend and see if the effects had faded. Now, I'd just get the same time off. So, my suspicions rose.

My cameras had shown nothing untoward so far, and I was confused. I wasn't drinking the coffee, I was only eating sealed items, and I hadn't seen anyone touch my food or drink. What was happening? Was I confused? Were my feelings really my own? No. They couldn't be. This was foreign and felt wrong. It was a love potion; I knew it was.

I had one thing to look forward to though—Gabe. At least I wouldn't have to worry about Scott seeing him pick me up from the house since I'd be at the bed-and-breakfast in town. I was concerned about Mr. Mittens being alone. I asked him to come with me, but he was reluctant because his power was reduced away from the land. He was also averse to letting me go without his protection though, so he was undecided. The bed-and-breakfast did allow pets, so it would just depend on his decision.

Friday morning after the workers arrived, I did my usual and took my cat out to practice my magic. He hadn't told me recently about any incursions, so I assumed things were improving. He told me things were quiet. I invited him to come with me again. He finally agreed. My magic was coming along, and my control seemed vastly improved. I was still cautious about using lightning, but I knew it was there if I needed it. I still hadn't found the remaining artifacts, and I continued to wonder if they'd been stolen before now. Was this weekend plumbing debacle to steal my magic? Nah, I didn't know much about construction, but I was smart enough to know you couldn't rip out old plumbing and put in new without shutting off the water. I'd know when they were done without a doubt.

After our walk, I went back and packed up for the stay in town. They were shutting off the water in an hour, and I was making sure I could get out without pressuring them to move their timeline back. They were supposed to be done by Saturday at quitting time. I sure hoped they were. I already missed my house.

It was a little exciting to leave and pretend I was having a vacation even if it was just in town and only for two days. Mr. Mittens was nervous, but he entered his kennel and didn't gripe at me. He'd debated back and forth whether it was better to watch over me or the house. I won out. I was his charge, not the house or my magic. I was lucky, even though I had a litter box, Mr. Mittens preferred to do his business in my toilet or outside, so I only needed him and his food, plus the toys he had yet to use to keep him from boredom. Maybe he'd like a minute being a regular cat and not having to chase off or kill my enemies.

Before I left, I wanted to talk to Scott about some ideas I had for the bathrooms, nothing big, but still important to me. I walked out to do so and realized he was just now pulling in. He didn't see me sitting on the back stairs. I watched as he picked up the ubiquitous coffee cup in his work-gloved hand and wiped it down with a rag. I wrinkled my brow. Why was he wiping it off? Was it leaking? Was he applying something to it? Why was he wearing his gloves in the truck? My suspicions rose.

He stepped out of the truck and frowned at me. I'd surprised him. He pasted on a fake smile and walked over and handed me the cup. I took it, then wondered if I'd made a mistake. If he was wiping something onto the cup, that was how the potion was being administered. From now on, I swore only to touch the coffee cup wearing rubber gloves.

"Hi," I said brightly. "Did the coffee spill all over your truck?"

He looked confused for a moment. "Oh, no it wasn't too bad. Just sloshed down the side and into the cup holder. No big deal." I could sense the lie. My heart fell.

"I can get you some paper towels, if you want?"

"Nah, I had a dirty rag in the truck, I got it all cleaned up."

"*Sure, you did*," I thought. I hoped my face didn't give away my suspicions.

"Well, I'm packed up. I'll see you guys Monday. Let me know how it goes."

I turned around and took the cup back in the house. I dumped the contents as usual, but this time I saved the cup. I examined it. No coffee stains. That confirmed Scott's lie. Maybe my cat could smell if the potion was on the outside, rather than in the coffee. Before, the smell of coffee was too strong.

I went over to where everything was waiting to go out to the car. "Mr. Mittens, I think he's applying the potion to the outside of this coffee cup. Can you tell by sniffing it? Since the cage door wasn't latched, he strolled out and sniffed the side of the paper cup in various places. Then he sat and looked contemplative.

I've never smelled a love potion, but I can sense magic to a degree. That cup is suffused with magic.

"Well, shit." I sat down next to him. "That bastard *is* dosing me. I caught him red-handed, too. Your feelings were right about this one."

I'm sorry, Brigid. I did hope I was wrong. For your sake.

I wiped my hand off on my jeans and reached over to pat his head. I thought better of it. I didn't need a lovesick cat on my hands. I nodded at him and got up to rid myself of the cup and wash my hands.

When I came back, my cat was back in his carrier. I latched it and carried him and my stuff out to the car. At least I knew how to avoid the love potion now and who one and possibly two of my enemies were.

Well, I had my cameras to watch if they did anything hinky this weekend. Screw 'em.

* * *

THE B&B WAS DELIGHTFUL AND CHARMING. I CHECKED IN WITHOUT any issue and set up in the room I'd be staying in for the next two days. Since Gabe was picking me up tonight, I took great care with my preparations while still looking casual. He picked me up promptly. He looked nervous but still him. Now that I knew I was under the influence of a potion, I listened intently to my inner voice. Yes, I was truly attracted and interested in Gabe. It didn't compare to the weird intensity I felt for Scott, but it felt like me and truth. I smiled.

"So, I thought we'd go for food first, and then the later movie, if you're OK with that," he said after he opened the car door and settled back into the driver's seat.

"Sounds great." I smiled at him.

He took me to a decent restaurant in town, not too fancy, not too casual, and we had a great time chatting while we ate. Both of us relaxed, and it was like we hadn't been separated by twenty-four years, the ease of being together and conversing flowed. The movie was a rom-com. I thought that was funny but had such a great time with Gabe I couldn't even remember the title. We shared a popcorn, and when it was done, we held hands like we were in high school again.

By the time he pulled up to the bed-and-breakfast, I knew. This was the man I'd been in love with since I was in high school, and I still was. The stuff with Scott was a total lie. A forcing of something that would never be. Anger filled me. Someone was messing with my mind, my life. They wanted to take my mental health, my control, and my magic. The unfairness of it all enraged me like nothing in my life ever had. Not even my ex had made me this angry.

Gabe followed me into my room. He greeted Mr. Mittens as he'd done every time he'd met him. That warmed my heart further.

I like this human, Mr. Mittens said to me.

I chuckled. "My cat likes you," I repeated.

He smiled. "He does? What about you?" he asked shyly. Almost surprised at his boldness.

"That's an easy question." I stepped up to him and molded myself into his body. I wrapped my arms around him, bolder than I'd ever been with anyone, even my husband who hadn't liked displays of affection that weren't initiated by him. "I like you, too."

His arms encircled me. I looked up at him; he bent down and kissed me. Unlike with Scott, the passion that arose from my core was gradual and real. It warmed me, caressed me, and reached out to fill both of us. We deepened the kiss, and the whole time I was in control of how I responded. My will wasn't taken from me. The rage I felt at that killed the mood quickly though, and Gabe pulled away confused.

"What happened just now?" he asked, unsure.

"I'm sorry, that wasn't you." I sat down on the bed, and he sat across from me in the plush chair. He looked concerned. Since I didn't want him to think I wasn't interested, I took a deep breath and told him what was going on. I told him about Scott, the date, me jumping him, the whole embarrassing thing. I wanted *this* man. I wanted a real relationship that was based on trust. Although I wasn't sure if he'd still want me after I told him this. I hung my head.

"Bridge," he started and paused. He looked at my face, into my eyes. "This isn't your fault." He stood up and walked over to the bed. He put his arm around me and pulled me close. "First, I know you. You would never lead someone on and tease or abandon them. I don't feel like you are pulling something over on me. So, stop thinking that. You were the most loyal friend, someone that I always trusted. Please don't think I'd ever think you would treat me or anyone that way. Second, what is being done to you is close to rape. Someone forcing your body and your mind to be attracted to someone at that intensity is wrong. If this weren't magic, I'd go with you to the police, and we'd have that bastard arrested." He pulled back a little so he could look at me. "Finally, you can always come to me with anything. Personal, magical, medical, I don't care. Even though this thing between us is new, or newly continued, you are my friend. I will always think of you that way whether things work out romantically or not. Though, I hope they will…"

As he said that, my heart filled with joy. "I hope that, too."

He was quiet for a moment, and I thought maybe he was done. I was warmed from everything he said, the shame fell away, and a great relief raced through me. I think I'd been terrified that he would reject me once he knew how I'd been with Scott. Instead, he was still the great guy I knew as a teen.

"I don't know if you want to have a relationship. I get that your divorce was brutal, and this thing with the contractor just adds fuel to the fire of suspicion towards a new relationship. But if you do, you should know something about me," he said. His voice and body language were troubled.

A wave of fear choked me. This was it, the thing that came after the line "if something looks too good to be true…" I swallowed the lump in my throat, the one that was gonna proceed the meltdown I'd have if this was too great a thing to get over.

"I think you should know about my past relationship." He cleared his throat, and I could tell this was difficult for him.

I tried to reassure him. "It's alright, take your time. You can't scare me away."

He smiled at me. "We'll see."

My heartbeat faster as fear hit me. What if it was bad? What if he wasn't the person I thought he was? No, he was who he appeared to be, I reassured myself.

"I told you I was married."

"Yeah."

He took another deep breath. He was struggling to talk about it. "I met her back East while I was in medical school."

"You went to Harvard?" I asked. I thought I'd heard that some-where a long time ago.

He smiled. "Yes."

This was starting to tie together with his back East comment from our first "date" since I'd been back.

"She was from Boston, not going to school there."

I nodded.

He stood up and started pacing in the small space between the bed and the chair. "It was a whirlwind romance. I fell hard for her."

I smiled up at him to continue. I couldn't feel jealousy over this, I'd married right out of college too.

Reassured, he continued. "She was…is a beauty. Long dark hair, blazing green eyes, the perfect classic figure. I'd never thought of myself as a shallow man, always judging a woman by her looks, but I was so attracted to her. I asked her to marry me six weeks after I met her. She agreed, and we got married six months later."

I still felt a twinge of jealousy. I brushed it away. Mr. Mittens strolled over and laid against me. I stroked his head.

"I wanted to start a family, I was finishing med school, I had a bright future. I'd paid my way and had some money set aside. It was a good time. We were young, and it was the logical next step," he said as though he were trying to convince me. I nodded.

"She kept putting me off with various, if logical, excuses. I let her, or I didn't press her. I figured we still had time. What I didn't know, was she never was going to agree or want children with me. I was a mark. She was a witch and had been given the assignment by her coven to bring me in and get me to commit to them. When I found out, I was enraged. I swore I'd never help the coven." He was silent for a while, pulling his emotions back in check.

"When she realized she couldn't convince me, and she'd failed at her *mission*," he spat out the word. "She packed up and left me. Just like that. Like our seven years together were nothing."

We were both silent for a moment. Then I stood and walked the two steps to him and threw my arms around him. He was breathing hard, upset.

"I'm so sorry."

His arms tightened around me. "Believe it or not. I'm over it. However, it damaged something in me. An ability to trust. My natural belief that humanity is good. I became cynical, even hateful. My bedside manner suffered. I almost lost my job. I finally had to leave and come back here to regain my sanity. And then here you were."

He stopped, and I looked up at him. He smoothed the hair away from my face. "You were just you. The sweet girl I remembered from before. You wanted nothing from me. You didn't even know about magic. You were even a big mess like me." He chuckled a little at my grimace.

I wanted to forget my meltdown.

"You didn't even want anything from me once you knew what I was, except for one desperate call to save someone else if I could. And that came out of being a good person, not because you wanted to control me for your own ends. That said more to me than anything."

He pulled me in tight and hugged me for a brief moment, then we both sat down on the bed.

"I don't have the energy to control anyone else. I can barely handle myself," I quipped to lighten the mood.

He laughed. "Trust me, Bridge. You're good people."

"Thanks, I should try harder, but I do appreciate you saying that."

He looked over at me and leaned in. I could feel his intensity like heat wafting off him. I knew he wanted to kiss me again, but he was waiting to see if I wanted it too. I let the delicious tension build, and then with a sigh, I tilted my face up, and accepted a gentle kiss. His hand cupped my face, and his other arm was around me. The kiss became less gentle, then demanding, and soon we were locked in an embrace. His mouth was hungry for mine. I met him in his intensity.

This felt right. This was the man I wanted, truly. How could I have thought for a moment that the feelings I had for Scott were real? This feeling started in my middle and suffused my entire being with desire and that aching want that drove you to touch the person you cared for with every part of your body and soul. All I'd felt for Scott was unadulterated lust.

We kissed like that for a while, both of us knowing that the other person was the one we wanted and had always wanted even if we'd found other people before. Finally, he pulled away.

"I should go, Bridge. I don't want to wreck this thing we have by jumping into bed too soon."

I nodded. I needed a moment before I could string a sentence together. I think I might have mumbled, "Uh huh." Or something equally stupid.

He stood up. I stood with him and walked him to the door. He bent and gave me another breathtaking kiss, then left. I stood in the doorway and watched him walk away. My stomach fluttered with butterflies. Once I shut the door, Mr. Mittens strolled out of the bath-room. He'd taken off when we started kissing. I guess he didn't want to witness that.

I threw myself down on the bed and rolled over to look up at the ceiling. He jumped up and laid down on my stomach and looked at me, his huge blue eyes blinking slowly at me.

I like him, he told me.

I stroked his head. "I like him, too."

He would be a good strong mate for you, the cat continued.

"Are you marrying me off?" I asked.

Well, it would help to have another magical being at the property. Particularly a healer. That is a rare and wonderful gift.

"So, you only like him because you want me to have a healer on site?" I questioned my opinionated cat.

He is also nice, and I don't sense any wrongness in him.

"Good to know." Not that I doubted that. I'd known Gabe as a teenager. If a teenager was good and dependable, then the man could only improve.

Hmpf. You should listen to me. I'm quite wise, he bragged.

I barked out a laugh. His face took on its grumpier look. I stroked his fur until he was forced to purr in pleasure. "Yes, you are wise. I appreciate that you bestow your wisdom upon the unworthy like me."

He closed his eyes, and his sleepiness lulled me into a stupor as well, and pretty soon, we were both sound asleep.

CHAPTER
FIFTEEN

When I returned home, the rough plumbing was done. Scott might be a lying, sneaky bastard, but he was a great contractor. I wasn't sure what to do. Now that I knew Scott was dosing me, it gave me a good reason to suspect my friend Sofia as well. She was part of the local coven. I'd ignored all the warnings by everyone not to trust the local witches, and it had burned me. Well, I wasn't the same timid pushover I'd been with my ex. I was taking care of this shit now. I called Sofia and arranged a meeting.

I wanted to do this privately, so I invited her to lunch. She agreed to come and acted happy. I hoped I was wrong about her. I asked Mr. Mittens to hang around and observe. I wanted his opinion later. I couldn't believe she might be the witch that had killed Craig. That meant every single thing she had done and said was a lie, and I was a trusting fool.

I prepared everything angrily. Trying to work it out so I could pull this off without it devolving into something I'd regret. Remembering her penchant for rabbit food, I didn't even bother with bread or meat, I laid out a salad spread of all veggies and ate a roll before she arrived.

The carbs didn't help.

She pulled up and came through the back door and into the kitchen.

I tried to act like nothing was wrong. We both prepared our plates in silence. As we sat down to eat, Mr. Mittens jumped up on the table. He kept a respectful distance from the food, so no stray cat floof would end up in our meals. I appreciated that about him. However, Sofia wasn't as amused.

She made shooing gestures with her hand. "Get down, cat," she addressed him. He gave her that aloof cat stare owners of cats have been getting for millennia.

When that didn't work, she turned to me. "Please get your cat off the table while we're eating."

My hackles were already up, but this was my house, and my pet that lived here could do whatever he wished, and I allowed. I'd asked him to be here to observe her, so I went from already annoyed to full on pissed in point two seconds.

"He's not anywhere near your food," I said, coldly.

She looked up at me, an odd expression on her face. "Is something wrong, Brigid? You've been on edge since I got here."

"I know about the love potion."

I watched her face and body language closely to see if she'd respond to my accusation. I thought she tensed up. But it was a small enough reaction, it could have been surprise.

"I don't know what you are talking about," she said calmly, and continued eating. That gave her away. Any normal person would have quit eating to get to the bottom of the issue.

I looked at Mr. Mittens. He gave an almost imperceptible nod. She was lying.

"Your cousin has been wiping a love potion onto a paper coffee cup every morning and giving it to me. I don't know what his endgame is. I doubt it's because he loves me, and it can't be so I'll stay enamored of his work. He does good work, and he knows it. It's not for those reasons. Still, it was an easy, logical jump to this one. I know you or both of you killed Craig Whelan."

She blanched. "How dare you?" She slid her chair back and stood up. She planted both hands on the table and leaned in so she could tower over me in the other chair. "I won't be insulted like this. I *was* your friend." With that, she grabbed her bag and jacket, but she didn't deny it.

"No, I was *your* friend, I just don't understand why. Why would you go to such lengths that you would take the life of a good man?" I asked, hoping she'd explain herself and her motives.

Her eyes blazed at me. "Of course, you don't have a clue, you stupid bitch. You never have. Everything in the magical world came to you so easily." She smiled a wicked smile. And changed tactics. "Just like you to mourn over some animal," she sneered. Then she left, slamming the back door as she went.

I cringed at her last parting shot. Craig wasn't an animal. He was a warm caring family man who had been kind to me. Maybe Gabe and my cat were right. There weren't any good witches. Now I'd blown my only chance to get more information out of her. I was still shaking with emotion after her outburst and revelations. I wasn't even sure how to define what I was feeling. Betrayal, of course, anger, disappointment at myself for being too trusting, maybe other things I couldn't put my finger on.

"What did you get out of that?" I asked my cat.

His blue-eyed gaze pierced me. *You were correct, she is behind the death of your werewolf friend. Also, she is probably the driving force behind your dosing with the love potion.*

"Any theories about why?"

He scoffed at me. *You know why. You just don't want to admit it. Witches only want more power. She is after yours. She must think that by killing your werewolf she could gain more access to the property. Which she has done by arranging to have her cousin work here. By dosing you, she guarantees your loyalty to him, and the continued access to your property. Also, a way to distract you and to keep you from digging too deeply into his or her motivations. A simple but effective plan.*

I sighed. I did know that. I didn't want to face that someone I knew and considered a friend could do something so *evil*. I shuddered. "What is wrong with her to make her so twisted?"

I got the equivalent of a mental shrug from my cat. *Witches aren't inherently evil. However, their need to constantly gain new sources of power to keep themselves from aging and burning up, corrupts most of them. The kind ones either never had much power or choose not to use what they have so they can live a normal life.*

I was still confused about how witch power worked. My power seemed to invigorate me, fill me with life. But apparently witch power was not as kind.

"Explain how it works, you know, for witches. I've been trying to piece it together from your and Gabe's comments, but I'm still not sure how it works. Please." I tacked that on, even cats deserved good manners.

Witches are born, like all magical creatures, with innate magic. It can be strong or weak just like other traits. Their magic is finite though. They only have so much in their magic well, and when it's gone, it's gone. This can be fixed by a healer. For some reason, magical healers like your Gabe can refill the well. If the witch is strong and uses their magic without healing, it alters them as the power leaves, eventually. If they don't have regular healing, or don't find another source to replenish their magical well, they age quickly, grow weak, and die.

I shuddered. "That must be awful. To have magic, and know you shouldn't use it because each time you do, you could die? No wonder covens keep trying to imprison Gabe. He is a marvel." I wrapped my arms around myself. "They'll stop at nothing to get my power, won't they?"

He gave me one quick nod.

I hadn't taken this that seriously. The motivation behind stealing the artifacts containing my power had seemed vague, not that great of a draw. I needed to get them all first and quickly. That was the way to end this.

"We need to find the rest of the artifacts, if the witches haven't found them already," I said firmly.

Haven't we been looking? he responded drolly.

"I was only looking half-heartedly. I need to redouble my efforts. The magic isn't safe until it's been returned to me."

They could steal it from you directly, you know. My cat dropped that little fact without a pause.

"What?!"

Yes, witches aren't limited in how they gain power. They've been developing methods since the beginning of your time.

I threw up my hands. Then I sat down heavily. "This is a disaster."

If you wish to feel better, the problem is no worse than it was yesterday. You just understand it better. He stretched out on the table. Front paws forward, back legs stretched out fully behind him in a sploot.

"I so want to be mad at you right now," I said.

He barely looked up at me having reached his comfortable "I might have a nap" position.

Why? he asked simply.

"It's irrational. I just need to be mad, and you're here, and you're the one giving me information. Late, but nonetheless there it is."

I've tried to tell you before.

I sighed. "I know. I wasn't ready to hear it."

That is true.

I stood up and started clearing away the food and dishes. "What do I do about Scott? She's gonna tell him, I know. I still need this house finished."

His eyes were completely shut, his head resting on his crossed front paws. *That is up to you.* He lifted his large head and yawned, showing all his brilliant white, pointed, teeth. *Threaten him? Use your mind magic? Or you could just talk to him. He isn't very powerful. I doubt he even had enough juice to make the potion.*

"So, the less powerful the witch, the less likely they are power hungry, evil despots?"

Not necessarily, but it could happen. He shut his eyes again, and I knew I wouldn't get anything out of him until he was done with his catnap.

I finished cleaning up and left him in silence. I had to think about what to do. I'd also promised Luke Whelan I'd let him know if I located the witch. I needed to call him.

I sighed. I'd never get a third company out here to finish. But was it right to continue with a person whose actions were so despicable?

No, I couldn't allow this. I should have ended this arrangement the first time I realized I was under the influence of a spell. I should have known that Scott was behind the potion. He was the only one I took a food item from. It made sense. Yet, I was naïve and trusting and let it continue because I wanted the house done, and I wanted everything to be pleasant. This was what I got for trying to avoid confrontation.

Now I had to deal with it, and the enemy was aware I knew about them. First, I'd warn Luke. The werewolves had been in the world of magic a lot longer than I had, and they might be willing to help with my witch problem. I picked up the phone and called him.

"Whelan Construction, Luke speaking," Luke answered.

"Hi, Luke, it's Brigid Donovan."

"Sure. Hi Brigid. How are things going?" he asked pleasantly.

"Uh," I wasn't sure how to answer that. "Fine" didn't cover it. "I know who the witch is," I blurted out.

He was quiet on the other end, then I heard ragged breathing.

"Luke, are you alright?"

He cleared his throat. "I'm fine. Who is it?"

"The leader of the coven, Sofia Kettle."

"Are you sure?"

"Ninety-nine percent," I answered firmly. I didn't dare say one hundred percent because I hadn't caught her in action, but my gut was sure.

"That's good enough for me. I need to talk to the pack, I'll call you back," he said, and before I could respond, he hung up.

I knew I'd shocked him, so I tried not to be annoyed at his brusque manner. I shrugged, made sure the ringer was up all the way, and continued down my list of things to do.

Next, I needed to locate my magic. And there was no more wishy washy, half-assed trying this time. I took a deep breath, reached out with whatever invisible magical sense I had, and marched to the top of the third floor. I opened the attic door and started searching.

So far, Gram's journals had led me to believe that our powers were the same. In that case, I was still missing air, ice, aether, reality, shadow, light, and time. If time was the ability to control time, or travel through time, I did not want that to be found by the witches. That was too monstrous a power and could be used against me. Not that I wanted any of my power used against me. I had no idea what aether or reality were or how they could be used. However, the rest were self-explanatory. I crawled to the very back of the attic and found a free space to stand. I stretched out my hands and my senses and demanded my powers come to me.

An electric sense of curiosity filled me. That was odd. Could the artifacts that held my power be sentient? I turned towards the feeling. It was coming from the wall. I had to wend my way through more junk and construction materials. They'd cut the hole for the elevator, and the mechanism was here, although it wasn't fully functional yet. So, there was a lot of jumble. When I reached the wall, I couldn't feel the pull. I looked around. I was standing directly below one of the original stained-glass windows. This one was tulips with a rose-colored border. It was lovely. I loved looking at them here and from the outside. I could reach about halfway up the window, and without a thought, I reached up to trace the flowers in the design.

When I did that, the pull began. My heart raced with excitement. One of the artifacts was here. I felt all over the window, trying to find the missing piece. There it was, next to the stem of the flower, a piece of rose-colored quartz came free and fell into my hand. Not a traditional piece of jewelry, but more a piece of stained glass even though it was obviously crystal. I studied it for a moment, and as it warmed on the skin of my hand, it flashed with a brilliant blaze like sunlight, and it disappeared into me. Warmth suffused me like a summer day, and I knew that this was the power of light. Clever, hiding it in a window. What could make better sense? Maybe I'd been looking for my power incorrectly. Maybe if I knew what they did, I'd have an easier time finding them.

I thought about it. Time. I should look for a clock, or another thing that represented time. I looked around the attic. There was a grandfather clock against the opposite wall, so I made my way to it. I vaguely remembered this standing in the grand foyer at some point. It'd been moved when I was in grade school. I always wondered why. I was just told it was broken, but usually something that expensive could be fixed. Maybe they put it away to hide my magic. A flutter of excitement began to build. I searched the clock top to bottom. Seeking with my eyes and my magic. Nothing. Was I wrong? Had this piece of my magic been taken? The workers had been in the attic a lot. I should never have allowed anyone up here without my supervision. Good grief, my grandmother and my father had made it impossible to even get in here unless you were family. I had been infinitely stupid.

I shook my head. The only way I could think to check if my power was missing was to wind the clock and see if it really was broken. That would at least give a reason why it was up here if it wasn't to house my power. I found the key and set and wound the clock. It's gentle ticking filled the quiet of the attic. Damn. It worked. A cold hand clawed down my back. Unless I was wrong, my magic was gone.

CHAPTER
SIXTEEN

I searched the rest of the house but didn't have any luck. Maybe it was because the wind was out of my sails, or there wasn't anything to find. Meanwhile, I needed to think about what I was going to do about Scott. Would he even show up to work once Sofia told him about our confrontation? Would he come and then proceed to do a terrible job? Or would he be belligerent? I didn't know how it would turn out. Did the witches have a better way to find my magic than I did? If so, would he tell me? All of this raced through my head Monday morning.

I was a little surprised when vehicles started arriving and the sounds of a construction crew getting ready filled the air. I figured I may as well cut this off at the pass, so to speak. I walked out to Scott's truck. He was on the phone in his cab. I walked around and to the passenger side and opened the door. I climbed in. He looked at me surprised and ended his call.

"Hey, Brigid. What's up?" he asked.

"You haven't spoken with Sofia?"

He wrinkled his brow in confusion. "No, why would I?"

I was quiet for a moment, building up my courage. Then I took a deep breath, gathered my magic, just in case, and plowed ahead.

"I know about the love potion, Craig Whelan, and that you guys are trying to steal my magic," I blurted.

His mouth hung open. "What?"

I'm sure I'd shocked him. But he did seem honestly surprised. Why was the question.

"Are you shocked that I know, or shocked because you didn't know?"

He sat silently and looked out his side window away from me. "Shocked that you know," he said finally.

Emotions roiled through me. I think I half hoped he'd been duped. I liked him. Not enough to date him, but he was very likable. Plus, the house. I needed him to finish. I sighed. Probably wasn't going to happen.

He thought the sigh was over what he said. "I knew it was wrong."

"You basically gave me a date rape drug."

"What? No! I'd never do that!"

"So, giving me a love potion that stole my choices isn't the same?"

"You keep your free will, and you remember what you did," he argued, sullenly.

"I'd have never made out with you, or even gone out with you without being under the influence of that potion."

"For it to work, you have to be attracted to the person," he argued.

"Think about it, Scott. How many people are you mildly attracted to when you meet? Even members of the same sex, I'm sure. We are social creatures. We wouldn't even have friends if we weren't attracted to others. It isn't fair to exploit that and make it sexual. I liked you. I found you attractive. I wouldn't have ever chosen to date you for many reasons, but that choice was taken from me by your potion."

"Oh."

"Yeah, 'Oh.'" I mocked him, but I was angry. "Even if I wasn't angry at you for that, and hurt, and betrayed, there's Craig. Now we've gone from crimes against me to just pure crime."

"What are you talking about? I don't know anything about your old contractor?"

"You didn't know your *cousin*," I spit out the word with venom.

"Killed him? She cursed him and stood there…" I pointed to the side of the house. "And directed her magic at him to cause brand new scaffolding to break and kept him from shifting long enough he died?"

"What? Sofia?" He shook his head. "She'd never do anything like that!"

"You're wrong. She did. She confirmed it."

"Look, Brigid. I told her I'd help steal your magical artifacts, and I'd use my job to do that. I'm guilty of that. I also agreed to smear that potion over the cup every day to keep you distracted so I could continue to search. But I'd never hurt anyone. I didn't want to do any of it, but she got me this job, and I needed it."

"I was desperate! I'd have taken you on even if she hadn't recommended you," I spat out.

He hung his head in shame or a good imitation of shame. "Do you want me to leave?"

I was quiet, thinking. Did I? Could I live with seeing him daily, knowing he was stealing from me? Knowing he had forced me to do what I did?

"No," I said, surprising myself. "I want this house done. You are doing a good job. However, you may not be alone at the house or in any part of the house. You must swear you will not take one single thing that isn't yours while you are here."

He nodded along as I spoke. "OK, yes, I can do that."

"Have you found any magical artifacts?"

He looked at me. Probably deciding if he should answer, knowing his cousin was a murderer. "Yes."

My heart fell. I was worried about this, but I think I held out hope that I'd find all my magic. "What did you find and take from me?" I asked with a hint of danger in my voice.

"Umm, we found a couple of pendants in one of the walls upstairs. A diamond, and an onyx."

Huh, nothing to indicate time. He must have found ice and shadow. At least that's what made sense based on the stones. That left me with aether, air, reality, and time, hopefully. "What did she do with them?" I demanded.

"Umm, I just gave them to her yesterday. She told me there's a whole ceremony spell thing she has to do to take the power. I'm not a great witch. I hardly have any power, and I've never learned to use it. Witch stuff is just too dangerous for my kind."

From what I'd found out this was a true statement.

"Don't go after them, Brigid." He punctuated this by shaking his head. "She is very powerful. One of your magic artifacts could power her for years. She wants it all. Once she unlocks those stones and takes that power, she's going to come after you and take all your power."

I grabbed the handle release in his truck. "Finish the house. I'll be fair with you. But if you take one more thing that is mine, or if I ever see you again after our business is concluded, it won't be something you'll enjoy. Do you understand?" I looked up into his eyes.

He had the decency to look chagrined. "Yes," he answered quietly.

I opened the door and jumped down. I think I heard him say, "I'm sorry."

I wasn't sure how much I believed him, but he had sounded sincere. Of course, I was a terrible judge of character as it turned out. Not that there's any surprise at that. I made a terrible choice for a husband, a new friend, and apparently a contractor. Ugh.

Now, I had to stop that new friend from stealing my magic and making herself so powerful as to be nearly unstoppable. How was I going to do this? I only had a cat and a healer on my side. What a part Fae, barely adequate magic user, a healer, and a Splintercat were supposed to do, I hadn't a clue. I walked back to the house, deep in thought, threw open the door and walked into the kitchen. Almost directly into the wolf apparition standing by the table.

I stopped short, startled. The wolf looked at me. I was scared; it looked so real, so solid. My palms were sweating, but I had to find out if it was Craig and what he needed to tell me. I took a deep breath. I wiped my hands down my sides to dry them and to gather my wits. Then I gathered my power. I should have spirit power now, whatever that meant, but if it meant I could speak to it, I needed to know, fast.

"Craig?" I asked.

The wolf cocked its head, ears flicked to front, and slowly the ghost wolf morphed into Craig Whelan.

"Yes," he said.

"I'm so sorry this happened to you. What can I do for you?"

"You're in danger," Craig's ghost said.

"You came back to tell me?" I asked, stupidly.

"A witch did this," he said.

I shook my head; I already knew this. "Yes, Sofia did this to you."

"Not just her," Craig said, while shaking his head sadly. "All of them. You need to leave. It isn't safe."

I could feel Craig's tenuous connection to reality. He was ready to leave. I needed to let him go. Maybe my magic had trapped him here. I didn't know.

"Thank you, Craig. You are a good man. I hear you. I release you."

He smiled. "This wasn't your fault," he said, and then with an increasing brightness of light, he faded and was gone.

"Mr. Mittens!" I yelled out, although I knew that wasn't necessary, I was deep in an emotional crisis. He appeared next to me and jumped up on the table.

"I saw the ghost wolf, again."

He blinked at me, waiting for me to finish my tale. I told him what had occurred.

His big blue eyes watched me intently until I had finished. *So, he believed more than one witch, possibly the entire coven is involved in this stealing of your powers?* he summed up.

"I guess. I don't know how he would know, but I don't understand ghosts either. Now he's gone, so I can't ask more questions either."

I can't help you with that. I am not familiar with how ghosts work, my cat said.

"Well, it sounds like the witches have to do some kind of ceremony to access the power in the artifacts, so until they do that, I can still recover them. They are mine!"

Mr. Mittens stood up and stretched. *Yes, they are. So, do you have a plan?*

I sighed. And walked around the table. "No."

189

Hmpf. That's probably the first step.

"Yeah, I know it's the first step, but I can't decide how to do it. I don't even know where to start." I slumped.

He stared at me, almost as though he were calling me an idiot. At least he'd stopped short of doing that.

Stop thinking like a human. You are a powerful fae. You have collected almost all your magic. Use it. With that he jumped down and sauntered towards the back door, tail erect and flicking back and forth with his swaying walk.

I swallowed the lump of frustration in my throat. Was it truly that easy? I just willed my magic to find the witches and their ceremonial spot? Then what did I do?

"Wait, Mr. Mittens!" I called out. "Will you help me if I can locate them? I think I could use a Splintercat."

He paused. I got one flick of an ear. He sat and wrapped his tail gracefully around, but he didn't turn. *It is my job to help and protect you.*

My eyes welled up with tears. I'd been alone so long, and this one phrase filled me with gratitude and a warm feeling of safety. "Thank you."

When I looked for him again, he was gone.

I debated calling Gabe and asking him the same. On one hand, I had no other allies, and I could use all I could get. Craig may have been one if he hadn't died, but without him and without Sofia whom I had thought of as a friend, I had one Splintercat, Gabe, maybe a griffin, and a really big maybe on a pack of werewolves against an entire coven of witches. Witches that had overstepped, but still an entire coven of trained magic users. On a good day I was still only half trained. I might not have the limitations they did, but they knew what they were doing, and I had no idea what that would look like in a fight.

I didn't know what a healer could do in a magic battle, but I guess if one of the fighters were injured, that would be convenient, especially if he could heal creatures that weren't human. I'd never asked. At least I could call and talk to him. I had no idea how to contact Brightfeather. She didn't have any obligation to me and could say no.

I took my phone out of my back pocket and scrolled through to Gabe's contact. I took a deep breath and hit send, praying it would go to voicemail. We had only a new and tenuous link to each other and for me, this felt extremely forward. Plus, I didn't want him to think I was taking advantage of him. I was surprised, when after three rings, he answered. I'd assumed he was at work.

"Brigid! I'm so glad you called." His bright answer filled my heart with warmth.

"You might not be after I tell you why I'm calling."

He laughed. "Nothing you say will change my mind."

"The coven has stolen some of my magic, and I was calling to beg your help getting it back."

The phone was silent. Just as I thought he'd hung up on me or the call had dropped, he responded. "Wow."

"Is that a 'wow' you'll help me, or 'wow' I can't believe you asked?"

He chuckled. "I'll help you. The wow was because you are willing to take on the coven. I'm impressed."

It was my turn to laugh. "Don't be. I am strong, but I have very little training, and no idea what the witches can do. This is stupid, but I have to do it. It's me, you, my Splintercat, a werewolf or two, and maybe a griffin—I still have to ask her. I'm probably going to get us all killed."

"A griffin?" He was quiet. "That is impressive."

"Only if she agrees."

"I hope she says she'll help then," he said. "Hold on, I have another call."

His end grew quiet, and I knew he'd switched over to his other call. He must not have had to work today since he was free to take calls. I wondered how to broach the subject of what he could do with only a healer's power. I was contemplating how to bring it up when he came back.

"Sorry, that was work. I'm on call, so I have to take those."

"Can your power do anything but heal?" I blurted out. Then embarrassed, I blushed, not that he could see me. I tried to backtrack. "I'm so sorry."

"Healers use the body and its lifeforce to heal. But using lifeforce goes both ways."

I shuddered. Did that mean he could take life as well?

"Using lifeforce is tricky. I can fill the well, and use that to heal, or I can empty the well."

"Does that mean you can take life with your power?"

"It's why healers are in demand by witches. We help with their magic issues, filling their wells so that they don't run dry from magic use. But those unscrupulous healers that join covens are often used to do the unspeakable."

"Are all witches evil?" I asked, my heart sinking with dread.

"I don't know. I'd like to think that all people are redeemable. But my experiences haven't been…pleasant."

"I want to believe that there is good in everyone," I said timidly, but I was losing faith.

"I do too," he replied.

"I guess we'll see. I'm going to try to find where and when they're going to meet to do their ceremony. I'll let you know what I find out."

"OK." He was quiet. Maybe my abrupt change in the conversation made him think I was trying to get him off the phone.

"I appreciate you wanting to help me," I said to fill the silence.

"I'll always help you."

"Thanks." I wanted to say more, but anything else felt too intimate for where we were in our relationship. So, I ended it with that.

I put the phone back in my pocket. Before I did anything else, I needed to get the last member of my team together, or at least see if she'd be willing to help. I went out my back door and walked over to where the trail to the waterfall started in the woods. Once I stepped in, I called out to Brightfeather. I waited. Nothing. I felt foolish. This was a large property, and she could be anywhere on it, or somewhere else entirely. I doubted she'd left, since I was giving her sanctuary, but you never knew. I called out again, "Brightfeather!" Nothing. I wandered along the trail further. I was nervous because Mr. Mittens made me swear not to wander in my own woods alone, but he'd left, and I needed to talk to the griffin.

I called out as I went. Soon enough, I was at the waterfall. It was loud here, but I called out dutifully, anyway. If I didn't find her soon, I'd have to go back. "Brightfeather!"

Even over the water, I heard a loud squawk, and a grey eagle drifted into view. The griffin transformed and landed in her natural shape. She bowed her head to me. *Lady Brigid.*

"Thanks so much for coming, Brightfeather. I hope I didn't disturb you."

No, but I was on the other side of your domain. Your magic is very powerful to call me from so far away.

"I called with my magic?" I didn't know I had done that. Mr. Mittens had said something like that to me before as well.

She gave a single nod.

"Oh, I'm sorry."

It is no matter.

"Uh, I'd like to ask you a favor. It will not affect our deal, no matter how you answer, you are welcome here, and I will honor your sanctuary."

She cocked her head in curiosity.

"The local witch coven has stolen some of my power. I would like to ask for your help in taking it back."

Her eyes opened wide. *You would entrust this to me?*

"Yes," I answered, confused.

It would be a great honor to assist you.

"I'm sure there isn't any honor involved, but I would appreciate it so much."

She acknowledged me with a bow again.

"I don't have a time or a place yet, if it's acceptable, I'll call you when I know."

That would please me.

"Thank you!"

She gave me another stately nod and then unfurled her wings, and by the time she was fully airborne, the griffin was again the plain grey eagle. A downdraft blasted my hair back, and I blinked with admiration at her ability to shift so effortlessly. Maybe it was a glamor, not a shift. I didn't know, but regardless, it was an amazing show of talent.

I hoped that Gabe and Mr. Mittens were correct that a griffin was a powerful and formidable ally, since I hadn't heard from the were-wolves and could only depend on the three of us against a coven of who knew how many witches with unknown strengths. I hoped I wasn't going to get us all killed.

With Brightfeather's agreement to help, my next task was to try and locate the site and the time of the ceremony. Mr. Mittens had indicated I could find it if I used my magic. Since I had nearly zero luck locating my missing magic before this point, I had no idea how to do it now. Since I was a computer person, I started googling. It wasn't like I had any other ideas.

Witches were a well-known and documented group. Though I wasn't aware of magic before I came back here, even I knew that people claimed to be witches. So, I googled "where would you hold a witch ceremony?" That got me nothing. The answer was basically anywhere you wanted. I changed my entry to "when." That was more useful. Apparently, witches had a lot of holidays, go figure. Since it was late summer, the obvious, the day after Halloween or Samhain, was out. That was the only one I knew. There was Lammas the first of August, but that was past. The next was the equinox, but that was further away than Scott had indicated. He said it was in a few days, not weeks. I could feel my frustration grow.

Didn't witches dance around fires under the full moon, or the new moon? I wasn't sure, so I changed my search again. This time I found that the moon played an important role, especially when waxing full or attaining full. I looked it up. The moon would be full at 2:36 am in two days. That sounded like a possibility. I had a when. Now if I could pin down a where, I was golden.

The search also talked about "drawing down the moon." After reading about what that was, I figured they'd have to be outside. They'd need an open area to actually see the moon to draw down its power. That narrowed the possibilities slightly, but we weren't far from the beach and that was a lot of area.

However, my power, fae power, was stronger near the forests, maybe they had to do it there? All I could do was guess. I had no idea how to use my power to find out where. My only other idea was to follow Sofia around town in the meantime and hope I could locate the ceremony that way. Maybe Scott could find out? I didn't know if he'd help me either. I still wasn't sure he wasn't in on everything. He *had* dosed me. So, I guess I'd follow Sofia. That decided, I put it out of my mind.

Just as I finished putting away my laptop, my phone buzzed. I picked it up and looked at the screen, Whelan Construction. I fumbled answering in my haste.

"Hello?" I said a little breathlessly. This call could make a huge difference.

"Brigid? It's Luke."

"Yes?"

"We want to know all you know. The pack is going to war."

"Well, I have some news." And I filled him in on my very shaky plan.

* * *

TWO DAYS LATER, WITH GABE, THE PACK, MR. MITTENS, AND Brightfeather informed of the time of the ritual, I had nothing to do but follow Sofia around to find the location. Since it wouldn't be until the early morning hours, I waited until evening. I knew where she worked —she had been my friend after all—and I waited there until I saw her get in her car and head out. I figured the next bit would be a long boring slog of me following her around before she headed to the ritual location.

It was. She went to the store, then she went home and stayed there for hours. I watched her house and car until the boredom nearly killed me. Luckily, Gabe texted me often to check in or it was possible I might have given up. Just as I was thinking that she'd found a way to sneak out without me knowing, she came out of the house. She had bags of things that she placed in the trunk. Ritual requirements? Maybe. Finally, around eleven, she started her car and left the house. I followed. I desperately needed to pee, but this was the time I was going to find her secret ceremonial spot, so I had to gut it up and hold it a while longer.

She wound her way through town, casually obeying all the stupid traffic laws and driving under the speed limit. Was she concerned the cops would catch her with witch supplies? Seemed dumb that a murderess would be worried about something so trivial as traffic laws. I giggled to myself, a little punchy. She headed south out of town on Highway 101. It was a beautiful drive; I knew because this was the road to my house.

She turned off before my property and pulled in where I had replaced the road with wilderness to block access to my property. Just great, she was performing the ritual on my land. Not only was she stealing my magic, but she was also trespassing. Again. The bitch! I texted Gabe.

"She's here, on my land!"

I couldn't really follow her anymore. She'd parked and was on foot. I turned and drove back to my house and parked. My anxiety notched up. I got out and called Mr. Mittens to me. He appeared. I told him what I'd seen and asked him to follow her and report on the exact location. He agreed and disappeared. I went to the bathroom, then walked over to the trail to the waterfall and called Brightfeather. She had been waiting, so she came quickly. I filled her in, and she also set off to watch my former friend. I went back to the house to get ready. Nerves jangled, and uncertainty twisted in my stomach. I walked in the back door, texting Gabe with the same information.

Something hit me in the back of the head, a bright explosion of light, and then nothing.

CHAPTER

SEVENTEEN

I woke up confused and disoriented. My head pounded, and for a while, I saw in photo negative. Nausea rose up and gripped my guts, and I nearly spewed my meager dinner. I definitely had a concussion. I was curled up in a heap. It was dark and damp, and it felt like wet leaves under my cheek. I tried to reach up and feel the back of my head, but my arms wouldn't respond. I realized they were tied behind my back. My shoulders ached so I must have been out for some time. I would have groaned my discomfort, but I was afraid I'd puke if I made any noise.

My vision finally adjusted, or my brain did, because I could start to make out shapes around me. Trees, so I was outside for sure, the leaves sort of gave that one away. Next, my hearing came back. I must have really been knocked upside the head, hard. It was swimming and throbbing with every beat of my heart. I was dizzy as well, but I could finally hear voices. They weren't distinct, so my head still hadn't cleared up all the way.

I blinked a few times. Flickering light filled the clearing. We were in a clearing somewhere on my property. If we were here, Mr. Mittens could go all Splintercat on them. I smiled. Even doing that made my head split. The witches had a fire. How stereotypical. That thought caused a giggle to slip out. A hysterical giggle for sure. I was trussed up like a sacrificial lamb by a bunch of evil witches on my own damn land where I was a freaking fae lord, and I couldn't do a thing about it.

Where was my cat? My allies? I looked around, trying to see what was going on. There were a bunch of people milling around. I couldn't figure out what they were doing. Maybe preparing for the ritual? No cat, no werewolves, no griffin that I could see from where I was lying. I sure hoped they knew where I was. I hadn't finished my text to Gabe past the one that said they were on my land before I got knocked out, so hopefully he was on his way with the werewolves, and Mr. Mittens would tell them how to find me.

My movements alerted someone because they reported, "She's awake."

I froze. Suddenly dozens of witch eyes focused on me. "Hi." I muttered, not knowing what else to say.

A boot connected with my lower back and my hands. "Shut up. If you say anything, I'll tie your jaw shut."

Pain exploded from my back, hands, and throughout the rest of my body, a groan escaped. Another kick.

"No sound," the rough male voice growled.

Did they think I needed sound to perform magic? Maybe witches had too, but as far as I knew and had practiced, I just needed to focus my will. Currently that will was shattered by the pain in my head and now in my back and hands. But if I could pull it together, I was going to unleash hell. Probably. Maybe. At least I wanted to.

My vision had finally cleared. In front of me was the large bonfire, and beyond the fire a stone altar. It looked old. Had it always been here on my land? The witches couldn't have brought it in, so it must have been here for a long time. I searched for a sign of my cat. I knew he had to be here somewhere, I'd asked him to find and follow Sofia. I thought of my ability to call him and other creatures to me. If I could clear my head long enough, that was the easiest and oldest of my magics. I could call him to me.

I closed my eyes and concentrated on Mr. Mittens. After some time, I called his name in my mind. Over and over, I called. I could feel the magic leave me. I opened my eyes and looked around. No Mr. Mittens. Had they captured him too? No, I couldn't see him in the clearing. Neither Ragdoll nor Splintercat shape. I tried calling Bright-feather. Nothing. Had they already stolen my power?

No, they couldn't have. The moon still wasn't fully risen; the ritual had not begun. Something else was going on. I scanned the clearing again. Several robed witches were encircling the clearing, facing out towards the woods, while others scurried about doing whatever pre-ritual tasks witches did—something with candles and other objects I couldn't identify. The robed witches were chanting something low and almost inaudible to me. Were they keeping out my friends? Creating a barrier of sorts?

My heart fell and despair filled me. If my allies couldn't reach me, what could I do? I was tied up, it looked like several dozen witches had captured me, and once the moon hit its zenith, they were going to steal my magic.

A screech filled the air. I looked up, Brightfeather was high above the clearing in her eagle form. I could only make her out because the flickering light from the fire caught her silvery feathers. I finally understood how she got her name. In the dark, they were truly bright with the reflected light. In the day she just looked grey, now she was a glowing silver. Her wings beat against an unseen barrier. A witch yelled out, "Here it comes again!" The chanting became louder for a few moments. I shuddered. I was alone.

Brightfeather flew off. I wondered if the barrier hurt her or just kept her out. I hoped she was OK. This wasn't really her fight. If she couldn't get in, I bet Mr. Mittens, Gabe, and the werewolves couldn't either. I sighed. Pain exploded in my upper back. Another kick by Mr. No Noise. I closed my eyes. Maybe I could call the lightning. That would show him. I concentrated my will. If I could reach out to my allies, surely, I could call on my magics. I turned my head to glare at him and willed the lightning to come.

He jumped back as though he'd been shocked. "Ow," he yelled.

Not lightning. If I could only conjure up a shock, what was holding back my power? Was whatever barrier the witches were chanting causing interference with my magic? At least Mr. Kickypants didn't put together the light shock with me doing magic. My back wasn't up for more full kicks. I'd have to soak the bruises away for a week if I survived this. Since that wasn't likely, I guess I'd have to bear the pain for now.

The kicker moved around to my front. I used the opportunity to attempt to loosen the bonds on my hands. They were tight, but not so tight there wasn't any play. Since my magic was weak, I didn't have much to draw on, but maybe I could draw on a small amount. A little fire maybe? I concentrated on the plastic and willed it to burn. Under full power, I might have set the forest on fire, including myself. Now I used all I had and slowly but surely, I could smell burnt plastic. I pulled and twisted my hands around until the zip tie broke. I sighed and rubbed my wrists carefully.

I didn't dare move my hands to the front, even though my shoulders burned and ached from having my hands behind my back for so long. I concentrated instead on melting the zip ties around my ankles. I needed to get free and run, not just make sure my shoulders didn't hurt. I'd only get one chance.

"Brigid!" Gabe's voice split the night. Several witches turned towards the sound. Mr. Kickypants turned and looked at me and made the international sign for "shut up you moron," he brought his finger to his lips and glared at me. I nodded. I thought harder at the zip ties around my ankles. The stench of burnt plastic filled the air. I grimaced. Hopefully my guard wouldn't notice it.

Gabe continued to yell my name, and my heart leapt with each call. The zip ties snapped audibly. My guard whipped around, but he was looking in the trees, not at my feet. My heart pounded with fear. He turned back to the fire.

Now I could see the wolves. The pack was larger than I'd thought. Their yips and growls added to the confusion outside the barrier.

Things were starting to happen inside. Sofia and a few other witches placed items on the altar and looked as though they were preparing their ritual. I swallowed. I had to do something soon, or I'd lose my shot. I rolled further onto my side so I could get my feet under me. I needed to stop the witches holding my friends out of the circle and keeping my magic suppressed. My plan was simple, jump up and ram the nearest one to stop the damn chanting. If that didn't work, I was going to try to short circuit the barrier with my body and every bit of magic in it.

Not much of a plan, but it was all I could do at the moment. I'd barely pulled up enough power for a shock and to melt some plastic. I watched Sofia. She was placing the two jewels that contained my magic on the altar. Damn that pissed me off. The kicker was still too close to me. If he wasn't slower than tar, there's no way I could get up and ram a witch before he stopped me. I looked around for a weapon. Other than a soggy leaf or two, there wasn't even a stick close enough to me to make a difference.

Maybe if I touched him, I could generate enough electricity to zap him into submission. It was a gamble though, and I'd only get one shot. The moon hit its zenith. I felt it like a cold blast of water drenching me. Sofia raised her hands, and white light bathed her in its cool glow. She began chanting. The kicker spread out his arms, as did all the witches, and they too began to chant. I scooted back, away from him. He couldn't hear me on the damp ground. The small sound my movement made was drowned out by the chanting as it grew louder.

The foreign magic itched under my skin. It felt wrong and tainted to me. I continued to put distance between me and the kicker, the witches distracted by their chanting. A tree stopped me. I used it to heave myself up to standing. My right side was numb from laying on the cold ground, and I was stiff and awkward. I focused on the closest witch, one holding the barrier, and raced at her. I took three steps close enough to almost touch her and something slammed into me from behind. The momentum carried me into the witch and the three of us— the witch, the kicker, and me—tumbled to the ground. I yelled, "Gabe!" with all my might, hoping that the barrier was down.

A fist smashed into my face. Blood spurted out my nose and probably my lip. I kicked and clawed and gouged at any flesh in my reach. A hand grabbed my hair and yanked my head back. I yelled out in pain. A hand came over my mouth. I bit it. A punch to my side dissuaded me from further biting, mainly because I couldn't suck in any air for a while.

The scuffle got the attention of Sofia. She called out, "Bring her here."

The kicker dragged me by the hair up to the altar. I kicked my way there, trying to take pressure off my scalp, but it felt like my scalp was separating from my skull. Tears poured out of my eyes in pain, and I clawed at the hand tangled in my hair.

He threw me into the stone altar once we were close enough, and the force knocked the wind out of me. I gasped for air, fighting the pain. Once I could take a breath, I shouted out for Gabe again. I didn't know if my breaking the chanting of one practitioner was enough to let my friends through, but I hoped.

The yell got me gagged. Stupid witches. I didn't need my voice to do magic. Sofia should know that. I thought. Maybe I'd never told her? I couldn't remember. It didn't matter, because I just needed my will, and now my head had cleared—I had will in abundance. There was one way to know if I'd disrupted the magical shield around this place. I called up lightning again. The rage behind that was immense. I told it to strike the other witches chanting around the barrier. I let it build in my mind and then, I released it. Electricity crackled in the air. I could actually see the static charge as it filled the clearing, held in by the weak bubble the witches had chanted up to protect their ritual. A huge "bang" rang out in the clearing, and most of the witches were knocked off their feet. Hair floated around heads, but most importantly, the barrier came down. I felt it like an audible pop in my ears like changing altitudes on a plane. Witches were standing around me, most angry and all looking at me.

Five strangers came at me. I kicked and clawed and twisted with all my might. But they lifted me up onto the altar and held my limbs still so I couldn't move. A few uttered words, and I was unable to fight at all. It was even impossible to blink. Tears of pain and frustration rolled down my face. I couldn't even control that.

I pulled myself together. I still had magic. Lightning helped, and the barrier seemed down for now, so even if my allies were held back before, they were free to come in now. I didn't want to zap them so I thought it would be a good time to start seeing if "mind" magic meant I could exert control over others. At the moment, that did not seem like an unethical pursuit. I concentrated on the witch holding my right arm. I gathered my will and mentally screamed, "Let go!" She twitched back, surprised, but she let go. I was still being held by the spell, but at least now I knew I had something to fight back with.

How could I break this spell? Was I strong enough to do it with only my inherent fae power and my will? I couldn't even close my eyes to help my concentration. I focused on the moon. Could fae call down the moon? Or was that specific to witches? I guess my power wasn't inherent to this realm so probably not. I could draw on the forest, my forest. I stared at the moon, and let my mind go blank. Then I gathered the power in my forest. I pulled on it, begged it, let it wrap me up body and soul, and when it felt like I could hold no more, I commanded it to free me from my spell bonds.

I felt them fall away and I took a deep breath. Sofia was chanting over me, holding the two pendants—ice and shadow. I reached up and yanked the black one out of her hands, she yelped. I shoved it in my jeans pocket and sat up. I jumped off the altar. Hands reached for me, trying to pull me back down. I was having none of it. I wasn't a violent person, and I hadn't ever taken any classes on fighting, but I also wasn't going to let them steal my magic and continue to beat me up. I kicked out at whoever was closest and heard a grunt as I made contact. I slapped the witch nearest me and caught her in the nose. She squealed and backed up. Sofia stopped her chanting and started directing them to contain me. I broke free of the grasping hands and started to run back to the safety of the forest.

A shriek ripped through the air and a silver dart passed through my peripheral vision and started tearing into witches. I grinned. My allies were here. I barreled through another witch, a smaller girl who went flying when I shoved her. I could see Mr. Mittens batting witches to the ground. And wolves seemed to be everywhere, chewing up witches left and right. Yes, we were going to do this. We could stop them. I looked over my shoulder. Sofia held up the ice pendant and chanted. A white nimbus started to form around her, and I realized she was going to complete the ritual soon. I groaned and turned back to her. I had nothing to stop her with. I couldn't think what I could call on that would shut her up and stop her. I looked around. No one was as close to her as I was.

I tried my mind magic, but it didn't have any effect. Whatever she was doing was protecting her. I tried to throw lightning, and fire at her. I had no water source, so that wouldn't work. Spirit was as worthless as mind. I hadn't let shadow absorb into me yet, so I couldn't use that either. All I had was my body. I reached her and tried to yank the diamond pendant from her hand, but I couldn't make contact. She had a shield of power around her. I tried to shove her, to push her down. Nothing. I shrieked in frustration.

Brightfeather heard me and headed over. She couldn't access Sofia either. And the entire time Sofia never stopped chanting, the moonlight bathing her and encasing her in light. The other witches, those not engaged in a fight with either the griffin, the wolves, or the Splintercat were chanting along with Sofia. Maybe if I stopped them? I changed my tactics and started attacking the witches assisting Sofia. They weren't protected. Brightfeather dispatched five to my one, and the wolves took out the rest. Soon witches were lying around like logs in the clearing, groaning and moaning if they were still alive and aware.

I hadn't seen Gabe anywhere. I didn't know if he was injured or dead. But chaos and bodies were everywhere. The fire was dying down now that no one was tending it, and the light changed to a sinister red.

Mr. Mittens was destroying the witches, his growls split the night and his eyes glowed in the red flickering light. He looked terrifying. I was glad he was on my side. Suddenly a blast shook the clearing and knocked me off my feet. I felt power ripped away from me. Even though the objects were separate from me and held my magic, they must have still been tied to me in some way. The wrenching of the power felt like someone ripped a piece of my soul away. I turned back to Sofia. She was glowing, a look of triumph on her face. The pendant was gone. She'd completed her spell and taken my ice magic.

Her eyes caught mine, and she sneered at me. I stumbled back up to my feet and lurched towards her. The ache in my chest where my missing magic should be, burned like an open wound, and I rubbed it with the heel of my hand. A growl of pure hatred escaped my throat. I reached for her. She spoke a word and a wall of ice formed in front of me. I ran into it and fell hard on my butt. I placed my hand on the ice wall and willed fire at it. It melted away. Sofia had disappeared. The rest of the witches still standing were fleeing through the woods after her. I curled up on the ground and wept.

CHAPTER
EIGHTEEN

M r. Mittens leaned down over me. He nosed me, probably deciding if I was alright. I wasn't, but I groaned, rolled over to my knees and got up slowly. The witches that were able had fled. The wolves chased after them, leaving Mr. Mittens and I to check the bodies lying around the forest floor.

"Are they all dead?" I asked.

Mr. Mittens sniffed. He didn't care, but I had to. These were people. How was I going to explain the deaths of several robed figures on my land?

Yes, he answered simply.

My shoulders slumped.

You can make the bodies disappear.

"I can? How?"

Have the earth swallow them. There will be nothing left for the humans to find.

That was right, I had earth magic. Mr. Mittens had encouraged me to practice doing things with the earth magic before. Besides talking to forest creatures, I could make plants grow and move the earth itself. "Are you sure they're all dead? I don't want to bury the living."

Yes, if they are not, they deserve to be buried alive, he replied.

207

Part of me wanted to think that too, but I couldn't do it. I had to check each fallen body. Maybe Gabe was lying here too. I still hadn't seen him.

"Have you seen Gabe?" I asked him.

I did earlier, but not since the barrier came down and the battle began.

I checked each body. They were mainly robed, but Gabe could have thrown on a robe to confuse them, so I needed to see every face. I recognized a few bodies from people I'd seen around town. A couple were on my construction crew, and that reignited the anger in my belly. No Scott though. Maybe he really wasn't involved in all of this beyond his already recognized sins.

One man was still alive. One out of about seventeen. No Gabe. I didn't know what to do with the man, because I couldn't pick him up and carry him back to the car to take him to the hospital. I left him where he lay and continued on. While we checked the rest, Mr. Mittens grabbed him by the scruff of the neck and snapped it. I gasped at his brutal action, but he scoffed at me.

They tried to kill you, he reminded me.

I closed my eyes and sighed. I'd think about it tomorrow.

"Stand behind me." I commanded him. The wolves were filtering into the clearing from their search and stood silently watching. Brightfeather also returned and joined Mr. Mittens. They stood behind me. I pulled up my magic, which felt wounded somehow, and asked the earth to swallow the bodies. It responded sluggishly, as though ripping the ice magic from me would require the magic to heal before it rose to my will as easily as before. The bodies sank, and the earth closed over them. No sign of their presence remained. I asked the earth to swallow the abomination of an altar, it obeyed sluggishly, but the altar disappeared. Then out of spite, I asked the forest to take the clearing. I pushed the magic out of me with force. The grass greened and rose from its crushed and broken state to new and lush; trees broke through and pushed their branches to the sky. Once no sign remained, I turned and with Mr. Mittens, the wolves, and Brightfeather started back to the house.

We looked for Gabe as we went, but even though I yelled for him, no answer returned. Mr. Mittens said he couldn't smell an active scent, and when I queried the wolves, head shakes confirmed that they couldn't smell him either. When Brightfeather returned from looking from the skies, she also had no news. I hoped beyond hope he was holed up at the house, having seen that we had kicked ass back at the clearing, but seeing the house dark and feeling its emptiness ended that dream. His SUV was still parked behind my house, and the engine was cold. He was missing.

I sat on the back porch steps in the dark. Mr. Mittens curled up next to me in his Ragdoll shape. Brightfeather landed on the railing in her eagle shape. The wolves were changing out of sight.

"Do you think the witches took him?" I asked. But that had to be what'd happened.

"I do not know, Lady Brigid," Brightfeather answered. "But I have seen no sign of any other humans since the witches fled."

"I think they wanted him and so they took him," Mr. Mittens said. "They will not harm him. They want his skills," he added.

I nodded. That was true. At least that was the history he had with witches everywhere he went. If nothing else, they were consistently creepy. I wondered why they had waited to take him. He'd lived here several months.

By then, Luke and his brother, Noah, the new alpha, joined us. "Witches." Noah spat. "They took him. We could smell him back there." He pointed. "But his scent disappeared into a vehicle."

I sighed. At least it was confirmed.

Was this my fault? Maybe acting against them had driven them to punish him this way? Or it was just an opportunity they couldn't pass up? Would they let him return to his practice or keep him locked up somewhere to do their bidding? I was too tired and drained to worry about it right now.

Feeling guilty, I pushed myself up and climbed the few steps up to the house. Regardless of what I knew I needed to do, right now I had to eat and rest, or I wouldn't be able to do anything to help Gabe.

I thanked Brightfeather, and she flew off. I opened my back door and invited Luke and Noah in. There were three other wolves, but at Noah's nod, they got in their cars and left. The two brothers came in and sat at my kitchen table. I fed my cat. Then, I offered the werewolves food, but they declined after seeing me in the light and left after they reassured me that they'd be looking for the witches that'd snuck off as well as continuing the search for Gabe. I thanked them as they walked out.

I ate something I don't remember, took some painkillers, stripped, and fell face down on my bed. I didn't even clean up the mud and blood from my face and hands. I slept until the pain woke me again. I took more painkillers and went into the bathroom to clean myself up. Big mistake.

I shouldn't have looked in the mirror. Half my face was swollen and distorted. Blood was smeared everywhere, and my hair was tangled and full of leaves, twigs, and dirt. When I peed, it was mostly blood. I got in the shower and let the heat soak away the mess and the aches. I got out and dressed. Then I stripped the bed. Too tired and sore to remake it, I wrapped up in a clean quilt and collapsed on the bare mattress. I fell back into a concussed sleep. I probably shouldn't have let myself sleep, but I couldn't fight it. My head and body had taken too much damage, and I couldn't stay awake.

If I woke up, I needed to call someone for help. I didn't know who, or what they could do, I was too out of it. But I needed help from more than a part time housecat and a griffin that couldn't leave my property.

I did wake up. I wasn't sure if I was happy about that, but Gabe needed me. Unfortunately, I needed someone as well, and I had no one here. The only person that came to mind was Megan. I hadn't told her anything about my magic or what had happened to me so far, and I wasn't sure about dragging her into this. It was dangerous. She was human. But I couldn't help my hand as it dialed her number. When she answered, all I could choke out was, "I need you."

She was quiet for about two seconds, then she said, "I'm coming."

CHAPTER
NINETEEN

The relief I felt was almost tangible. My body relaxed, my mind focused, and I knew I'd done the right thing for me. Now I needed to find something to protect her while she was here. I pulled my hair back gently from my swollen face, took the elevator to the third floor, and climbed the few stairs painfully into the attic. This time, rather than search, I used my magic, and I called my grandmother's books to me. I needed to master my magic, and I needed to do it yesterday. I stood near the top of the stairs, closed my eyes, and pushed out my will to the entire attic. Then I called. When I opened my eyes, ten books lay at my feet. They were slim volumes, so I gathered them all up and took them to my room.

Before I dove into them, I fed Mr. Mittens and asked him about protection for my friend. He didn't know anything about the magic part but did mention that he knew of protection charms. So that guided me in what I should look for in Grams' journals.

I ate something, but still was vaguely nauseous, probably because of the concussion. I tried to search the journals, but I couldn't focus and fell back to sleep. When I woke up, I felt a lot better, although I was far from one hundred percent.

I found protection charms in the third journal I searched. Grateful I didn't have to look through them all since focusing on the print was difficult, my eyes had trouble focusing, and reading made my head pound, I made note of how to do it.

Luckily, making a protection charm was a simple process since I didn't feel like I could do anything complicated. I was also grateful they didn't take much time since I didn't know when Megan would get here—I wasn't even sure if she was driving or flying. When I thought about it, I supposed she must be driving since she didn't ask me to pick her up at the airport. It was a fourteen-hour drive if you drove straight through from Utah to the Oregon coast, so I wasn't expecting her in one day.

The protection charm required me to have an object that would accept the magic. The book suggested silver. Apparently, the fae magic I had liked silver, which made sense since every one of my magical artifacts was encased in silver. Either I needed to find something I already owned, or I needed to go to town and buy something. After seeing my face, I figured it was best to find something I already owned. I did have my grandmother's jewelry box, which was quite large and full of beautiful pieces.

I dug through it. Megan was my best friend, so I wanted something that was valuable and pretty. Something I knew she'd like. I removed each piece and examined them. The sapphires went aside, since they were a set I didn't want to separate, but I found a gorgeous silver chain with an Alexandrite pendant—rare, expensive, and exquisite. I wondered if the Alexandrite would hold the magic as well as silver. I shrugged. Only one way to find out.

This was the perfect protection charm for Megan. I prayed it would work. The book's only instruction was that I push each facet of my magic into the charm while focusing on protecting the wearer. That seemed easy—if time consuming. I also didn't have all my magic, so I could only use what I had.

I took the charm and sat down in my comfortable leather chair in my reading nook. Wrapped up in my fuzzy blanket, trying to gather all the comfort I could around my aching and sore body, I concentrated on the charm. My injuries distracted me. I think even my hair and eyelashes hurt. Reaching up, I brushed a finger over my eyelashes. Sure enough, they hurt. I almost smiled, but since it felt like my face would crack and fall off, I didn't.

Focusing on the charm, I grasped the necklace in my hand and concentrated on my earth magic. It was the first one I'd reintegrated, so I figured it was the best one to start with. I pushed it into the new charm and focused on it protecting Megan. I felt the magic leave me and the necklace glowed in my hand.

"Huh," I said. "It worked."

I returned my focus back on the charm I was creating. I was a little shocked since I was still new at magic and was always a little surprised when something worked. I continued with all the magic I currently bore. Sadly, she wouldn't be protected from ice.

When that thought entered my mind, the rage rose again. I would take it back from Sofia's hide. I also couldn't protect her from reality or aether—still no idea what they were—or time. Hopefully, those wouldn't be an issue. Suddenly, I remembered that I'd snatched back shadow and rose slowly from my chair. My clothes were still heaped in the bathroom, and I hobbled my way there and found my jeans. They were stiff with mud and blood. Thrusting my hand in my pocket, I found the onyx. I took it out and set it in my hand, so that it touched my skin and soon enough, it flashed darkly and sunk into my skin and disappeared. The strangest feeling overwhelmed me. Not of darkness or depression, which I sort of expected, but of warmth and comfort. I was confused. Why would shadow be warm and comforting? I'd think about it later.

I added protection from shadow to the charm and set it on my vanity so it would be ready for my friend. I hoped it worked.

* * *

I spent the next two days resting and sleeping. I really couldn't do much else, but worry about Gabe, since I was so beat up and ill from the experience with the witches.

I barely fed myself, and I couldn't get out of bed. Why didn't I have healing magic? Was that a fae thing at all? Who knew? I occupied my time between sleeping bouts with rereading my grandmother's journals and looking through photo albums. I worried about Gabe.

Luke and Noah came and checked on me. Their mom sent over casseroles and other comfort food—most went uneaten. They'd continued to search for Gabe but couldn't find him. In the meantime, they worked on identifying members of the coven by scent and were slowly building a list of the bastards that had been on my property.

Mr. Mittens was concerned about me, and he spent more time lying next to me on the bed than doing patrols. When I asked him if that would leave the property vulnerable, he replied that Brightfeather was helping. She was also concerned. When I did get up and take care of myself, I hobbled around like a ninety-year-old in poor health. There was a very good possibility that some ribs and maybe my jaw were broken. I couldn't even drive myself to the hospital, and the fact that Gabe wasn't around took more wind out of my sails.

Megan texted at some point that she was almost here, and I wept with relief. I needed my bestie. She was the only person in the world that I associated with comfort. She loved me unconditionally as I did her. If she were here, I'd be able to face my defeat, the loss of my magic, and the search for Gabe.

You must eat. Mr. Mittens huffed at me for the second time today.

I'd have shrugged noncommittally, but it was too painful.

If you do not, I'll bring you a mouse.

The thought of that made me shudder. "You wouldn't."

He gave me a slow blink, but his eyes were steely. *I would.*

"Fine." I groaned my way up to my feet and went into the kitchen to make a cup of cocoa and a piece of toast.

Just as the toast popped up, I heard the gravel crunch, and an engine roar up my driveway. My heart leapt in my throat. Toast forgotten, I hobbled out the kitchen door and onto the back porch. Megan had finally arrived. Everything would be okay.

The End

JILLEEN DOLBEARE

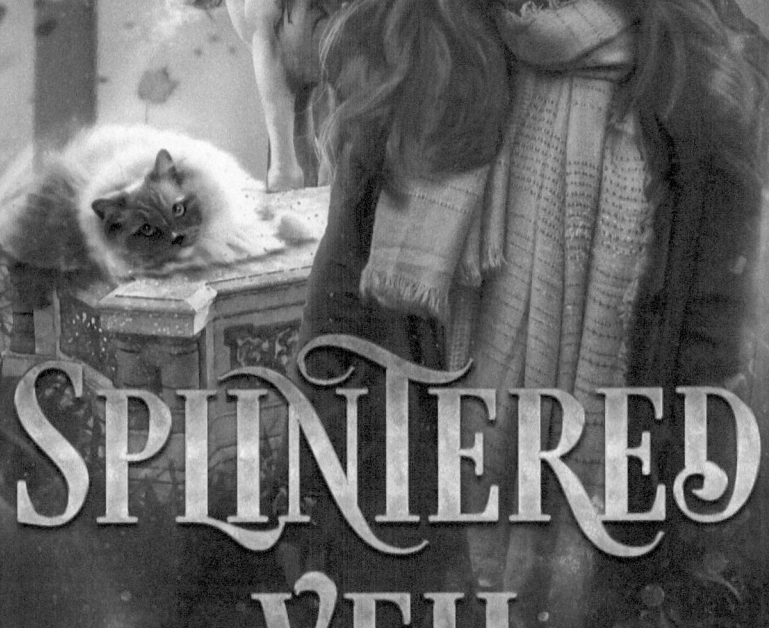

SPLINTERED
VEIL

Splinter Veil
Jilleen Dolbeare

ICE RAVEN
PUBLICATIONS

Copyright © 2023
Editor: Cissell Ink
Cover Designer: Crimson Phoenix Creations
Interior Art: Rose Rasmussen

I dedicate this book to the people that have supported and encouraged me along the way. To my mom, who taught me to love sci-fi and fantasy. I wouldn't be anything without you! To my husband for not getting upset when I'm busy with the books. To my Mastermind Group, thanks so much! To my niece, Baylee Rose who read everything, kept me focused, made suggestions, and for her brilliant art. And to all my alpha and beta and ARC readers. Thank you all!

CHAPTER
ONE

I turned the kettle on for hot water and put dry cocoa mix in my mug. This was my first time out of bed in three days. The witches had done a number on me. I'd been beaten within an inch of my life, and although I wasn't a doctor, I bet my ribs were cracked, and my jaw was broken. The only reason I was up was because my cat had threatened me with a mouse. I didn't have the energy to take care of a dead rodent, and I definitely didn't for a living one.

Megan texted that she was close. Only the desire to see her and feel the comfort of her presence kept me from going back to bed. I'd cleaned up and gingerly washed my tender face. There wasn't anything I could do with my hair, so I twisted it into a messy bun, where it wouldn't bug me. Even my hair hurt. That might have been because a male witch had dragged me across a clearing by my hair and used it to throw me into an altar. I'm sure several hunks of hair were missing. I couldn't bear to look.

Gravel crunched outside. I hobbled to my kitchen door as I followed the sound around back, stepping out onto the porch. Excitement and relief filled my broken body. Megan waved at me from her

SUV. I started to wave back, but the pain in my back and my ribs screamed, and I yanked my hand down quickly. She didn't notice. Damn those witches and their evil agenda.

Megan bounced out of the driver's side and opened the back door, reaching into the back seat for her bag and a pillow. She turned and rushed to my back porch.

Her dark hair was in a high ponytail, and her favorite sweats encased her shapely figure. I would have grinned at the sight, but my face hurt too much. I groaned. I didn't even have a place for her to sleep. She could spend a few nights with me in my bed, but I'd have to order a mattress for her. I was a terrible friend.

She flounced over the gravel and up the stairs to the porch. She finally looked up at me and gasped.

"Oh my God, Brigid. What happened?" She tossed her things down and wrapped me in a careful hug.

I burst into tears. She held me awhile as I sobbed. After what must have been forever, I calmed down. She let me go, and I invited her into the house. She gathered up her things and followed me into the kitchen. I must have inadvertently called Mr. Mittens, or he was hungry. Either way, he met us there and leaped gracefully up onto the table. Megan jumped back.

"That scared me," she said, then noticed the cat. "Oh my, what a gorgeous cat!"

He was beautiful—long creamy fur with blue-grey points and two front white mittens.

He blinked at her with enormous periwinkle blue eyes and m'rowed. Then he leaned in for her to scratch his ears and give him a thorough pet.

I wasn't sure how to explain what had happened without first telling her about magic. Since she was as unlikely to believe he could talk as I had been at first, I needed something to assist me. It would be awesome if Mr. Mittens could talk to her.

That gave me an idea. I told Megan to wait there and hobbled my way to the bathroom, where I picked up the charm I'd made to protect her. I held it and focused my magic on it, telling it to allow her to hear magical creatures. And the pendant flashed.

I took it back to the kitchen. She was still petting my cat, who appeared to be in ecstasy. The harlot.

"Hold out your hand," I said.

She looked at me curiously. "Okay." She held out her hand.

I dropped the necklace into her open hand.

"What's this?" she asked and studied it. "Is it Alexandrite?"

I gave a very small smile, my face aching. "Yes, I know you love it."

She tried to hand it back. "I can't take it. That's a large stone and I know how much you spent on it."

"You're wrong. I didn't spend one dime on it. It was my grand-mother's," I said, proudly. I knew she wouldn't take it if I'd spent too much money on her.

Her face twisted up in horror, and she thrust the necklace at me. "Now, I really can't take it!"

"Why not?"

"It's part of your inheritance. You can't give me something that was your grandmother's!"

I pushed her hand back towards her. "She left me a ton of jewelry. This wasn't even close to the most expensive piece, so you can take it without any guilt. Please take it. It'll make me happy."

She took it back, reluctantly.

"Please put it on," I encouraged. Then I stood up and walked behind her so I could help her with it. She looped it around her neck and handed me the ends. I fastened them.

I sat back down. My breath rasped, my knees and arms were weak, and I felt like I'd been kicked again. Everything must have shown on my face because Megan looked concerned, then asked me again what'd happened.

I took a moment and caught my breath. Feeling better prepared because she was wearing the charm, I started my tale from the moment I'd arrived until now, focusing mainly on how the witches had played me, stolen my magic, beaten me to a pulp, and then taken Gabe. Megan let me continue without interruption, although her face betrayed every emotion and her disbelief. Once I was done, she stood up and began pacing.

"I know you don't believe me. But I can prove it." I looked at my cat, who had splooted over the table throughout my whole retelling. "Mr. Mittens, you're up."

He gave me a bored, blue-eyed gaze. *What do you wish me to do?* He spoke into my mind.

"I imbued Megan's necklace with the power to hear you. Please, speak to her," I said.

He turned his face to her. I watched her as she heard him speak into her mind. Her eyes flew open wide, and she sat back down, hard.

"What?" she gasped.

I knew I hadn't believed the cat was speaking the first time, so I turned to him and asked out loud, "I think maybe you should show her your true form."

As you wish.

He hopped lightly to the floor and found an area big enough to transform.

Megan yelped and leapt onto my table. I probably should have warned her. "That's, that's…" She pointed at my cat. "A saber-toothed tiger!"

I giggled, then coughed, as the movement was like a new kick in the ribs. Not only did he not look like pictures on the internet I'd seen of saber-toothed tigers, but Mr. Mitten's expression was disgusted at the implication he could possibly look like something so lowly and earthbound as a saber-toothed tiger. This time, he spoke to both of us.

I'm most certainly not, he huffed. *I am a Splintercat.*

His four hundred plus pound shape filled my large kitchen. He looked a little like a gigantic bobcat. He had a round pumpkin-shaped head with four-inch canines that hung from his top jaw to below his bottom jaw. His front end was a little higher than his back end; he wasn't as long bodied as wild earth cats, although he looked balanced. He was spotted like a jaguar, had tufted ears like a Maine Coon, and had a bobbed tail that was approximately a foot long. He twitched it in irritation at Megan. His eyes remained a blazing periwinkle blue.

Hmpf. He snorted with disgust, then morphed back into his Ragdoll shape and wandered out of the kitchen.

Megan climbed down and returned to her chair. "Magic is real."

"Yup."

"Wow."

"Yup."

I couldn't say much else. She needed some time to process and accept. Her hand drifted up to the necklace, and she grasped the stone and slid it along the chain, her face blank, staring into nothing.

After a few minutes, she looked at me. "So, this necklace does what?"

"Well, I imbued it with the pieces of magic I have. Hopefully it will protect you from almost all magic but ice, air, aether, reality and time."

"OK."

"Don't take it off. I have no idea what the witches will do if they know you're here."

She nodded.

I knew she needed a break. This was a lot. It had taken me several days to absorb the truth.

"Do you want to tell me why you brought a trailer?" I asked.

She grinned. "I finally did it. I quit my job and told that bastard ex of yours to take a giant leap."

A wave of relief washed over me. I'd begged her to do this from the moment I told Evan I wanted a divorce. I knew he'd do everything in his power to punish her once I was out of his reach.

"I've come to throw myself on your good nature and be your slave for life. You only have to support me until I find a new job." She smiled uncertainly as she spoke.

I knew that was hard for her to say and do. She hated being beholden to anyone. But at the same time, my heart swelled with happiness. I had my best friend! I'd support her forever just to have her close to me again.

"Trust me, I'm dancing a jig on the inside," I said. "And you already have a job."

"I do?" she asked, confused.

"Yes, I'm starting a new business, and you are in on the ground floor. I think that immediately makes you vice president."

"Yay! I demand a raise."

We both giggled.

"Well, you can only go up from zero," I said.

"True. What's the business? I probably should ask before I make my new business cards."

"I'll show you later. It's in the same field, so you'll fit into the work environment perfectly. You'll do great around the water cooler."

"So glad. I don't want to be the odd woman out."

"Too true, but since the other employees are a Splintercat and a griffin, you're already the odd one."

She laughed, a little wild eyed, but still she laughed.

She sobered up quickly once it was clear that laughing hurt me. "We'll talk about the business later," she said. "First, let's take care of you. Your face could have broken bones in it. We really should take you to the doctor."

"No." I started to shake my head but thought better of it. "I can't go anywhere. I don't know who the witches are, or where they'll show up. I think one or more might work at the clinic."

She opened her mouth to protest. I held up my hand. I took a breath. I couldn't sustain long speeches since I couldn't take deep breaths. "Plus, I need to find Gabe first. He's still missing. He might be worse off than me. I have no way of knowing. The werewolves are looking, but they don't have the magic to help if it comes to another fight."

When she didn't look convinced, I continued. "If I find him and he's alright, he can heal me. If he's not, I'll go to Portland or some-where to get looked at. I promise."

She gave me a judgmental look, trying to decide if I was lying or not. I must have passed because she nodded. "OK for now. But we need to do something soon."

I needed to change the subject before she had me agreeing to something I didn't want to agree to. "So, what's in your trailer? You didn't have time to pack everything!"

She smiled. "Naw. I packed the essentials. Frankly, just everything I wanted to keep. I hired a company to empty the house, either junk what's left or sell it. When they're done, I'm selling the house. I'm out of there!"

"Wow, when you make a decision, you go all out," I said.

"I took my cue from you. You were out in what, a week?" She knew; she'd helped me pack. I'd done much the same thing. Packed what I wanted, had a junker do the rest, and sold the place remotely.

"Something like that."

"So, when we decide, we move on. That's what I did." She threw up her hands in excitement.

"Cool. I don't know if I can help you right now, though."

"Nothing is too heavy. There's no furniture, just keepsakes and some books. I can haul it in without help."

"I don't have a room for you yet, but you can choose one. I still have to order the mattresses for the finished rooms."

"No worries, I can crash on the floor."

"You can sleep with me until the mattress gets here. It's a king-size bed. Although Mr. Mittens still manages to take most of it."

She laughed and shrugged. "Whatevs."

"I don't know if the workers will come back and finish." I sighed. "There isn't much left to do, at least."

"They better not come back, not after the stunt the witches pulled and that bastard Scott. I can't believe you took him back after he gave you the potion."

Sofia, the head witch, had installed her cousin as the head of my renovation team after she'd murdered the local werewolf alpha and head of Whelan Restoration, who'd originally been working on my old Victorian house. Then, she'd mixed up a love potion to keep me enamored of Scott and distracted so they could steal the missing pieces of my magic. All of that culminated in my current state when I'd tried to stop her.

"I know," I said. "But I had to get the house finished. I couldn't find anyone else to do it in less than a year. Now, the jobs left are so small, I could probably get a small-time contractor here and there to finish. Just some painting, and some finish electric and plumbing. All the big stuff is done."

"Cool, the outside of the house is gorgeous. I love the paint scheme. Can't wait until you get the landscaping done."

It was beautiful. I'd had it painted in classic Victorian colors—dark green, dark red, and tan.

"Yeah, it'll be a showstopper." I sighed again. I just saw more work. But I'd signed up for it. "Ready to see the inside?"

"If it looks as good as this kitchen, I can't wait!"

I wanted to be out looking for Gabe. However, the wolves were on it, and I was still too injured. I needed another day to recover or more. If I was honest with myself, it would probably be weeks. At least I kept telling myself just one more day so I could enjoy Megan and the comfort she brought with her presence.

"OK. The second you see the room you want, let me know. It's yours. Don't just choose one because it's finished. Promise?"

"Sure. I can share for a while to get the perfect room." She looked at me oddly.

I didn't think she'd choose a room just because it was finished. I wanted her to know she didn't have to settle. I had a room I thought she'd like, but I didn't want her to say no because it was the best room besides mine. If she knew I planned to turn this into a bed-and-breakfast someday, she might choose the smallest room or the ugliest. I'd have to nudge her in the right direction. I thought I'd turn the second-floor primary bedroom into an apartment by closing off the turret and the unfinished room on that end. Now that she was here, I wanted her to have her own space. I smiled in delight.

"Let's start on the third floor and make our way down." I stood up painfully, and hobbled, bent over, to the back of the kitchen and the stairs.

Megan gasped in alarm. "Can you do the stairs in your condition?" She hurried over and reached for my elbow to help.

"I don't have to. I have an elevator," I said, proudly.

"Seriously? That's so cool."

I led her out of the kitchen to the elevator door under the grand staircase. She released my arm and walked around the entryway, looking up.

"This entryway is amazing," she said as she gazed all about, her face looking up at the top of the house.

"I know. I'm going to find the biggest Christmas tree in the state and put it in here," I said.

"Can't wait to see that!"

"Me either."

I hit the button, and the door swished open. It wasn't a large elevator. Big enough for two people and a couple of suitcases. So, we were comfortable on the short ride to the third floor. We came out at the top of the staircase. I started her down toward the end of the hall by the attic entrance. The door was standing open.

"Is that the infamous attic?"

"Sure is. I'd take you up there, but it's just more stairs and storage. So maybe later when I feel better."

"No worries. I don't need to see it now."

We opened the first door to a new suite. The rooms up here were mostly finished, although the furniture was a jumble, and the finish plumbing needed to be completed. But they were formed, and the beauty was showing through.

"Wow," Megan exclaimed after each room. She adored the turret room as well, and that made me smile.

We took the elevator down to the second floor. It was only my second or third time using it, and I was happy it ran smoothly and quietly. Again, we started at the room furthest from the turret room and made our way around.

"These rooms are mostly finished; except I have an idea that's going to need a little more work." I looked at her from the corner of my eye.

She just nodded.

I had my furniture pieces in each room, although none were

arranged, and the beds didn't have mattresses. The bathrooms were all finished, and most had been cleaned of all the construction dust and debris.

"These are so beautiful!" she exclaimed at each room with its individual paint scheme. Finally, the third suite door was ahead of us, next to the turret. She had gushed over the turret, and I smiled. Then, I let her open the door and step inside the room I thought would be her favorite.

She gasped. The room was done in seafoam green, and all the wood was painted white. Every other room had natural wood, refinished and stained. Here, I had all the wood done in gleaming high gloss white. The floor was still the original oak, refinished to a high gleam. The furniture that was in the room was also white. It needed a good cleaning and probably new paint, but you could see the bones and what this room could be. The bathroom was magnificent. Almost a twin to mine. The original claw-footed tub from this floor had been re-enameled, and everything inside the bathroom was gleaming white marble. The new modern glass shower had a million shower heads and was large enough for four people. It was a dream bathroom.

"I love it! This is the room!"

I smiled. "I knew it."

She jumped up and down a little.

"There's still some work to be done. If you like this room, which you do, how about we enclose it with the turret and make a little apartment? You'd have a sitting room or reading nook and the bed and bathroom. We'd still have to share the kitchen, but what do you think?"

I stumbled a little through the speech; I wanted her to love the house and to stay so much. It was still a good idea even if she wanted to leave eventually, because enclosing the turret would make this a larger space for families. I could add a pull-out couch or something if Megan ever left.

She squealed with delight. "You really want me to stay?"

"More than anything."

"Yes, yes, yes!" And she did a little happy dance.

I laughed. "I'm so happy. I'd dance with you, but I'd probably not survive."

"I'll bring all my stuff up here. Is the bathroom ready to be used?"

"Yeah, the water is hooked up and everything works."

"I'd sleep up here if there was a mattress." She looked around.

"Well, all the furniture needs a wash and paint. We can order the mattress of your dreams tonight. And by the time it gets here, we should have the furniture all done."

"Perfect."

We both looked around.

"So, what do you have for food? I'm starving."

"Me too." I frowned. "How about we order something? I haven't felt up to cooking."

"Whatever you choose, I can go pick it up if they don't deliver out here."

"I know who delivers." I gave her a list of choices, and we made a decision and ordered.

While we waited, she started to unload her tiny trailer. She really hadn't brought much. Every piece of luggage she owned was full, and maybe ten to twelve additional boxes and totes. She brought things in and loaded the elevator.

I felt bad I couldn't help, but she was so happy to be here, she kept telling me not to worry about it.

I helped her organize her bath things. She was thrilled with the beautiful bathroom and declared she could live in it. I smiled.

After everything was done, we went back to the kitchen. The food was late, luckily, since it gave us time to get her stuff organized. She would have to live out of a suitcase until we got the furniture squared away. Her closet was finished, but it also needed the construction dust cleaned out before she unpacked her clothes.

The pizza finally arrived. I put out salad and soda, and we tucked in. Megan had the disgusting habit of dipping her pizza in ranch dressing. I shuddered.

"Do you have a plan to find Gabe?" Megan asked as we ate.

I put my slice down. I'd done nothing but think about this. "First,

229

we have to find him and figure out what the witches have done to him." My appetite had disappeared as the anxiety and worry built up in my gut.

"They probably have him in chains in a dungeon somewhere," she said.

I blinked at her. "No. They can't do that. He's a doctor. An upstanding community member. They'll let him go when they're done," I explained. Not sure why I was so positive. It just made sense. This was a small town. Maybe five thousand people lived here. A missing doctor would be noticed.

She shook her head. "No way. How else would they control him? They can't just let him go. He'll tell on them. Get them arrested for kidnapping, get a restraining order. I'm telling you, they're keeping him in chains somewhere."

"Those are good points." I shook my head. "But you're forgetting something. It's easy to do, I struggled with it too. Magic."

"What do you mean by 'magic'?"

"They can do something to control him with magic." After what I'd told her about everything that had happened and witnessing Mr. Mittens' transformation, I was confused at her inability to grasp what magic could do.

"What?"

"That's the scary part, I don't know. I'm very much a noob at this. And I don't know much about witch magic. But after what I've seen them do, they aren't limited by scruples."

"Yeah, I guess not." She looked me up and down, all beaten and bruised as I was.

"I didn't mean just what they did to me, I meant what they did to Craig Whelan and the stuff with the love potion."

"I know," she said.

"So how do a human and a Fae lord go about freeing a hot doctor from a bunch of unscrupulous witches?"

I sighed. "I'm not a real Fae lord. My cat just likes to mess with me."

"Come on, let me have this! It's so cool, like a fantasy story or something."

"I'm going to regret telling you that, aren't I?"

"Yes, yes, you are."

"You are so lucky I love you, or I'd Fae lord your ass."

"Sounds kinky." She winked at me.

"Ugh, go dunk something in ranch dressing."

She looked at me and dunked her last bite of pizza in the ranch and shoved it in her face. She was trying to act seductive, but she ended up missing slightly and smearing ranch over her mouth and cheek. Then, we both cracked up, and she spewed ranch covered pizza bits all over the table. I grabbed my ribs firmly but couldn't stop laughing.

After we cleaned up the mess and the remains of dinner, she said she was going upstairs to break in her new bathroom.

I assumed that meant taking a bath or shower, so I nodded. After she left the kitchen, I pulled out my laptop and started looking for mattresses. I found and bookmarked a few for Megan to look over. After that was done, I pulled up the proposal for my new business and emailed it to her. With nothing else to do, I started googling all I could on witches. I needed to be better prepared, or as prepared as possible.

I couldn't find anything to help me. I should have guessed. I needed a witch in my pocket, but I couldn't trust the witches around here, and probably not any witches anywhere.

Megan came down as I was pounding swear words into my laptop in frustration. She laughed when she saw what I was doing. It was something I'd done to avoid swearing at Evan when we were married. He didn't think swearing was dignified. Which generally meant that swearing at *him* was disrespectful. I don't think he understood the point of getting cussed out.

It used to be my only way of expressing my frustration, but it wasn't working at the moment. Now, I could scream cuss words at the sky, but no one cared. But it wasn't solving my problem of finding or saving Gabe.

I still had the gut feeling that they would turn him loose to go back to his life after some heavy spell layering. I just had to wait it out. I could check on him. I knew where he lived and worked. Tomorrow, I'd call his work. If he was missing, I'd go to his house. I told Megan the plan, and she agreed. Exhausted, we went to bed.

Mr. Mittens curled tightly against me—his warmth and security a comfort. Megan snored lightly. I thought I'd fall instantly asleep having done more today than I had in days, but instead, I stared into the dark, eaten up with worry about Gabe and what the witches were doing to him.

CHAPTER
TWO

The second I knew the clinic opened, I called. Eight a.m. sharp. The receptionist answered with a sleepy good morning. I told her I wanted to set an appointment with Dr. Ambrose. She was quiet for a moment. My heart raced. He had to be there; he had to be okay.

"Dr. Ambrose doesn't have an open appointment this week. Would you like to see someone else?" she asked.

"No, I'd really prefer Dr. Ambrose. Is he out of town?" I prompted.

"No, he was out sick for a couple of days, but he's back now, just behind. If you like, I can add you to his cancellation list."

"No, I'll call back. I need to think about it." Relief caused me to slump as all my tension dissipated. He wasn't free of the witches, of that I was sure, but he wasn't in chains in a dungeon like Megan believed.

The receptionist probably thought I was nuts. You either needed a doctor or you didn't. It wasn't a dinner reservation.

I ended the call and looked up at Megan who was sipping coffee with her feet up on the chair and one arm around her knees.

"Gabe's at work."

"Well, blow me down."

I laughed. "Yeah." She'd picked up that saying from me.

"So, are you going to go see him?" she asked.

"No, I couldn't get an appointment. But I'm wondering if I should go to his house later."

I thought of his SUV still parked behind my house. I wondered what he was driving and what the witches told him about the missing car. Otherwise, why wouldn't he have retrieved it? Weird.

"You should. We both should."

I looked at her, assessing. "You just want to check him out."

"I never!" She flipped her long hair back. "I resemble that remark."

"Yes, you do."

We laughed. The relief of joking with my bestie helped ease the knot in my stomach.

"I just want to make sure he's *fine…*"

I threw her the look.

"I mean, uh, alright." She grinned.

"I know what you meant."

"So, now that Gabe is tooken. What other hot men have you found in town? I gotta catch up to you."

Her body language was still tense, worried, even if her tone was light. Bless Megan. She knew I was terrified of whatever the witches had done to him, and she was doing her darndest to take my mind off it. I gave her a grateful smile.

"Scott is the only one I've met, but you want to avoid him like the plague." I thought for a moment. "The Whelan brothers are pretty fine. I don't know if they're involved or married, though. And they're a little younger. At least two of them are closer to our age, but I'm not sure exactly."

"Intriguing. Werewolves, huh?"

"Yes."

"Are they hairy?"

"What?"

"Like do they look a little on the wild and wolfy side when they're human?" She wiggled her eyebrows.

"No, they look like men." I yawned. I wasn't quite ready to be awake, the yawn made my sore jaw ache and grind. Darn, it was most likely broken. "Fine, muscular, dreamy men." I fluttered my eyelashes at her. That was the only thing that had fully recovered. My eyelashes. My eyelids still hurt though, part of the joy of two black eyes. Joking helped my heart, if not my aching body. I could forget my worries for a moment.

"Why didn't you get a doctor's appointment?" she asked after watching me wince and rub my face.

"I only want one with Gabe."

Megan had her stubborn look on. "Well, you should have made one even if it's for later, tell them you want in if there's a cancellation."

"OK, Mom."

She watched to make sure I called back. I made the appointment and asked for anything that came open earlier, the receptionist put me on the list, and that was that.

"See, that was easy. If you get him to heal you before that, you can cancel."

I started to roll my eyes, but I was afraid one might fall out, so I didn't.

"I'm going to go get us some breakfast," Megan announced.

"What? Why? I have food here we can make," I protested.

"Do you feel up to making it?" she asked, hands on her hips.

"No, not really."

"This is my treat to you and myself. I just got here and I'm not ready to work. I need a mini vacay. Plus, I have to return the trailer."

"Fair enough."

She grabbed her purse and borrowed my rain jacket since it had started to drizzle again. She wasn't prepared for this much rain.

I left her a note that I was soaking in the bath in case she came back before I finished, which was likely. Then, I went to soak away some of the pain. When I saw myself in the bathroom mirror without my clothes, it scared me a little. I was so black and blue from the beatings, that if I'd seen someone else like this, I'd have notified the police and taken them to the ER.

I didn't want those damned witches to know how bad I was hurt though, and I couldn't trust them to not be everywhere I wanted to be. I hadn't seen enough faces, but there had been so many of them they could be anywhere or everywhere in this town. I'd told Megan that was one of the reasons why I didn't want to go to the clinic or the hospital. I thought I'd recognized a witch I'd seen at one of those places. I shuddered. But that hurt. I ran the water as hot as I could handle, dumped in an entire bag of Epsom salts, and slid down into the glorious tub.

I woke up when Megan grabbed me and hauled me to the surface.

"What are you doing!" I yelled when the water cleared out of my eyes.

Megan's eyes were wild, her face flushed. "You were underwater. I thought you'd drowned!"

I blinked. "I was fine." This was new. I'd been underwater, and I didn't know for how long. Could my water magic help me breathe underwater? Did I grow gills or something? I reached up and felt my face and throat. Everything felt the same.

Megan sank down on the fluffy rug next to the tub, her breathing ragged. "This was another magic thing, wasn't it?"

"I don't know. I have no idea how long I was under. How long were you gone?"

She looked at her phone. "About forty-five minutes."

I felt my heart skip a beat. I remembered about five minutes of being in the bath. I may have been under for nearly forty minutes.

"I think it may be a magic thing. I think I was under there a lot longer than a couple of minutes."

I had her hand me a towel, and I stepped out of the tepid water and let it drain. I dried off and wrapped my long auburn hair in a towel and myself in my robe. *Mr. Mittens*, I thought loudly. I knew he could sense me on this land and hear me just fine.

Sure enough, a couple minutes later, Megan and I were seated at the table with our breakfast when he strolled in.

You bellowed?

I laughed, and Megan looked at me. "I was laughing at him." I pointed at the cat, my mouth half full. I finished my mouthful. "Do you have your necklace on?"

Her hand darted to her neck, which was bare. She paled. "No, I took it off last night when I took a bath. I'll be right back."

She dashed off, her steps pounding loudly up the stairs. She came back wearing the necklace.

"Now, you can hear Mr. Mittens," I said, trying not to reprimand her after I'd practically begged her to wear it all the time.

Are you ready to tell me why you called? he asked drolly.

"I fell asleep in the tub."

He blinked his large blue eyes at me, waiting for more of the story.

"Underwater."

His eyes opened ever so slightly larger.

"For forty minutes."

He blinked. *That is interesting.*

"Yes, do you know why I'm not dead?"

Magic?

"Very funny. Do you know how it works?"

I don't. You keep asking me about your magic. I'm not a magical Fae *cat.*

"I know, but you've been around a long time, and you've seen more than I have."

Hmpf.

"Did my grandmother ever hang out underwater?"

Not that I'm aware of. She may not have known this aspect of her power, or she wasn't as strong as you are.

"Oh well, I guess I don't have to worry about it unless I fall asleep in the bathtub again."

Is that all, my pet? he said with a large yawn.

Megan's eyes flew open. "Pet?"

"Yeah, it's our thing. I'm his charge. He likes to call me his pet."

"Hey, before we go check out your doctor tonight, can I meet your griffin friend?" Megan asked.

Mr. Mittens looked at me, so I waved him away to let him know we were done. Of course, that was after a chin scratch and an ear rub. He wandered off.

"Sure, why not."

I walked out to the porch and called for Brightfeather. Bright-feather had explained to me that she heard my calls and would came as quickly as she could, so I didn't worry when she didn't show up immediately. She would come as soon as she was able. We drank our coffee out on the back porch, watching the rain—me in my robe with my hair in a towel, and Megan in her sweats. By the time we were finishing up, a great, grey eagle drifted in and landed on the porch railing.

Hello, Lady Brigid. Is all well with you?

"Yes, Brightfeather. Is all well with you?"

Yes, thank you. How may I serve you?

That woke me up more than my coffee. I didn't need a servant. I thought of Brightfeather as a friend.

"Umm, you don't have to serve me, Brightfeather. I just wanted to introduce you to another of my friends." I gestured to Megan. "This is Megan. She is human and doesn't have magic, but I want you to know that you can show your true self to her. She knows everything." I turned to Megan. "Megan, this is my dear friend, Brightfeather. She is a magnificent griffin. She is not my servant, but my friend," I said pointedly.

Brightfeather shifted into her real form, and Megan gasped. She stood and looked as though she was going to reach out and pet the grif-fin. I put my hand out, but she stopped herself, realizing that it was rude to pet a sentient creature, unless it was a ridiculous Splintercat who liked to walk around as a Ragdoll.

Brightfeather looked a little off balance since I'd made it clear she wasn't a servant of the Fae lord of the land. I wanted to swat my cat a little for telling everyone that—but not too much, because he could remove my head with one claw.

Brightfeather, with her courtly manners, dipped her head in a bow to Megan, and spoke into our minds. *I'm pleased to meet you.*

"You are the coolest creature I've ever met," Megan gushed.

Thank you, Brightfeather preened.

I laughed. "You are amazing, and thank you for helping the other night, you saved my life."

It is my pleasure. I have sanctuary and freedom on your land. It is a small price to pay for such a gift.

I bowed my towel-covered head to her. "It is a small gift; I wish I had more to offer you. I do want you to think of us as friends."

Thank you, I like having you as a friend, Lady Brigid.

She gave us a respectful bow, then shifted back into her eagle form and launched herself from the porch and out over the woods.

"What else do you have in your woods?" Megan asked after Brightfeather disappeared from view.

"Umm, bears. Lots of dead invaders apparently, unless Mr. Mittens eats them. I'm afraid to ask. The only one I know that is friendly is Brightfeather. I think there may be other supernatural creatures out there, but I haven't met them. My cat is the boss of that." I waved away the question with a flick of my hand.

"Your life has seriously gotten weird."

"Yet, it finally feels right for some strange reason."

We sat in silence for a while.

"I know you told me your story, but how do you find the rest of your magic?" Megan asked.

"I don't know. I have my gram's description of the objects that contained her power, so I have an idea of what form they might take, but I've searched the house multiple times, and I don't think they're here or know where they could be. I also don't know for sure what they do. Time and air seem self-explanatory, but what does aether and reality do? It's confusing. Plus, how do I get back my ice magic from that bitch of a witch? I'm out of my league. I also don't know what to do about Gabe. If he were still fully himself, he'd call or come get his car or something. I don't know what the witches did to him or if I can undo it. I wish I had someone to talk to!"

"I know I'm not much, but I'm here." She reached over and grabbed my hand and gave it a squeeze. "Here's an out of the box thought." She stood, put her coffee cup on the railing and faced me. "Your cat said that your great-grandfather, the Fae lord, could live for thousands of years. Couldn't he help you?"

A frisson of shock ran through me. I hadn't even thought of him.

He would know everything about my magic. He used to come here years ago to visit his wife and daughter. Would he see me? Had he been here since she died? I had no way of knowing. But there was one problem. "I don't know how to contact him."

"You said you had your grandmother's journals. Didn't she contact him? Could she have left instructions, even unknowingly, in her diaries?"

"Huh. I have some journals, true. I haven't noticed anything in them like that. But we could look in the attic and see if we can find more."

I finally had something, a plan to help me and help Gabe. We looked at each other, then dashed into the house. Well, Megan dashed, I hobbled, but the intent was there. I left my coffee mug on the table and shuffled to the elevator. Megan took the stairs. I met her at the attic door.

"That is so cool!"

"What?" I asked.

"The door didn't appear until you were like three feet away from it." I'd closed it on our first foray up here.

"I forgot for a moment, of course, it only shows up when it senses me or my magic, not sure which."

"Didn't it show up before you got your powers?"

"Yeah, but Mr. Mittens seems to think I have some inherent magic even without my active powers."

"Oh."

"It's not important. It works, if someone needs to get up there, I can leave the door open like it was the first time we came by."

She shrugged. We climbed the few attic stairs and stood in the vast space. She gasped.

"Wowzer."

I laughed.

"I bet all this antique furniture is worth a fortune."

"It might be, but I was hoping to use most of it to furnish the house. I've sold a few pieces already, I know I sold them too cheaply, but they're gone, and I don't have to worry about them. I had to make room for the elevator equipment."

She made a beeline for the old trunks. "These are so neat."

"Yeah, but I've already searched them. I haven't done much in the back; we should start there."

She nodded, and we wove our way to the back through the stacks of old furniture and boxes of who knew what. I hadn't done any work in the back. I'd gone there and felt around to see if any of my magic called to me, but it hadn't. I hadn't looked through any boxes and just marked furniture to be removed for sale. There could be journals back here. There weren't any more trunks, but plenty of boxes.

"I haven't searched the furniture or boxes back here," I said after we were at the back wall. I'd also called some books to me before— my grandmother's journals. I doubted anything from her was left. I had no idea if my great-grandmother had even written journals.

"Let's get started," Megan said, the light of the hunt sparking in her eyes. She actually rubbed her hands together in glee. I had forgotten how much she enjoyed antiquing. This must look like heaven to her.

"If you see anything you want for your room, just tell me."

"Oh, I will."

We each chose a box and got started.

Several hours later, we were grubby, grumpy, and thoroughly sick of antiques. We did have several more books to search through, though. But first, we had an appointment at Gabe's house.

We showered, dressed, and met downstairs to head to his house. I had Megan drive her car, and I drove Gabe's car. That was our excuse, we were returning it.

I led the way, and she followed carefully. Of course, it was pouring rain, and my thick, wavy hair, that I'd carefully smoothed and tamed, was now a floofy frizzball. But it didn't matter since half my face was swollen and black and blue, gradually changing to purple, yellow, and green as well. I was lovely.

I wasn't sure how I felt as we pulled behind his house. His spare truck was there, so he had to be home. My guts were cramping, my hands were sweating, and my throat was closing off. I stepped out of the car nervously, his keys clutched in my hand. Megan followed me to the back door. I looked at her for reassurance and knocked. Footsteps echoed, coming gradually closer, then he was at the door. He looked down on us with an inquisitive smile on his face.

My heart stopped.

"Hi, can I help you?" he asked.

I'd been looking away, the ugly half of my face hidden by my hair. I turned and looked up at him. He was perfect. His handsome face was unmarked and unbruised. His brown hair dusted with a little silver at the sides was slightly mussed like he'd run his fingers through it. His hazel-green eyes were full of gentle kindness. He looked at me oddly. Like he was trying to remember who I was. Fear clawed its icy path down my back. What if he'd completely forgotten about me? How would I restore his memories?

"Wow, that's some bruise, what happened?" he asked. Frowning at me professionally.

"I was beaten by a bunch of witches," I answered truthfully.

His face filled with shock.

"Witches?" he repeated quietly.

"Yes, thank you for helping me. I brought your car back." I held my hand out with the keys in it.

"Car?" He sounded uncertain, drugged.

"Who are you?" he asked. "I know you, don't I?" He shook his head as though he were trying to dislodge something.

"Yes, I'm Brigid. Brigid Donovan." I gave him my maiden name. Maybe they hadn't tried to rewrite his *entire* memory.

"Brigid," he said uncertainly. "I think I used to know a Brigid."

He gestured for us to come in out of the rain.

Once we were in, boots and coats off and seated on his sofa, I tried to jar his memory.

"Yes, I'm Brigid, we used to date in high school. We started dating again recently."

He stopped me by putting up a hand. "That's not possible. I wouldn't date you. I have a girlfriend."

I jolted back in surprise. A girlfriend? My heart sank and my stomach clenched. No. That wasn't possible.

"Her name is Sofia; she's on her way over right now." He looked confused. "No, that isn't right." He put his hands to his head and closed his eyes tight. "If you ladies don't mind, I have a splitting headache." He stood and gestured for us to leave.

I reached over to hand him his car keys. "Here are your keys."

"Keys?"

"Yes, to your car? We brought it back from my house?"

"I don't have a car."

"You do, it's in the driveway. You can check the registration. It's yours."

He shook his head, then clenched his eyes shut again. I could tell he was in pain. Megan's eyes narrowed. She kept looking at him, then me. I felt like I'd been gut punched. I was on the edge of tears. He escorted us out and shut the door behind us.

Megan supported me as we walked to the car. My legs had gone weak and useless. Her face was grim and concerned.

We climbed into Megan's car, and she started the engine. We drove out in silence.

CHAPTER
THREE

I swallowed the lump that kept rising in my throat and focused on my rage. "That unbelievable, self-serving, witch whore," I said once the shock wore off, and I had control of my emotions.

Megan laughed. "You are definitely more relaxed away from Evan."

I smiled at her. "I guess you're right. But it's still true. She's put him under some spell, is trying to make herself his girlfriend, and made him forget me."

"I'd have gone with bitch whore, plus a few more," Megan said smugly. "So, what do we do?"

"We're going to do what we planned. We'll search those books, call up my great-grandpa, and use my magic to save Gabe from her claws. I have no choice. You saw what that spell was doing to him. Who knows if it will kill him, eventually? He's obviously fighting it."

She nodded. We'd already hurt him by exposing him to some truth, even if it was just a car and the fact his girlfriend wasn't Sofia, the raging bitch whore.

She'd wanted him, my house, and my magic for who knew how long. Maybe since high school. I can't believe I thought she was my friend. I pounded my hand on the dash and then moaned in pain. That movement hurt my hand, my ribs, and my back.

"So, what do you want to do to Sofia?" Megan asked after my outburst.

I opened my mouth to deliver all kinds of torments to the witch from hell, but before I could start, Megan stopped me by putting up a hand.

"Realistically." She threw me the side eye. "I know what you want to do. I'm sure that there are all kinds of torture and torments that you can dream up, but what can we do to her to make her pay, that we can get away with without doing twenty to thirty at the state pen?"

I closed my mouth. I hated reality. But Megan made sense. I wouldn't survive captivity. Just my hair would drive me mad without having the proper products. And I really doubted I'd get enough reading or computer privileges to satisfy me either. So, torture and murder were out—unless it was on my land where I could hide the body. I sighed.

"I just don't know. As a witch with Fae magic to power her, she's unstoppable. The only thing that keeps witches in check is the state of their magic—having a limit and having to be careful. She's beyond that now."

"Don't forget, you are Fae. You have that going for you. Plus, you have friends." She looked over at me. "You have more than one piece of Fae magic, what makes her stronger with only one?"

I looked at her. "She's not limited by morals. She's already a powerful witch, now she'll have years of power that won't drain her personal power well. Also, she has an entire coven, and she's taken Gabe, whose power added to hers is significant."

"So, your friend part is weak, but you do have a Splintercat," she added weakly.

"Yup, I have a cat, a griffin, part of a werewolf pack, an unfinished house, and a bestie. We're gonna win for sure." Despair welled up, and I almost lost control of my emotions again.

She slugged me lightly on the arm. "That's the spirit." I groaned dramatically, although it hadn't hurt much.

We were *so* going to die.

* * *

WHEN WE GOT BACK TO THE HOUSE, WE TOOK THE BOOKS AND searched through them. Right away, Megan found an interesting passage. The books were mixed. Some were my grandmother's, but the interesting one belonged to my great-grandmother—who'd been a witch. She was the one who'd found herself a Fae lord and married him.

Megan read the passage out loud. "'I found the spell book to summon a fairy. From what I've studied, the Fae folk can grant magic to a witch. This removes the risk of draining the witch's magic and will permanently eliminate the need to refill the witch's well.'"

She looked up at me. "This might be it, Brigid."

I nodded at her. "Keep going."

Megan continued to read from the journal, "'My parents kept the book hidden. I don't know why. If they had this, why haven't they used it? My mother is aging much too fast. She's using too much magic. When I capture the fairy, I'm going to demand it grant her magic first.'"

Megan stopped reading, and her eyes scanned the book. "There's a lot of stuff along this line, I'll skip ahead."

"K."

She scanned a few pages, moving her finger along the line as she read, then stopped. "'You must enter the forest and prepare the altar.'"

"Altar?" I asked, my mind racing. After the battle with the witches, I'd made the earth swallow the altar, and I'd hidden the clearing it had been in by telling the forest to swallow it up. Had I eliminated the one item I needed to call my great-grandfather forth? Could I pull the altar back from the earth I'd buried it in?

"Yeah, it says altar."

Would my great-grandmother have come to this land, which wasn't yet hers, to perform this ritual? Or did her family own some of it then? I didn't know. Mr. Mittens had told me that Fae gold had purchased this land. I shrugged. Not important. I needed a forest and an altar. I knew where to get them.

"OK, sorry I interrupted."

She nodded and continued, "'It would be best if the altar has a natural fairy ring, but if you can't find one, you can create a faux ring. Place items that are attractive to the fair folk in a ring around the altar and as offerings upon it. The Fae are partial to cream, honey, sweet cakes, and wine. Next, to protect yourself, make sure you have a ring of salt and iron around you. A fairy can be harmed by these items and is thus repelled by them.'"

She looked up at me. "Do you think she really did this? This ritual sounds fake."

"Don't forget that she married a Fae lord. Something worked."

"Yeah, I guess you're right." She shrugged and started reading again, "Blah, blah, blah, sweets, ring of salt, ah this is where I was. 'After you are protected, wait for the full moon to hit its zenith. Then, prick your finger and allow three drops of blood to wet the altar and say these words. "Come to me fair one. Help me with this task. See me, obey me. Grant me what I ask."'"

She looked up. "There's a page of symbols that you're supposed to add to the altar, and a page of motions you're supposed to perform as well."

"You're right, it sounds stupid." Disappointment took the wind out of my sails. This was a joke. We wouldn't even be able to call a pizza delivery with this stupid ritual. How was I going to save Gabe now?

She showed me the page of symbols.

"These don't look like anything to me but doodles. This can't be right," I said. Despair eating deeper into my psyche.

She agreed. "I'll keep reading. This sounds like a silly girl thing. But we know something worked, so maybe I'll find it."

I watched her read further, her brow wrinkled with concentration. A few moments later, she spoke. "It worked apparently. It's a real spell. Of course, she had her witch magic behind it, maybe that made the difference."

Something sparked in my mind. Excitement warmed my heart.

Spells were just a way to focus your will and intent. Sofia had taught me that. So even if this spell sounded like a young girl's fanciful attempt, that young girl had the magic to back it up and make it work. I had the magic that would make it work. Confidence filled me.

"It'll work," I said suddenly.

Megan looked up from her book. "It will?"

"Yeah, you said it. She had the magic to make it happen. And I have *his* magic. That has to be even more potent." I stood and paced. "Mark that page; we're gonna have a lot of work to do to recreate that ridiculous spell." I paced some more, thinking. "First, I have to raise an altar from the earth." Stupid me. Why did I bury it in the first place? "Plus, it's a walk—and not an easy one—I buried the clearing and caused the forest to regrow." I rubbed one of the sore, bruised spots on my back.

She marked the book and stood up. "Well, a walk is good for sore backs. Let's go check it out."

I sighed. I was sore, but she was right. You only healed if you kept moving. "OK."

We put on our mud boots and rain jackets, and I led her to the site of my failure—where I was beaten, lost my magic, and lost Gabe all in one night. At least it was rainy, muddy, and miserable to match my mood.

On top of that. I forgot to tell my cat, and I got us lost. It's amazing how one patch of forest looks like another. Before, there was a clearing —it was pretty obvious. Now, there was nothing.

"I know I saw that tree before," Megan said. "It has that patch of moss that looks like a T-Rex." She stepped toward the tree and reached out. "Especially now." She removed a tiny piece of moss near the T-Rex's mouth. Now, it really did look like a dinosaur.

I tilted my head to the right to get a better view. "Huh."

"Yeah."

"So, since you figured it out with your fantastic paleontology skills, you might as well know."

"Know what?"

"We're lost."

She rolled her eyes. "Yeah, I know." She sighed and removed another piece of moss from the T-Rex tree to make it even more obvious. "What do you do when you get lost in your own woods?"

"Well, the last time it happened, I swore that the next time I'd call my cat."

She raised an eyebrow. "Does he carry a phone?"

It took me a minute to decide if she was serious or making fun of me. I decided she really was confused. He did talk after all. "No, I just think at him, and he shows up."

She tensed. I saw her head come up and her gaze focused past my shoulder. "I hope he's fast, cause that is not good." She pointed.

I whirled around as fast as I could with my injuries. Coming at us was a real-life unicorn. And it was not what the fairy tales had told me. Propaganda. Just like Mr. Mittens warned me. It did have a single horn and the general appearance of an equine. But that's where the similarities ended.

"Get up a tree!" I yelled and stumbled towards a tree of my own. "Mr. Mittens!" I bellowed and prayed he was fast. His warnings raced through my mind as I grasped a branch and tried to haul myself up. But I was too injured. I couldn't force my body to work properly. I was spry for forty-two, and although I wasn't a gym rat, I fancied myself fairly fit.

Megan was already a third of the way up her tree. I couldn't even get up to the first branch of mine. I put the tree between me and the quickly approaching beast. Why had I wanted to see a real unicorn? Had I inadvertently brought it here to my woods with my wishing?

I tried to power up my injured magic. I could talk to animals, right? That was one of my powers. Did unicorns count as an animal or were they too *magical*? I concentrated my will and tried to connect to the raging creature as it galloped towards us—its eyes blazing red and its horn glowing with unholy fire. Shit, I'd never seen anything so terrifying. It wasn't as large as a regular horse, more pony sized, but it had clawed feet, not hooves, and it was eerily silent in its approach. Maybe climbing a tree wouldn't make a difference.

I didn't know if unicorns came in different colors. You always saw the perfectly white creature that represented purity. This one had black feet that faded up its body into white on its back, neck, and head. Its tail and mane were black. But it wasn't black in color, it was black fire. Its whole body and horn were blazing with a strange black fire. As it ran, it left little patches behind it that faded into real red and orange flame as it passed. I was lucky the woods were soaked or the whole forest would go up.

I looked around, trying to find an escape. But the unicorn was too fast, and soon, it was right on us. My magic did nothing against it, or it wasn't listening to me yell "stop" at it telepathically. I started yelling "stop" out loud, but that didn't help either. The unicorn was pissed. I had no idea why.

"What do you want?" I yelled in frustration since it wasn't listening to me yell, "Stop."

It slid to a stop just like a reining horse, rump down, back feet extended, front feet walking out to a complete stop. Then, it shook its head, and its flaming mane blazed high and hot, then faded out. It pranced around my tree and tried to poke me with its horn. It snorted, and flames shot out at me. I backed up in a panic and put another tree between us.

"Do you speak?" I pushed out with my magic.

The unicorn reared and pawed the air, its front claws glinting like knives in the light of its fading flames.

I do not speak to the filthy Fae. Its voice pierced my mind.

Great, a bigoted unicorn. Just what I needed—as if the horn, claws, and fire weren't terrifying enough.

Where was my cat? I threw a quick glance around, hoping to see him.

"Then, how do you explain what you want if you won't speak?" I asked the creature. I figured I'd either reason with it or delay it long enough so that Mr. Mittens could arrive and save us. Megan was all the way up the tree now.

"Brigid, get climbing!" She yelled down.

"I can't. I'm too hurt," I yelled up.

The unicorn charged at me again. I circled the tree, keeping the unicorn moving with me. It's unholy fire flaring up and causing the grass and fallen leaves around the tree to burst into flame. Since the flames were short lived in the damp, the smoldering leaves put out extra smoke, and I started to wheeze and cough.

"Mr. Mittens!" I coughed out the best I could, adding an extra burst of magic to the shout.

I'm coming. His gruff and put-out voice echoed in my mind.

A wave of relief flowed through me. I just had to keep the unicorn busy until he arrived. It couldn't take long, he always seemed to materialize when I called. I wondered what had kept him so long, although it couldn't have been more than a minute since I'd called him.

Another snort and burst of fire raged over me. This time, I felt the little hairs on my arms burn off, and I reached up to check my eyebrows. Still there. A wave of fury swept over me. I had fire magic, too, dammit. I almost called it up, but I stopped. This thing already used fire. It probably had defenses against fire magic. But I also had control of water, and between the rain and damp around us, there was plenty of water.

I focused my will and gathered up all the water I could hold and shot it at the unicorn. The water smacked it right in the face and washed over its body, drowning out the creature's natural flames. Just as I extinguished it, a giant cat launched itself through the air and landed on the unicorn's back. Razor-sharp claws grasping and teeth flashing as Mr. Mittens deployed them and gripped the back of the unicorn's neck. Mr. Mittens' weight, which I judged to be around four hundred pounds or more based on his size, pushed the unicorn's front end into the muddy earth.

The unicorn made a sound suspiciously similar to a roar, and using its powerful haunches, it lunged forward—awkwardly getting its front feet back under itself. Mr. Mittens ripped and tore at its back with his claws. The unicorn, having regained control of its legs, went down and rolled over Mr. Mittens trying to crush him with its weight. Even though it was pony sized, it still had to weigh close to a thousand pounds. It was solidly built. Muscles rippled, and unlike the propaganda, it was stout and stocky. It was closer to a tank than the waifish, delicate representations on tapestries I'd seen. I was beginning to wonder what happened to all those virgins the unicorns wanted to attract? I shuddered. It couldn't be good.

As it rolled, Mr. Mittens jumped clear between two trees. They were too close together, and now he had nowhere to go. If he tried to jump over the unicorn, it would gut him. If he ran forward, it would skewer him. He could back up, but I doubted he could do that fast enough, and he'd only be caught tighter between the trees. The unicorn charged.

I had to do something, or the evil beast would kill my cat. Terrified, I ran at the unicorn, approaching from the side. It would have to pass me to get at Mr. Mittens. I called to my magic with everything I had and lashed out with lightning.

The air crackled, and the woods lit up with a great flash. I couldn't see. Megan yelled out. I'd forgotten her. I hope the lightning didn't zap her, too. She was human, and I doubted she could survive a lightning blast without the talisman I'd made her. Leaf litter and dirt exploded around us. I closed my eyes. When I opened them, the unicorn lay twenty feet away. It had been knocked into a tree and stood slowly, acting disoriented. Its front feet were splayed and its head down. It breathed hard. Then, it shook its head and began to sort its feet.

Mr. Mittens growled. This time *he* charged the unicorn, and then in the last ten feet or so, he launched himself. His head was down as though he was going to ram the beast like a goat. Only, he sailed through the air, and when he hit the unicorn, it flew and slammed into a tree so hard, its body bent around the tree until its tail and head met. The snap of breaking bones filled the air, then the foul creature fell and lay crumpled on the ground, its fire snuffed—dead.

Mr. Mittens stood over it, his sides heaving. I noticed that the unicorn had gotten in a few blows—his sides were covered with deep, blood-dripping scratches. I stumbled over to him.

"You're wounded!" I reached out and grabbed his head and looked into his eyes. "Thank you."

The wounds are no matter. Here, on this land, I am the most powerful creature in this realm.

"You are magnificent," I said, stroking his ego. He'd earned it.

I watched his scratches. They were healing and looked old. The blood had stopped already.

Why are you in the woods without me? he asked, perturbed.

"I'm very sorry. I didn't mean to cause you trouble." I looked away. Megan was coming down the tree, and it wasn't gracefully. She was swearing like a sailor, and tree litter fell on us. "I wasn't thinking. We came to find the altar I buried and got lost. I was going to call you when the unicorn attacked us."

We both looked at the broken body of the evil beast. I shuddered. I didn't think any horse could scare me like the unicorn had. I never wanted to see another one. Why had I wished to see one?

Unicorns are dangerous, he reminded me.

"I see why you told me that."

"No shit," Megan added in, huffing and puffing from her exertion. A final crash told us she was down.

Hmpf. He reached back and licked some of the blood off his fur. The wounds were nearly closed. *How did you get lost in your own woods?* he asked casually as though he were amused.

"Well, it all looks the same."

You are the lord of this land. You should be able to go anywhere you desire with minimal effort. You are magical.

And an idiot, apparently. I never even considered using my magic or linking to my land to find my way. I blushed at my own stupidity. I guess Evan was right about me. I wasn't cut out to be a leader.

By then, Megan had picked herself up and joined us. "Why did a unicorn attack us?" she asked. Obviously confused and angry. Plus, her pants were torn, and she was covered in tree sap and bark.

Mr. Mittens turned his head to her but spoke into both of our minds. *Unicorns are the nastiest of all the creatures that inhabit this realm. You should avoid them.*

"I avoided alright. I haven't climbed a tree since I was fourteen." She brushed dirt off her clothing, frowning. "So, what do you do with the body? I don't think unicorn carcasses are common in this part of the world," Megan said. I could hear the irony in her voice.

I looked at Mr. Mittens. I still didn't know what he did with the creatures he killed, but I suspected he ate them. He nodded. I called on my earth power, and the earth pulled the carcass down until nothing remained.

"Wow." She stared at me. "I know you told me about your magic, but the lightning, and now that…" She pointed at where the carcass had lain. "That was freaking amazing!"

I smiled. Maybe I perked up on the inside, at least a little.

"So, I've seen you and your cat in action. I wish I hadn't been so freaked out. I would have videoed it all on my phone."

I frowned, and my cat let out a little growl. "No, you can't film any of it," I said. And Mr. Mittens nodded.

"I wouldn't have shown anyone," she whined. "It doesn't matter, anyway. I was too busy holding onto the tree and trying to wish the unicorn away."

Hmpf. Mr. Mittens shook himself, and when he stopped, he was in his Ragdoll shape. He started to walk away, looking back at us, and encouraged us to follow. We looked at each other and followed him. Of course, he was my protector. I should never have brought my human friend into these woods without him. A wave of gratitude washed over me, and I sent a thought full of love and thankfulness to him. His tail shot up, and the tip flipped back and forth in his kitty acknowledgment.

He led us to the former clearing we'd been searching for. It wasn't that far away, and frankly, we'd probably walked through it a couple of times without recognition.

Mr. Mittens stopped, his tail swished a few times, then he sat and looked at me. *The altar is here.*

"Thank you."

My cat was rarely curious about me, so I was surprised when he asked me why I needed to come back here.

"I'm going to summon my great-grandfather. Your friend."

His eyes opened wider. *Why?*

That caused me to doubt my reasoning again. But I couldn't see another path.

"I need to know about my magic to help Gabe and to just *know*. I don't have anyone else to ask."

He looked thoughtful. *Hmpf. I'm not sure summoning a Fae lord is a good idea.*

"Why not? He's my family."

The Fae are not as you are.

"How so?"

They are less emotional. More driven by duty and honor. Your grandfather may not be happy that you summoned him. He could punish you.

I second guessed myself again, worried I was putting the three of us in unnecessary danger. But he was family, and I had no other options.

"Did he punish his wife? His daughter?" I argued.

They did not summon him when I knew him.

My thoughts were dark. I didn't have a choice. I couldn't see another answer. To save Gabe, I had to know my abilities. I couldn't face a witch with power equal to mine. She'd lived her whole life knowing her limits, using her magic, and understanding it.

"I don't see a choice," I said, finally.

He acknowledged my decision with a swish of his tail. Then, I reached for my earth magic, seeking the altar deep in the ground. Once I sensed it, I ordered it to rise again. The earth slipped around the stone altar and lifted it almost as though it were floating to the top.

Once above ground, I straightened it and cleaned it with a thought. Then, since we'd need the space, I ordered the greenery around it for twelve feet to return to the ground, and it did. Finally, the altar sat on a small clear patch of earth.

"Well, there's the altar," I said. "We can't wait for a full moon, since we just had one, and I'm not waiting a month to save Gabe. Plus, I doubt that's really important. It will just have to be a waning gibbous. However, we should still do it at the moon's zenith."

Megan nodded along with my commentary.

"I think your magic will make up for the moon," she said.

I guessed I'd impressed her.

256

"Let's hope."

Or not hope, if what Mr. Mittens said was true. If I were snatched from my realm, I'd probably be grumpy, too. I took a deep breath and let it out slowly. I wasn't up for this. I just wanted to sleep and heal, but I couldn't leave Gabe in this mess. He'd just been helping me. It wasn't fair to him. I strengthened my resolve, and the three of us headed back to the house to prepare for tonight and the not so full moon.

CHAPTER

FOUR

I put all the supplies we'd gathered into a bag. Megan was going to carry it, since I was hurting a whole lot worse by nightfall. Unfortunately, the moon wasn't going to hit its zenith until 3:23 a.m. The witching hour indeed. I giggled.

We tried to sleep some, but we were too wound up or scared for that to happen, so we just lay in my bed and talked like schoolgirls at a sleepover until it was time to leave. Mr. Mittens escorted us to the altar. Megan was excited to see more magic and a real fairy. But I was terrified. If Gabe's life and independence weren't at stake, I'd bail on this endeavor. I knew some magic. I could get by. But I couldn't bail on him. I cared about him. Also, I knew how he felt about being controlled by witches, I couldn't let that go.

Megan held the lantern so I could read the symbols and copy them onto the altar. I'd practiced the movements earlier, and I did again so when the time came, I'd be ready. Even though the night was cool and a breeze drifted through the trees, I was sweating. What if this didn't work? I didn't have a backup plan to save Gabe. I'd just have to go after Sofia directly, but I'd probably lose. What if it did work? From what I'd read in fiction, the Fae were fickle and alien. This could be worse than attacking Sofia directly. I shivered. What if I conjured the wrong Fae? How would I know? The bad outweighed the good. I just had to trust that by using my blood, he'd be the one summoned. My great-grandmother just got lucky.

The moon cleared the trees and beamed down on us. Its cool light touched me with a physical weight. The comforting, cool magic enveloped me, and I knew it was time. I used my pocketknife and pricked my finger with the sharp blade tip. I let three drops fall onto the altar. I did the initial movements, although I felt silly dancing around the altar. Plus, it hurt. A lot. Megan held the light over the book, and I read the spell, pushing my magic into it and completing the final arm movements before the altar.

"Come to me, fair one. Help me with this task. See me, obey me. Grant me what I ask." With all my might and the magic he'd given me, I willed that my great-grandfather would appear.

I stepped back from the altar. I grabbed Megan's hand and held on tightly. The glacial moon bathed the altar with its cold light. I was trembling, terrified. Nothing happened.

Megan and I looked at each other. "Did I say something wrong?" I asked her.

She shrugged. "Nope. That spell was simple."

"What about the movements?"

"You did everything that the book said, perfectly. The spell is just stupid."

"Yeah, and she was a wi—"

BANG

A blast of light and sound hit us with the force of a truck. We flew off our feet and bounced on our hind ends painfully.

Megan groaned. I was groaning. All of my pain sensors screamed.

"Who dares to summon me!" A voice rumbled through the forest. A bright halo of light surrounded the figure.

I stood and brushed the dirt off my backside. Then, not knowing what else to do, I raised my hand. "I did."

The figure frowned.

I had no idea what I expected my grandfather to look like. Both my great-grandmother and my grandmother had said he was handsome.

So, I'd pictured him like Legolas from the *Lord of the Rings* movies. Long flowing blonde hair, perfect, glowing skin, with a lithe figure dressed like Robin Hood with a bow in his hand. Graceful and poised in all he did, and perfect, pointed little ears peeking through his hair. I was *extremely* wrong.

The figure before us was domineering. That was the only word for it. He was tall and powerful and looked more like a Viking than a lithe elf. His hair was short and dark red. His grey eyes blazed with fury. Hard leather armor over some silvery chainmail covered his body. His shield was slung over his back, and in addition to the ax in his hands, a sword was strapped at his waist. If he didn't look like he was going to kill us with the ginormous ax in his hands, I'd have called him handsome.

"Hello, great-grandfather," I choked out, my voice squeaky and unsure in front of this monster of a man. Where were the pointy ears? This must be like a unicorn. Total propaganda. Little people with wings, my eye.

"Who are you?" the voice boomed.

"Umm, I'm Brigid. The great-granddaughter of Niamh, grand-daughter of Lucy Rose, daughter of Aiden."

His frown deepened. "What do you want of me, child?"

"This is a long story; do you want to come to the house for some tea?" I asked politely. Megan was still on the ground, trying to look small and disappear behind me.

"I was preparing for battle. I cannot stay."

"Well, I've just had a battle with a coven of witches. They are stealing my magic, and they've taken my boyfriend. That's why I need you. My family is dead. I didn't know about magic, and I have to learn fast. You're all I have left."

He contemplated me, taking in the bruises and swelling in my face, and the painful way I stood.

"I will come for…" He looked like the word was distasteful. "Tea."

"Thank you, grandfather."

He put the ax in a holder on his belt. I wondered if all that metal pulled his pants down if he wasn't holding on to it, but the belt was hefty and looked tight. Probably part of why he was grumpy. I gritted my teeth and pulled Megan up. Mr. Mittens had stayed out of the way, but now he led the way back, his glowing fur lighting the path.

I opened the door for my grandfather, and we followed him in. I turned the kettle on. He sat at the table and crossed his massive arms over his equally massive chest. I was not going to believe a single fantasy story ever again.

Mr. Mittens stared at my grandfather. Eventually, they nodded at each other. Maybe Mr. Mittens and my grandfather had been communicating. I'd ask the cat later. Mr. Mittens leapt up on the counter, out of the way, but didn't leave. Megan sat as far from my grandfather as she could. I sat next to him.

"This is my friend Megan, she is helping me," I started the conversation.

My grandfather sneered. "She is human."

"Yes, so? She's a good friend."

He looked at me. "I cannot teach you all about magic in the few hours I can spare. What is it you want from me?"

His attitude was understandable but wearing on me. I needed him, he was family, and I shouldn't have to beg for his help. I was growing increasingly irritated.

"Look, gramps, I have had a whole magical heritage hidden from me, I have witches breathing down my neck, I can't get this house finished, and I have to free my possible soulmate from the evilest bitch I've ever known. I need to know how to free someone from a witch's control. And I need it without the attitude and the intimidation." I must have really lost it. I was standing and leaning over the table and in his face. I had no idea what had come over me.

He smiled, but it wasn't a warm smile. "You have spirit, child of mine."

"Thanks." I sat back down.

"You may call me Lugh."

"Is that your name?" I knew enough about the Fae that I doubted he'd give me his name.

"It is near enough."

I nodded. Just what I thought. His name hadn't been written in any of the journals, only that he was a Fae lord. I didn't really know what that meant, but if they lived in a feudal system, probably someone with some power that reported to a king.

"Can you help me with this witch problem?"

"I cannot remain in your realm for long. I have responsibilities I must not shirk. And this place drains my power and makes me weak. Your training may be long and would best take place on my land in my realm. However, I can help you free your mate."

"Really? How?"

He stood and reached out. I leaned back, away from him. He took back his hand. He sighed. "I need to touch you to give you the knowledge you require."

I gave him a sheepish smile. "Sorry. I don't like to be touched." I leaned back in.

He placed his hand on my head and closed his eyes. Megan was quiet, but drinking it all in, her eyes flicking between us. Mr. Mittens was curled up on the counter. He looked relaxed, but I was more attuned to him, and every cell of his Ragdoll self was focused on us. He didn't appear alarmed, so I also shut my eyes.

The magic hit me like a bomb. Fire raced from my head to my toes. I might have cried out. But then knowledge on how to break a witch's spell surged through my synapses. I panted with the pain of it all.

"That should be what you need," Lugh said. "Knowledge absorbed this way is painful. It will require time to settle in and be sure in your mind. Sleep, child. You will know what to do when you awaken."

"Thank you, grandfather," I choked out. My head pounded with the beat of my heart. This was worse than a migraine. I blinked at him.

"I will contact you about training your magic," he said.

The kettle whistled. I grabbed my head as the sound sent a spike of agony through it. Megan stood and shut off the burner.

"I'll make your tea," I said to my grandfather and stood to do so.

His eyes flicked up to the left, as though he'd heard a summons. "I must go."

Before I could say anything else, a blinding light exploded around him, and he vanished. I gasped at the additional pain the light caused. I sat down heavily, holding my head in my hands.

"Let's put you to bed," Megan said.

I waved my hand to acknowledge her, but I couldn't speak. She helped me up and guided me to the bedroom. I couldn't see, the pain was so severe. She tucked me in, and I fell asleep quickly, my mind and body overwhelmed by my grandfather's gift.

CHAPTER
FIVE

I woke up late. The headache was gone, and I knew how to break the witch's spell. Megan was already up, I could hear dishes banging and smell food, so she must be cooking breakfast. I stretched and got up.

Megan looked at me oddly when I came in. I was smiling, so that might have been why.

"Your bruises are gone," she said.

I reached up and felt my face. All the swelling was gone, and I noticed I had no other pain. I started to laugh.

"Why are you laughing?"

"My grandfather must have healed me, and I can break the spell on Gabe," I said smugly.

"OK. Can you stop the witch? Can you get your magic back from her?"

I frowned; she was killing my mood. "No."

"I didn't mean to ruin your day, but until we have a plan, are you sure we should break the spell on your Gabe?"

I sat at the table and drank the coffee sitting in front of me. Should I break the spell? I thought for a moment. Remembering back to what

Gabe had told me about his marriage and the previous encounters he'd had with witch covens, I had only one decision to make.

"Yes, we need to break the spell. Then, he can decide what he wants. We can't leave him without the opportunity to make his own choice."

After that, I felt a wave of relief wash over me. I took a breath and let it out. Then we ate. As soon as Gabe was home from work, we had a witch's spell to break.

* * *

JUST LIKE BEFORE, WE PULLED BEHIND GABE'S HOUSE AND KNOCKED on the door. He answered. No sign of recognition lit his eyes. We were strangers, again. I sighed. Oh well. As long as he kept the door open for a minute, I could do this thing. Megan and I had discussed a plan to keep him busy while I worked the magic I needed to.

She babbled on with some story she concocted on the fly about being lost and trying to meet someone secretly and blah, blah, blah. Meanwhile I gathered my will and reached out to the spell resting on Gabe's mind. Just as she was coming to the end with "...so can you tell us where that is?" I pushed with my magic, and the spell snapped. At least that is what it felt like to me—an inaudible snap like a rubber band pulled back and released quickly. Megan's amulet flashed at the same time, and she reached up to grab it. Gabe wobbled back a few steps and blinked several times. Then, he stood up straight.

"Brigid?"

"I'm here."

He looked disoriented. I'm sure he was. I thought he'd ask me what had happened, but his countenance turned dark and angry.

"Come in, we don't have very long."

We both walked in, and he closed the door. We sat on his sofa.

"Sofia will be here at six thirty," he said. "She has to come every day and 'freshen up' her spell on me. By evening, I have terrible headaches. I've been fighting against the compulsion she keeps on me, the block against my freedom."

"Gabe, I'm so sorry. I didn't know how to free you before."

He crossed the room from the chair he was in, to the sofa, and pulled me up. He wrapped me in a hug and held me tight, his face buried in my hair. "I knew you'd find a way. That hope was trapped in my heart under her spell. I may not have remembered you, but somewhere, deep inside I knew you'd come."

Emotion grabbed my heart and squeezed until it was hard to breathe. It took all I had not to cry at his confession.

"Thanks, Bridge," he said softly.

He released me, and I smiled up at him. "Always."

"She'll come and put the spell back on me," he said.

I nodded my head. "That's why you should come with us."

He shook his head. "I don't know if I can. She'll find out, and it'll be worse for you."

"Gabe, I'm so sorry. If you hadn't helped me, this wouldn't have happened to you."

He shook his head. "She'd have found a way. This was always her plan. Don't fool yourself." He walked us back to the door.

Megan walked ahead. He leaned down and kissed me.

"You, it's always been you I've wanted. No matter what she says, don't forget that," he said ominously.

A wave of nausea overwhelmed me. He'd called Sofia his girlfriend before. What else had she made him do?

He noticed my face had gone pale. "Come by in two days. She's going out of town. You can unwhammy me, and we'll plan our next steps." Then he kissed me again and closed the door.

I had many questions. If she had to "whammy" him daily, how could she leave for two days? What other kind of nasty thing was she setting up? I understood his reasons for remaining behind—he was protecting me. That broke my heart. I knew how much he hated being controlled.

As we cleared his street and pulled out on the highway, we passed Sofia. She looked directly at me. I felt ill. Did she know I'd been at Gabe's? Was she going to do something more to hurt him because I'd been to see him? Should we turn around and take him with us? No. I had to trust he knew what was best, but I cried all the way home, knowing I'd made the wrong choice. Megan desperately tried to comfort me.

When we returned, Mr. Mittens was waiting for us on the railing of the back porch.

Your grandfather has sent you a gift, he said. His mental voice was off, uncertain.

My crying jag had drained me, as had leaving Gabe to the sadistic wiles of the bitch witch queen. My curiosity barely piqued.

"Oh?" I said. Not completely engaged in his agitated body language.

I went to open the door.

You may want to walk in slowly, my cat said. That gave me pause.

This time I was curious. "Why?" I asked pointedly. It was my house after all.

He sent your magic teacher.

"Oh, that's nice," I answered. I twisted the knob to enter.

I took one look inside, then backed out and shut the door.

"Mr. Mittens, what is sitting at my kitchen table?"

He licked a paw, attempting to be nonchalant, but I could tell he was also shaken by the thing my grandfather had sent to teach me. *That is a Kelpie.*

"A Kelpie," I repeated. From what I remembered from high school English class, a Kelpie was a water horse—a creature that enticed humans into the water and drowned them. Why would my grandfather send such a thing to me? He'd healed me, and helped me, surely he wasn't trying to kill me?

She is technically only half Kelpie. The other half is Fae, Mr. Mittens corrected. *She's your great grandfather's mistress of magic.*

"My life is strange," I mumbled.

Megan's face lit up. "It might be, but it's sure a lot more interesting than before!"

I gave her a sidelong glance. "That's the understatement of the year."

I had to save Gabe. To do that, I had to learn magic—apparently from a Kelpie, a Scottish-Fae monster.

I'd thought that to accomplish my goal, I'd learn something quick and be done. I needed this to help Gabe. I hoped he could hold on. I sighed and opened the door to face my fate at the hands of my teacher.

"Hi, I'm Brigid."

The half Fae looked up at me. She'd obviously made herself at home; she had a cup of tea in her hand and a pastry. I didn't even know I had pastries. The Kelpie had long curly green hair and a faint greenish tinge to her skin. She had the pointed ears, go figure, but they were distinctly horsey—long, pointed, and on top of her head—they flicked around with any sound. Her hands had long fingers, six of them on each hand, and long claws. I wondered how she held such a delicate cup with those things. Her lashes were long, but they covered eyes, which were as black as night, and there was no white sclera at the edges. She could not pass as remotely human.

She looked up at me, unimpressed. She nodded her head in a slight bow of acknowledgement. "You can call me Dana." She had a thick accent I couldn't place. There was a burr and a lilt to it like a cross somewhere between Scottish and Irish, although I wasn't any kind of expert.

"Umm," I said, uncertain where to start. "Mr. Mittens said my grandfather sent you?"

The Kelpie nodded. "He did."

I waited for more information, but none was forthcoming. I had the distinct feeling that not only was Dana not impressed with me, but she wasn't very happy to be here.

"I'm happy you took time out of your life to help me learn magic," I prompted.

Her shark eyes bore into me. "I'm not here out of a sense of magnanimity. I was ordered here by my lord. We aren't going to be friends, and I expect you to do exactly as I say when I say it."

I looked at her for a moment. I didn't have time for this. Yes, I needed to learn magic yesterday, but I couldn't be locked down while I did it. I had werewolves to talk to, a boyfriend to free, a house to finish, and a business to get off the ground. I couldn't spend twenty-four seven being a slave to a creepy magic teacher.

Instead of accepting her terms, I asked. "What will this entail?" Megan gasped slightly behind me.

The Kelpie finished the last bite of her pastry and licked her fingers. Her green tongue was long and pointed. Yuck.

"While we practice, you will obey."

"How long each day will it take?"

"It depends on how quickly you learn."

I sighed. "OK."

My new teacher looked smug. She stood and clip-clopped to the door behind me. I realized that her feet were horse's hooves. She was clad in an ivory silk robe, and I wondered briefly if she had a horse tail as well.

She threw all three of us a disdainful glance and said, "We'll start at dawn." Then in a golden flash, she vanished.

CHAPTER

SIX

"Mr. Mittens!" I bellowed after the Kelpie's dramatic exit.

Yes, he sighed. As he strolled in the door left open by the Kelpie.

"What did my grandfather say to you?" I demanded. Obviously, they'd spoken more about me than I'd thought the evening before.

We discussed you, of course. I'm your protector.

"That's not gonna fly this time. Explain to me what that means, and what you and he discussed, *exactly*." My hands were on my hips, and I stared down at him.

His face seemed to become grumpier before my eyes, which wasn't an easy feat. He always looked a little grouchy.

Well, he began. His eyes shifted to the door.

He'd better not be planning to escape.

Megan and I leaned in to hear what he was going to say, even though it was in our heads. My cat could work a room.

I just explained to him how much you were struggling with magic without anyone to teach you, he finally admitted.

I looked at him a minute longer before speaking. I wasn't sure I believed him. He probably made me out to be much more pathetic than

I was, but I couldn't read his cute kitty face, and he was sitting on his fluffy tail so that couldn't give himself away.

"Hmmm, are you sure that's all?"

He blinked, the picture of innocence, and then was silent. He wasn't an idiot. He knew I'd catch him in a lie if he kept talking.

I doubted my patheticness would be enough to convince my great-grandfather to send me his "mistress of magic," so I knew that Mr. Mittens had told him something else, something important. I could be wrong, maybe I'd guilted him into helping me, but you never knew.

"So, I need to know about this Dana. What do you know about her?"

She's powerful and terrifying. She'll hate you for taking her away from her duties, which include torture and finding new ways to break your grandfather's enemies through magic. He looked away again.

I was starting to think he wasn't looking for an escape but looking for danger. "What's the matter? Why do you keep looking at the door?"

I'm sensing an incursion. I must go.

He walked to the door and looked at me, so I knew to open it for him. "Fine, but remember, ask before you kill."

He raced out, and I shut the door. Megan looked at me strangely when I turned back around. "What did that mean?"

I sighed. "He thinks something dangerous, think unicorn, has popped up on my property."

She rolled her eyes. "I know what he meant. What did you mean by 'ask before you kill'?"

"Oh, when I first met Brightfeather, he was trying to kill her. I stopped him. After talking to her, we realized she was only here for sanctuary, not to kill me," I answered distractedly. My mind was already on the list of things I needed to do before I met with Dana in the morning.

"Okaaay."

"Yeah, I love my cat, but he thinks he's badass."

"He is. You saw him take out the horned pony from hell."

"Yeah, I guess he is."

"You're distracted, what's going on in your head?"

I shrugged. "I need to contact the werewolves and let them know what's going on. We're working together on the witch problem. Their dad was fond of Gabe, too."

She nodded. "OK, call them."

I looked at the clock. "You don't think it's too late, do you?"

She gave me a hard look. "It's seven thirty. You're avoiding it."

I was. I was nervous since it had taken me so long to recover. I didn't want them to think that I wasn't pulling my weight after they'd fought so hard against the coven. I was a pathetic ally. "No, I'm calling now."

I pulled out my phone and dialed Luke. He answered after two rings, so I knew he was anxious.

"Hi, Luke. It's Brigid."

"Brigid! I've been worried about you. Are you feeling any better?" At that, all my worry melted away. It'd been a stupid thing, mostly a leftover from years of emotional abuse. He didn't think I was worthless, just hurt.

"Much better. Thanks so much! It really helped that my friend came out to help me."

"That's nice. What a good friend."

I looked at Megan. She really was a good friend. I smiled at her. Luke was also a good friend. He'd taken the time to ask about me even though I'm sure he was anxious about what I'd discovered.

"I saw Gabe. He's physically well," I started the conversation.

"Yeah, we checked at the clinic," Luke responded. "Brigid, how would you feel if we met quickly? That way everyone can hear what you have to say."

I looked at Megan. I wasn't sure how she'd like being bombarded by a family full of werewolves. I hit the mute on my phone. "Would you be OK if the wolves came over?"

She looked a little intimidated, but said, "Sure, if they're as good looking as you promised."

I rolled my eyes, then I unmuted. "Do you want to come here?"

"Sure, have you and your friend eaten? Does she know?"

273

"Yeah, she knows everything, we can talk freely. No, we haven't eaten."

"We'll bring pizza. See you in an hour." He hung up. I looked down at the phone with a frown. He hadn't even ended with a goodbye. Oh well. He must be busy.

"They'll be here in an hour," I said to Megan.

"Good grief," she replied and ran upstairs to fix herself up.

I went to my bathroom to wash my face. Hopefully the swelling in my eyes from crying would go down before anyone saw me.

* * *

To my surprise, the entire Whelan clan showed up with several pizzas. They weren't the entire pack. I'd learned from Luke earlier, there were several other families that completed it, but they were the leaders. I introduced Megan to everyone, and I could tell she was smitten with both Noah, the new alpha, and Lucas, the second oldest brother. The other Whelans, Anna, the mother, Michael the third, and the two sisters, Isabella and Madison, made up the rest of the party. Anna was one of those timeless, handsome women, and her daughters took after her with their blonde hair and green eyes. The boys had varying shades of blonde hair from dirty blond to dark honey blond on Luke. But all of their eyes were the clear, bright shade of green like their mother's.

Luckily, my table could hold eight people, if I brought back the extra chairs I had doing extra duty around the house. The two eldest Whelan brothers weren't that tall, probably in the average range, but they were physically intimidating. They were strong and broad shouldered. Michael, the youngest, was slightly taller and leaner. The girls and their mother were all shapely, but not that imposing physically. It was strange to think that this family of normal looking people could transform into terrifying wolves, twice the size of normal ones. If I hadn't seen it myself, I'd never believe it.

Once everyone had food and was eating around the table, Noah started. "Thanks for having us over, Brigid, we're happy to see you looking so much better. Is this." He waved at my face. "Because of Gabe?"

I shook my head until I swallowed the bite in my mouth. "No. I saw him, but he doesn't remember me."

They all stopped and looked up, my newly healed form, forgotten.

"What do you mean?" Isabella said.

"When I saw him, he knew exactly who I was," Noah added with a frown. He was the

serious one of the family.

"She doesn't want him to remember her," Megan said with around a mouthful of pizza.

They all looked at her. She shut her mouth and looked abashed.

"It's true. We saw him twice. The first time he couldn't remember me at all, or his car that we returned. When he almost broke through, he had a terrible headache and told us to leave. The second time, I broke the spell on him. He told us that she was keeping him in a controlled state that she had to renew nightly," I said.

I was growing more and more upset and stopped before I started crying again. I took a bite of my pizza, even though it tasted like ash, to hide my growing emotions.

Megan noticed, as did Anna. While Megan filled in the rest of the story, Anna patted my hand comfortingly. I felt guilt rise up to join my other churning emotions—she had just lost her husband. I should be comforting her. That gave me the boost I needed to shove down the emotions and answer the questions everyone had.

"So, why is Sofia leaving him for two days? That sounds rather convenient if she's having to renew her spell every night," Luke said.

We hadn't had time to question Gabe; he'd shooed us out too quickly. It had been eating at me as well, so I figured it was best to see if anyone else had a possible explanation. My gut was saying she'd concocted something nasty in place of her spell.

"We don't know," I answered for me and Megan. "But I have a bad feeling. What do you all think?"

The werewolves looked perplexed and muttered some things to each other. Finally, Noah spoke up. "She's got something up her sleeve. So far, she's out planned us. If she's leaving him alone, she's going to do something to keep us away and to keep him from coming to us."

That was exactly what my gut was saying, so I agreed. "What do we do about it?"

Noah looked around at his family. "We'll be there. We'll set up a watch around his property and attempt to keep him safe." He gestured at Isabella. "Izzy will follow him to work and home."

My heart rate accelerated. I was causing them to take time from their lives. "What about your jobs?" I asked. "I'm free, and so is Megan, we can follow instead."

Noah shook his head. "No, we both saw how badly you were injured, and Megan is human. The witch and her coven would chew her up. We're werewolves. We may not have active magic, but we're tough. Plus, Sofia already knows you, and who knows how she'll react if she sees you around Gabriel."

Isabella chimed in, "I'm free right now—we're in between jobs. We've got the time, don't worry."

I accepted their reasoning, but I still felt bad. Their husband and father had been killed so the witches could steal my magic. Yet, the Whelans were still loyal to me and willing to help. I didn't deserve their friendship and kindness.

"I know I'm the lone human, but Sofia doesn't know me. I'm a total stranger. Wouldn't it make sense that I'm involved?" Megan asked.

Everyone looked at her. I was afraid. She was my best friend, and other than the protection in her charm, totally defenseless against a witch. But she was right, and looking at all the faces around me, the wolves agreed. They'd been trying to keep her out, but it made too much sense to not involve her.

Noah gave a terse nod. As the new alpha, they all looked at him, and that was that.

"She can go with me. That way, she can drive, I can go wolf, and we'll cover all the bases," Isabella said.

"That'll be great," Megan confirmed, but her face was a shade paler, and I knew she was scared.

"OK, we've got a plan." Noah sighed. "I think we also have a complete list of the coven members."

I stiffened. That was good news. "Yes?" I prompted after a moment. Then because it had been weighing on me I asked, "What are they saying about the dead members? I haven't heard anything about missing people in the local news."

Madison answered. "My job was to find out that particular information. Apparently, they've gone on a two weeklong 'retreat.' I'm guessing something will go horribly wrong to explain why they don't come back."

"Yeah, like they messed with the wrong werewolf pack." I heard Luke comment under his breath. The Whelans were definitely as angry at the coven as I was.

"I'm so sorry," I blurted out. "I didn't know this would happen when you came to work for me. I'd give anything to bring him back."

Anna's eyes filled with tears. She wiped them away unselfconsciously and reached over to grip my hand. "Don't go there, dear. It was not your fault. It was the witches, and don't you forget that. Not one of us"—she looked around at her family—"and I mean no one in this family blames you."

I stood, leaned over, and hugged her. She returned the hug. I sat back in my chair. "Thank you. You don't know how much that means to me."

They all nodded, faces full of love and care, and I believed them.

"I'll email you the list we've compiled," Noah said. "They are in just about every business in this town," he added, ominously.

My stomach churned, and I wondered if I'd be able to hold down my supper.

They finished the pizza and sat around chatting about anything else except for witches and magic. I noticed that Luke and Megan had hit it off. They were talking quietly in the corner of the kitchen, he was leaning with his back against part of the counter, Megan was leaning on the opposing one, and they were oblivious to the rest of us. I smiled.

Izzy, after Noah had called her that I couldn't think of her any other way, pulled me aside for a moment.

"They look cozy."

I looked over at Megan again and smiled. "Yeah."

"Luke had a bad breakup a year ago, and this is the first time I've seen him even look at another girl." She sipped her drink and watched them. They remained oblivious.

I nodded. I didn't know what to say to that. Megan was a good, dependable soul, and he could do a lot worse.

"Yeah, she was upset because he 'kept secrets' from her. Her words. It was the werewolf thing. It's agreed in the magical world that humans must remain ignorant."

Was she telling me that because I broke a rule? I must have blanched because she placed a hand on my arm.

"Don't worry, we don't have a police force." She smirked. "I was telling you that because that's already a barrier gone for them, if this" —she gestured at them—"goes further." She paused and sipped her soda. "I'm happy, Brigid. Don't worry. I won't let him hurt your friend. He's a good man, too."

I already knew that. Of all the Whelans, I felt closest to Luke. We'd been the ones that had spoken the most about the house, and I'd been with him when his dad died. Craig, the Whelans' dad, was the perfect example of a great family man. He loved and cared for his family so much. Just looking at them now, all close and loving, was enough to let me know that Luke had a great example. He'd be a great boyfriend, or more. I'd feel good about it if he and Megan chose each other. Of course, this was their first meeting, so both Izzy and I were probably far ahead of the game, but it filled me with warmth that we were both hoping for them to get together.

"I didn't come over here for that, I just want to reassure you that I'll look after her."

I shrugged. "I know you will." I smiled at her. "You Whelans are good people."

"Are you sure? We can be ravening beasts."

She looked so sincere at that, that my face must have shown the surprise I felt.

She laughed. "Don't worry, we can control it, but your face! Priceless."

I realized she was joking around with me. Since previous to this, we'd only worked professionally, and Isabella was *very* professional, I laughed, too. Maybe I'd made a new friend to replace the one I'd lost.

"Izzy, do any of your pack know anything about Kelpies?"

She blinked at me. "Uh, I don't, but I'll ask. Are Kelpies something we need to worry about along with witches?"

"No." I laughed and shook my head. "That seems to be a particular problem of mine."

CHAPTER

SEVEN

My alarm went off before it was light. I wanted to be dressed, ready, and full of warm food and coffee before my strange teacher arrived. Megan was sleeping in, and I was careful not to disturb her. I was nervous, and truth be told, a little terrified.

I was finishing up my coffee, when Mr. Mittens licked the last morsel from his bowl and looked up, so I was prepared when a flash of light announced her arrival.

Her imperious expression froze when she saw him. Then to my surprise, she gave a stiff little bow in his direction. "Xrsrphn," she greeted him.

He returned the bow with a slight dip of his head. "Mistress Dana."

I raised a questioning eyebrow at him, and intoned, "Xrsrphn?"

It's my true name.

I wanted to ask him why he hadn't shared his true name with me, but before I could, my new magic teacher cracked her whip.

"Xrsrphn, you will guide us to the place of power," she commanded.

Place of power? What was she talking about? My eyes were on my cat. Only the swish of his tail betrayed his annoyance at her demand.

But he led us out the kitchen door, down the porch steps, and across the gravel drive to the waterfall trail.

I followed behind my new teacher, apprehension tight in my throat. We passed the place where I'd run into a black bear and her cubs, passed the spring, and continued towards the waterfall. Is that where we were going for sure?

I pushed a question out from my mind to his, *Is the waterfall a place of power?*

It is. This is why your grandmother hid the trail.

How much power are we talking about, and what kind of power?

But instead of an answer, I got his usual annoyed *Hmpf.*

We marched along a little further. I kept my eyes on him because I could feel his anxiety. I couldn't figure out what it was about. He was obviously acquainted with Dana; he didn't seem afraid of her. I understood a moment later, when he stopped in the middle of the trail and faced us.

I must leave you here. There is an incursion. He looked at Dana. *Brigid will lead you to the place of power.* With that, he twisted into his Splintercat form and bounded away.

I sighed. I wasn't comfortable with my magic teacher. I'd been hoping his solid presence would be with me. That's the real reason he'd been tense not the incursion. He didn't want to leave me alone with her either.

The Kelpie frowned but motioned for me to take the lead. I took her up to the waterfall. I hated having her in my personal sanctuary. I'd always been most at peace in this location. The thrum of the water, the way the sun always seemed to shine on my favorite boulder perch, the smell of the rhododendrons and evergreens always whispered "home" to me. I stopped at the edge of the small pool and looked at her expectantly.

A small creeping trickle of fear trailed down my spine as I realized I'd brought a water horse to a pond. But I pushed it down. Surely, my grandfather wouldn't send her here only to kill me. He'd been helpful.

"Let me see what you have learned so far," the Kelpie said. "This is the heart of your power; you'll have the most control and strength here. Amaze me."

Great, a snarky Kelpie who hated me. At least she hadn't attempted to kill me yet.

Since I'd practiced here many times, I figured I'd start with water. I turned to the pond and coaxed a stream of water to rise from the pond. I sent it in a swirl, and it rose and gamboled through the air. Then I formed it into the shape of a butterfly and made it beat its wings in a circle before I released it back to the pond. I was best with water, and I smiled at my perfect display of control. I looked at Dana, she gestured that I should continue. No praise, no criticism—tough crowd.

OK, next. Fire. I looked around. There was a bunch of tree litter on my favorite rock. I silently directed the fire in me to consume it. When it lit up, I ordered the fire to form a flower, and then I let it burn out, cleansing the stone. I was proud of myself, that fire flower was a perfect replica of a rhododendron bloom. Before my teacher could demand more, I confidently instructed the earth around my boulder to burst into wildflowers. Then, I commanded a single bolt of lightning down from the sky. It hit the water, which splashed and boiled and sprayed us with water. I grimaced. I hadn't intended to get us wet. I glanced at my teacher briefly to gauge her mood.

She still frowned at me. I had no way to show her mind magic or spirit. In fact, I barely understood those aspects of my power. I'd lost ice, I'd never done anything with shadow, and I obviously had little control of lightning. The last one was light. I hadn't practiced that one much, but I funneled the light from the sun to come down and twinkle in a ball in my hand. I tossed it up, caught it and dispersed it. When I was done, I looked at my teacher—hopeful she'd find that I wasn't a complete loser.

"That's all?" she intoned, and my stomach sank. I was a failure.

"Yes?" I squeaked.

"Is that a question? Don't you know?" she asked with an imperious tone.

I didn't trust my voice, so I stood there and waited for more judgement to land like blows.

"My master was right, you are wholly ignorant and unprepared," she muttered to herself. "Pathetic," she spoke directly to me.

I sighed. I already knew that. The witches had kicked my butt less than a week ago. I had power. I knew that. But using it? Just like she said, pathetic. The little bit of confidence I'd pulled from fled.

"We have a lot of work. The only magic you seem almost competent at are water, fire, and earth. So, we'll start there to at least raise you to competency at something."

It looked like a long road ahead.

"First, what are you using to focus your energy?"

Focus my energy? I'd only been using my mind and will. I didn't know I was supposed to use anything else.

"Umm, nothing?"

"No wonder. For you to advance, you need to start small and precise. A focusing object would be best." She looked at me and tapped one of her horse hooves against a stone. "Do you wear any jewelry consistently?"

I looked down to the spot my wedding ring used to be. I'd tossed that over a bridge in a fit of pique during the divorce. It was dumb, but it made me feel good. I'd begged my husband earlier in our marriage to replace it after we'd had monetary success, but he'd ignored me. One of the many red flags I'd ignored throughout our marriage.

I shook my head. "No, but I was used to wearing a ring. I can start again." My grandmother had left me a lot of jewelry. I'd pick something I liked with *good* memories.

"Fine, we'll start there. Call the ring to you."

"What?"

This time my teacher sighed. "Your ignorance is daunting. You are Fae. It should be part of your inherent magic. Call the object."

I didn't want to be called any more names, so I pictured my jewelry box, and focused on grandmother's engagement ring. It was a pretty thing. Art déco. A classic cut diamond surrounded by filigree. I'd assumed it was white gold, but now? Maybe it was silver. She was part Fae as I was, and the Fae had an affinity to silver. I pictured the ring firmly in my head and called it to me.

I remembered that Mr. Mittens had told me once I could call anything. But there were rules. It had to exist, and I had to be careful in case it was ripped from someone who didn't believe in magic. This exercise meant I was safe from exposing magic.

I opened my hand so the ring would have a landing spot. Nothing. Great, one more thing for my teacher to complain about. Just as I was about to try again, something flashed by my face and tinkled as it landed on my favorite boulder. I looked at the rock. Sure enough, the ring lay there twinkling in the sun. I grinned. I wasn't a complete magical disaster. I slipped the ring on.

"Hmmm. That was adequate," Dana remarked. "Now, you will call a single drop of water. Focus through the ring. Concentrate on it and lift a single drop from the waterfall."

Great. I could sometimes do small magics, but I'd never done anything that small. We were probably about to get drenched. I focused through the ring, as she'd directed me. That was an odd feeling. I was used to looking at what I did, but now I had to rely on my will and imagination. I reached out and called a drop of water to me. My magic reacted—a coolness in my chest that I associated with my water magic. I lifted the water. My eyes flicked to it. Sure enough, not a drop, more like a cup. She frowned. I released the water, and it splashed back into the pool. I tried to keep my thoughts positive, but Evan's voice echoed between my ears that I would never be good at this. I shook my head. He was wrong. I'd already accomplished so much. I could do it, I just needed practice and instruction. I kept at it. Plus, I did not want to disappoint Dana or more importantly my great-grandfather. For one, I wasn't sure she wouldn't just drown me in my own pond. Kelpies had that reputation.

It took a couple of hours, but I was finally able to call one drop of water consistently. Once I was pronounced "adequate," she left in her usual blaze of light, promising more delights tomorrow. My magic usually exhilarated me and left me full of energy, but today? I was drained. My mental facilities hadn't been strained like that in a long time. I'd exhausted myself fighting my self-doubt, and I'd taxed my concentration. I dragged myself down the trail, forgetting to call my cat.

As I strolled down the path, mind elsewhere, I was stopped by a snake. I knew that there were snakes in Oregon, although I'd never seen many here. We'd had rattlers in Utah, so I was cautious near snakes, but not really worried about them. However, before I just skipped around it, my mind finally caught up to me, and I realized it was bright red. That registered as *not* normal.

I stopped and studied the creature. It seemed like a normal snake, coiled on the ground watching me. I moved to the right to take a wide berth around it, it swung its head to the right. My heartbeat increased. That was fine, I'd just go around the other way. I took two steps to the left. Sure enough, the snake moved to the left. Now I was worried. My heartbeat sped up a little more. I took a step back. This time, I'd go back to the waterfall and wait for Mr. Mittens. If this was a normal snake, maybe it would be gone before my cat arrived.

As I went to turn around, the snake slithered forward. Once it was uncoiled, it began to grow. Shit. I gave Mr. Mittens a mental scream, and I started to run. The snake continued to grow. An enormous head punched through the trees next to me and blocked the path. It wasn't a snake. My heart beat so fast, I felt lightheaded. I slid to a stop.

Bright yellow eyes froze me in place. The slitted pupils of the reptile thinned to almost nothing in the bright light of the noon sun and focused on me. I called for my cat again. I began to focus almost frantically on the creature's fine scales. They lay with precision, so tight against each other they appeared almost drawn on with a fine pencil. Overall, the creature was red, but up close, each scale was almost a rainbow of reds. I noticed a fine pattern along the top of the head and the neck, a slightly darker shade that formed a pattern like a diamond-back rattler. I swallowed hard.

I looked carefully away and followed the sinuous neck behind me, which had grown and flattened trees on either side of its immense body. It had four legs and a set of neatly folded wings. This wasn't a snake. It was a dragon. My knees almost gave way. What did Mr.

Mittens say about dragons? Oh yeah, they were exactly what the legends said. Big scaly reptiles that breathed fire and collected hordes.

This creature was so gargantuan, even Mr. Mittens in his Splintercat form couldn't do anything against it. I was going to get eaten, and if Mr. Mittens showed up soon, I'd get him eaten, too.

Remembering that I kept reminding Mr. Mittens to talk before he killed, I addressed the dragon—even though neither I nor my cat had a chance of killing it.

"Hi. I'm Brigid. How can I help you?" I asked politely. I figured it couldn't hurt. Maybe I'd get a couple of seconds before it ate me.

A puff of smoke billowed from its nostrils. Then, like all the other magical creatures I'd met, namely my cat and Brightfeather, it spoke into my mind.

Hello Brigid, Fae lord of this land. You may call me Goch.

Okay. What? The dragon spoke. Did that mean it wasn't going to eat me?

"How do you know I'm the lord of this land?" I choked out. Before I died, I should at least get information from him.

The Splintercat said I should introduce myself. I've been granted asylum here.

I tilted my head at him.

"Why did you seek asylum?" I was curious now. Surely this wasn't a case of a bad marriage like Brightfeather's.

I have angered my wing, and I've been exiled, he stated, a hint of sadness in his mental voice.

"I'm very sorry. May I ask what you were exiled for?" My mind went to a group of dragons attacking Oregon because I didn't ask the right questions.

His eyes closed slightly, and I could feel his shame.

I failed in battle. I am considered a dreamer, and I caused harm to befall another because I was dreaming when I should have been paying attention to the fight.

"Oh. I'm very sorry, Goch. You are welcome here. Is the red snake the shape you chose to show if a human comes along?"

Yes. I'm sorry I frightened you. I was trying to get your attention.

287

"Thank you. There aren't any red snakes in Oregon, at least that I know of, so I was concerned that you were an imported, venomous snake."

I am venomous! he said eagerly.

That wasn't really helpful, but I gave him a wan smile. "I'm sure that will come in handy."

Just then, Mr. Mittens came galloping up.

What is wrong? he asked.

Afraid to anger my new dragon responsibility, I mind-spoke back. *You failed to explain this, and I was afraid when he plopped in my path.*

Mr. Mittens's eyes flicked to Goch. *Hmpf,* he said. *I asked you to wait until I could inform the lord of the land,* he addressed the dragon.

Goch continued to look ashamed, his huge head drooped, which was difficult when it was inches from the ground. *Forgive me, my lord.*

I rolled my eyes, this "lord of the land" thing was growing old quickly. "Goch," I said aloud. "You do not have to address me as lord or lady. I'm Brigid. Please, make yourself at home, just remember, you should use your snake form if anyone that you don't know is around. You may show your true self to me, Mr. Mittens, and my friend Megan. I'll introduce you later."

Goch's head rose at that. His eyes widened. I got the distinct impression that Goch was young for his kind and still sought recognition and was eager to please. *Thank you, my...um, Brigid! I'll be the most perfect dragon!*

I gave him a small nod to acknowledge him. Goch spread his massive wings, and with a tremendous leap, launched himself into the air. The wind from the beat of his mighty wings almost knocked me down, but I recovered and watched the dragon disappear over my trees. I sighed.

"Is there enough room and food here for a dragon?" I asked my silly cat.

Mr. Mittens looked away.

"What do dragons eat?" I asked, hands on my hips.

Well. His eyes darted to the left. *They eat whatever they wish. You saw how big that one was, and he is only half grown.*

"That is not an answer."

He huffed. *They eat meat. Lots of meat. I think that I'll have to teach him to realm walk so he can hunt elsewhere.*

Great, there wasn't nearly enough food here. "If he has to be taught to realm walk, that means he's from…"

Yes, dragons live in this realm. Mr. Mittens finished my thought.

I shivered. Crap. "How, where?"

They are rare beings. Only a few hundred are left. That is why I granted Goch a home on your land. His voice was soft and sad in my mind.

My annoyance faded. That made sense, I'd have done the same. Instead of telling him off, I said, "Thanks for talking before killing."

Hmpf.

I'd have to ponder on dragons for a while. I'd always thought the idea of dragons must have come from some ancient human seeing dinosaur bones or something instead of a real honest to God flying lizard. This was no pterodactyl, either. Well, as I'd learned, there are stranger things in heaven and earth, or however that Hamlet quote went. I shrugged and followed my cat down the trail towards home. At least my new life was never boring.

EIGHT

E ven though it was lunchtime, Megan was warming her hands around a cup of coffee when Mr. Mittens and I walked into the kitchen.

"Hey! How was your first magic lesson?" she asked with a yawn.

"Did you know that there are dragons in North America?" I replied.

She sputtered. And the coffee she'd been sipping came spurting out of her mouth and over the kitchen table.

I frowned at her. "I guess that's a no."

"Dragons?" She was awake now.

I sighed. "By the way, we have a new creature courtesy of Brigid, Fae Lord." I looked pointedly at my cat.

His blue eyes gazed up at me without shame, and he jumped up on the counter and looked at the fridge. He didn't even bother to talk to me. Just did the bossy cat thing. I got out a clean dish.

"A dragon?" Megan asked hopefully. Then she frowned. "This isn't going to be disappointing like the unicorn, is it?"

"I sure hope not. But in this case, I don't know if that's a good thing or a bad one."

"Why don't you start at the beginning."

So, while I prepared Mr. Mittens's premium meal, I recounted the whole day starting with my first lesson.

"Huh." She thought for a moment, her eyes distant. "You know…"

I put up a hand, because I knew where this was going already. "We do not ride sentient creatures that can eat us."

"You shut that down way too fast," Megan said. "It's almost like you already considered it."

"Well, a telepathic dragon—of course I *went* there."

"You're sure we can't ask?"

I shook my head. "You can ask if you dare. Just remember he's a *teenage* dragon. I don't trust human teenagers to drive, let alone fly me around."

"There's that. Damn." She blew a stray hair out of her face. "This was my chance!" She flung up her hands and shook her head. "I'm never gonna fight Thread now."

I grinned, joining in. "You can still fly to the Red Star, I'm sure."

"Hell, no! I know how well that went."

"Guess you should go back to harping then." I laughed.

"You know I can't sing for shit." She mopped up the coffee from the table.

"Oh, yes, I do."

She threw the damp rag at me. We devolved into giggles, the ridiculousness of the situation getting to us.

We made lunch and ate. Mr. Mittens had finished his meal earlier and was curled up on my lap, getting stray scratches and head rubs. As we were sitting there, finishing our food, Megan said, "I've been thinking about your bed-and-breakfast idea."

I raised my eyebrows at her. "Yeah?"

"Instead of doing a straight, boring, basic B&B, why don't we cater to the supernatural community?"

I stopped chewing and swallowed. "What do you mean?" I'd kinda had this thought, too, but I hadn't fleshed it out.

"Well, just in this small town, you have a good-sized werewolf pack and a large coven of witches. Plus, there's enough weirdness going on around here that you know there are all kinds of other types, and not just from this 'realm.' Don't other races vacation? If I was a city werewolf, wouldn't I like four hundred untouched acres to run in for my two weeks holiday every year?"

"Eight hundred," I said off-hand, deep in thought.

"Eight then. Geesh."

One of the ideas I'd thought of, once Gabe was rescued and the witches were subdued, was to open up the B&B idea to include not just humanoid races, but magical creatures.

"Two hundred of those acres are an old dairy farm. It's been out of commission and is overgrown, but I'd like to change that into a kind of stable for magical creatures as well." I looked at her, and she narrowed her eyes at me.

"You already planned on doing this."

"Sort of, I haven't gotten very far, but as the vice-president of Lady Brigid, Fae Lord, Enterprises, LLC you should write up your ideas and present them at the next board meeting," I said with a fake English accent.

She raised her hand. "First item is to change the company name, the current one's much too long and overly descriptive."

"Added to the agenda." I made a mark in the air.

"Mr. Mittens, as the resident realm walker, would you in your travels, enjoy an inn set up with your needs in mind?"

He yawned, the heavy meal and pets setting him on the path to dream land. "Would there be premium cuts of fish, chicken, pork, and beef, with a side of cream available?"

"Yes." I rolled my eyes.

"It sounds lovely." He nodded back off.

Then, while the idea was fresh, we both brought out our computers and started writing up ideas and plans. I felt better about this than the new computer business idea. This fit my new life, the one I'd made for myself, free of Evan, and I was excited about it. We had one more day before we met with Gabe again, and then we'd defeat the evil witch coven, save Gabe for good, and have a plan to open a place that catered to others like me. Everything was looking up.

* * *

SINCE MEGAN AND I WERE EXCITED ABOUT THE NEW PLANS, I thought that we'd better go see the old dairy and what kind of shape it was in. I'd had such a hard time getting my house renovated, I couldn't imagine what I'd have to do to get the dairy revamped into a livable space. I had a Splintercat, a griffin, and a dragon living on my property, and if I had that great a variety of clientele, I wasn't even sure how to house them. It's not like they all came in one convenient size.

We waited until Mr. Mittens was done sleeping off his lunch, and since it was a lovely day, decided to walk out to the dairy.

"Do you know the way?" I asked my cat.

He "hmpfed" at me, and I cringed. *You are the Fae lord of the land; you should be able to find a specific blade of grass whenever you wish*, he chastised.

"OK, I'll give it a go," I said. I'd die of embarrassment if I got us lost—again.

Megan saw the uncertainty on my face because she smiled. "No biggy, it'll be an adventure!"

"Great!" I said with false cheer.

It was warm enough for short sleeves. So, we walked out the door and into my woods, wearing jeans, t-shirts, and boots for the inevitable mud or muck we'd encounter on the way. Even though I led the way, Mr. Mittens strolled along for protection. You never knew what you'd find in my woods.

The dairy was on the western side of the property. I don't think it had been an active dairy since the seventies, so it didn't have much modern equipment. However, there were a lot of buildings. I didn't know much about dairies, but I had grown up in a dairy town, so I had a general idea what each structure was for. To one side was a modest farmhouse, which had been used as a rental in years past. Then, there was the milking barn, that was obvious, the feeding barn for winter when the cows weren't at pasture, the calving barn, and a covered hay barn. There were various sheds for tools and equipment, and fenced pastures. Everything was grown over and returning to nature. At least the large structures looked solid.

"Boy," Megan said. "This looks like a lot of work."

I nodded. I was a little discouraged because it did look like a lot of work. There was the cleaning and taming of the pastures and the outside of each building. I could probably handle the grounds with my magic, but I needed someone to come in and check out the structures and make sure they were as sound as they looked, and then an idea on how to turn them into creature stables. I didn't really have a clue for that one.

"Mr. Mittens, do you have any idea what mythical creatures would need in a structure?"

He turned his periwinkle gaze at me. *Shelter from the elements, a soft bed, and plenty of food.*

That sounded about right. He wasn't picky where he slept, since he slept on the table, on the floor, in the middle of my bed, really any place he felt tired. For a supernatural being, he sure acted like a regular cat.

"That's helpful." I rolled my eyes, making sure only Megan could see.

I took a few pics with my phone camera, and we went to look inside each building. We started with the barns, since the house would be good for a caretaker or two but wouldn't be part of the guest facilities. We took more pics and talked about what would need to be done. After we checked out the outbuildings and barns, we headed to the house.

The door still had the realtor's lock on it. I had the code; I just hadn't been here to check it out since I'd moved. It wasn't high on my list. I punched in the code on the lockbox and took out the key. The door squeaked eerily when I opened it, and we were greeted with dust and cobwebs. The power wasn't on, but enough light filtered through the uncovered windows, that it wasn't much of an issue.

The house also looked solid, and I was grateful. It would need a whole new electric and maybe a plumbing update, but other than new appliances, paint, and flooring, and of course a thorough cleaning, it looked great. I needed to get an inspector in to check if it was safe to have the water and plumbing turned back on, but since the house had been lived in within the last five years, unlike the dairy, it was probably not an issue.

It was a simple two-story farmhouse, three bedrooms upstairs, the living room, a half bath, kitchen and mudroom on the main floor, and a full basement. I doubted the basement would be light enough to explore without the electricity being on, but Megan and I had the flashlights on our phones, so we decided to brave the spiders and check it out. When I suggested it to Mr. Mittens, he gave an annoyed swish of his tail, but his curiosity won out, and he followed us down the basement stairs.

Like a lot of basements on the coast, it smelled dank and musty. I wondered why there was a full basement, since the water table was so high. It was a rare thing to find here. But it was extra space to be used, so down we went. It was dark, and our phone flashlights barely pushed back the gloom. It was spooky too, and I shivered. The short sleeve t-shirt I was wearing was not enough after the warmth of the bright sunlit day and the upper floors.

"It's cold down here," Megan echoed my thoughts.

I nodded. Just then, Mr. Mittens froze. I froze too. Anything that scared my cat, doubly scared me.

"Megan, get behind me," I said.

She turned and frowned at me, but then she noticed my cat and slid behind me and out of his way.

"What's down here?" I asked him.

I'm not sure, but it feels bad, he answered.

"Bad, how?"

But he didn't answer. There was a low growl emanating from his direction, which sent more icy shivers trailing down my back. I motioned for Megan to start back up the stairs. She scooted one foot back, and I followed, keeping my eyes peeled for whatever my cat was sensing.

Nothing but darkness.

Run! Mr. Mittens announced into our minds.

Megan turned to start up the stairs but tripped and fell onto them. Since I was right behind her, I fell on her. Which was a good thing, because as I fell, something dark passed over my head, brushing my hair. I yipped.

Mr. Mittens followed, still in Ragdoll form, but his eyes flashed, and his claws were out, and they were much larger than those of a regular house cat. I rolled off Megan, and she started to scramble up the stairs. I got my feet back under me, but I turned to see what Mr. Mittens was chasing. I saw a shadowy figure, but with the lack of light, I couldn't tell what it was. Now I was good and aware that there was something down here with us, I realized that the atmosphere had become heavy, and fear was pressing me down. Megan was at the top of the stairs.

"Come on, Bridge!"

I shook my head. I wasn't going to let something I couldn't see dictate what I did. I had light magic. Time to illuminate the issue. I hadn't practiced with it much, so when I called it up, it filled the basement full of light so bright, it temporarily blinded me. Mr. Mittens squawked, I'm sure it really hurt his cat eyes.

After my eyes adjusted, I saw what he'd been chasing, and I wished I hadn't. I didn't know what it was, but it had a shiny black spider body like a black widow, but a human-like face. Only the human face had spider mandibles, fangs, and four jeweled eyes. The light had also stunned it, luckily, because I didn't want to get Mr. Mittens eaten. It was frozen, but I could see the tiny hairs along its legs quiver, and I knew it would be moving again soon. I wondered once more why my cat hadn't transformed into his larger Splintercat form.

"What's wrong, Mr. Mittens?" I called out.

He shook his head like you did if you're disoriented. *The creature bit me*, he slurred into my mind.

"Uh oh."

It appears to have injected me with some kind of neurotoxin. I can't transform.

He wobbled. I wondered if it would kill him.

"Let's get you out of here," I said. "Before that thing comes after us again."

It's afraid of the light, he added, then fell over on his side.

A wave of fear ran through me. I didn't want anything bad to happen to my cat. What would I do without him?

The spider moved a leg. I blasted another wave of light magic, and the spider froze again, the hairs on its legs vibrating. I scooped up Mr. Mittens and held him like a baby. He was limp. Too limp. This wasn't the typical Ragdoll flop, this was boneless. I pressed my hand against his stomach, it rose and fell slightly, weakly. I raced up the stairs and slammed the door at the top.

"Megan, he's been bitten," I yelled as I raced forward through the kitchen and out the side door. "Let's go!"

She gasped but fell in behind me.

"Call the vet, see what we should do for a black widow bite," I called as we ran back towards the house.

"On it." She was punching things into her phone, then I saw her select and dial. She told the technician the issue and waited to be connected to the vet.

She was quiet, listening. Then she said, "OK," and hung up.

"He said, wash it with soap, put ice on the bite, and get him there ASAP, they are waiting with antivenin."

"Shit, I don't know if that thing had black widow venom, it wasn't natural!"

"I know. Hopefully, they have general medicine."

We were both huffing and puffing. Frankly, I walked around a lot, but I only ran if I was chased. Megan did some mild jogging some-times, so she was better off than I was, but I didn't want my cat to die. I dug in and kept on.

Mr. Mittens was moaning now—both in my mind and out loud. He was panting as well. Not good signs. We surged into the house. I washed the wound on his leg, and Megan grabbed ice. I snatched my purse and the keys, and we piled into my car and raced down the long drive to the main road and help.

CHAPTER
NINE

B y the time we pulled into the vet, Mr. Mittens's leg was swollen, he was salivating badly, and he was having muscle tremors. I rubbed his head, trying to give him comfort, but he was out of it.

A vet tech took him from me, shaved his other leg, and inserted an IV. The vet came in.

"Tell me what bit him," he asked, looking at me over his glasses.

"I'm not sure. I thought I saw a spider scurry away," I replied vaguely. I wanted to tell him, but he wouldn't believe me.

"The bite is large, but I only see one puncture hole, so hopefully, he didn't get a full venom load. It helps that he has a large body. Without knowing the spider, I don't know which antivenom to give."

I bit back a sob. "What can we do?"

"We treat the symptoms and hope he's strong."

I hugged myself and looked at Mr. Mittens. He was strong, right?

The vet put him on fluids and pain meds. Apparently, spider venom could create a lot of pain. That explained the groaning. I sat next to him and stroked his head. He was too strong for this, no way could a stupid spider bring him down. He fought unicorns and commanded dragons. I was gonna squash that spider thing—although it was probably over thirty pounds. I'd get a big ass boot. If I had too, I'd burn the house to the ground. I could bring in a manufactured home for the caretakers. No one wanted an infestation of spiders or venomous spider things.

We waited with him for hours. I'd cried until my eyes were almost swollen shut, and Megan wasn't much better. The vet and the tech constantly checked on him. They were about to move him into the back and kick us out when Mr. Mittens's eyes fluttered open.

I need to transform. A weak Mr. Mittens said into my mind. I bolted upright. I looked at the vet. He continued to frown at whatever he was looking at.

"Will it help?"

The vet gave me a strange look, and I cringed. I'd said that out loud.

Yes. My size will change, and the poison will disburse quicker.

"I'll get the vet out of here, unless you want to go home?" I replied to him in my mind, concentrating so my mind magic would work.

Yes. Home. His voice went quiet, and I saw he was asleep again.

"What are his chances if I take him home?" I asked the vet. My voice quavering.

"I can't promise anything. He'll be in pain once the meds wear off, and he'll need fluids. If you feel you can do that at home, he can go. But I don't recommend it."

The vet didn't understand I had a magical cat. But I had to do what I could to save my protector and friend. I nodded. "I'm gonna take him home. If anything changes, I'll bring him back. I just think he'll be happier there."

The vet's expression said he disapproved, but he didn't argue. He just nodded and had the vet tech prepare a take home kit with medication and a bag of Lactated Ringer's for subcutaneous fluids, which they showed me how to administer. I took the bag of stuff and handed it to Megan. I picked up and cradled Mr. Mitten's limp body gently in my arms, and we walked back to the car.

I shouldn't have taken him to the vet at all, but I was so scared. Megan was, too. He laid in my lap, limp as a wet rag. His breathing was rough and shallow, and his drool wet my leg. I was still scared, but I believed that transforming was better for him. He was magical. He had to get better.

When we got to the house, I took him in and laid him on my king-sized bed. He'd need the large space. He sighed when I laid him down but didn't awaken.

"Mr. Mittens, wake up," I said softly.

He moaned.

"Wake up," I said louder. Worried now that he hadn't stirred.

I looked at Megan; she frowned.

I was starting to panic.

I put a knee on the bed and shook him gently.

What? A grouchy voice croaked into my mind.

"We're home. You can transform," I answered.

He stretched out to his full length, and his body shimmered and went right back to his Ragdoll form.

"Mr. Mittens? Can you transform?" I asked nervously.

In answer, he rolled over and lay panting. Then, he pulled his feet up and stood, wobbling on the bed. He weaved back and forth as he tried to maintain his balance. His head hung low, and his eyes looked dull.

He shook his head. Panic gripped my heart. What if he couldn't do it? Would he die? I reached out a hand to steady him.

He huffed and shimmered again. This time when he failed, he collapsed back on his side, exhausted.

I need a minute, he said. *I'm weak.*

"What can I do for you?" I asked, willing to try anything so he could get better.

He was silent, and I panicked. I leaned in and put my hand on his side to see if he was still breathing. I wished with all my might he could transform and get well. Under my hand, his body grew. I stepped back, as the shimmer over his body exploded, and his Splintercat form lay panting on my bed, filling the entire thing.

Thank you, Brigid, he said. *I needed the boost.*

"I helped you?" I asked, surprised.

Yes. You lent me some of your magic. It was what I needed. Now I must rest. His panting had slowed, and his drooping eyes slammed shut.

I looked at Megan. She shrugged.

"I guess we're out of a bed tonight," she said with a wry smile on her face.

"Yeah, I guess so." I'd sleep in the car if it meant Mr. Mittens would get better, so I didn't care. We laughed—the stress leaving our bodies. I was shaking. I turned off the bedroom light and closed the door—not tight, in case he needed to get out in the night, but enough so the light and the noise from our talking wouldn't disturb him. His breathing had deepened, and he snored. I grinned, relieved, and followed Megan into the kitchen.

"Maybe your bed will be here tomorrow," I began.

She nodded. "Yeah, but we're out of luck today."

"No, we're in luck if Mr. Mittens is OK."

"You're right. I'm starving. Let's eat."

I nodded. As we ate, the exhaustion hit. It was late, and I had to get up and face my magic teacher, meet with Gabe, and come up with a plan to defeat the witches. I needed to rest. I didn't even have a couch to lay down on, and I doubted I could sleep on the hard floor and wake up refreshed.

"If you can stay with Mr. Mittens, I'm going to run to town and get us a couple of air mattresses," I said after we were done.

"Are you sure? I can go if you're too tired," Megan offered.

I shook my head. Even though I was exhausted, my mind buzzed, and I hoped the car ride would relax me. I'd take her with me, but I really didn't want Mr. Mittens to be left alone. I checked on him. He'd turned over. He was lying on his back, his front legs straight up, but relaxed paws flopped down, and his rear legs stretched out like a person. He was drooling on my pillow. His breathing was smoother, and his snoring had died down to deep breathing. I breathed a sigh of relief, grabbed my purse, and headed to the store.

CHAPTER
TEN

I picked out two of the best queen air mattresses sold at Freddie's and a box of pastries for my magic teacher and checked out. I took my packages to the car and loaded them up. I had coffee for the morning, so hopefully, this would be enough to keep me on Dana's good side.

It started to rain, hard, on the way home. That wasn't surprising, I lived in the temperate rainforest on the north central Oregon coast. I turned onto 101 and started south towards my house. As I passed through the green light crossing Highway 6, I saw a truck coming down it. I accelerated because it looked like he wasn't going to stop. He wasn't. He sped up. My heart hammered, and I screamed as I punched the accelerator. I couldn't get out of the way or maneuver in time. I had all of this magic, things were finally going my way, and I was about to die in a car accident. The truck bashed into the side of my car. My car bucked up and slid and spun across the road. I was yanked back and forth against my seat belt, and all the curtain airbags deployed.

I sat there, blinking. Trying to figure out what happened. Several cars stopped, and someone pounded on my window. I hit the button and rolled the window down. I must have still been stunned, because it took me a minute to decide what the woman was saying to me. Then, like a fog lifting, I heard her. "Are you OK?"

Was I? I blinked some more. I couldn't quite decide or get the words together. I was alive, that was good. I grabbed the door handle and opened the door. The woman came around it. She looked me over.

"I'm a nurse. I saw the wreck."

"OK," I said, finally finding my voice.

I unlatched the seat belt and swung my legs out. When I tried to stand, they wanted to buckle, but I tamed them and stood. I was sore, but nothing seemed broken, and I wasn't bleeding. My car was a mess though. The side was bashed in, and the wheels were canted from being pushed so hard across the street and into a curb. I frowned at it. I was swaying, I think, because someone grabbed my arm and maneuvered me, so I was sitting in the driver's seat again.

"Thanks." I looked around. "What happened?" I asked next.

The lady helping me frowned. "That truck was going fast. Way too fast. It sped off after hitting you. The guy over there..." She pointed. "Called the cops."

Once she said that, I noticed the sirens, and the crowds of looky-loos watching me from the sidewalk, a few with phones taking pics. I blushed, suddenly embarrassed by all the attention.

"Umm, I've got to go," I said to the lady, and moved to swing my legs in and start up the car.

"Honey, you aren't going anywhere. That car is done for, and you are not thinking straight."

I remembered the car and nodded. I put my hand up to my head and felt a huge lump on the side of my forehead. When the truck hit me, I must have smacked it on the side window. Or the curtain airbag had hit me. I didn't know. "Ok," I said.

The police and ambulance arrived. The police took witness statements and asked me what happened. I told them the best I could remember. Then the ambulance put me on their stretcher, loaded me up, and checked me out before transporting me to the small hospital in town. I had one of them call Megan.

Once there, they did all the doctor things, including a CT of my head to check for a concussion. It was clear. I was surprised, because I knew I was still goofy and acting erratically. I hated that Megan had to leave Mr. Mittens to come and get me, and I had her wait an hour before she came so I would be cleared and ready to leave. Luckily it was a slow night at the ER, and I was treated quickly. By the time Megan arrived to pick me up, I'd been released and some of the events came flooding back to me.

Megan was quiet until we got in her car. Apparently, mine was totaled.

"What happened?" she asked softly after I told her my head was pounding.

I looked at her for a moment and then back to the road. I was shivering, the aftereffects hitting me hard. "I was just going through the light."

I looked at the oncoming headlights and shrunk back against the door. She reached out and gripped my hand.

"It was a big crew cab F-350. I saw it at the last moment. When I realized, it wasn't going to stop for the light, I punched the accelerator. I think it was planning to hit my door." I looked at her. "Whoever there were was trying to kill me."

Megan's knuckles turned white on the wheel. "That son of a whore."

I chuckled. "Yeah."

"Did you see the driver at all?"

I thought back. Yes, I did. At the last moment, once I knew I wasn't going to avoid a collision, I saw his face clearly. It was the kicker from the night the witches stole my ice magic.

"That sadistic bastard!" I said loud enough that Megan jumped.

"Who?"

"The guy that hit me is the same cruel bastard that beat me up before you got here. A freaking witch!"

She huffed, angrily. "What's their problem?"

"Sofia," I answered simply. "I'm probably on the coven's hit list."

"Don't they need you alive to steal your magic?" she asked.

I shrugged. I didn't know. Something to ask Dana tomorrow. I slumped. Dana. How was I going to do a magic lesson with the Fae teacher from hell?

I must have groaned.

"What's wrong?" Megan asked anxiously, expecting me to collapse from my injuries on the ride home. I was sore and battered, but not really injured, not like the witches had done to me before.

"I have a magic lesson tomorrow, and I don't know if I can do it."

"Oh."

"Yeah."

"Well, I got all your stuff out of the car before I came over, so at least you can sleep comfortably!"

That jolted me. "How's Mr. Mittens?" I asked belatedly.

"He was still snoring when I left."

"Good." I breathed out in relief. "I don't think I'm thinking straight."

Megan barked out a laugh. "Really?"

"You aren't very funny," I grumped. I pressed my fingers to the side of my head, feeling the nice sized lump. "My brains got a good sloshing."

She sobered. "I know. That must have been so scary."

"I don't think I was. Scared I mean. It happened too fast. I only had time to accelerate, and that saved my life. The truck hit the side behind me, instead of into me."

"Yeah, the car was smushed behind your door. I had to get everything out of the back from the passenger side," she agreed.

"I liked that car. I'm adding it to the list of items that I'm taking out of Sofia's hide."

"You do that. She's seriously making her way onto my list, too." Megan sniffed.

She reached out a hand and squeezed mine when I slipped it into hers. I smiled at her. She turned onto the long gravel drive up to the house, and after she parked, I hurried in to check on Mr. Mittens.

He was still asleep, but he'd rolled over, so his legs weren't in the air. He was on his side, his breath sounded normal now, and I breathed a sigh of relief. He'd make it. I brushed a cautious swipe down his spotted fur, and he twitched slightly, but didn't awaken.

I walked out and partially shut the door so he could have as much quiet as possible.

"I'm going to call Luke," Megan said.

"Because of the wreck?" I was baiting her a little. She probably just wanted to talk to him.

"Yeah, if the witches are going after you, that means Sofia is up to something, and they might know what," she replied.

That actually made sense. I really wasn't thinking clearly. She called and let Luke know, and he said that the wolves would check it out.

Megan and I made up our beds in the huge entryway, and exhausted, I fell asleep.

CHAPTER

ELEVEN

I awoke and rolled off the air mattress onto my hands and knees. I struggled to my feet, every muscle in my body screaming. The wreck must have jostled me around more than I thought. I stretched slowly. It took the walk to the bathroom and into the kitchen before I could walk without shuffling.

I brushed my hair and teeth, got a cup of coffee and a pastry. In the middle of my breakfast, a flash of light announced the entrance of Dana.

"Are you ready?" she asked imperiously.

I sighed and waved at the pastries. Her eyes lit up at the treats, and she selected one with a sigh of pleasure. I grinned, facing away from her so she wouldn't see. She wolfed it down along with two more.

"This realm has delightful food," she remarked.

"We do have good pastries," I said.

She gave herself time to enjoy one more before barking at me to move out.

When I groaned involuntarily as I stood, she frowned at me. "What is wrong?" She spoke sharply.

"Witches keep trying to kill me," I answered truthfully.

Her face reflected rage, her green skin blushing darkly, her eyes narrowing. "Who is this witch?" Her voice was deeper and more resonant.

"The same one that kicked my ass a week ago. A member of the coven that is trying to steal my magic."

She grew quiet, thoughtful. "Then we shall, what did you say? Kick their asses first."

That's what I was talking about.

Megan looked at me, her eyes wide. She mouthed over the Kelpie's head, "What the hell?"

I shrugged. "OK," I said.

I checked on Mr. Mittens before we left for the waterfall. He stretched and hopped off the bed from his huge Splintercat form into his Ragdoll.

I'm hungry, he muttered.

"Megan is making your breakfast right now. I have a date with my magic teacher. We'll be at the waterfall."

When you return, I request your assistance in destroying the creature that bit me.

I nodded, wondering what I could do, but I owed that spider thing a good smoosh with my boot.

As we walked to the waterfall, Dana asked me what happened. I gave her a blow by blow. Of course, that required that I explain what a car and truck were which was interesting. I agreed to take her for a ride after our lesson.

Today wasn't as beautiful as the day before. The sky was overcast and threatened to rain.

Dana had been deep in thought during the second half of the walk after my tale. Just before we took the turn off the trail to the waterfall, we stopped at the spring for a drink. A red snake lay next to it, his eyes alert, looking at me for permission to speak.

"Hello, Goch, how are you today?" I asked politely with a side glance at Dana to gauge her reaction to the bright red serpent.

She held her hands aloft, as though she were going to smite the creature.

"Stop!" I yelled at her, and she glared at me.

"That creature is masking his true form."

"I know. He's a dragon. I've asked him to use his snake form around strangers."

"Hmmm."

"Goch, you may show your true form to Dana. She is a Kelpie from the Fae realm."

"Half," Dana added.

I nodded. I didn't think that Goch cared, I just wanted him to know she wasn't human.

He unfurled to his full length and grew into his immense dragon form. "Thank you, Lady Brigid," he said in his eager to please voice.

"It's just Brigid. How may I help you, Goch?" I asked, staring up and up into his face.

"Brightfeather told me about the witches and asked me to report to you if I saw any strange humans come onto your land."

"What did you see?" I asked, becoming concerned. Were those damned witches still sneaking onto my land?

"Two were looking around the house earlier this morning."

"Oh?" I sure hoped he didn't eat anyone. Unless it was Sofia. But it could be someone like a meter reader or something, and I wasn't sure how to explain that to the power company.

"Were they in a car or truck?" I asked.

He looked at me for a minute. "I don't know what that is."

Right, magical creature. Why would he know the terms car and truck?

"Thanks, Goch. You did the right thing by letting me know."

His eyes lit up. He was so eager to please, and he ate up the praise. "I'll keep an eye out!"

I smiled up at him. He leapt up and flew off, the dust and forest detritus swirling up around us.

"You have a dragon?" Dana asked, flatly.

"I don't own him, but he's welcome on my land. He's just a kid," I added, quickly.

"Dragons are very useful creatures," she said, the light of avarice burning in her eyes.

"What do you mean?" I was growing concerned with the way she watched Goch fly off, and I was worried she would try something that would harm the young dragon. I vowed to keep her and the dragon separate when she was here.

"No matter." She brushed it away. "Let's go to your seat of power."

It may not matter to her, but now I had to think of ways to keep Goch away from her. I didn't want him to be injured or killed because of me. He'd come to me for help.

We finished the journey to the waterfall, and I prepared myself for another mentally draining day making tiny gains.

"Do you have access to shadow magic?" she asked.

"I do, but I don't know how to use it."

"If the witches are making attempts on your life, it would be best to skip elemental control and move into shielding first and then offensive magic."

Yes! I thought that would be amazing, but I just nodded at Dana.

"Shadow is the perfect shield," she added.

I looked away for a moment and when I looked back, Dana was gone. "Dana?" I asked, confused.

"Yes?" Her voice hadn't moved from where she was, but she was not visible.

Her form popped back into my vision.

"Was that shadow magic?" I asked, amazed.

"Yes."

"How does it work?"

"Shadows are naturally concealing. So, the magic just enhances that quality. Let your shadow magic envelope you in its warm embrace, and you'll fade from view."

We practiced for our allotted time, and finally, I was able to call up and wrap myself in shadow so completely that Dana pronounced me, "adequate." I expected Dana to disappear in a flash, but instead she stood and stared at me. Right, she wanted to ride in a "metal beast of burden." I nodded in silent agreement and headed back home to face that and all the other tasks of the day.

I opened my back door and called for Mr. Mittens. Megan's car was gone, so I assumed she'd gone to town on an errand. Since my vehicle was wrecked, I couldn't take Dana until Megan returned. I made some lunch for the three of us, Dana, myself, and my cat, and before we finished eating, a delivery van arrived. Mattresses. Dana agreed to stay in the kitchen out of view, while the delivery guys hauled several mattresses up the stairs and laid them on the awaiting beds. One step closer to opening my magical B&B. Megan's mattress was a couple of orders of magnitude nicer than the guest ones, and the delivery guys placed it on the bed frame in her newly cleaned and organized room.

I looked around. We were so close. A few more items to cross off in the guest rooms, but I had a list of handymen to call for those, and the house was done. Now to get a crew for the creature quarters, but before that could be done, we had to rid ourselves of a nasty venomous beastie.

Megan came back soon after the mattress guys left, and I showed her my new trick.

"That's the coolest!" she exclaimed. "You can turn invisible!"

"Not really, I'm just cloaked."

"Like the Predator?"

I frowned. "You watched those movies?" I asked. "I thought you only watched rom-coms and action flicks."

"I watch sci-fi and fantasy movies too."

"Uh, the last time I asked you to go with me, you said, and I quote, 'It's too scary. I'll have nightmares.'"

"I got over it."

"Uh huh."

"OK, you caught me. When I told you that, I had a blind date, and I didn't want to tell you in case it was a total disaster."

"Was it?"

"Yes, that's why you don't know about it," she huffed.

"That's ridiculous. As your best friend, you can't deny me the right to mock and denigrate a terrible blind date."

"In my defense, you were distracted by your divorce, I was sparing you from the disaster of my own love life."

"What about Luke?" I asked suddenly.

She blushed. "He asked me out for Friday, if everything goes well tonight with the Gabe thing and there's nothing else going on."

I smiled at her; a thrill of excitement ran through me for my friends. They'd be so cute together. "I'm excited for you, Luke is great."

"Thanks. It'll be weird knowing I'm dating a guy who transforms into a giant wolf, but it's also sort of exciting, like the ultimate bad boy."

"I get that." I nodded at her. It was true, you got the bad boy who treated you well. The perfect man. Couldn't beat that. Then, because Dana was watching our interaction and glaring at me, I asked, "Can I borrow your car?"

"Sure, why?"

"I promised Dana a ride. She's never been in a car."

"I thought Fae couldn't be near 'cold iron'?"

I looked at Dana. "Are you alright being inside an iron beast?" I rolled my eyes inwardly that I had to say that.

"I'm only half Fae," she said stiffly.

That didn't answer my question, but I didn't dare ask her anything else.

"OK, let's go." Megan tossed me her keys, and I led Dana out to the car.

I walked to the driver's side, and Dana followed me. Ugh. I walked her around to the passenger side and showed her how to open the door, where to sit, and how to buckle the seat belt. Then I went back to the driver's side and climbed in.

"I'm gonna push this button," I said demonstrating, but not pushing. "Once I do, the engine will start, and you'll hear it and feel it through the seat. Are you ready?"

She nodded. Her hands gripped the side of the seat, and she looked frightened—an expression I doubt her face had ever made. I pushed the button, and the engine roared to life.

Dana stiffened and jerked in surprise.

I laughed to myself and started rolling slowly around the house to the long gravel drive. I went very slow, maybe fifteen miles an hour. I couldn't really go too fast on the drive. Once I hit to the road, I turned left and sped up to fifty. Dana pressed herself into the seat as far as she could and started screaming, "Stop!"

I pulled over. "Are you alright?" I asked, my heart pounding.

"That was so fast. How is this possible?" She looked shaken. Her hands quaked, and her lips trembled with fear.

"It's not magic. It's technology."

"I don't know that word, tech-no-logy," she repeated slowly.

"It means we are good at building machines."

She nodded. Then in a flash, she disappeared. I guessed she was done with the driving lesson. I shrugged, flipped a u-ey, and returned to the house.

Once I got back, I opened the back door.

Megan looked up at me. "Where's Dana?"

I shrugged. "She didn't handle the car very well, she left."

Megan went to the back door and pulled on her high rubber boots.

"Well, you ready to go squash a nasty spider?"

I pointed to my hiking boot encased feet. "Sure am."

"What's the plan?" Megan asked.

"We go in, find it, squish it, and burn the place to the ground."

"How about we just set it on fire from outside the house?"

"I like how you think." I shuddered. I really didn't want to see that thing again, and none of us could afford a bite. It had almost taken out my Splintercat, and I didn't think anything could do that.

I don't think you can burn it, my cat added.

"Why not?" I asked.

"I think it's a Xkrgny."

"A what?"

He huffed. *A soul spider.*

"That means nothing to me." I looked at Megan.

"Me either."

We looked at him expectantly.

Hmpf. He sat and laid his tail gracefully around his feet, the shaved spot on his leg a stark contrast against his usual fluffy perfection. *A creature that can vary its presence between here and elsewhere.*

That was as clear as mud.

"Um, I still don't understand," I said.

It can slip in between realms with a thought. It's difficult to kill because it can phase from material to immaterial.

"Good hell." I put my hands on my hips and paced. "How do we kill it then?"

We must catch it when it is solidly here, he said, like it was an easy thing to do.

So armed with our cowardice, we headed out. Mr. Mittens in the lead, his floofy tail blowing in the gentle breeze.

CHAPTER

TWELVE

Instead of the cute farmhouse I'd seen the first time, the house had a sinister air. I shivered. This was all in my head. That spider thing, whatever Mr. Mittens had called it, was still there, haunting the place—apparently in more ways than one. I guess it sort of was a ghost since it could go immaterial at a whim.

We stopped and stared at the house before we marched up the few steps to the front door and pushed inside. I removed the realtor box. We'd left in such a hurry before, that it wasn't locked. I put my hand on the knob of the basement door. "Are you ready?" I asked my two companions.

I got a nod from Megan and a "*yes*" from Mr. Mittens. I twisted the knob, and the door swung open with a creak. That didn't add to the atmosphere at all. I shivered again.

I stared into the darkness of the basement. We were better prepared today, we wore headlamps, and I immediately added my light magic to act like the missing light bulbs. The basement was quiet. Where was the ugly spider?

I stepped down the wooden stairs, the creaky door was backed up with creepy creaky stairs as well. If we got rid of the spider creature, this would make a great haunted house. My heart was pounding in my ears. Megan put her hand on my shoulder, and I jumped.

"Sorry," she whispered.

"It's OK," I replied. But my skin crawled, and I resisted the urge to run my fingers through my hair and scratch all over. Images of invisible spiders and creepy crawlies flashed through my mind. My "ick" factor was on high alert.

Mr. Mittens brought up the rear, even he was being cautious after almost dying. I heard skittering, and my head whipped towards the sound in the darkest corner of the basement behind the stairs. I sped up. If it snuck up between the stairs, we wouldn't see it until it was too late.

We made it to the concrete floor and spread out, our headlamps piercing the gloom as we searched every dark corner. I whirled when I caught an old box moving out of the corner of my eye. "There!" I pointed.

The box stilled. We all faced it. "Maybe you should transform," I whispered to Mr. Mittens.

The space is too small, I can't maneuver as well in my natural form, he replied.

It would be tight, but I was freaked out about him almost dying. "Are you sure?"

Hmpf.

Where was the damn spider? I swept my head back and forth, trying to illuminate the space with my headlamp. Nothing. Had it phased? A cold feeling of being watched prickled the back of my neck, and I whirled. That creepy creature had phased behind us. Everyone else either reacted because I did or felt they were being watched as well, because they also turned, and the spider was there looking at us. It was easily the same size as Mr. Mittens in his Ragdoll form although with longer spider legs. To make it worse, it had ten legs rather than eight. Because more legs made it less creepy, right? Wrong.

It hissed at us and spat something that was yellowish green. The glob shot forward about three feet, falling short of us and hissing as it struck the concrete. Great, it was venomous and spit acid. What other nasty tricks did it have? I had a strange thought and sent out a mental call. Maybe we already had help available.

How were we going to fight this thing? We had no weapons, no ability to stop it from phasing, and it could poison us or melt us with acid. I looked at Megan. She'd always had overdeveloped arachnophobia, and she appeared frozen. I reached out a hand and squeezed hers in comfort.

The spider thing faded from view. "Maybe we should stand back-to-back," I suggested, and Mr. Mittens and Megan hurried forward, and we stood in a triangle form so we could observe the room.

"There!" Megan yelled, and sure enough the spider materialized in front of her. It stalked forward until it was in range with its acid spit, and Megan jumped out of the way just in time. It faded again.

"This was a bad idea," I said to my companions.

"Yeah," Megan agreed. Her shoulder brushed mine, and I could feel her tremble.

If we can anticipate where it will show, we'll get it, Mr. Mittens said.

"Uh…How?" I asked, but we didn't have time to worry because it appeared again. Once again, we jumped out of the way just in time. I swear the creature was playing with us, probably laughing or whatever spiders did when they found something funny.

It kept fading and reappearing, but it made a mistake. It was forming a pattern. Once it faded out again, I said, "Next time it appears, I'm going to try to hit it with my fire magic."

I got a quiet assent. We were starting to get tired.

The spider appeared, and I sent a ball of flame at it. Its four eyes widened slightly, but it faded quickly.

"Damn!" I've got to anticipate it!

I'll attempt to jump on its back, if I'm holding it down, maybe you'll get enough time to set it on fire, Mr. Mittens offered.

"I don't want to set you on fire," I responded.

I will heal faster from that than from its venom.

I cringed but nodded. "It's going to appear in front of Megan in three, two…" Mr. Mittens maneuvered to where he could easily pounce, and the spider creature began to fade in. The second before it was perfectly solid, Mr. Mittens launched his large house cat body and came down directly on the back of the shiny black carapace. The spider body sunk to the ground, its legs splayed, and I hit it with the hottest fire I could conjure. The spider screamed an eerie squealing rasp like metal being twisted and torn. Mr. Mittens leaped away and rolled the flames from his fur. I applied more fire.

The screaming stopped, and the creature melted into the concrete— black sludge and green goo being consumed by the white-hot flame.

"Awesome!" Megan exclaimed.

I shuddered but turned to her to take the fist bump.

"Mr. Mittens, is the house clean? Are there any other nasty creatures here?" The bottom line was I didn't really want to burn the house to the foundation, but I would if there was another nasty beastie here.

His eyes went still, and his inner eyelids partially closed. His little grey nose wiggled a little as he sniffed.

I don't believe so, he answered after a few minutes. *However, all I can smell is fried Xkrgny.*

"I'll take it. A fried one is better than a live one."

On that, we all agreed. We did a thorough search of the basement, overturning boxes and looking behind shelves. We found a few regular spiders and insects, but no more soul spiders. We took another turn through the house, searching for more nasties, but it appeared clean. I breathed a sigh of relief, and we went back to the house for the next task—meeting with Gabe.

On the walk back, a dragon landed in the pasture by the dairy.

"Goch!" I said, in surprise, then remembered I'd sent for him. "We handled it, sorry I called you for nothing."

My lady, there are a couple of humans at your house. Come quickly! he said, proud that he could warn me.

I thanked him, and he flew off, promising to be near, but out of sight. The three of us ran back to the house.

THIRTEEN

W e arrived panting. There was a van parked in the gravel area behind the house next to Megan's red SUV. Two men stood on the back porch. I paused and Megan stopped with me. Mr. Mittens stood behind a tree, keeping an eye on the intruders and growling softly.

Before we stepped out of the woods and into view, I examined them. One of the men, who was short, but stockily built, scanned the yard. He had dark hair and a darker complexion, probably Hispanic. The other had his back to us. He was taller, well-built, muscular, and had white-blond hair. I froze. Scott. It had to be.

"I think the blond is Scott," I said to Megan. "I wonder what he's doing here."

"Scott, the asshole?" Megan asked.

"Yeah."

I suggest that you go back to the farm. I'll deal with the intruders, Mr. Mitten snarled.

I couldn't let that happen. Scott was a bastard, but he wasn't anywhere near Sofia's level of evil and didn't deserve a full on Splintercat confrontation. He had no protection. He was a witch, but not one strong enough to wield magic.

"It's OK," I said to my cat. "I'll go see what he wants. You guys stay here in case something is hinky."

Megan nodded. It took a little more soothing before Mr. Mittens agreed. I stepped out of the trees and walked towards the house.

Once the other guy saw me, he elbowed Scott who turned and waved at me. I frowned. We weren't that friendly anymore, but he had kept his word after he promised me. I wondered what he wanted.

Once I was close enough, he took a step towards me and said, "Hi, Brigid."

"Hi," I said warily back. "Who's your buddy?"

Scott looked at his companion as though he'd forgotten about him. "Oh, this is Jorge, he works for me."

Jorge nodded and held out his hand. I looked at it, but then I grasped his hand and shook it cautiously.

"What do you want, Scott?" I didn't make any effort to keep the disdain out of my voice.

"Umm, well…" He thought for a moment. "I'm sorry my crew and I weren't back after the thing with my cousin, but it wasn't my fault. She forbade me to come back. I just wanted to apologize and see if you still wanted us to finish up. This is *my* business, and I don't have anything to do with her anymore."

I shook my head. I didn't trust him as far as I could throw him. "I don't think so. Send your final bill, and I think we don't ever have to see one another again," I said firmly.

Scott looked down, and I think he truly looked contrite. "I really am sorry. I let her blind me. I was stupid. I hope you can forgive me someday. I brought Jorge because I thought you might say that. He's a good dude. He doesn't know anything about…um…Sofia or her… dealings. So, if you don't want me, please consider him. He's trying to set up on his own business, and he's a good guy. Just consider this a peace offering. Again, I'm sorry."

This was weird. Why would he bring this guy? He had to be nuts to think I'd let anyone associated with him back into my life.

"Here's his resume. I helped him because his English isn't that great." He handed me a creamy sheet of paper. "Come on." He gestured to Jorge, and both of them climbed into the van. Scott waved as they turned and drove down the drive. I clutched the paper, wrinkling it in my hand. I gasped. What was I doing? Why would I touch anything he'd hand me? I started to shake with fear. Then, I searched my feelings, had anything changed? Not that I could tell. I reached out with my magic. Was the paper imbued with a spell or a potion? I didn't feel anything except fury building.

Megan and Mr. Mittens slunk out of the woods and joined me at the back porch. I sat down and stared at the paper in my hands. It was indeed a resume with all of Jorge's building and restoration experience, nothing more. Why did I get all the strange ones? Why had Scott brought him by, and did he really expect me to hire him? I wadded the paper into a ball and clutched it in my hands.

"That was weird," Megan said as she sat next to me. "I couldn't hear it all, but Mr. Mittens filled me in. He really had the balls to ask you to take on a guy that worked for him? Is he nuts?"

I nodded, still stunned. "Yeah."

"Alrighty then."

I shook it off and stood. I walked into the house, tossing the paper in the recycle bin.

"What time are we meeting the werewolves?" I asked Megan, since she'd been the one coordinating with Luke.

"Luke said to be ready, he'd call once Sofia left."

"OK."

I stepped wearily into the house. I grabbed a glass and filled it with water from the fancy fridge and drank it.

Megan was watching me oddly. "He really did a number on you, didn't he?" she asked.

"Yup. And I let him." I rolled the cool glass over my forehead. "I knew better. After everything with Evan, I should have been more wary."

"You can't blame yourself. You were drugged or magicked or whatever. Not your fault."

"Doesn't stop me feeling like this."

"Yeah, I know. Sorry." She looked miserable. "I just hate seeing you like this. Look at all you've accomplished on your own." She waved at the house. "You discovered your magic and became a badass. You don't have any reason to feel bad."

Even though it shouldn't have, her speech buoyed me a little from the depression I felt coming on. She was right. It wasn't my fault, and I could take care of myself. I had friends now. True ones. Mr. Mittens, Megan, the Whelans, Brightfeather, Goch, and Gabe—as soon as I freed him. My old life was done. I didn't even need to look back at it. I could move forward.

I sat in the kitchen chair and finished my water. "Thanks, Megan." I put all of my love and gratitude for her into that simple phrase. She leaned over the chair and hugged me.

Her phone rang. She stood back up and pulled it from her back pocket. She looked at the screen. "It's go time," she said, then answered the phone. "Hey, Luke."

I couldn't hear the other side, but they didn't talk for very long. Megan's face was serious and angry. She hung up.

"There's a problem," she said. "We've gotta go now."

My heart accelerated. "What's wrong?"

"I'll tell you on the way, let's go."

I followed her out the door. Mr. Mittens jumped up on the balcony rail. "Are you coming?" I asked.

I do not have much power away from this land, he reminded me with a head shake.

"I know, but you are always welcome to be with me."

His chest puffed up a little, and I could see that my statement made him proud.

Be safe, pet.

I patted his head as I passed and headed down the porch stairs. "I will. See you soon."

I climbed in the passenger side, and Megan turned the car and headed down the drive.

Once we were on the way, I repeated my question. "What's wrong?"

"It appears that Sofia did have a plan for Gabe during her two-day trip. She encased Gabe in ice. Madison must have tried to stop her, because she is also frozen in a block of ice."

I gasped, involuntarily. "What?"

Megan shrugged. "That's what Luke said over the phone. He was in a panic. I said we'd get there as soon as possible."

"I don't know how to thaw anyone out safely!"

"Well, you have between here and Gabe's to think of something."

That sent me back down the rabbit hole of self-doubt. If Sofia froze Gabe, she must have a safe way to unfreeze him. I doubt she'd leave him like that forever. If she wanted him dead, there were easier, less obvious ways. I didn't think she wanted that though. In some sick way, she had a thing for him.

Good grief. I was a beginning magic user, not a powerful well-trained witch. How was I going to do this? I mulled it over, becoming more and more agitated as we drew closer. I had no way to contact Dana for help, calling my grandfather required the moon at its zenith and a ridiculous ritual. I didn't dare just try to melt them or set them on fire. I could kill them.

I guess I needed to assess the issue first. We pulled into Gabe's driveway and around to the back of the house where the parking area was. I climbed out. The Whelans were there, milling around the back-yard. As we approached, I could see that the reason the Whelans were agitated. They were looking all around Madison who stood unmoving with a thin film of ice surrounding her.

I joined the family members. "When did this happen?"

Noah stepped forward. "Sometime in the last hour. It was her shift to watch Gabe. When we didn't get a report within thirty minutes, and no answer on her phone, Luke came out to check on her and found this." He gestured to Madison's frozen form.

"Gabe is inside."

I followed Noah into the house. Gabe stood frozen in place, leaning against the kitchen counter staring off into his adjoining living room. He was the same—frozen in place with a thin barrier of ice encasing him. Luke was staring at the Gabe statue, examining everything he could to find a way to thaw the two people.

I joined him in looking up close at Gabe. His eyes were staring straight ahead, but something was odd. I reached into my back pocket and flicked on my phone flashlight. Then, I shined the light in Gabe's eyes. Slowly, his pupils shrunk in response to the bright light directed at them.

"Did you see that?" I asked.

"Yeah," Luke said. His face inches from mine as he stared into Gabe's eyes.

"They're still alive and reacting, if very slowly."

"So, what do we do?" Luke asked. Noah moved closer to hear the answer.

"Umm, I don't know. I'm afraid if we thaw them too quickly, it'll hurt them somehow—burn them or something, and I don't know how dangerous that would be. If we do it too slowly, they might suffer from hypothermia. I just don't know!"

I started to panic, to breathe too fast, and my heart pounded. I didn't want to be responsible for this decision. I wasn't a medical professional or a competent magic user.

Luke put his hand on my shoulder. "We'll put our heads together, come on, let's go outside with everyone else."

I nodded, grateful, and followed the werewolves out to the statue of Madison. Once outside, I needed to determine if Madison was also reacting and alive in her case of ice.

"Has anyone noticed any reaction?" I asked the family standing around and studying her.

They shook their heads. I tried the light thing with Madison, but she was in the sun, and her pupils were already pinpricks. I ran back in the house and grabbed Gabe's jacket from a hook inside the back door. I put it over Madison's head and waited for one minute which I timed on my phone. After the minute ended, I yanked off the coat and studied her eyes. I breathed a sigh of relief. "Her pupils have expanded. She's alive," I announced.

The family seemed to sag in relief. That was the immediate concern, that she was alive in the ice. The second one was how to free her from it while keeping her unharmed.

Luke ran inside. We followed. He dug through the kitchen drawers and came out with one of those long stick lighters for candles, or barbecue grills. Before I could stop him, he held it up to Gabe's arm, clicked it on, and let the flame touch the thin barrier of ice. I gasped. He held it there long enough the thin ice should have melted, and the flame should have caught his sleeve on fire. But nothing happened.

"Regular fire doesn't do anything. It might have to be magic fire," Luke said.

Megan and the Whelan's all stared at me. I swallowed, the blood rushing out of my head. I swayed.

I stumbled back outside, sucking in air so I didn't pass out from the weight of the family's need to save their sister and daughter.

I stopped by Madison's frozen body.

Anna, the Whelans' mother, came over to me. She placed a comforting hand on my arm and looked me in the eye. "This is a lot of pressure, Brigid. We know. Whatever you decide, we'll support you." That was a brave thing for the girl's mother to say, but it added to the pressure instead of relieving it.

I smiled weakly. "I wish I had a book or guide that went with all of this, but I don't. Whatever decision we make, I'll have to live with it."

I explained the dilemma about either burning them or causing hypothermia. After much discussion, they decided that burning them would be best, because if we awakened Gabe, he could heal them both. Whereas hypothermia would be scarier if we couldn't get Gabe active and aware quickly. I nodded, still too terrified to try. I wished Mr. Mittens had come, his presence always reassured me and gave me confidence.

What I really needed was advice from someone with Fae magic like mine. Even though a witch had done this, she'd done it with my ice magic. I didn't know if that changed the use or how to undo it, but it had to factor in. I explained my reasoning to the Whelans.

When they didn't appear moved, I added. "I can call my grandfather at the moon's zenith."

"We don't know how safe it is to keep them in this state," Noah argued.

I looked at him and realized my hands were clasped together. I let them fall. "No, but Sofia wants Gabe alive and well, so I assume they'll be safe for two days at least. If I can wake them up tonight, we'll still have time to make plans with Gabe," I replied.

Noah stared at me for a second, and then the Whelans spoke amongst themselves while I waited with Megan.

Finally, they came back. "We can wait, it's probably safer if we have guidance from someone familiar with this magic," Noah said. Then he pointed to Michael and Luke. "Let's get Madison in the house, out of the sun in case that does anything weird to her or melts her too soon."

The boys picked up their frozen sister gently and placed her in the kitchen next to Gabe. I didn't notice any water or evidence the warmth from the house was melting Gabe, so maybe the magical ice would hold up to natural heat and sunlight as well as to flame. I didn't know. When Sofia had made an ice wall to block me from attacking her, I'd melted it with my fire magic without any effort. I didn't dare do that to people, but I was afraid that was what it would come down to.

Anna decided to stay and guard her daughter and Gabe, and the rest of the wolves, Megan, and I went back to the house to wait for the moonrise and another call to my grandfather for help. I hoped he was in a good mood.

CHAPTER
FOURTEEN

L uke and the other Whelan's looked at me strangely when I explained the ridiculous ritual. When I googled when the moon would be at its zenith, it was early in the evening, 5:16 p.m. It would still be light. That would be a change. It also didn't give us much time to prepare. So, after I explained what would happen, I quickly gathered the supplies I needed and hurried out to the altar.

Megan decided to stay behind with the Whelans at my house. Mr. Mittens accompanied me because he insisted on "protecting" me from my own woods. It was a good idea since I still wasn't over the unicorn incident.

I set up the altar and danced my dance before I said the stupid rhyme. I felt better this time, and the movement didn't hurt. At the end of the chant, my grandfather, without a delay, appeared in a blaze of light. He wasn't dressed for war this time, but he was still grumpy.

"Why did you summon me?" he demanded, his voice thunderous in the still clearing.

"Forgive me, grandfather. I don't have any way to contact you or Dana, and I have a pressing magical emergency," I said, nervously.

"Well, what is it, child? I cannot stay long," he answered and crossed his huge muscle-bound arms over his equally muscle hard torso.

Mr. Mittens jumped up on the altar and folded his tail neatly around his legs, watching with his luminous blue eyes. It started to mist. I shivered.

"Umm, the witch that stole my magic, used my ice to freeze two of my friends into statues." I opened my phone and showed him the pictures of Gabe and Madison encased in their thin veil of ice.

He held the phone with a frown, examined the device carefully—as though it was going to burn him—and finally looked at the photos. I flipped the page back and forth so he could view both victims.

"What is this clever device?" he asked.

"It's a smart phone. A small computer that allows me to make phone calls and access the internet. It also acts as a camera, and lots of other things."

"Phones when I was last here were simple machines," he intoned. "I do not understand computer?"

"Yes, phones have changed a lot in the last few years." I put the phone back in my pocket and looked up at him. I had no idea how to explain a computer, so I ignored that part of his statement. "What about my frozen friends? Is there a way to unfreeze them safely?"

"Yes, we should conclude our business quickly. I can explore the changes in this realm later. As for unfreezing them, there are two possibilities. You melt them with your fire magic, or you reverse your ice magic."

I opened my mouth to interrupt him and remind him I'd lost the ice magic, but he put up a hand to stop me. "I know the issues with your ice magic. The fire magic is a difficult one, as you'll have to be careful not to burn your friends. You will need to apply a thin layer of magical fire to the ice and melt it swiftly. As soon as the ice is gone, you should place your friends in a warm bath and bring their body temperatures up swiftly."

I cringed, terrified that I would either burn them or not get their core temperatures up in time. "Is there no other way?" I asked, hope flaring at his "reverse the ice magic" statement.

"If you wish to wait a day or two, I can have my mistress of magic attempt the task; however, I warn you that she will not be as worried about damage to their frail mortal shells as you will be."

That was the problem. At least I'd been on the right track, and I knew there was no other way out of this mess.

"Is that all, child?" he asked. I was surprised at how reasonable he was being after being summoned against his will.

"Grandfather, is there another way to contact you or Dana if I have a need? This way requires time, and some things are time sensitive."

He tilted his head in thought. "I will think on it. My mistress of magic will bring you the answer."

Without even a goodbye, he vanished in a flare of light. I sighed wearily. Mr. Mittens hadn't said anything, and I was surprised, although he and my grandfather had shared a quick glance, and perhaps a quick mental word.

"Did he say anything to you?" I asked him as we walked back to the house.

Nothing pertinent to the problem, he responded.

"Was it about me?"

It was...personal.

I looked at my cat. He didn't seem upset or worried, so maybe it had just been a greeting or catch up between friends. Maybe someday he would fill me in on his backstory and how he became trapped in this realm as my protector.

Suddenly, a thought came to me. I'd assumed that my grandfather and my cat were friends, maybe their relationship was different than that. "Are you friends with my grandfather?"

We are friendly, he answered or evaded. I wasn't sure, but his tone implied he didn't want to talk about it. I let it go. Not my focus at the moment. Now, I had to perform precise magic that could end in the maiming or death of one or both of my friends.

The house was full of nervous werewolves and Megan. They all waited impatiently to hear what the answer to our problem would be. I still wasn't sure what to do. Should I attempt to thaw them? Should I depend on Dana to show tomorrow morning and have her do it for me?

331

Or just have her close to guide me? I couldn't decide, but when it came down to it, I didn't have to decide alone. I told them everything that my grandfather had said, including the choices we had—my magic fire, waiting for Sofia to do it when she showed up in two days, or waiting for Dana to show me tomorrow or the next day.

"Sofia is out," Luke said, and everyone agreed, including me.

"Yes," Noah agreed. "I think we should wait for the magic instructor."

"But, there's no guarantee she'll be here in time or be gentle or careful with people she doesn't know," Luke added.

Izzy nodded. "I agree. I think that Brigid should try. We know she'll be careful."

"But I'm a newbie!" I protested. "What if I burn them, or don't do it right and they freeze to death? Maybe we should wait for Dana, if you don't want her too, at least she could instruct me and guide me."

Megan jumped in. "No, she isn't human. How can you trust her? Plus, she might not get here until Sofia is back."

Even though I didn't think Dana would care about helping humans, she cared about pleasing my grandfather—and she'd been punctual so far. However, it sounded like my grandfather might have her tied up for a day. But she was still a risky choice. I explained my reasoning to the group.

Luke acknowledged us both with a tilt of his head. "I agree with Izzy, Brigid, I think you can do it. You'll be careful, even more so because you care about Gabe and Madison. And best of all, you can do it now."

Michael, Luke, and Izzy were onboard. I looked at Noah, desperate for him to nix the operation. It would be better if Dana did it. She may not care about them, but she was a master magic user. I shook my head.

"Fine, I trust Brigid as well," Noah said to his family. "Brigid, you have all of our faith."

My eyes flew open wide; I swallowed hard and looked at Megan. She gave me a sympathetic look. "I believe in you," she said.

I took a deep breath and let it out slowly. "OK. I'll try."

With nothing else to do but give it the old college try, we decided to go. Everyone filtered out, and we headed back to Gabe's where we'd see if I could unfreeze them.

CHAPTER
FIFTEEN

I visualized what I would do, just as my grandfather had instructed. I'd need to have a tub waiting with warm water, towels, and maybe a car running in case we needed to get them to the ER as quickly as possible. I wasn't sure how I'd explain severe hypothermia when the weather was mild, but we'd cross that bridge if we came to it. I wavered between which one to attempt the thaw on first. If I thawed Madison first, I'd have the practice to work on Gabe, who was most important because he could heal her if something went wrong. However, maybe I should thaw Gabe first, so he'd be available if something went wrong with Madison.

Since I couldn't decide, I put it before everyone. The final consensus was to thaw Gabe first. He was the healer. He could heal himself and be ready for Madison once she thawed.

"Do you want to do it in the kitchen?" Megan asked me as we examined our two frozen friends.

I hadn't gotten that far in my plans.

"Hmmm, if we do it here, then we have to carry them to the bath. Plus, there's a chance I'll burn down the house."

"We could do it in the bathroom and have the fire extinguishers ready," she suggested.

It was a good idea, so I nodded, and the werewolves picked up Gabe and carried him to the main floor bathroom—the only one in the house with a tub. We placed him in the middle of the floor so I could walk around him and filled the tub with room temperature water. If he was hypothermic, we'd need to gradually increase the temperature, otherwise he'd be in agony.

The bathroom could only hold Gabe, me, and two werewolves, and that was a little too chummy for me, but we needed those fire extinguishers on hand. The others waited outside the bathroom, all in various states of nervousness. If this didn't work, Madison would likely have to be thawed by Dana, and that unknown wasn't something they wanted to face.

With nothing left to delay me, I faced Gabe. "Please forgive me," I said to him, and then I closed my eyes, and gathered my will. Once I thought I was ready, I focused on my ring and called the fire. Grandfather said to do a fine even layer all at once. So that's what I told my fire to do. Once the ice melted off of his skin, we had to get him in the water. I could warm that gradually from the faucet, so hopefully, he'd be OK once we made it that far.

The fire came, and at first, it was too much. I scorched his bathroom tiles and ceiling, before I found the right balance. The ice evaporated. Or just plain disappeared. It was strange, when you melt ice, you expect water to be the next state of matter, but the ice didn't melt, it just went away. I knew it was gone when I smelled the burning of Gabe's clothing. I cut off my magic, and Luke and Noah lowered him into the tub. He was still not responding. Hopefully, with the magical ice gone, he'd stir soon.

The water put out his steaming clothes. Two minutes passed, three…

I was beginning to get nervous I'd failed, and Gabe was dead, when he took a sharp intake of air and began to thrash.

"Gabe, it's Brigid! Calm down," I begged. It took him a moment to realize what was going on.

"Brigid?" he asked confused.

Ugh, he'd forgotten or been forced to forget again. I placed my hand on his head and undid the spell as I'd done once before. Again, it took a moment, then the memories came flooding back, and he realized who I was.

"Brigid!" he said again, recognition in his eyes. "What's going on?" He looked around, seeing the wolves, me, and finally himself in the bathtub, fully clothed. He lifted his arm, the water dripping from it. He began to shiver. I turned the water fully to hot and allowed the bath to gradually warm, letting water out as needed, until he indicated that he was warm.

I sighed with relief.

"How are you feeling?" I asked once the shakes had stopped.

"Better now. I'm warm, finally. I can't believe she encased me in ice."

"Yeah, me either. Unfortunately, you aren't the only one she did it to.

Gabe looked at me his eyebrows pushed together. "Who?" he asked, stunned.

"Madison Whelan. We had her watching the house. Well, all the Whelans have been taking turns, but it was on her watch. Somehow, either Madison confronted her, or Sofia caught her and froze her as well. Once you're able to get out of the tub, we're going to thaw her as well. We figured it would be best to have a healer on hand."

"Yes, of course." He stood, the water falling off his clothes, and I handed him a towel. He wrapped himself in it and moved into his bedroom to change in privacy. He came out a few minutes later, his hair tousled, with dry clothes on. He had a bundle of wet clothes wrapped in his towel, which he tossed into his laundry room.

He couldn't avoid seeing Madison, still frozen in his kitchen. He examined her visually, then reached out a hand to press it against the ice.

"She's still alive," he said in wonder. "She's not fully frozen, everything is still functioning, only very slowly. Her heart is…ba… bump…ba…bump." He said each sound, taking several seconds for each, drawing out the sound of her extra slow heartbeat.

I watched, fascinated. "You can do that because of your healing ability?" I asked, although it was an obvious question.

"Yes. I can 'hear' all of her body sounds. She is still functioning, only in extreme slow motion."

I looked at her family, who were anxious to bring her back.

"OK, let's get her into the bathroom."

Her brothers picked her up and placed her gently in the spot where I'd thawed Gabe. The tub was still full, and I let some water out and refilled it until the water was lukewarm.

This time, I had the feel of how much fire to use to thaw the magical ice, and I did so. No fire extinguishers needed, and only a spot or two on her clothes that were scorched. Once done, her brothers lowered her carefully into the tepid tub.

When she came to, it was with her hands flung forward screaming, "No!"

Luke knelt beside the tub and spoke to her until she realized where she was.

"What happened?" she asked, looking at all of us, her face a mask of confusion. "I was waiting for Sofia to leave, then..." She looked away, remembering. "Then I don't remember. She put her hands out, and I thought she was going to throw a nasty spell at me, and now I'm here." She used a hand to indicate the tub.

I nodded, and Luke took her hand. "She froze you in ice."

"Ice?" She shivered. "That explains why I'm so cold."

"I can fix that," I said and turned the heat all the way up, adding it to the tepid water already in the tub.

It took a few minutes before she indicated that she was warm, and we helped her out. Her mother took her into the spare bedroom, and she came out in dry clothes a few minutes later, her wet things in a reusable grocery bag. I drained the tub while we waited. We went out to Gabe's living room to talk about what to do next.

"What was she thinking, freezing you?" I asked. "She knows you'll be missed at the clinic!" I started off.

He shook his head. "I don't know. She's so worried I'll leave her or plot against her."

"And that's what we're going to do," Luke added.

Gabe smiled. "Yes, we are, but I need to call the clinic first."

Gabe found his phone, went into the kitchen, and made his call. From the sound of it, he was on call, and just checking in with a sorry excuse that his phone died, and he didn't notice. That was stupid—of course, he'd never be that irresponsible.

Once his call was done, he came in.

"Everything was fine, there hadn't been a call in, so it worked out. I can't imagine how I'd explain an entire weekend without being available when I'm on call. Sofia has gone too far."

I agreed, she'd been going too far for a long time. Freezing both of them, killing Craig, stealing my magic. It was all too far.

We settled back down on the living room furniture. Noah looked angry. That was a rare look for the new alpha. All of Craig's sons were happy, well-adjusted individuals, and it showed in their sunny smiles, warm greetings, and generally contented natures. Noah's grim face, tight lips, and the burning in his eyes was scary.

"What do you know of her plans?" Noah asked.

"Her plans are just what you think. She plans to capture Brigid and take the rest of her magic." Gabe stood and paced the large living room. "She hasn't spoken about all of her specifics, but she has plans for the next full moon, and she has members of the coven watching you…"—he gestured at me—"all the time. Even on your property."

I jerked. How? I wondered. I had Mr. Mittens, Brightfeather, and now Goch watching for intruders. That seemed nearly impossible. "How?" I murmured. But the sharp ears of the werewolves perked up. They all looked at me, which caught Gabe's attention.

"She hasn't said, but she is powerful. Perhaps some kind of concealment spell."

I hadn't considered that. I could do a kind of invisibility spell using my elemental magic, but who's to say there weren't other ways to do it. I knew nearly zero about witch magic, and even my teachers probably didn't know much more. We weren't witches.

"Oh," I said. "That makes sense. I wish I knew about witch magic. It would be helpful."

Gabe nodded. "I know about some, being the recipient of the nasty things more than once." He sighed.

I couldn't imagine how awful it would be to always be on the lookout for some witch coven or the other. Always looking over your shoulder, trying to stay off their radar. They always wanted him for what he could do—fill their magical wells. It was disgusting. If they'd only asked, he'd be willing, instead they had to control and twist everything with their evil little hands.

"Are all witches so…evil?" I mumbled. I wasn't thinking. I knew that comment would hurt Gabe. His ex had been a witch, and she'd done a real number on him.

Luckily, only the wolves heard, and when they looked at me, I waved it away as the rhetorical question it was. The answer was most of the time they were all evil. There might be a few out there with glowing pure souls, but not here. Here they were all involved in this plot. They'd already murdered for it and would stop at nothing until their goal was met—drain me completely of my magic and then kill me.

I lost the train of the conversation in my musings. When I came back to it, Noah was speaking.

"…with you."

"I don't know for sure, other than the obvious," Gabe said. "But she is acting like I'm her boyfriend to the coven and to the people at work. It's disgusting. I resist even under the spell."

I picked up on what they'd been talking about.

"Gabe, it's time to get out from under her control. We can't ask you to continue this…" I added.

"I want to leave. But I'm the best source of information right now. We'll be fighting her blind if I don't stay."

"Then we'll fight her blind," Luke replied.

The ache in my chest was starting to melt. We could do this. We could defeat her. Even if we didn't have inside information. I was getting more control with each lesson. I didn't know spell work or anything like that, but I had raw power, and I was gaining control with each attempt to work my magic.

"We have more allies now," I added. Although one dragon seemed to be a little thing despite his size.

They looked at me.

"Yes?" Noah asked. Confused.

"The other day..." I started and trailed off. How did one explain running into a dragon while on a nature walk? "I ran into a red snake, only it wasn't a snake, it was a dragon."

There was a collective gasp.

"Dragon?" Noah repeated.

"Yeah, a huge red dragon. His name is Goch. I think a dragon is a good ally, even if he's only a teenager and a little distractible. His heart is in the right place though." I was babbling. I'm sure none of that made sense to the group. I blushed.

"Dragon?" Luke repeated. I think they were a little stunned.

"Yes. A real live, fire-breathing dragon. Oh, and he's big. Did I say that already?"

"Yeah," Luke said.

"Where do you put a dragon?" Izzy asked. "If he's that big, how do you hide a bright red dragon?"

I shook my head. "Around anyone that isn't approved, he has to appear as a red snake. So, easy to hide in eight hundred acres of mostly wilderness."

She nodded. "OK."

Noah cleared his throat. I guess he'd snapped out of it. "A dragon is a great ally. We'll have to ask him if he has any kind of spell resistance."

That question got my mind swimming. Spell resistance?

"Is spell resistance a thing?" I asked.

Every head nodded.

"Do werewolves have spell resistance?" I know that Craig had succumbed to a spell, but it had taken a nasty fall for that to happen.

"Generally, we are resistant to a lot of things, unless we are weakened somehow. Like Dad was," Noah added quietly.

"I wonder if Brightfeather is as well," I said aloud, but it was just a passing thought. I figured my cat was, he'd taken down a lot of critters that should have killed him, and he'd prevailed. And during the fight with the witches, he'd come out unscathed. Something to ask all of my magical creatures.

"Please come with us, Gabe," I begged, although it caused my heart to race just to ask. I didn't know what I'd do if he refused. "You can stay in the house, or if that makes you uncomfortable, you can stay at the dairy in the house there."

All the Whelans also invited him to stay with them.

He looked at all of us, considering. Finally, he conceded with a sigh, "Yeah, this isn't working with Sofia. She isn't giving me enough information that living like this is viable. Freezing me and Madison, that's just taking it too far," he repeated.

"Yeah," I agreed.

He stood. "I'll pack a bag and lock up here. Brigid, I'll take you up on that offer."

A knot in my gut lessened. I'd been so worried—mainly about him being with Sofia but partly because of the thought of being rejected. Now, we just had to keep him free of her clutches while he was at work, but he'd be safe at home once I informed my guards what to look out for. At least, I had plenty of room.

CHAPTER
SIXTEEN

Dana didn't care what day of the week it was. I didn't know if in the Faerie realm they even had a weekend. Or, for that matter, if they had equivalent days of the week. I also didn't dare ask her, no reason to make her grumpier if I was taking her weekends. She showed up bright and early, cleaned us out of pastries, and away we went to my "place of power." I wish I felt powerful. But my instincts were right, she'd have been here in time to save Gabe and Madison if we'd have waited.

Shockingly out of character for her, she'd actually engaged me in conversation for a few seconds. "Did your friends thaw properly?" she asked after we arrived at the waterfall.

"Yes, it went well," I replied.

She grunted in acknowledgment, another version of "adequate" I assumed.

She thrust an object at me.

"This will allow you to contact us in case of an emergency," she said. I took the object, and so I wouldn't annoy her, I placed it in the pocket of my jeans.

"How do I use it?" I asked.

"Hold it in your hand and focus on the recipient. In this case either myself or your Grandfather. Once the object lights up, you can speak your piece, and the message will be transmitted."

"OK, that seems easy."

"Yes, even you can't make a mistake using this." She sniffed.

At least she was consistent.

Since we'd already worked on a defensive magic with shadow, she taught me how to throw fireballs as an offensive weapon. I was better at this than the other things she had me do—at least at forming them. My throwing was another issue, but she didn't dwell on that, and we were done earlier than usual. She must have another pressing issue to let me get away with it. After she flashed away, I walked myself back to the house, Mr. Mittens trotted along in front of me, watching for threats.

"Do you have any magic resistance?" I asked since I'd been curious.

He stopped and threw a glance back at me. *Yes, I have some resistance here on this land.*

"Do you think that Brightfeather and Goch do as well?" I continued, filling the looming silence.

Most likely. Magical creatures usually have some kind of magical immunity based on their species, but for more specifics, you would need to ask them.

That made sense, so I nodded, although he couldn't see me, and we continued to walk. "What specific immunities do you have?" I asked after a moment or two.

Hmpf. His usual response if he were thinking or annoyed. Probably annoyed, I was distracting him from his "patrol." *I am immune to most spells, although not to direct elemental attacks.*

"So, you could resist anything a witch threw at you, but not a Fae?"

I got the impression of a shrug in my head, so most likely, but not a perfect yes or no.

It depends on the strength of the attack, but most witch spells have no effect.

That was interesting. I was glad he was safe in this conflict I had with Sofia; I couldn't bear to see him sick or dying again. The spider bite still scared me when I thought of how close I came to losing him. In the short time I'd had him with me, I had grown extremely attached.

We continued to saunter back to the house, not in a great hurry. Gabe was at work, and although he was staying in the house, things had been if not strained, then uncomfortable. He'd had to flee his home and come stay with me and Megan, knowing that he'd been acting as Sofia's boytoy for a short time. He had suffered trauma and had to face Sofia once she returned. All not his fault.

I breathed out a loud sigh, and Mr. Mittens glanced my way. *What is the matter, pet?*

I didn't know how to put all my frustrations into words, but the cause of everything was easy to identify. "Sofia."

Ah. Yes, she is a problem. If she comes back to this property, I will consider her a creature to be destroyed, he said matter-of-factly.

"Me too." I tripped over a rough patch on the trail. He waited until I was steady, and we continued our walk. "Unfortunately, if it were that easy, we would have already eliminated her."

Yes. It is regretful.

I agreed with that as we quickly approached the house. "Oh, I almost forgot. Gabe told us that we are being watched by coven members on this property."

Mr. Mittens stopped short, and I almost ran into him. His tail whipped from side to side in irritation.

How is this possible? he asked with a growl.

"Gabe said they are using concealment spells to hide themselves from us."

Mr. Mittens's growl grew louder as if he were Splintercat size. *I'll be back, pet.*

I chuckled at his unintended Schwarzenegger impression and watched him fondly as he disappeared into the trees. I wondered what he was going to do. Impulsively, I bellowed after him, "Bring them *alive* for questioning."

Megan was on the phone when I entered the kitchen through the back door. "Yeah, that works, see you then."

I opened the fridge to find something to drink. I pulled out a can of Diet Coke and popped the top open. "What was that about?"

"We have a handyman coming, I called one from your list. He's going to check out the little things we need done here and look at the dairy house as well." She beamed with pride.

"Cool, I can check that off. Did you find out what licenses and things we need to open the B&B?"

"Yup, they've been sent to your email, we are on our way!"

"That's great. I'll look at them after I shower and clean up."

I climbed into my shower—I had to say my bathroom was my favorite place in the house—and cleaned up, scrubbing away the sweat and effort learning magic cost.

Once out, I retrieved my laptop and looked at the items we needed to complete before opening. The list was daunting but exciting in a way. This new project was the first thing besides restoring the house that filled me with anticipation. How would the B&B do? Would the supernatural community respond well to the idea? Were there others like it in the world, and probably the most anxiety causing thought, how would I advertise?

Megan was going to use her considerable computer know-how to see if she could locate other businesses that catered to the supernatural community. They had to exist. I couldn't be the first one to come up with the idea.

Before I took a deep dive into my computer, I heard Mr. Mittens in my mind.

I have one for you, pet, and yes, it is alive…

Well, shit.

"Megan!" I said, maybe louder than I intended.

"Yeah, what's wrong?" She looked up from her computer with a start. Mr. Mittens must have just sent that message to me.

"We need to meet Mr. Mittens outside."

She finished typing a few words and closed the laptop, following me out the door. In the protected gravel drive behind the house, Mr. Mittens stood with a large Splintercat paw pressed on the chest of a man dressed in camouflage. The man was writhing around, trying to escape, but it appeared my cat held him down with little effort. I shivered. At least the witch was still alive.

Megan looked at me and crossed her arms. "He's one of them, isn't he?" she asked. "A witch."

I nodded. Her face darkened with emotion.

We approached until we were looking down on him. He stilled.

"What are you going to do to me?" he asked, his voice cracking.

I looked at Megan, and then my cat. "It depends."

Mr. Mittens growled, and I saw the paw on the witch's chest flex, and the claws extend enough to just puncture the skin. The man tensed, then thrashed around again.

"OK, OK, I'll do anything!" he gasped.

"How many of you are watching my place?"

"Just me. I swear!"

"So, you come one at a time, or does it vary?"

Mr. Mittens extended his claws a millimeter more. The witch froze and drew in a sharp intake of breath. "It varies!"

"Continue…"

"We have up to three at a time. This is just in the middle of the day when everyone is at work."

"How are you hiding yourselves from me and my protector?" This time my voice was hard, and I had changed from crossed arms to hands on hips—my power move.

"We have a concealment spell. Sofia designed it."

I looked at Megan and Mr. Mittens as though I were considering their input.

It is true; the witch was concealed. Should I kill him now? Mr. Mittens asked.

I addressed the witch, "Is that all or should I let my cat kill you? He's hungry."

"No, no, ummm, Sofia, she's got a plan to take more of your magic!" he stammered out.

I waved a hand at Mr. Mittens, and he retracted his claws. "Tell me more."

"She'll kill me," he whispered.

I used my earth magic and had the ground move until he sunk slightly into it. His legs, bottom, and part of his chest were half covered.

"Wait!" he yelled.

"You don't think that I will kill you? Or my cat? Foolish." I released the earth, and he was lying on top of it again. Mr. Mittens licked his chops and dipped his head, his eyes lighting up with his intent.

"Everyone always discounts me," Megan said with a pout and lifted my best, eight-inch, kitchen filet knife.

My eyes flew open when I looked at her. I had discounted her as being the kind one. I shouldn't have. She knew this was deadly serious.

I nodded. "Sorry, I shouldn't have forgotten to mention you." Apparently, she wasn't only my ride or die friend, but also my ride and kill friend.

She smirked. "That's right."

"So, what else do you have to tell us?" I really didn't know what to do with him when we were done, I guess I'd let Mr. Mittens decide, although that was the witch's death sentence, but I couldn't let him go. Or could I? If he went back, maybe he'd terrify the others into leaving me alone. Of course, if he said anything Sofia would probably kill him, but at least that would be off my conscience.

He reached for his pocket. Mr. Mittens growled, and his claws extended again.

"I have a paper with the spell and the schedule, but it's in my pocket," he said.

I nodded at Mr. Mittens, and he allowed the witch to reach into his pocket. He pulled out a folded piece of notebook paper, and he reached up so I could take it.

I opened the paper, and sure enough, there was a handwritten schedule with a simple spell. "Sofia can't use a spreadsheet?" I asked, incredulous.

"She doesn't let us write things down, usually, evidence you know, but I kept forgetting my rotation."

"What about her plans to steal my magic?" I continued.

"I just know she has plans, but I'm not in her inner circle. I don't know what they are—I swear!"

I was disappointed; we already knew she had a plan from Gabe. I looked at the fear in his eyes and didn't think there was much more the witch could tell us. So, I gestured for Mr. Mittens to let him go. He growled but took his paw off the man's chest.

"I c-can go?" he stammered.

"Yes, you will leave my property. If we ever see you again, or you tell the other witches I know about the rotation, I'll let my cat eat you on sight."

He brushed himself off and bolted back to the trees, probably to wherever he had parked. Hopefully, he found his way quickly because as soon as I released Mr. Mittens, I doubted he'd get a second chance at escape.

"You caught him quickly," I remarked to my cat as he transformed once more into his Ragdoll form.

Hmpf. It was easy once I knew they were using a spell, he said with disdain.

"Have you talked to Brightfeather or Goch about the witches?" I asked.

Yes, they are aware and will be more vigilant, he replied.

"Thank you."

He nodded and strolled away to do whatever he did—I hoped it wasn't eating a stupid witch.

CHAPTER

SEVENTEEN

G abe came in with another load of his things. I'd put him in a finished room on the second floor. He was still uncomfortable with me, and I didn't know how to make it right. I followed him upstairs.

"Are you OK?" I asked, as he put his bag on the floor.

He looked at me and smiled uncertainly. "I feel like we just barely restarted our relationship, and then I cheated on you."

That's what I thought it was. "Gabe, I don't blame you. You were under her spell. I blame her." I looked him straight in the eyes. "If you want to see what we can be to one another, I'm still willing. You remember what I went through with Scott and the love potion? You didn't blame me. This is worse. Not your fault, and I don't blame you at all. There is zero to forgive. I know your heart, you're caring, loving, and giving. I know you would never have done this under your own will. I truly blame her. She's evil. You are not. Please believe that. Let's put this behind us."

"I also know how you feel about cheating. After your husband…" He trailed off, his eyes intent on my face, trying to read any insincerity there.

"You didn't cheat. You didn't do anything wrong. You were

spelled. You need to quit putting blame on yourself," I answered firmly, making sure I made constant eye contact, so he knew I was telling the truth.

He looked at me for a few moments more, then he nodded, and let out a breath. "Thanks, Brigid. None of this has been fair to you. You are too good."

I huffed. "I'm not good. I just threatened a witch with death by cat earlier today."

He laughed. "I'd have liked to see that."

"Yeah, too bad it wasn't Sofia."

His face darkened.

"Sorry, shouldn't have brought her up," I apologized.

He nodded. "It's OK, I'm still…" He waved a hand, but I understood. "So, was it a coven member spying?" He changed the subject.

"Yup, we didn't get specifics out of him, he told us he wasn't in her inner circle, but we have this." I pulled the paper with the names and rotation schedule out of my pocket and handed it to him. "You probably know more of these people than I do. Maybe you can identify if any of them are working at the clinic?"

He studied the paper for a few moments, his frown deepening. "That bitch," he whispered finally, almost so quiet I didn't hear him.

"What's wrong?"

He pointed to a name. "This woman is one of my medical assistants. This is how Sofia is always one step ahead of me."

"I'm sorry," I said.

He shook his head. "I'm taking care of this one, right now."

He took out his phone.

"I'll give you some privacy," I said and began to walk out of the room.

"You don't need to leave; this will only take a moment." He manipulated the phone and put it up to his ear. "This is Dr. Ambrose," he said. "Can you connect me with Sierra Curtis, please?"

There was a pause for a few moments. His hand was tense on the phone, his face grim. "Sierra? This is Dr. Ambrose. I know you've been spying for the coven. I want you out of my office. If you transfer,

I will give you a good word, if you don't I'll fire you. Decide." He hung up. I could hear a protest on the other side before he ended the call.

I felt a momentary twinge for the hapless MA, but it only lasted a second. She'd spied for Sofia. She was probably on my land during the ceremony to steal my magic, and she'd certainly not offered up any medical services after my beating, so I shoved any sympathy down where it belonged.

"Good riddance," he said, his voice hard. He was one of the sweetest people I knew. So, having him this upset just cemented that my reaction to the witch earlier was warranted. I nodded.

He pointed to several other names he recognized, and he told me what businesses they worked at. There were a few more that were at the clinic, but no one else that worked directly with him. Who could believe that the evil witches in the coven would work in jobs that served people? It was so out of character. I wondered again if all witches were truly evil.

I had to let it go. The witches in the local coven, except for those too weak to use magic, were evil. They'd tried to kill me and my allies. They'd enslaved Gabe. I had to remember that. I told him that the Whelans had a more complete list of suspected coven members, and he nodded.

Time to up the protection on all eight hundred acres with three humans, a Splintercat, a griffin, and a dragon. That was a lot of area to cover. However, if the witches were smart, they were mainly watching the house, so I needed my protectors literally closer to home. Time to call a meeting.

"Gabe, I'm going to call a meeting. Do you want to join?"

"Sure," he said uncertainly, probably not knowing what I was talking about.

I smiled. "Come on." I put out a mental call to my protectors and led Gabe down to the kitchen and out the back door. We picked up Megan along the way and sat on the steps while we waited for the others to arrive.

Mr. Mittens was first. He probably hadn't gotten too far away after the witch, or he was patrolling around the house looking for more of them. Brightfeather and Goch were close behind, flying in. I'd given Goch permission to show his true form around Gabe, and he was grateful. Luckily, there was a large enough patch of tree free gravel back here from all the construction activity where he could land and stand comfortably.

"Wow," I heard Megan murmur. She hadn't met Goch yet and was still living in her fantasy of being a dragon rider. Frankly, dragon riding looked like it would be difficult, and require lots of muscle from all the jerking around that taking off, landing, and flying caused from what I'd observed of Goch's movement. Brightfeather was much smoother and more graceful. Although, Goch was young and would probably improve with age.

Goch's bright red coloring was flashy though and impressive upon first sight. I wondered if he could be seen from the road when he flew in. I'd have to ask him.

"Goch, how do people not see you flying?"

He lowered his head down to my level, which was nice, but horribly intimidating. *Dragons have magic that conceals us when we fly. That's why we are mostly just myths to most humans.*

"But I can see you."

You are in the know. The magic doesn't work well when people truly believe or have real knowledge of us.

"Huh," I replied.

Megan hung on every word. "How old are you Goch?" she asked. I was curious as well. So, we both waited for him to answer.

I know I'm young, but I hope that doesn't mean you won't let me help, he replied.

"That's not why I asked," Megan replied. "I am just curious. I don't know anything about dragons. I have no idea how long you live."

Goch looked abashed, which was interesting since he was already red in coloration, and didn't blush, his expression changed minutely, and he looked away slightly. *I am one hundred and thirty years old. Dragons can live for several thousand years. I know that I am young, but I am fierce!* He showed his impressive teeth. They were as long as a person and brutally sharp.

I gulped.

"You are the fiercest dragon we know," I reassured him. He appeared to preen a little, his eyes lighting up and his mouth curving slightly upward in a draconic grin.

Brightfeather also added her approval, and I continued with the meeting.

"Thank you, friends, for coming. I just wanted to let you all know that the witches are still spying, and they are using a concealment spell. They are watching me specifically, so if you are looking for them, I feel like they will be concentrated near the house. If you wouldn't mind checking it out on your daily sweeps, I'd appreciate it. Mr. Mittens..." I waved a hand at him, and he straightened up taller in his seated position. "Caught a witch earlier today. We discovered that they have a rotation to watch me here on my land. We have the list, so we know about how many witches will be here and when. Also, we do know for sure that she has a plan to capture me and take more of my magic. She'll be back in town tomorrow, so we should be prepared since we don't know when or what her plan entails."

My allies nodded grimly, and I knew they understood.

We are happy to help, mistress, Brightfeather said.

Goch also acknowledged that he would help.

"You can report to Mr. Mittens. Thank you, friends! Is there anything I can do to help you?" I asked.

Goch and Brightfeather were fine, but Mr. Mittens grumbled, *You can stay inside, my pet, and quit wandering around.*

I leaned down and scratched behind his ears. "You know I can't always do that. But I know you are just worried for me."

He purred. *I want you safe, my pet.* His face turned up to me, his eyes half shut, and he rubbed against my leg.

Warmth filled me at his words, and I ran a hand over his soft cottony fur.

Ok, here we go, I thought. Time to plan faster and harder than Sofia and have something ready this time around. I knew what ceremony she had to perform, she'd done it before, I knew when, same as before, and I knew where. I assumed she'd still do it at my altar in my woods—my magic was strong here, and she wanted it.

We had approximately one more week to go before the next full moon. And this time, I didn't want to be helpless and without my allies.

"We need to set a trap this time," I said to my companions. "And we'll have to set it by the altar. That's where she's going to attempt to strip my magic. Can you all search around that area to see if she's set anything up?"

They nodded and left.

I turned to Gabe and Megan. "She has to be looking for the missing pieces of my magic I'm still looking for as well. We need to find them first. So, that's our first step. I'm still missing air; it will have swirly markings. I guess any of them can be in the shape of a necklace, ring, or bracelet. Aether will be quartz stones, reality is unknown, and time will be represented by some kind of clock, so a watch or something similar. I've searched the inside of the house, the rest is either outside or in the woods."

I looked thoughtfully at the house. Just then, I heard a vehicle coming up my drive. I stiffened, and Gabe's face grew dark. Who was it now? Scott back to thrust more workers at me? Another witch trying to spy on me? That was dumb. They'd have to be sneakier than coming up a gravel driveway.

A white work truck with "Whelan Restoration" drove around the house and into the back parking area. I relaxed when I saw Luke and Izzy in the truck.

"Hi, guys!" I greeted them brightly, happy for their company and help searching.

Frankly, Luke was probably here to see Megan, but it was nice to have Izzy around.

We were becoming friends, and I liked to be around her.

Megan smiled at Luke, who came over and stood by her.

"What's up?" I asked.

Luke shrugged. "Just thought we'd come by and check on everything. Especially since there could be witches hiding and wandering around. Thought you might like a wolf or two to check."

"That'd be great. We'd love it. Actually, Mr. Mittens brought us a fine specimen earlier."

Luke started, and Izzy frowned with dismay. "What?" she asked, surprised.

"He took our comments about them being concealed to heart and flushed out a witch. We got a copy of their rotation plans and of the concealment spell and sent him on his way."

"Wow," Izzy said.

"Right now, we were going to start a search for the rest of my magic while we know there aren't any witches watching. If we can get it all first, we'll be better prepared for the next full moon."

"You think that's when she's going to try again?" Luke asked.

"I do." I had nothing to prove it but a gut feeling, but I'd been learning to trust that more and more.

"We'll help," Luke volunteered, and Izzy nodded.

"Cool, thanks."

Since this was as important as stopping Sofia, making sure I was completely armed, we spread out and started with the exterior of the house. Since Luke had the company truck—and it had tools, ladders, and scaffolding inside—he pulled out a ladder.

"I'll start with the roof," he said, and carried the ladder to the porch roof, where he could easily access the rest.

The rest of us spread out to cover the main floor porch and the patch of garden where I'd found the gris gris bag.

I don't know why I hadn't asked for help before now. I guess before the incident with the witches, I hadn't been serious enough about it, and then I'd been hurt and worried about Gabe, but it was time to drive the stakes up a notch. Fully magicked was how I could outpower Sofia and her coven.

I used my inherent magic, as Dana and my cat called it, and sent a call to my magic, to the jewelry that contained it, and I asked it to come to me, to show itself to me and my friends. I stood next to the house by the roses, arms wide, face to the sun, and let my magic pull the other parts of me home. When I opened my eyes, I saw a glint next to the house behind the roses. I was drawn to it, so I made my way through the rose garden.

Once I was near, I bent over, the glint was gone, but the pull was there. I reached out to the siding on the house, recently recovered with shiny new paint. So odd that the workers who'd been looking hadn't seen this. A single silver thread peeked out, I tugged on it, and a small velvet bag followed. I opened the bag, which was dusty, and partly painted, and out tumbled a ring into my hand. I gasped. It was a strange stone. When I gazed into it, I could see what felt like the universe, but a quick glance showed that instead it was a simple glowing blue jewel, and nothing more. Unable to resist the pull to study it more, I slipped it on my finger, and a wave of heat and longing for the unknown swept over me. I shivered and pulled my arms around myself. Reality. That was the piece. I hadn't known what the jewelry would look like, but when I gazed on it and re-integrated it, I knew.

The experience was eerie—that was the only word that came to me. Eerie. I had no idea what *reality* magic did, but it had an *immensity*, an ancient *pull,* to it that I had no idea what to do with. I took a deep breath, trying to steady myself, and leaned against the house, its solid realness re-attaching me to the now and the moment and the whatever that made this place what it was.

I cleared my throat after a moment and found I could speak. "I found one!" I yelled, and Izzy came around the house to give me a thumbs up.

"Any luck?" I asked her.

She shook her head. "I'm going to try the crawl space," she said.

"Really? It's dirty and there are spiders," I replied. I'd been a little weird about spiders since the soul spider incident.

"I've done worse," she said and smiled. Then, she took off her jacket, rolled up her sleeves, and headed for the small door hidden under the porch that led to the crawl space.

"Good luck," I called after her, and she waved briefly before disappearing into the gloom under the porch. I checked on Megan and Luke, but they were intently looking, and I didn't want to disturb them. I tried my call again, but something about finding the last arti-fact was keeping me distracted, and I couldn't connect like I'd done before. I went to the kitchen and made some sandwiches and drinks. I could be a good hostess, while everyone was working so hard to help me.

Just as I was finishing, I heard a call and rushed out. Luke was coming down the ladder. Once on the ground, he held up a necklace of quartz stones. It glittered and shot sparkles in the sunlight, and I clasped my hands together. Two pieces of magic in one day! Why hadn't I asked for help before?

Quartz, this must be Aether. Whatever that meant or did, but I gazed at the stones as my magic called to me to take it into myself. Luke watched my eyes and realized that I couldn't be in its presence for long without trying to pull the magic back inside of myself.

He held out the necklace, and I kept myself from snatching it, barely. I held it briefly until the compulsion was too much, then I slipped it over my head. The necklace flashed, and a light citrus scent wafted over me, and the feel of a sunny day breezed through me. Aether had a light touch which I was grateful for, especially since fire had been brutal.

"Ah," I sighed out.

Luke looked at me strangely. "What does it feel like? Reintegrating your magic like that?"

I looked at him. "Why, what did you see?"

He shrugged. "I saw a flash, and then your expression appeared… blissful, I guess is the only way to describe it."

"Yes, this one was blissful. They're all different. Each one has given a different sensation. Some have been unpleasant, but this one was light and easy."

"Interesting."

I nodded but felt slightly embarrassed. My cheeks warmed.

"I made sandwiches, if you're hungry," I said, changing the subject.

"Sure, I can eat. You'll find that offering food to werewolves is always welcome. We're usually hungry." He winked.

I laughed. "Anytime, I'm not much of a cook, but I can manage the basics."

He went inside and came back with a plate that had two sandwiches, a pile of chips, and a Coke.

I left him eating and went to gather up everyone for a break. I grabbed Megan and waved at Gabe to come in and sent them to the kitchen. I yelled for Izzy under the porch, and she called back, "Just a minute, I think I found something."

My heart sped up a beat. Three pieces of magic in one day? That would be the record. I'd be only one short if that happened, minus the ice magic Sofia had stolen, of course.

"Come under here, I can't quite reach it. You have longer arms."

I shuddered. After running into the soul spider, I had no desire to go where spiders lived, but it was for my magic, and that was more important than my newly acquired arachnophobia. I sighed and crawled under the porch and into the dark underbelly of my house. I could see where Izzy had crawled. The dust was disturbed, and I could see her light up ahead. There was more headspace under here than I'd imagined when she'd first crawled through the door. I could almost stand, or at least crouch down without hitting my head on the supports that held up my house.

She was looking at me and waving for me to hurry. She seemed excited. I wondered why. If it were a piece of jewelry, then she should react, but there was more excitement than that.

I crawled up and knelt next to her. "What is it?" I asked, because I didn't see anything at first.

"Oh, sorry." She pointed her light back into a hole between supports. About three feet back, I could see what looked like a metal cigar box. I was only an inch or two taller than Izzy, so I wasn't sure I could reach it either. There was also no guarantee that a piece of my magic was in there either, because the box looked older than me by a lot. If my magic had been stored here at the same time as the box, it would be older than me, so nothing but a red herring.

Plus, I didn't want to stick my arm in a spider hole. I was still getting over the last one. My whole being was yelling *ick*.

But the box called to me. I was drawn to it as surely as if it did contain...*something*.

I reached my arm in, fighting the desire to run, strip off my clothes, and brush out my hair. I grazed the edge of it with my middle finger, but it was out of my reach.

"I can't reach it," I grumbled.

"Uh!" Izzy exclaimed. "We'll have to find a stick or something. I don't think my brother's meaty hands can fit. I'll be right back."

She crawled around me and headed out. I shivered and felt the desire to flee the spider infested crawlspace, but I held it together for the few seconds she was gone. She came back, finally, with one of those grabber things that short people need to reach the top shelves of tall cabinetry. I'd forgotten I had one of those in my kitchen. Vaulted ceilings were lovely, but they made it hard to reach my extended cabinets.

"That'll work," I said, and made room for her to shove the grabber in and grasp the box.

She handed me the flashlight. "Hold this!" I obeyed and held it so she could see the box and reach into the hole to pull it out.

I heard the grabber clink as it grasped the tin box, and the rasp as she pulled it out of the tight hole it was in. Finally, it lay between us, mysterious and old.

"Well?" she asked. "Open it."

"Me?"

"Yeah, your house, your box, your magic," she said.

I nodded. Of course, I was being silly. It was all of those things, maybe.

I reached out a hand. The box zinged under my fingers, and I snatched them back. There had to be a piece of my magic within. I opened it. Inside were a bunch of old photos. Photos of my family from when I was a small child. Probably near the time my magic had been taken. I shone the flashlight on them, and tears welled up. There was my grandmother. I hadn't realized I looked like her. In her nineties, she looked nearer my current age. She was smiling, and her auburn hair was falling around her face in waves, her bright blue eyes laughing. I'd thought she was so old then. Ha.

Then my mother and father gazing on me with love. I clutched the photos to my heart. I hadn't had many. I guess because they were still here at the house, and my heart swelled with love for my dead family. I pulled them all out and carefully laid them on my lap. The last item was a pocket watch. Time. It had to be. I held its silver case in my hand. Then, because I didn't know how to wear it to activate the magic, I opened the lid, and the timepiece was exposed for a moment. Then in a flash, it disappeared into my skin. My body buzzed with energy. It was the most invigorating feeling I'd ever had. I wanted to run, jump, laugh, and fling my hands to the sky.

I must have laughed out loud, because Izzy looked at me oddly.

"Time is a rush," I said, and she probably thought I'd gone over the edge.

We crawled out from under the house.

By then, the rush had worn off. I sighed, and we went into the house to eat.

CHAPTER
EIGHTEEN

The next day, Sofia was supposed to be back. We weren't sure when exactly, so I went to my lesson. I let Dana know I'd acquired Reality, Aether, and Time. She gave me an odd look when I asked her what they did. I sort of got Time, that one seemed obvious, but I didn't have a clue about the others.

"Reality," she said. "Is many things, but most importantly, it will allow you to walk the realms."

"Realm walk?" I asked, excitedly. That meant I could go visit the Fae realm and see my grandfather and how he lived. I was going to go visit too, once this conflict with Sofia was over. I could also go to Mr. Mittens's home realm. I'd been curious about it, since he was so closed- mouthed about his origins.

"Focus." She snapped her long extra jointed fingers in front of my nose.

I jerked my head back.

She appeared to be in a horrible mood.

"Yes, well. Realm walking is dangerous and not important right now. First, we must master the magic you need for the witches. That is my task to teach you. Xrsrphn can teach you to realm walk on your own time."

I nodded. She scared me more than a little, so I didn't argue. I was still dying to know what Aether was, but I supposed it could wait for another day. I had it and that was the most important thing. I was starting to feel whole for once and my magic less wounded.

She declared me adequate with fire, water, and shadow, and now we were working on light. Frankly, water, shadow, and light seemed like small potatoes next to Sofia. I thought we should be working on lightning, since that was my big scary power. At least it scared me.

"You're not paying attention," she yelled.

I wasn't, so I concentrated. My mind was with my friends and the weak plan we had to bring Sofia down in a few days when the moon was full once more.

I wove the light again. This time I kept my mind on it, and she declared me adequate and flashed away. I wondered if I would flash once I learned to realm walk. The first time my grandfather had appeared, there was a huge flash of light and a concussive force. That hadn't happened since, so I imagined he'd done that on purpose since he was pissed I'd summoned him.

Mr. Mittens met me at the spring, and we walked back to the house together. He, watching for intruders, and me, lost in thought over our coming conflict with the coven.

We made it back without any interruptions. We were going to meet with the werewolves later, since they were staking out Sofia and trying to figure out her plans. The coven must have already told her about Gabe, since he'd blatantly told off the coven MA from his office. I was sure she wasn't going to let him go without a fight.

He was at work. I had to trust he was safe in public at his own office. Even she'd not dared mess with his schedule too much. He was well-known and liked in town. The handsome, local boy, who came back to serve his community. No way she could interfere with that.

Megan was holding down the fort. The handyman she'd hired had begun the finish work we still needed done on the house. I was letting her take point, since we never knew how long my lessons with Dana would take every day. Megan was competent, so I wasn't worried.

When I came in, I heard the welcome sound of construction work from above, and Megan was on the phone and the computer at the same time. I was glad I'd hired her, not that there was a chance I wasn't going to. She was taking up all the slack and was going to get this business up and running while I was lacking in time.

I caught the tail end of her conversation as I walked in and realized she was talking to Luke. My heart warmed a little for my friend. She and Luke deserved happiness. I sure hoped they could make this thing between them work.

She hung up.

"Luke and Megan sitting in a tree…"

She rolled her eyes. "Grow up, Bridge."

I laughed. "I couldn't help it; you should see your gooey eyes when you talk to him on the phone."

"Well, he's pretty dreamy, you know." She smirked. "Besides, I'd like to cover him in gooey chocolate."

I laughed. "I bet."

A couple of sharp bangs came from upstairs.

"So, the handyman showed?" I asked.

"Yup, only it's a handywoman," she replied.

"Really? That's cool. What happened to the other guy?"

She shrugged. "He couldn't do the job, backed out. The handy-woman has good references and was willing to take on this rather large project, so we are grateful to have her."

"Yes, we are," I affirmed. Even Megan didn't know how grateful. From the beginning, my main goal was getting this house done. Now, I had the additional goal of having it ready to open as a B&B before spring.

"So, what did Luke say about Sofia. Is she back?"

"Oh, yeah, she's back, and apparently, she's raging. That witch you sent back to her?"

I nodded.

"Well, the Whelans aren't sure what is happening to him, but he's locked up in the coven's warehouse, and the coven are all heading there tonight to decide his fate."

I shivered. I knew this would happen when I released him. I figured

Sofia would do something awful, but at the same time, I wanted the coven to be frightened of us as well. Any doubt we could throw their way had to be good for our side.

"If they are busy infighting, maybe they'll forget about me."

"You wish."

I nodded. It was a stretch. I still knew she was coming for me, and it would be in just three more days. Somehow, I had to make sure that all of us were ready.

"The Whelans can't get inside to check. The witches know about them and are watching for them. Luke said there's a ward on the warehouse," Megan continued.

"Well, that sucks." I sat at the table.

"Yeah, I was kind of wondering if the ward is just against magical types, and if I could sneak in," she said quickly, almost flippantly.

"I don't know. That's too dangerous, Megan. I'm not sure about that."

"No one knows who I am, if I get caught, I'll just say I was lost or something." Her jaw was set, and I knew she'd already decided she was going to try.

I stood up and put my hands on the table.

"So, you're going to do it, anyway? Is that what I'm hearing?" I said, my voice a little too high and loud as panic set in.

"You know me so well. Come on, you can be my backup."

"Not if I can't get through the ward."

She smiled at me. "Luke says if I can get inside, it's possible I can bring the ward down. Then, I'll have you and the werewolves as backup."

Damn Luke, I was gonna strangle him.

"How?" I put my hands on my hips, this sounded like a ruse to get me off her back.

She smirked. "Simple. I just need to break the circle. It's a requirement of a witch ward."

I huffed at her. "Do you know where the circle is? What if it's painted on? What if it's guarded?"

She frowned; she hadn't thought that through. Then, she shrugged.

"We'll cross that bridge when we come to it."

"You're going to get yourself killed or sacrificed or something. The witches aren't playing." I started to pace.

"It'll be fine, Bridge, I have faith in you and Luke's family to get me back safely." Her tone was matter of fact. She didn't even act scared.

I wasn't going to win; she was determined. "When?"

She looked at her phone. "Two hours. I'm waiting for Luke to be ready."

I threw up my hands and called my cat. I needed his advice on breaking witch spells. He probably couldn't help, but he knew more than me.

"And Luke is OK with this plan?"

She lifted her hand and waved it back and forth to indicate so-so.

"Hmpf." Now, I sounded like Mr. Mittens.

Mr. Mittens came around the corner, just like a regular house cat on his own agenda. *You rang?*

I wanted to keep my mad going, but that made me giggle. I remember I would curl up in a chair with him when I was very small, and we'd watch reruns of *The Addams Family*. Apparently, he remembered too.

Megan must have heard him as well because she rolled her eyes. My cat was becoming more ridiculous by the day. He had a better sense of humor than I had first thought though.

"Yes," I said to him. "Megan is going to go crash the witches party at their coven's warehouse. It's warded, apparently. Do you know anything about breaking a witches' ward?"

I thought back to when they'd captured me and kept me bound and contained under a ward. That had been an active working though, so I didn't know if they were the same. He couldn't get through that one, but several witches had been chanting and using magic to hold it against him, Brightfeather, and the wolf pack. Maybe a passive working would be easier to break.

Hmpf. I am not a witch or a Fae, he grumbled.

I sighed. "I know, Mr. Mittens, but you were the protector of a witch, and you've seen more magic than I have. I was just hoping you'd have more information than I do."

He cocked his head and blinked his enormous periwinkle blue eyes at me. *I do.*

That was an understatement; he was somewhere around two hundred years old.

"About wards and witches?" I prompted.

Basic wards such as you describe, simply need the circle broken. In my experience, the problem is getting to the circle.

That aligned with what Megan had described. "OK. Sounds easy."

He stared at me. *Witches never make things easy. Don't forget that, pet.*

That I believed. Then something he said hit me. "You said, 'basic wards' what's not 'basic'?"

I got the impression of a mental shrug. *Witches can make their wards to do more than one thing, pet.*

That gave me a chill. What was I sending Megan into?

"What do witches usually make their circles out of?"

He blinked. *Usually smelly stuff. Things they use in their potions and such. I don't know specifics.*

Of course, a cat would notice smells. That made sense. "Any ever use paint in your experience?"

He licked a paw and chewed around the claw. Once he was satisfied he'd cleaned whatever was stuck on there—I shuddered at the thought—he answered, *Not in my experience, but this is a different age. They could have adapted to the times.*

Not what I wanted to hear. I looked at Megan. "Did you hear all that?"

"Yeah, but we won't know unless we try. We don't even know if I can cross the ward, so no sense worrying about what else it can do, or if I can destroy it until we try."

There was a certain logic to that. Even if it was the wrong kind.

CHAPTER

NINETEEN

I was ready to pounce on Luke when he pulled up to the house. How dare he put these ideas in Megan's head? She had nothing to protect herself with if she made it through the ward. However, I should have known that he wouldn't be that thrilled about the idea either. This was pure Megan. He was trying to dissuade her before I got up close enough to chew him out. So, I didn't light into him.

"I'm going to do it," Megan said, with finality, and put up a hand to stop any further argument.

Luke wilted. I recognized that look, he'd given in to her will. Since I'd already folded, I couldn't really get mad at him for doing so. Short of tying her up, we had no way to stop her, and if we did that, we weren't any better than Sofia.

It was supposed to be Megan, me, the Whelans, and a few other members of their pack. I didn't know their names. I'd feel safer with Mr. Mittens, but he had no real power off the land. So hopefully, things worked out in Megan's favor. Frankly, I hoped she couldn't get in.

Luke drove, and Megan and I crammed into the front of the work truck next to him.

"Are the others meeting us?" I asked after we pulled onto the highway.

"No," Luke answered. "They are out on a job, but they'll keep their phones close if we need backup."

We drove in silence, mainly because Luke and I had lost, and Megan wasn't listening to any more arguments. The warehouse was on the north end of town, I lived south of town, so it was about a fifteen-minute drive and some winding through town to get there. Kilchis wasn't very big, so our "industrial" area was also small—a few warehouses, a logging yard, a boatyard, and a combination boat repair and dealership were all that surrounded it. The road on one side and the sea on the other left little space for any greenery or trees, so the warehouse was fully visible if you wanted to look for it. I wondered why the witches met here.

Maybe it was cheap and large enough to host their coven meetings? Maybe they had a share in either a boating or logging business? I had no idea. I knew that Sofia had some kind of high-powered job, but that didn't mesh with the kind of businesses in this area, so maybe she did something outside of the coven. When we'd been friends, she'd been vague about her job and hadn't wanted to talk about it. She'd hinted that she was in charge of a lot of money and people, but no clue in what area of business. She could be a glorified fishmonger for all I knew.

We pulled up and parked at an adjoining business so we wouldn't be noticed. We probably should have brought Megan's car, because "Whelan Restoration" was splashed all over Luke's truck. Oh well, this is why we weren't professional investigators. We clambered out and walked over to the witches' warehouse. When we got within two feet, I could feel the ward humming. I reached out a hand and bumped into a solid, cold surface.

"I can feel it," I said. But it was obvious that I'd stopped. Luke walked until he ran into the ward, and then he growled deep in his throat. That's right, werewolf. I threw him a sidelong glance; it was hard to remember that not everyone I knew these days was human—including me.

Megan was three paces behind Luke. I looked at her, and although her face was set and her eyes hard, her hands were trembling. I knew she was terrified. Maybe our arguments had set in some.

She paused and straightened her clothes as though she were only going in for a job interview. Instead of trying the ward on the wall, we'd stopped at a spot which was devoid of windows, she walked around to the front entrance and marched up to the front door—a glass, two-door entrance that was a common sight around here. There was an open sign in the doorway, so at least she'd have an excuse once she went inside. This must be one of the witches' businesses after all. I wondered what they really did inside.

She handed me her alexandrite pendant, just in case—more shivers and bad vibes passed over me as her meager protection evaporated. She passed through the ward. I wondered for a moment if that meant the main door wasn't warded. It was a business after all, but when I approached wrapped in my shadow magic, I was still rebuffed. I slunk back to the truck which was positioned so we could see the door.

She went inside and disappeared. Now, we waited. She was going to text us if she got the ward down, and then we were going to sneak inside. If she couldn't get it down, she was going to do whatever spying she could without getting caught. I hated to wait. I wished Mr. Mittens were here, but he probably couldn't get through the ward either. Minutes ticked by.

After I checked my phone for approximately the three-hundredth time, she came strolling out. She looked normal, not frazzled or upset, and my heart leapt in joy. She was safe.

I wanted to leap out of the truck and grab her, but instead, I waited until she was in the truck to hear what had happened.

She shut the door and then sunk into the seat. "That was terrifying."

I gave her back the pendant with a sigh of relief. She fastened it back on. Luke reached out and grasped her hand over my lap in the close quarters of the bench seat of the work truck. He held onto her for a moment before letting go.

"So, what happened?" I asked a little impatiently.

She grabbed her water bottle from the drink holder and took a long drink. "The front is normal, like any business, complete with a receptionist up front filing her nails. It's like they don't know what a real business should look like, so they used a stereotypical one from the media." She dismissed their foolishness with a wave of her hand.

"I told her I had an appointment and just breezed past her. She barely looked up and didn't protest, which struck me as odd. Maybe she's an illusion or construct or something."

I didn't know if those were possible on that scale, but neither did Megan so I just grinned and waited.

"I went to the back, looking for the witches' circle so I could break the ward spell. I found the door into the warehouse proper; the front was just a few offices and a unisex bathroom. I looked back there, but it was full of witches. I mean *full*." She emphasized the lack of space by spreading her arms and crowding us more.

"I looked around, but couldn't see where the circle was, but there were so many people I could have easily missed it. I walked into the back room and slunk around the walls where it was darker. Everyone was so busy, I didn't think I'd be seen. There were stairs to a loft and more offices. I figured I could see better looking down, so once I located the stairs, I headed there. The stairs were your typical industrial metal steps, nothing aesthetically pleasing at all."

"And…" I tried to hurry her, but she was taking another drink.

"And I went up to them. Duh."

I rolled my eyes at her. "Come on, Megan, what did you see?"

"I could see the offices were dark, so I figured no one was up there, which was good since there was nowhere to hide, and if anyone looked up, they'd see me. And I stood out. They were all wearing dark blue coveralls, and hair nets, because they were processing fish. It stunk in there, I'll tell you."

That explained what business the coven worked in. Maybe Sofia *was* a glorified fishmonger, huh? Since Megan was wearing stylish jeans and a long-sleeved t-shirt, she would have stood out.

"So, I looked down. The circle wasn't literally a circle. It was just bits of stuff along the edges of the walls of the warehouse. Once I found it, I hurried back down where I wasn't so exposed, and snuck over to the edge of a wall to try and disrupt it. Unfortunately, even though the stuff looked like it was loose, it was stuck pretty tight in some kind of adhesive. It must have taken the witches a long time to make the thing. I did break it up, I think, but I won't know until you get close enough to try to get through it. I would have texted, but someone saw me, and I had to put on my act and be 'lost.' That's when I left."

"No one tried to attack you?" Luke asked.

"I'm here and fine, I think."

"Yeah, still that's scary. I should probably see if I can sense any witch magic on you before we do anything else," I said.

"You know how to do that?" Megan asked incredulously.

"No, but I think I can. I've sensed witch magic before." I was thinking of the gris gris bag and its foul contents, as well as Mr. Mittens hint that wards could do more than one thing.

"OK, sense away!" she said and closed her eyes.

I snorted. "Is there a reason you need to close your eyes?"

She opened one and peered at me. "Yes? I'm concentrating."

I laughed and reached out with my senses. It took a while to clear my mind, and I did end up closing my eyes, but I finally could feel a little something. I opened my eyes. "Turn around," I ordered her.

She frowned. "What's wrong?"

"There's something on your back, just turn around and I'll look."

She tried to twist around, but it was too tight in the truck. We climbed back out and once Megan's back was to me, I brushed away her hair. Holding my hand an inch away from her clothing, I felt all over until I sensed the sharp ping of witch magic. I plucked something from her shirt and held it out for her and Luke to see.

"What is it?" Megan asked.

I didn't know, so I shrugged. "A magical bug, I guess."

It did resemble a bug, but not anything I'd ever seen. It was dark green with an iridescent shimmer, and it had six legs like a real bug, but those appeared more for gripping than movement. It didn't have eyes, wings, or antennae, so I knew it wasn't a living thing. It gave off a slight magical pulse, and when I looked at it with my senses, it was a small thing, nothing too complex. It probably was just a homing beacon.

After we examined it, I tossed it in a bush and checked Megan over again. She was clean.

"Huh, I guess the ward did do more than one thing. Kept out the magical and marked any non-magic types with a bug," I said.

"Let's go see if that ward is still up," I announced, and we slunk over to the windowless wall to test it. Sure enough, I could touch the warehouse now without anything holding me back. The ward was broken.

"Good work!" I told her.

She beamed and buffed her nails on her shirt and then looked at them. "That's right, I'm your secret weapon."

I wanted to shake her because she could have died infiltrating the lair, but she had been successful and deserved to gloat a bit.

"Yeah, but it's still dangerous, and I don't want this to be a habit. What if instead of a tracker, they'd done something to you?" Luke asked.

I looked at him, he was falling for her, and he was truly concerned.

She recognized it too, because she threw her arms around his neck and gave him a firm kiss square on the mouth. "Thanks for caring about me."

Luke looked stunned. Like totally gobsmacked. I gathered they hadn't kissed before now, and I wanted to chuckle at the light pink blush that rose up his neck and over his cheeks.

He pulled her in close and returned the kiss with heat. I heard Megan gasp in surprise, and then groan deep in her throat as she returned the kiss with fervor.

I gave them a few seconds before I cleared my throat. "Ummm, I'm still here. And there are witches."

They broke apart.

"Yeah, witches," Luke repeated as though his mind wasn't quite back in his head.

"Let's go set up a listening device of our own," I said.

The plan was easy, if maybe stupid, but it's not like we had high tech listening devices to plant or magical bugs. We'd picked up some fancy game trail cameras with sound capability, and we were going to plant them in unnoticeable spots in and around the warehouse. The benefit of using them was they were easy to acquire, if pricey, they didn't require permits or anything fancy, and we'd get audio and visual information sent to our phone apps.

The problem was sneaking them inside and placing them somewhere no one would notice. At least we could all get inside now. Luke climbed a light pole and secured the first one, looking down on the warehouse parking lot and the front door. That one didn't have sound, mainly because all we'd hear would be road noise, and the beep-beep-beep of big trucks backing up. No one wanted that.

Once he was done, we were going to go back in to secure the others, which was the scary part. Sneaking past the receptionist wasn't going to work twice, I assumed, and the other entrances were for trucks at the back. Luke had suggested we wait for one, so Megan and I took our backpacks with the cameras and slunk around back to wait. Luke went for fast food, mainly because he was hungry, and I could nervous eat anytime as could Megan. We found a place out of the way on some logs that were being used as a makeshift divider and sat. There were other people about since it was approaching the end of the workday. Some were going to their vehicles, and a few were also sitting on the logs, taking a break, so we fit in.

Luke came back a half hour later, and we sat and enjoyed our food, while waiting. Finally, a truck pulled around the back of the warehouse with a big reefer attached to keep the fish cool for wherever it was being transported. It started to back up. We had to time it right so we could enter before the driver came around back, or the crew inside lined up to transfer their fish boxes to the truck. It was going to be tricky.

Since I had my nifty new shadow magic, I volunteered to go up and give the all-clear for the others. I waited until no one was looking my way and wrapped myself in shadow. Megan gasped lightly when I disappeared from sight, so I knew I was invisible. I boldly walked up to the truck, hefted myself up to the unloading dock, and waited for the delivery door to open.

The big semi-truck backed up expertly, and once it was near, the rolling door opened, and I peered inside. A coven member was operating the door, but after it opened, he disappeared into the warehouse, probably to get his crew. I texted Luke and Megan, this was our chance.

They snuck around the building, hopefully out of the eyesight of the truck driver, but since he was busy backing up, that wouldn't be a problem until they were in view of his big mirrors. I hoped he wasn't nosy; there wasn't any way to avoid him seeing them if he cared.

I wished I knew how to include them in my invisibility spell, but I was still a novice. Luke helped Megan up onto the loading dock, and then he easily jumped up. We slid inside the door just in time. A forklift was heading towards us, laden with fish boxes. We looked around for the best place to hide our cameras. There were some good areas, hard to see, but that would provide good coverage. But the best spot was a post near the main office where I was sure we'd get the best intel. The only problem was it could be clearly seen by everyone. This was going to be tricky enough with Luke and Megan fully visible. Placing it would be easy for me since I could keep myself unseen, but the camera would be highly visible. I waffled on whether or not to find another place for it.

Megan found the spot she wanted to place her camera and was slinking off behind some equipment. Luke looked after her, as though he wanted to follow, but then he went to his spot instead. I stood there, staring. It was the best place, and it would get the best information. I climbed the metal stairs so I could reach the pole.

Just as I got to the top, a door in one of the upper offices opened, and Sofia walked out. My breath caught, and unexpected fear froze me in my tracks. I knew she couldn't see me, but I was still terrified. She was standing three feet from me. I held my breath, irrationally.

A minion stepped out of the office after her and Sofia barked orders at the mousy coven member who was making notes on her electronic tablet. I looked for somewhere to hide before I remembered I was invisible.

"I need that information, now!" she barked at the poor minion.

"Yes, I'll be right back with it, sorry!" The poor mousy woman scurried away to get whatever information Sofia wanted.

Sofia was dressed impeccably as always in her power suit, makeup, and perfect hair. How could she work here and dress like that? It didn't seem practical. Probably why she never talked about it. Dress for the job you want, and all that. She sighed and looked over her kingdom from above, making sure everyone was busy. She frowned. Uh oh. I looked over the rail. Luke was clearly visible, and Sofia knew him. She knew all the Whelans. This wasn't good. Megan could hide in her anonymity, but Luke was too obvious.

She continued to scan, but her eyes didn't stop anywhere else but Luke.

I wanted to yell, "Run, Luke!" but that would give me away as well. The other cameras would be a bust, this one had to count. And now that I knew where her office was, I could simply place it there—where it would get the best info.

Since she was distracted by capturing Luke and because I couldn't do anything at the moment, I ducked into her office and looked for a good spot to hide the camera. It wasn't a huge thing, but a lot bigger than some fancy high-tech bug would be. I held it in my hand, weighing it, and wondering how I could place it. The corner of the office had some painted over pipes running through it, but it would stand out like a sore thumb. I dragged a chair over to the corner and tried to set it so you couldn't see it. That was a no go. It was just too obvious.

I sighed, and my heart beat faster. I had no idea how much time I had. It had to go here. I used the straps to belt it on and activated it. I stepped down and returned the chair. I looked up. I saw it plainly. Anyone who looked up would see it.

I was magical dammit. I should be able to conceal it. I gathered my shadow magic into my hand, whispered at it to hide the camera and tossed it at the unsightly thing. It stuck, and the camera disappeared. Unfortunately, so did a section of the pipe. But it took a moment to notice, and that might work in our favor. I didn't have time to attempt to fix it or redo it, because the door opened, and I had to slip through before she closed it again. She was on her cell phone, so I slipped out before she slammed the door to her office. She was talking to security. I had to get to Luke before security did. I could probably hide him and Megan now.

I was so stupid, I should have tried this before we snuck in, but I'd been too hesitant and without confidence to do so. I spotted them from the railing and raced down the metal stairs. I couldn't hide the sound, and I accidentally bumped into the mousy woman on her way up, and she slammed into the railing and gave a loud, "Oomph." She looked around with wide eyes, but I was past her and gone before she could react.

I dodged through people and equipment before I made it to Luke.

"She knows we're here!" I said to him, and he started.

Invisible, I had to remember. "I'm going to try to hide you, so hold still for a moment, then we've gotta get out of here fast!"

"OK, do you see Megan?" Luke asked, but he held still.

I didn't answer, because I had to concentrate, but after I coated him in shadow, and he disappeared, I whispered, "Yes, she's over by the door, let's go."

We made our way back to the door where loading was still taking place. Megan was standing crouched behind the forklift, out of sight, but she wouldn't be that way for long. As soon as they finished, they'd want to go back for more.

I grasped her arm and whispered, "It's me," at the same time so she wouldn't react. I assumed Luke was close by, but I couldn't see him. "If you hold still, I'll make you invisible, then we gotta go."

She nodded.

I concentrated and coated her in shadow. I started to see Luke faintly, so moving around was wearing the shadow magic away. Probably from me as well. We'd have to move fast. We headed back to the loading door. Just before we reached it, an alarm went off, and everyone froze.

"There is an intruder. Bring him to me," came over the loudspeaker.

Time was up.

CHAPTER

TWENTY

L uke jumped down first and helped both of us. We ran for the truck before all of our shadows disappeared. I hoped the shadow on the office camera kept it hidden. I assumed as long as no wind wore it away, it would stay invisible. But I had no idea, this was new to me.

We were panting when we piled into the truck. Sofia had seen Luke, so we knew the jig was up, but she hadn't caught us, and we hadn't been hit by any nasty spells. Luke started up the truck and pulled onto Hwy 101. While he drove, Megan looked up the app that connected with the cameras on her phone.

"Got it," she said once the real time feed connected.

"Well, what's happening?" I asked.

Luke grunted.

"Hold on, nothing yet."

She stuffed her earbuds in her ears since the truck and road noise were keeping her from overhearing anything important.

She held up a finger. "Sofia is *pissed*." Megan laughed. She was quiet some more.

"Ooo, this is good." Another stretch of silence, and Megan's face turned glum. "Shit."

"What?" The suspense was getting to me.

"Hold on," she said impatiently.

We waited a while longer, town coming into view, then we were out and headed out to my house.

"Turn around," Megan yelled suddenly. Luke checked his mirrors and swerved to the right, hard, swinging wide so he could make a left-hand turn and not have to back up on the narrow highway.

After he'd completed the turn, our hearts racing, I yelled, "What's going on?"

"She's going after Gabe at the clinic. We gotta get there first. Call Gabe and warn him. I'll call Noah."

I pulled out my phone and dialed Gabe's cell. No answer. He was probably with a patient. I tried the office, but they sent me to his voice-mail. I left a text and hoped he'd see it soon.

"I couldn't get him, what about Noah?" I asked her after I hung up.

"He's still out of town, but he's heading in. He'll be there, eventually."

We were silent the rest of the way, worried we wouldn't make it in time to beat Sofia and the coven. They already had people in position. People who worked there. Maybe it was too late already, Gabe wasn't answering. I took a panicked breath. No. That kind of thinking wouldn't help. He was just with a patient. He was a doctor.

I tried to calm my breathing and my heart, but it wasn't working. Megan reached out and grabbed my hand. I squeezed gently in gratitude.

"We've got this, it'll be OK, we'll arrive in time," she chanted softly to me. Probably to convince herself as well as me.

Luke pulled up to the clinic, and we jumped out. The clinic was a large, ugly tan and brown building in the shape of a U. It was two stories high and housed doctors' offices, instacare, the lab, and the imaging departments. We skirted around the instacare door and marched into the clinic. We were stopped by two receptionists at the front desk, demanding our appointment information.

I looked at Luke and Megan. "Umm, I'm here to see Dr. Ambrose?" I said uncertainly.

"What's your name and date of birth?"

"I don't have an appointment; this is a personal question. If you could just page him, I'd appreciate it."

The receptionist gave me a hard look, turned and whispered to the other lady, and smiled knowingly at me. "Is the doctor expecting you to call?"

This was a trap. If I said no, she'd dismiss me coldly. If I said yes, she'd make me wait until Gabe was free, and then go ask him. We didn't have time for either.

"Look, this is very important. Could you just ask him?" I begged.

"Dr. Ambrose is extremely busy with patients. If you want to leave a message, I'll be sure he gets it when he's free."

Yup, she was writing me off. I'm sure that Gabe had women throwing themselves at him. He was handsome, single, straight, and a doctor, but this was truly important—a matter of his life and freedom. I needed her to listen to me.

"Look." I glanced at her name tag. "Evelyn. If Dr. Ambrose does not get this information, soon, it will be upsetting for him. I only need a moment. Then I'll leave." I left out the part where I was going to take him with me. "If he doesn't get it, it could mean life and death."

She squinted at me. "Who are you? Are you here from the lab?"

I wondered why she'd jumped to that. I wasn't wearing scrubs, or a white coat, or any type of badge or identification. But, since she brought it up, why not? "Sure." I smiled sweetly.

"Is this about the patient I sent over this morning?"

I sure hoped I wasn't about to cause someone heartache or harm, but I said, "Yes."

"Hang on, and I'll see if he's available, Ms.…?

"Donovan."

She nodded and pressed buttons on her complicated office phone. I watched like a hawk. She waited. "Doctor, I have a Ms. Donovan here with some test results? She'd like to speak to you if you are free for a few moments? You are? OK, I'll send her back."

She waved me towards a closed door, and I opened it and walked through. Luke and Megan settled themselves in the waiting room chairs as I closed the door behind me and headed down the corridor. Before I had to choose a room or run out of the hallway, Gabe stepped out and gestured for me to join him in a room about halfway down.

"Gabe!" I said a little louder than I intended. My adrenaline was up after the ordeal with the receptionist.

"What's wrong?" Gabe asked, frowning. "What test results?" His brows were drawn together in confusion.

"I don't know about test results; your receptionist just started asking me questions, and I said, 'yes,' so she'd let me come back here." I took a deep breath. "We were spying on Sofia, and she's sending witches here now to put you back under the spell. We gotta go!"

I reached for his hand. He looked at me for a moment. "I have a patient waiting in the next room. I can't leave yet."

"Can anyone fill in for you? I don't know what'll happen if she catches you."

He stiffened. "Yeah." He rubbed the back of his neck. A gesture I recognized from when we were kids, he'd do it any time he was uncertain.

He thought a moment more. "I'll inform the front that I'm leaving after this patient, and they can either reschedule, or I'll see if the PA can fill in for the last two of the day. I'll meet you in the parking lot in fifteen minutes."

I looked at him, "Are you sure?"

"Yeah, I can't walk out on the people in need, and I can't let the coven dictate my life," he said with a sigh.

I nodded. There wasn't anything else I could do. "OK, see you at the car."

I walked back to Megan and Luke. "He's going to meet us in the parking lot after this patient. Let's go wait by his car."

They stood and followed me out.

I leaned on Gabe's car; Luke and Megan were driving over from the other side of the parking lot to park nearby. I figured I'd have to wait fifteen minutes, since that's how long it seemed an average doctor's appointment went for something routine. After a minute or two, I saw the truck turning the corner to this part of the lot. And coming right at them was a streak of light. I opened my mouth to shout a warning, but they saw it. Both bailed out of the truck on opposite sides as whatever it was rammed directly into the front of the truck.

The truck exploded into a ball of light, and the blast pushed me back. I bounced off the hood of the car and rolled to the ground. My ears rang, and I felt as though someone had punched me in the chest. I groaned and rolled to my hands and knees to slowly stand up. My heart hammered, and terror blazed through me. Was Megan alive? Luke? Once on my feet, I swayed a moment before I could stumble forward to where the truck burned, a searing, white heat. This wasn't a natural fire.

Luke had shifted into his wolf. I gulped. We were blocked on one side by the fire, but anyone who looked from the other three sides would wonder what a huge wolf was doing in the parking lot of the local doctor's office, but he was standing over Megan protectively. I shuffled towards them until the disorientation from the blast passed, and then I ran towards my friend, lying motionless on the ground.

"Megan!" I yelled.

Luke growled and scanned the parking lot for whomever had attacked us. I got to her and bent over. She was breathing, but she had a smear of blood on her head. She must have hit it when she bailed out of the truck. Her eyes fluttered open.

"What happened?" she mumbled, and her hands moved to her head.

"We were attacked," I answered and helped her sit up.

Luke paced around.

I looked around briefly but didn't see anything. I could hear sirens in the distance, the fire must have been reported already. Megan stood slowly. I put my shoulder under her arm to support her, and she wobbled on her feet. Once I had her, Luke took off, his nose to the ground to find our attacker. I shuddered. It had to be a witch. That had been a ball of light, not a grenade, or a rocket. It'd been magic. Plus, it was eating the metal of the truck. Soon nothing would be left of it but a scorch mark on the pavement.

If they hadn't bailed…I shivered again. I wouldn't think about it. We were vulnerable with only one side blocked from view. We needed to get out of here fast, before they aimed at us directly. I hurried, pushing Megan to limp along faster.

Luke's form meandered in and out of view as he wove through cars in the parking lot, silent and intent.

I pulled Megan next to Gabe's car, and we crouched down. We were in between two cars with a short space and the building behind us. Megan shook. I grasped her hand to give the little comfort I could. I pulled shadows around us to hide us further, but I'd just remembered to do it, so if anyone had seen us, they'd know we were still here.

I concentrated, for the first time using two of my magical abilities at once. Grabbing hold of my greatest offensive magic, lightning, I kept it in my mind, ready to strike. A slim, perfectly dressed figure stepped into view. Sofia. My teeth clacked together as I clenched them. The fury rising up and filling my body with rage.

I let go of Megan, tied off the shadow magic around her, and stepped into view. Sofia's eyes flicked to mine, and she grinned. Grinned. I let the lightning I held go and aimed it directly at her.

CHAPTER

TWENTY-ONE

The only sign she gave that she was surprised was a brief widening of her eyes, then she blocked my blast with an ice shield. I shook with rage. That was my ice. Mine. I sent a stream of fire at her, and the ice melted. She took a step back.

I smiled. This time, she couldn't out magic me. She was alone, and I was gaining better control daily. I sent another stream of fire at her. She paled. I called the lightning. I grasped it in my mind and focused. This time, I would hit her. I didn't care if it killed her at this point. I'd rather have my friends safe, than get back my piece of magic. But before I sent it after her, two more witches stepped into view.

Megan reached out and grasped my hand, trying to pull me back down between the cars. "Brigid, get down here!" she whispered urgently.

I sent the lightning at the three witches and ducked back down. I could fight one witch, but three? I wasn't crazy. They'd thoroughly kicked my ass the last time we met up. Before my head sunk below the edge of the car, I saw Luke's grey fur shoot by behind the witches.

"Shit, Megan, Luke's behind them."

I couldn't see her behind the shadow shield, but her hand tightened on mine. "We can't let him stay out there alone."

I nodded. I wrapped the shadow around me as well, and we ran out, crossing the parking lot to the next row of cars—close to the witches. Sofia was barking out orders. They still hadn't seen Luke or us. Just then, Gabe strolled out of the back door and headed towards his car. He hesitated when he saw the burning truck in the parking lot, but before he could compute what was going on and react, Sofia spotted him.

Several things happened at once. The fire trucks turned off the main road and pulled into the parking lot, Gabe turned to look at them. Luke leapt up and hit one of the witches and rode him down to the ground. Sofia put up a hand and aimed a spell at Gabe, as I screamed a warning, followed by a blast of fire.

The fire truck took my blast, and my view was blocked as it passed by me. I sobbed out a cry of disbelief and anger. Once it passed me, I could see what had happened. Luke was lying on the pavement, unmoving, and Gabe and the witches were gone. I screamed in frustration. The shadows fell from us, and Megan ran to Luke. I followed, stunned. Sofia'd beaten me again.

Before we reached Luke, he'd shifted back. Megan ran over to the car and picked his clothes up off the ground. He was lying very still. I stared at his chest, willing him to breathe. I relaxed slightly when I realized he was. I reached out to touch his shoulder to make sure, and the moment I made contact, he leapt up and growled at me, his eyes aglow. I fell back on my ass with a yelp.

He apologized, and Megan handed him his clothes at the same time Luke and I realized he was naked, and my eyes were aimed directly at his junk. I looked away quickly. Megan took a little longer, I noticed, since my eyes went to her face. Once she looked away, she winked at me and grinned. I rolled my eyes at the total inappropriateness, but the humor eased the pain in my chest at losing Gabe again.

Luke hurriedly dressed between two cars, then helped me up off the ground. Since neither of them had a phone—as both phones were both currently cooking down to atoms with the rest of the truck—I handed mine to Luke, who dialed his brother to see how far away he was. Meanwhile, the firemen poured water ineffectually on the magically burning truck from a safe distance, while others kept the crowd away.

We wandered away from the action. Since there was nothing identifiable as belonging to the Whelans anymore, we acted like onlookers until Noah showed up with his company truck, and we piled in.

We filled him in again, and we all came to the consensus that the best thing to do would be to come at her when we knew when and where she would be. The full moon. The altar. My property.

The thought made my hands curl into tight fists, and the blood pound in my head. I wanted to punch her, pull her hair, make her pay. The thoughts disturbed me. I'd never been violent. I'd been the kind that took it and took it, mostly without complaint.

I was quiet the rest of the ride home. Megan kept throwing glances my way, knowing me all the way through, she knew I brooded when I was deep in it. I climbed out and let Megan say her goodbyes to Luke. I stomped into the house. Mr. Mittens was on the kitchen table, looking for all the world like he was expecting me to walk in the door at that moment. I stopped, startled.

"Hi," I said, glumly.

Something is wrong, he said.

I nodded and burst into tears. His eyes opened wider, briefly, then he ducked his head and gave me a firm headbutt. I scratched his ears, and he purred. The sound and vibration rumbled through me and after a few moments, I calmed down. A cat purr was magical in its own way. I leaned in and picked him up. He flopped over my shoulder, and I hugged him. Eventually, he gave a squiggle, so I put him down, and he rubbed against me.

Do you feel better? he asked.

"Yes, thanks."

What happened to make you so upset? He sat back on the table and curled his tail primly around his feet, his large eyes intent on my face.

I told him what had happened.

I will eat her, he said after I was done.

That made me smile finally. He meant it, too. There was no joking or doubt in his mental tone.

"I'll let you," I replied.

He huffed a little, not trusting my tone I supposed. *Tonight is the full moon, do you and the wolves have a plan?* He asked after a moment.

I shrugged; it was more of an outline than an actual plan. Sort of, get there first, take out witches, rescue Gabe, but I wanted my cat to think better of me, so I didn't say anything.

Hmpf.

I guess my shrug wasn't as reassuring as I thought.

This is what you will do.

Then my cat went on to present a devious plan. No wonder my property was clean of dangerous creatures.

I agreed, because what he presented was an actual plan, not just a vague outline full of hope. My job was to give everyone their assignments, so I contacted the wolves, Brightfeather, and Goch to do that. Then, I was to go conceal myself and Mr. Mittens ahead of time at the altar site. After I left a few magical traps behind as a diversion— nothing dangerous or difficult, just some light explosions to disorient the enemy—Mr. Mittens and I took up our hiding spots, and I concealed us with shadow.

This time, I didn't know what Sofia was up to other than putting the whammy back on Gabe. She didn't have me captured and couldn't steal my magic. I had it all except ice and air. Had she found my air magic? If not, she'd have to drag the rest out of my cold dead body.

She must have something up her sleeve, why else would she come back here? I shuddered. Something was going on, something we hadn't guessed at yet.

I stroked Mr. Mittens fur. I could feel the soft rumble that was his purr through my hand, but otherwise, he was nearly silent, waiting. Since the moon was reaching its zenith early in the evening, there was still some light when the witches started to gather. I hoped all was set up as we'd planned. As far as I knew, the others were readying themselves and waiting patiently for the signal.

The witches continued to show up. Even though we'd killed several, there must have been replacements, or more coven members were involved this time. It looked like the entire town was here to do whatever nasty thing Sofia had planned, however, it might just be that the clearing was now smaller since I'd regrown the surrounding forest. Finally, as more and more shuffled into the small clearing, Sofia arrived.

Like before, everyone was robed in a long black, hooded gown over their clothes. This time, Sofia's was decorated with silver thread along the edges. I couldn't see the design from my position, but I could see enough to differentiate her from the others. She directed the coven into their positions and had others lay out objects on the altar.

I realized my hands were clasped into fists. I forced them to relax, but it didn't prevent my heart from beating out of my chest, and the sweat from pouring off me. To make it worse, the finale of Sofia's conquest was being dragged into view. Gabe.

He was covered in a black robe. The only reason I knew it was him, was because I caught a flash of his face briefly, when his head flopped back, and his hood briefly fell from his face. Sofia barked something out, and two other coven members came forward, and together they lifted him onto the altar. He was much bigger than I, being over six feet and broad shouldered, so his legs dangled from the knees, and his arms hung over the sides. He must be out cold, because the position did not look remotely comfortable, and he wasn't moving.

It was growing darker. The sun had sunk below the trees, and I could feel the cool moon rising even through the clouds. I shivered. It wasn't at its zenith, so we still had time before whatever evil plan Sofia had formed would come to pass.

To make everything just that much more enjoyable, a cold rain started. I sighed. Although I couldn't see him, I imagined Mr. Mittens's face grew grumpier. Even non-earth cats hated water. I had on a rain jacket, and my boots, but still, the cold slithered down my neck and added to my discomfort.

"Bring the athame here," Sofia barked, and a hapless witch brought her a wooden box.

An athame was a knife. My eyes flew open. What was she going to do? Surely, she wouldn't kill Gabe? The coven needed him; *she* wanted him. If only to spite me.

She made the witch stand next to her and positioned others around. I realized they were all holding a wooden box. Were they all knives? I should have had her explain witch magic when we were friends, but I was too involved in my own magic and problems to ask.

Thirteen witches now surrounded the altar, Sofia, and Gabe. Thirteen witches holding thirteen wooden boxes of unknown contents. Sofia moved to the top of the altar. I'm sure directions were important, but I had no clue which way the altar faced, or if it was still the same as it was before I sunk it and reraised it. I hoped my changes screwed up her ritual. I grinned at that thought. Of course, the moon was rising in the east. Damn, why did I know that? That meant she was at the north end of the altar, and it was still true to the cardinal directions. What should I do? What were they up too?

The twilight was pouring purple shadows, and true dark was breathing down our necks. The coven members not in the inner circle were lighting honest to goodness fire burning torches to light the area, several more moved forward and lit a bonfire in the center of the clearing. I hadn't even noticed the brush pile there, hidden as it was behind black clad bodies. The flickering firelight added to the horrific ambience.

All the witches returned to their positions and turned toward Sofia, waiting. I realized I was holding my breath and let it out. Should I give the signal now? I wasn't sure. I asked Mr. Mittens and was rewarded with a gruff, *"Not yet."* The moon continued to rise in the sky, and I knew it wouldn't be long. Full dark had slammed down at some point that I hadn't noticed, since the firelight was keeping the clearing well lit. It looked to me like they were ready for whatever they were up to, so they weren't going to wait until the moon hit its zenith in a few hours.

Right as I was going to ask my cat for further advice, Sofia's voice rang out. "Brigid. I know you're here. Show yourself."

I shrank down, foolishly, I know, since I was invisible to her. I put my hand out to Mr. Mittens, and I could feel his muscles bunch up, ready to protect me.

She continued, "Brigid, I know you're listening." She paused for dramatic effect. "I knew I wouldn't have to do anything; you'd come to me."

What was she talking about? I wasn't going to hand over my magic. What did she think, I was stupid?

"You see, I don't need the doctor anymore. He's handy for the rest of the coven, but no longer necessary."

There was some confused muttering, but she silenced them, mumbling a few words I couldn't hear.

She gestured to one of the box bearing coven members, who came forward. She reached out, opened the box he was holding, and pulled out a long dagger.

I gulped. She held the knife high, so I'd be sure to see it. Its bright blade reflected the flickering light of the fire. She brought it back down and tried the edge with her thumb. "It's very sharp."

She stepped up to the altar and threw off Gabe's hood. She brushed the blade along his cheek like a straight razor, and I imagined the sound as it scraped along his whiskers.

"Sharp as a razor!"

Then she put the point at his throat. "This is what's going to happen." She kept the knife pointed at him and moved back to her place at the head. She had a better stabbing angle now, and my breath caught. "You have a few seconds to make a decision. Is your magic worth his life?"

I shook my head, although she couldn't see me, they'd never let Gabe go. I wasn't entirely sure she'd kill him, but I already knew I was going to walk right up to her and let her strip me of my heritage and birthright to save him from the slim chance she would.

I stood, and Mr. Mittens growled low in his throat. I let the shadow magic fade off of me, although I kept him covered. Gabe wasn't his responsibility.

"There you are." Sofia smiled her snake grin at me. She kept the athame at his throat. "Come on over, you know how this will go."

I did. She'd have us switch places, and she'd steal my magic. All of it this time. Why didn't I give the signal? I'd waited too long. I didn't see a way out of this, unless my allies were waiting and watching. We might have a shot while I switched spots with Gabe.

She showed more teeth. With her free hand, she gestured to the coven members, and they started to chant. My ears popped. I realized they'd raised a ward like they had the first time, and I cursed. My friends weren't able to get through it before, how were they going to now? Were they in position? I doubted it, I hadn't given them the signal. Shit.

I was close now, and two coven members grabbed me by the arms firmly so I couldn't escape. Mr. Mittens was still inside. I kept that thought as a beacon of hope. If he moved too suddenly though, the shadow around him would fade quickly. I had to trust he could take care of himself. Magic resistant, I reminded myself over and over so the fear for him didn't overwhelm me.

The witches dragged me towards the altar. Gabe was still lying there, Sofia's knife hovering over him. Were they going to move him and put me in his place? Could I use some of my magic to keep him from being stabbed? I searched through my arsenal of magic tricks. Water? Not much of a barrier. Fire? No, but I could throw it at the witches and hope they moved back. Earth? That was a possibility. Could I use my earth magic quickly enough so I could block Sofia before she stabbed Gabe? Maybe, but I'd have to time it right. I needed to wait for the switch.

They stopped me right in front of the altar, facing Sofia. The fire had made her hooded face look sinister, but now I was facing her, she was as perfect as ever. Her hood had fallen back, or she'd pushed it back in the time it had taken the witches to drag me forward, and her hair was twisted back in a perfect chignon, her makeup was flawless, and I'm sure that under the robe, she was dressed as immaculately as always. She liked to keep up the outward perfection. Probably to hide the hideous monster underneath.

Sofia used her non-knife hand to gesture that the coven members needed to remove Gabe.

He still wasn't moving except for the shallow rise and fall of his chest. What had they done to him? Was he drugged or under a spell? I stared at him, trying to read his face and search for magic, but I got nothing. So, not a spell.

I glared at Sofia. Four men came forward and grasped Gabe's limbs. Sofia stepped back momentarily and lowered the knife. Even if she never ate a carb and had a perfectly toned body, even her arm had to get tired. This was my chance. I reached out with my earth magic, and…nothing. I tried again, using my ring to focus, and only a tiny tendril responded. A slim stream of earth started to rise, and I dropped it. Whatever they were doing with the chanting had limited my magic. Damn, it had done that before. I'd have to break the active working to use my full power. I looked around, but I wasn't close enough to the outer ring of coven members.

Mr. Mittens! I yelled mentally. I hoped beyond hope that my weak magic would reach him. He'd have to stop them himself.

If you can hear me, take out the outer ring of witches! I can't use my magic! I kept yelling in my head over and over at him.

No reply.

I felt the helpless tears start to run down my cheeks, warm after the cold rain. This was it. No help was coming. Mr. Mittens either couldn't hear me, or he was also disabled by the magic dampening of the ward.

The four men dumped Gabe on the ground, out of the way. My breath caught, but he landed bonelessly, so I doubted he was hurt too badly. At least he was away from immediate danger, Sofia was now focused solely on me. I struggled and attempted to break free. The grip on my arms increased to painful levels, and I knew I'd be bruised. Once that didn't work, I used my lightning magic, and sent surges of shocks through my skin into their hands.

They dropped me, and I scurried back, but that didn't last. Sofia barked out a few words, and I was frozen in place. Not literally in ice, just unmoving. Try as I might, I couldn't move. I couldn't even blink.

"You didn't think we'd be prepared this time?" Sofia said, with triumph in her voice. "We are prepared for all of your tricks."

I threw all of my hatred into the stare I gave her.

"This time, there is no escape. Your friends are out there." She gestured with a sweeping movement of her hand. "You are in here, and entirely, at my mercy."

She said something, and I could move my head, blink, and take a breath.

I gasped for air for a moment.

"Any last words?" This was different. She'd also learned I didn't need my voice to activate my magic.

I looked around. "None of you think this is wrong? That killing an innocent person is evil? What is wrong with you?"

One person yelled out, "You aren't innocent, you're Fae. You don't deserve the power you've been given."

That was it in a nutshell. I wasn't going to reach them by appealing to their consciences, they didn't think of me as a person.

"Put her on the altar."

They lifted me like I weighed nothing and wasn't kicking and flailing and screaming with all my might. Probably because even though I sent the commands to my body, I was still held completely still by Sofia's spell.

Then, I felt the cold hard stone beneath me, and I was lying on the altar, staring up at the cloud covered moon, and Sofia's smarmy face. I spit up at her. It was the only defense I had left.

The spittle didn't even come near her but fell harmlessly back onto the altar beside me. Her smile increased.

The witches fell back into their positions. She nodded at them, and said, "Let's begin."

The witches of the inner circle began to chant. It was like I was being crushed in a vice. The chant was pressing in on me from every direction, and I panted with the pain of it all, unable to draw a full breath. Then when I thought I'd pass out from lack of air, I could feel the pull that was Sofia stealing the magic from me.

I screamed.

All hell broke loose.

There was a pop in my ears, like the change of altitude on a plane. The pressure ceased, and I drew a deep breath. I could move, so I sat up, and I saw what was happening. Mr. Mittens had transformed and was slaughtering witches. They ran around to escape him, but when they stopped chanting, the barrier came down, and my friends were free to come in.

Mr. Mittens was bad enough, but a fire-breathing dragon? The witches didn't stand a chance. They fled into the woods. Careful so he didn't set the place on fire, Goch kept to the clearing, but Brightfeather and the wolf pack had nothing to hinder them. I grinned and turned to see Sofia attempt to flee.

She wasn't getting away this time. I chased her. She had picked a random direction and was now running towards my house. Wrong choice. We slipped into the trees. Unfortunately, Sofia was a runner, and I was not, but I had the benefit of being on my own land. I connected with it flawlessly, using everything I had to cut her off.

Finally, I commanded the ground to block her, and she turned around to face me. Before I could say anything, she flung a barrage of ice darts at me, and I threw up a dirt shield to stop them. I hadn't thought fast enough to counter with fire, but at her second blast, I brought my fire up and blasted back.

She grinned, and I blanched. She muttered something, and I could feel her magic try to trap me again. This time she didn't have the coven's dampening field to help, so I shrugged that off and sent a lightning bolt at her. She blocked it with an ice shield.

We were evenly matched. I probably had more power at my call, but she knew how to use hers. I threw lightning, fire, water, and earth at her, and she blocked each spell. She tossed ice shards at me and spells that felt nasty, but I didn't recognize as I pushed them into the earth. The surrounding plants and trees blackened and rotted before our eyes. I was growing tired, and I figured Sofia had to be as well when Mr. Mittens stepped up next to me.

Sofia took a step back. She threw a hasty spell at him, and he walked through it. She blanched. His growl rumbled out from his massive chest, and she look frightened for the first time.

I'm going to eat you. He directed the thought at Sofia. I wasn't sure if she could hear him, but her eyes got a little wider. It could have just been his presence.

I put my hand up on his flank. To have him wait.

"What is your end game, Sofia? We were friends. Gabe would have filled your well if you'd just asked. Why do you have to hurt people?"

My questions came out soft and pleading. I flinched. I really did want to know. What was her motivation to do all of this at the cost of everyone that had been kind to her?

She stared at me like I had two heads. "Everything is easy for you, isn't it?" she sneered. "Born with life giving magic, a fearless protector, and wealth? I deserve some of that. Since fate won't give it to me, naturally, I've had to learn to do it myself."

She raised her hand and started flinging spells at me. I couldn't block them all. She fired them so quickly, I barely got up a barrier and couldn't think fast enough to throw back offensive magic at her. Spell after black spell struck the earthen wall, blasting it apart a little at a time. I was pouring my energy into keeping it erect. Eventually, her attack wore me down, and I sunk to my knees. The barrier crumbling. Mr. Mittens jumped in front of me to block the attack with his body, but even with natural spell resistance, he was getting hurt.

His help gave me some breathing space. I put a last burst of energy into the earthen wall to block her attack, and the second it went up, Megan ran to me from the side. She tried to pull me back into the shelter of the woods, but I couldn't leave Mr. Mittens, and I couldn't let Sofia get away. I gathered myself for one last desperate attempt. I launched myself at Sofia and landed on her. Both of our breath whooshed out, and she scrambled away from me. I hit the dirt, but before I did, I grabbed her by the hair. She fell off balance to her knees, and she lashed out with her fingernails, catching me across the face. I socked her in the jaw. Her head snapped back, and then forward. Her eyes flashed, and she snarled a spell at me. Megan reached out to put her hand over Sofia's mouth to stop whatever nasty thing she was flinging at me, I grabbed both of them. Mr. Mittens leapt at us, trying to get in between me and the spell. I grabbed at my magic. I didn't know what I wanted it to do, but it obeyed. There was a bright flash.

CHAPTER

TWENTY-TWO

"Aargh." I groaned and sat up, clutching my head. It pounded with such force I swear it was going to blow apart. Plus, my face burned where Sofia's nails had raked it. My hands were on the soft grass or moss of the forest. I looked around. Megan and Mr. Mittens were sprawled with me. But something was off. I looked around for Sofia. She'd been right next to me.

She too was sprawled on the ground, but further away than I remembered. I blinked and tried to clear my head again. I checked that Megan and Mr. Mittens were breathing, then turned my attention to Sofia.

Her hair had half fallen out of its twist, and some was spread around her. I wondered why she never wore it down, it was long, shiny, and lush. Of course, it was currently a tangled mess, and her make-up was smeared. I smiled a brief grin at that. She'd hate being such a mess, I guessed she had to control every part of her existence. I shrugged. She was also breathing. I rolled over to my hands and knees and tried to stand. I staggered up, but my knees wouldn't hold me. I sagged and plopped back on my butt. Mr. Mittens stirred.

I reached out a hand to run down his spotted fur. He blinked his luminous eyes at me, then suddenly bolted up onto his feet.

How did we get here?

His mental question was loud and bounced around inside my head painfully.

"What are you talking about?" I groaned and clutched my head tighter.

Megan stirred and sat up slowly. "What happened?" she groaned. "My head hurts."

"Sofia was throwing a spell at me," I said, confused, and I...

The truth was I wasn't sure what I'd done. I'd gathered my magic up for a spell, and then released it. But I'd been wishing...

She's realm walked us to Faerie, Mr. Mittens finished.

"I what?" I asked stupidly.

He blinked his eyes at me. *You've taken us to Faerie.*

Sofia stirred. Then because she must have realized she was lying down, she sat up in a jolt and stared around at us. She brought her hands up in a defensive posture. I just stared at her.

I reached for my magic. Although I could feel it and the air seemed to tingle with the free magic of the realm, I couldn't touch it or bring it to bear. I tried again. Nothing. Sofia's face was confused as well.

"Mr. Mittens, why can't I use my magic?"

You realm walked without knowing that you have to guard yourself. Your magic was stripped away, and it will need time to recharge, he said simply.

"Grandfather and Dana never seem to have issues with their magic," I pointed out.

They know how to guard themselves. You have never been trained, he said with a mental shrug.

Story of my life. I sighed. Oh well, magic was new to me. I could live without it just fine. Sofia, however, continued to attempt spells, if her muttering was any indication, and was growing steadily angrier and more scared as she went.

"Are you OK?" I asked Mr. Mittens, sudden fear grasping me that I might have damaged him, my magical friend.

Yes, I've been realm walking for centuries, he replied, a little disgust at my question coming through his mental voice.

I breathed a sigh of relief. "Good, I was worried."

His gaze softened at that, then he turned to Sofia. He stalked towards her. She stood and ran into the woods. Mr. Mittens crouched as though he were going to chase after her, but then he turned his massive head at me. *Do you wish me to bring her back?* he asked.

I looked at him dumbly. "Uh, no."

He shrugged and gave me a wide cat grin. *She won't survive here long without magic.*

I'd worry about her after I took care of us.

I gulped. "How long before it...you know...comes back?" I asked nervously.

He gave me another kitty shrug, a sort of head bob. *It depends on the user. You, as a born Fae, probably a week or two, her? I don't know but could be a lot longer.*

"A week or two? Will we survive that long?" I shuddered.

He stared at me. Then in a blink, he morphed from his true form to that of a tall man, with tawny golden hair and pointed ears.

I blinked at him. "Mr. Mittens?" I asked hesitantly.

"Yes," he answered with actual words. "This is my Fae form."

"I didn't know you could do other forms beside your Ragdoll and Splintercat forms."

"I'm a shapeshifter on all the realms that are infused with magic," he said. "I can only do the two forms on earth because the magic there is weak, outside of your land, that is."

"Oh." I didn't know what else to say.

"You've been here before. What should we do?"

Megan had been watching this all with wide eyes. She chose that moment to speak, as though everything had just registered through brain fog. "We're in Faerie? Faerie?" she repeated.

We nodded.

"This is so freaking cool!" she shouted and popped to her feet. "I'm standing on another world!" She danced a few steps and laughed. Then, she looked at Mr. Mittens.

"Why do I feel giddy, almost drunk?" she asked, puzzled.

I realized after she said it, that part of my disorientation was the same. A light tipsy feeling but with lots of energy behind it.

"This world is suffused with magic, and the air is purer, richer, than the air on earth," Mr. Mittens answered.

Megan sucked in a few deep breaths. "Sweet."

I heard something in the distance. "What's that?"

"Horses," Mr. Mittens said, alarm growing on his face.

"There are regular horses on this planet?" I asked, not registering his growing fear.

He nodded. "They come from here. Or the originals did, thousands of your years ago." He looked around, and sniffed, then as suddenly as he had before, he shifted into this Splintercat form. *We must run.*

"Run? Why?" I asked.

Because that group has felt our arrival, and they are coming for us.

I finally felt the fear that was emanating from him and spun to Megan in alarm. She grabbed my hand and dragged me after my cat. Afraid to speak out loud, I asked him questions as we pushed deeper into the strange wood. Now that I had really looked at it, the trees were slightly off from the trees of home. The color, deeper, the shape slightly different. Even the grass and sky were richer in color.

Who are they? I asked.

I don't know, but everyone here, everyone, has their own agenda, and you can trust no one.

What about my grandfather? I asked, alarmed.

We will try to make it to his lands.

Do you know the way? I huffed out, even the richer air wasn't making up for my lack of running ability.

Once I see a landmark, I'll know, he answered uncertainly.

Great.

The pounding of hooves was growing closer. Mr. Mittens was in front of me, and I ran into him when he stopped suddenly.

"What's wrong?" I moved around him, Megan behind me.

We've run out of woods, he said.

I could see that. In front of us was a lake and rolling green hills. On the other side of the lake rose a gleaming white castle.

"Whoa," Megan said.

"Is that a big enough landmark?" I added.

Yes, Mr. Mittens bit out.

He hesitated. The hoof beats were upon us, I turned, and I could see glimpses through the trees.

"Let's go down there, maybe they'll help!" I said, desperately.

Mr. Mittens sank onto his haunches, his head low. *In your colorful vernacular, we are thoroughly screwed.*

The horses burst from the trees and surrounded us. I looked up at them. They weren't horses, after a double take. They were centaurs, and they had us pinned down, their bows drawn and arrows pointed at us.

I nodded to Mr. Mittens. "Yes, we are."

The end.

JILLEEN DOLBEARE

SPLINTERED FATE

Splinter Fate
Jilleen Dolbeare

ICE RAVEN
PUBLICATIONS

Copyright © 2023
Editor: Cissell Ink
Cover Designer: Crimson Phoenix Creations
Interior Art: Rose Rasmussen

I dedicate this book to the people that have supported and encouraged me along the way. To my mom, who taught me to love sci-fi and fantasy. I wouldn't be anything without you! To my husband for not getting upset when I'm busy with the books. To my Mastermind Group, thanks so much! And to all my alpha and beta and ARC readers. Thank you all!

CHAPTER
ONE

T he centaurs marched us by force down the hill towards a
white castle gleaming in the sun. I dripped with sweat and
shook with exhaustion and terror. Their weapons, mainly
crossbows and spears, remained trained on the three of us. I'd always
assumed centaurs would be mainly male, but these were all female.
They were tall—their heads were probably two feet above mine—not
that I was taller than average. I was surprised that their faces and what
I could see of their torsos were remarkably human looking except for
their ears, which were elongated and pointy—even sharper than the
Lord of the Rings elves I kept waiting to see.

They wore intricately embossed, bright silver armor on their human
torsos and their horse bodies as well. I wanted to take a closer look, but
the fierce-looking leader kept us moving, and since I'd been poked
once with a very sharp spear, I took it seriously—I wasn't sure if I
should be regularly afraid or over the top terrified. I think I was a bit
shocked that I'd accidentally realm walked us to Faerie. Who knew I
had that kind of juice?

"What is that place?" I asked Mr. Mittens, who trotted along
silently in front of me in his fearsome four-hundred-pound Splintercat

form. The gleaming white castle looked gigantic in the light of the foreign sun.

It is the castle of the High King, he answered into my mind.

"The High King?" I trailed off when I stumbled and got poked again with the spear of the centaur apparently assigned to me. "Dammit." I yelled back at her, but she only poked me again.

"What do you think he'll do to us?" I whispered this time.

Mr. Mittens's mind voice was strained. *I do not know.*

"Do you think he knows my great-grandfather?" I continued to press.

Yes. He does.

That sent my mind on a tumble. I didn't know what to think about it. Did that mean they were friends? Enemies? Frenemies? I shivered. Megan bumped me from behind.

"Sorry," she mumbled.

I'd have reached back to comfort her, but I didn't dare. I already had three holes in me and didn't want a fourth. Who knew what kind of germs those wicked-looking spears had? At least they'd put away the crossbows. I could imagine the damage one of those would do if they went off accidentally—or on purpose. I shivered.

"What do they want with us?" Megan gasped behind me. We were marching along a well-used road and going a little faster than we were used to walking. It was hard on top of our general exhaustion.

"I don't know. Mr. Mittens said we are going to the castle of the High King."

Mr. Mittens didn't add anything.

Megan gave an exasperated sigh but didn't ask any more questions. She was probably also tired of getting poked and deep in her own set of worries. Mainly, what had she gotten into when she'd agreed to come to Oregon to help me?

I was worried for us, but part of my mind also worried about Sofia running loose in Faerie. What kind of mischief could she get up to, and what would it mean for us? I should have had Mr. Mittens eat her when we arrived, but I'd been too surprised, and a bit muddle headed from the air and the magic. Also, I wondered if Gabe was OK? I'd left him with the rest of the coven, unconscious and unable to take care of himself. Hopefully, Brightfeather, Goch, Noah, Luke, and the rest of the werewolves had helped him escape safely. I could only hope. Despair weighed me down, and my shoulders hunched.

With nothing much to do but wallow and walk, I studied the scenery and the back of the two centaurs in front of us. Faerie was lush and beautiful. The sun was warm, but not overpowering, and the green of the surrounding forests and grasses were intense. The breeze smelled of flowers and the sweetness of spring. In contrast, the centaur females were fierce and hard looking. They wore elaborate helmets that caught the light. The helmets looked more decorative than useful, since they left their ears free and didn't cover their cheeks or nose. The shine from the silver armor gleamed so much you could see them from space if Faerie had satellites. I had to blink and look away often to avoid blinding myself. The helmets and armor must be some kind of ceremonial wear I couldn't imagine sneaking up on an enemy in all that bling.

The centaurs in front of us also had long elaborate braids under the helmets that swept down their backs like a horse's mane. Maybe that was the effect they were after, or maybe their hair actually did go down their backs like a horse's mane. The braids seemed secured to the armor, or their flesh, since the hair didn't sway back and forth as they walked. I wasn't close enough to see if the hair was attached to their backs or just secured to the armor.

Huh. If we weren't in terrible danger, I'd love to spend time studying these creatures. They were strange but majestic.

I stumbled again and got another poke for it. I took it back. They were not majestic, sadistic, maybe. I threw an angry glare at my poker but knew better than to swear at her again. She didn't even look at me. Hell, I didn't even know if we spoke the same language, or if they could even speak at all. We'd climbed a hill and were now looking down at the trail around the lake. It was lovely, well-maintained, and park-like. The trail seemed groomed, and the grass trimmed to an even length. The leader turned and headed down the hill.

They stopped us once and let us drink from the pristine waters of the lake. I tried not to worry about parasites or bacteria or anything else; I was too thirsty. Hopefully, being from a different world would protect us from the local infections. I looked through the crystal-clear water at the gem like rocks underneath the surface. A brightly colored fish sparkled in the depths. I might have smiled—I don't know for sure; I was too tired and scared—but the beauty around me kept surprising and delighting me regardless of the dangers. I scooped up water in my hands and drank what felt like a gallon. My thirst eased, I rinsed off the blood spots on my skin from getting poked, threw water in my face, and that was it. Time was up. The centaurs sped up and kept us marching until we reached the castle.

I took back my thought that this place *wasn't* like *The Lord of the Rings*. The architecture of the castle would fit right in. Lofty, sweeping, and ethereal, the intricate carving and design of the place was CGI worthy. It was so beautiful, and I yearned to be part of it. I couldn't even put into words the incredible spectacle it was. My mind wasn't clever enough to even create a place like this in a dream. It *was* Rivendell. Had Tolkien been here? Probably. Hope a centaur poked him. That's what he deserved for crushing my dreams about elves. I was still ticked that my grandfather hadn't looked like Legolas. Maybe I should be mad at Peter Jackson. *Hmmm.*

The walls were gleaming white like sun-bleached bone. I wanted to touch them, see what they were made of, but the centaurs kept us moving through the courtyard without pause. They finally stopped before a large, intricately carved door. It was covered with fantastical beasts and scenes that I didn't recognize—probably because I was on an unfamiliar world. Just as the doors began to open, I thought I caught a carving of some unicorns—the nasty bastards—but I wasn't allowed the time to study if that were true. On the other side of the door were more guards, two-footed this time, still in fancy shiny armor. They took over our care and marched us into the interior of the castle. At least we'd slowed down a little.

I looked at Megan. She looked at me. Fear reflected in her eyes, as I'm sure it did in mine. Mr. Mittens slowly shrank until he walked by us in his Ragdoll form, his glowing fur more noticeable on this magic rich planet. I wondered if that was emotion or design on his part. He'd been reserved since we'd been captured, and this made him seem scared. I'd *never* seen my cat afraid for himself before.

We were eventually ushered into a massive chamber. The ceilings were almost too high to be seen, and it was easily as spacious as an indoor professional sports arena. I looked around. People and unfamiliar creatures, wearing intricate robes in riotous colors and lush fabrics, milled around. The guards forced us forward. I stumbled and almost fell, but Megan grabbed my arm.

At the far end of the massive room, up on a dais, a robed and crowned figure sat. The High King, I assumed. I gulped. Megan slid her hand down my arm and grabbed my hand. Mr. Mittens's solid warmth pressed against my legs. He pressed on me so hard, I almost tripped again. We walked forward in our tight group, touching each other for comfort.

Finally, they stopped us and forced us to kneel before the dais. I trembled, as did Megan beside me. Mr. Mittens seemed smaller than his usual self, but when the king addressed him, he walked forward boldly, head and tail raised. I couldn't understand the king's words, and I felt a momentary panic, but then I realized his voice echoed in my mind and I could understand the meaning. I looked around. Did magic act like a universal translator here? I checked the ceiling. Was the room a universal translator? I didn't see anything that proved it *wasn't*.

"Xrsrphn, did we not banish you from this realm?" The King's voice was thunderous.

I thought I saw Mr. Mittens flinch. *Yes, sire.*

That was the reason he was so reluctant and afraid. Now that I knew he'd been banished, I was afraid for him. Would they take him away from me? Was this how they found us so quickly?

"Why are you here?" The king truly sounded as if he was curious. He didn't sound angry or accusatory. I felt a surge of relief.

I was brought here accidentally by my charge. His tail flicked at the tip, his anxiety palpable to me but probably not to others.

The King's gaze landed on us. He dismissed Megan, and the full weight of it landed on me.

"You are the progeny of my Pendragon?" he asked.

Was this a trick question? If he asked, he had to already know. He knew my cat and the terms of his banishment. Mr. Mittens had told me he was under a geas to protect my grandfather's progeny. So, that identified me immediately.

What was a Pendragon? I wasn't sure what that title meant here. I remembered that King Arthur's dad was Uther Pendragon. Did that make my grandfather a prince here? Wow, if that were true.

"Y-y-yes?" I stammered, uncertainly. I wondered if my single word was translated into the king's head as his were in mine.

He looked me up and down. Not the typical look you got from a man checking you out but an assessing look. And I didn't make the cut. I felt a teensy bit annoyed at that. Sure, I was a mess now, but I didn't think I was a total hag.

"Interesting."

I guess that answered my question about the universal translator.

His gaze flicked to a servant standing nearby. The servant hurried over. The king issued a command I couldn't hear, and the servant scurried off to fulfill it. I shifted my weight from foot to foot in nervous anticipation.

"What have you brought with you to my Kingdom?" he finally addressed me again.

I wasn't sure what he meant, and my face must have shown that because his gaze flicked to Megan and back.

"This is my friend, Megan," I said, not knowing what else he wanted.

"This is a *human*?" he asked, stumbling over the word "human" slightly.

"Yes, we both are," I added. Then I realized that might not be true. I wondered how much of me was actually human. By birth, I'd say I was an eighth Fae, seven-eighths human, but I had all of this power. I didn't really know what would show on a DNA test. Did Fae genes overwrite human ones? It was something I would only investigate in a private lab—if I owned one—once we were home.

He didn't answer for a moment, staring at us both. He looked remarkably similar to a human. Humanoid, for sure. Two arms, two legs, both races appeared similar in height. It was hard to tell since he was seated above us, but I'd put him at around six feet tall. He had long golden hair that was swept back. He did have slightly pointed ears, but I'd seen humans with equally pointed ears, so he could pass if he dressed like a modern human.

He was richly dressed in a long golden gown that was belted with a soft cord. Over that, he wore a large robe type garment that was made of some kind of fur. It was thick, white, and looked incredibly soft. He stood and walked down the three steps from his throne to us. Our guards straightened and became even more alert. They moved their weapons closer to us until the king waved them back. I breathed a sigh of relief. He came close enough to sniff us. Which he did. That startled me the most. I recoiled slightly, not enough to anger him, but enough he looked at me with surprise.

"You smell Fae," he said to me.

He sniffed Megan again, and his lip curled. He backed away. Just then, the servant that he'd sent came jogging back into the throne room. He cast about, looking for the king. When he spotted him, he hurried over.

"Sire, he is on his way." He then bowed and scraped his way back to where he'd stood originally.

The king glanced at us one more time and returned to his throne. He waved a dismissive hand, and we were guided back to a spot along the wall. Two guards remained, weapons trained on us, but we were forgotten for the moment.

People came and went, meeting with the king, but we were so absorbed watching and trying to figure out the local culture that we missed much of what the king was doing. I wondered what would happen to us, what the king would do to us when he remembered we were here.

It felt like hours that we stood there. If we slumped or looked like we would do more than shuffle our feet, the guards would force us back to attention. It was exhausting. I didn't even know I could get more tired, since I was exhausted *before* the centaurs had captured us.

On top of it, my feet hurt and my back ached. I could tell that Megan was uncomfortable and tired as well. Even Mr. Mittens drooped a little. We'd been through a battle, a transport to another world, and a forced march over miles of varied terrain. We were too tired for this standing at attention crap.

Just before I burst into tears of exhaustion and frustration, the court stilled, and all the background noise stopped. I'd thought it was quiet considering all the people packed into this room before, but the deafening silence that followed proved me wrong. All eyes were drawn to the door we'd walked through initially. The door swung open, and a massive red-headed man walked in.

He was built like a brick—tall, solid, and menacing. His presence drew everyone's gaze like a moth to a flame. Even mine. He was in a shiny suit of linked mail, covered with hard leather armor. He had an ax strapped to his broad leather belt, along with a sword. It was a wonder he didn't clank when he walked or lose his drawers. I tittered. I'd had the same thought the first time I'd seen him. No way a *non-magical* belt was holding up all that metal. But since he wasn't walking bare-assed into the throne room, he must have a secret to keeping his pants up.

The crowd parted before him. My great-grandfather did not stop or slow until he stood before the throne.

He bowed his head respectfully but didn't kneel. I thought that was telling.

"Sire," he stated. "How may I serve you?" His voice boomed to every corner of the room. The crowd seemed to hold its breath and wait to see what would happen. Including me.

The king looked at my grandfather fondly. "I believe I have something of yours, my dear Pendragon," he stated and gestured to the guards. They grabbed Megan and me by our arms and roughly dragged us back to the throne. Mr. Mittens trailed in our wake. If they knew that Mr. Mittens was much scarier than us, they'd have rethought that move and grabbed him instead.

My grandfather frowned at me. Then looked away dismissively. My heart sank.

"Thank you, sire. I have no idea how this came to be. I'm very sorry to have troubled you," he said.

"No bother. My Scáthanna picked them up while training—once they felt the portal open and the presence of the cat. They needed the practice responding quickly to threats." Ah, that must be what the female centaurs were called. The king's tone was flippant, not bothered, and I sagged with relief on the inside. Maybe we weren't a big deal, and we'd be allowed to leave. I looked down at Mr. Mittens; he had sunk even closer to the ground and looked completely miserable.

This time, my grandfather gave a deep bow. "I am honored that you would watch over them, sire. I'll remove them from your gracious care."

"We will speak later." The king waved him and us away.

My grandfather froze briefly, then gestured at us. I grabbed Megan's hand and followed him closely—Mr. Mittens in tow. I could feel the concentrated worry and rage rolling off my grandfather's back as he walked stiffly in front of us and out the doors of the throne room. I'd really done it now. Feeling like a naughty child being picked up from school by an angry parent, I marched behind him. I was forty-two —way too old for this crap.

CHAPTER
TWO

We entered a room in the High King's castle. It was plain white like the rest of the building but contained nothing except an elaborate circle emblazoned on the floor and us. I reached a hand out to the wall; I still wanted to know what the material the palace was made of. The wall felt smooth and cool to the touch, like marble, but it wasn't marble. I frowned. I wasn't even sure if it was stone, bone, or a super hard wood. My grandfather waved for us to move inside the circle. We did. The circle was of a silvery metal with runes and hieroglyphs embedded in it. I wanted to lean down and touch it too, but I didn't have time. He closed his eyes briefly and mumbled something. A flash surrounded us. I blinked the light from my eyes and looked around. We were in a new but similar room, except the stone walls were now a silvery grey, rather than the white of the high king's palace. My grandfather strode forward, opened the door, and walked boldly down a corridor. We followed, not knowing what else to do.

He ushered us into a large room with a huge fireplace and comfortable seating. One wall was floor to ceiling bookshelves complete with a rolling ladder, just like an old-fashioned library on Earth. There was also a heavy wooden table—carved and ornate. I'd call this a library or at least a private den or study if we were home. Megan was squeezing my hand painfully, probably as terrified as I was. At least we'd not been executed or accused of anything—yet. However, my grandfather was still holding back his anger, if his high color and flashing eyes were any indication.

"What are you doing here?" His voice was quiet, firm, and demanding all at once.

I looked at Megan; she looked at me. Mr. Mittens was standing extra quietly behind me, out of range, I assumed.

I cleared my throat. "Well, it wasn't intentional." I scuffed my feet, glancing up at him briefly before continuing. "Umm, we were fighting the witches. I think we were even coming out on top, but I panicked and accidentally brought us to Faerie. Now, I have no magic," I added as an afterthought. I threw up my hands.

"Hmpf," he said. That startled me. Did Mr. Mittens get that particular response from my great-grandfather or vice versa? Something to think about.

He was quiet, tension radiating from him. He turned his back to us and faced the fire. The fireplace was easily as tall as my grandfather and wider than my large sofa at home. You could roast a whole cow in it, if Faerie had cows—I didn't know. After a moment, he moved away, pulled out his ax and sword, and laid them on the heavy wooden table. He stretched his back. I was right, all that metal had to be uncomfortable. He loosened his wide, heavy sword belt and added it to the pile, along with the hard leather armor and shiny mail. Underneath, he wore a simple black high-necked tunic and pants.

Then he sat in a comfortable looking chair by the fire.

"Sit," he commanded.

We chose seats away from him on the opposite side of the fireplace and sat—none of us daring to disobey. He sighed loudly.

"You don't know what kind of position you have placed me in," he began, wearily.

I must have made a noise because he threw me a glance that would have shut up much scarier people than me. I shut up.

"The High King did me a favor. I will owe him."

I felt terrible. I had no idea what the favor would entail, but I hated anyone feeling like they had to do anything for me. I had some slight control issues.

"You do not understand our culture. I know that, and I didn't expect for you to come here until you were fully trained and cognizant of our ways."

That seemed more like he was talking to himself. But I hadn't *intended* for us to come here either.

"This is a dilemma. I'll have to present you formally at court. There will be other…repercussions. I might be able to delay until your magic regenerates. We'll see. I'm hoping the king forgets, but this was unusual enough, I'm afraid he will not."

I gulped. I had no idea what that meant or what it would mean for us, but my grandfather's worry terrified me.

His gaze swung to Mr. Mittens, who visibly flinched. "You have my permission to use your shifting magic in my presence during your time here."

Mr. Mittens looked relieved, like he was waiting for a blow, and it didn't come. He bowed his head and shifted back into the Fae form he'd shown us briefly when we landed in Faerie.

"Thank you, my lord," he said and gave a slight bow.

It was disconcerting to see my cat in this form. I knew he was a cat or cat adjacent, and seeing him with two arms and two legs threw me. His eyes stayed the same though; that was comforting. I noticed his feet were still bare and grinned to myself. He'd probably still sleep in the middle of the bed and jump in boxes. What had he done to anger the Fae?

"I must think on this," my grandfather said after a long pause. He pulled on a rope dangling near his chair, summoning a servant.

"Take them to the guest quarters, and send some food as well."

The servant bowed and gestured for us to follow.

Before I was sent to my bed, I turned and faced him. "What is a Pendragon?" I was curious, and I felt I must commit a small defiance.

He glanced at me, then away. "I'm the High King's Commander." Then he dismissed me with a wave of his hand.

Commander? Did that mean he was like a general or something? I had so many questions.

The servant led us through the keep. We wound our way through corridors and up multiple types of stairs. I was profoundly lost after the second spiral staircase. The castle—that was the only word for it—was mostly grey stone with dark wooden accents in the doors and wainscoting lining the corridors in some places. Someone had made an effort to decorate the corridors and make the castle feel homey with portraits, landscapes and occasional huge vases with flowering plants and vines at regular intervals. I tried to look at everything once I realized I'd never find my way back without a guide.

Finally, we stopped before a door; the servant opened it and gestured for Mr. Mittens to enter. He walked in, gave a slight bow to us, and shut the door. The servant dropped Megan off at the next door, and she looked at me nervously before entering. I told her I'd check on her. The next room was for me.

I didn't know what to expect from a Faerie dwelling. Particularly one in a castle. So far, my grandfather's residence seemed like a normal Earth castle, though lacking electricity. The window coverings were open, and light streamed in. The room was large, and the focus was on an enormous bed with rich furs and forest green coverings. I sighed. I wanted to sink into it and forget everything, but I was dirty, sticky, and sore. The rest of the room could qualify as a type of medieval hotel. There was a large wooden table with chairs, a wardrobe, and a few comfortable chairs covered with colorful tapestry type fabric near the window with another small table and a lamp. That area would make a comfortable reading nook. The lamp had oil and a wick, I discovered, as did the lamps on the bedside table. I didn't see a way to light them, and since my magic was gone, I couldn't use my fire magic either. I shrugged; I'd worry about it when it got dark. For all I knew, there was a servant in charge of lamps.

I looked around for a bathroom; there was another door in addition to the one we came through. I opened it. There was a chamber that fit the bill. A large coppery colored tub dominated the room, and I wondered if there was such a thing as hot water on this strange world. Shouldn't anything be possible with magic?

The tub did have a faucet and handles, not much different than in my home. I turned on the tap and found hot water. A grateful sigh escaped me. I plugged the tub and let it fill. On the outside wall, near a window, was a doorless closet—a garderobe. I walked over and examined it. It was basically an ornate wooden seat with a hole. It didn't smell, so wherever the waste went, it was far away. I shuddered. But I used it quickly. I was full to bursting. If I hadn't been dehydrated, I'd have never made it through the ordeal at court. There was a cabinet with towels and soaps, so I stripped off my filthy and torn garments and climbed into the tub. The warmth was glorious, and I sank under the water until nothing was exposed. *Great tubs are deep enough for a thorough soak,* I thought as the warmth melted the ache from my back muscles and sore feet.

Once the water started to get cold, I hurriedly lathered and rinsed. I climbed out, dried, and wrapped myself in a towel. My clothes were toast, too filthy and tattered to put back on. I fumbled around the room, searching for something else to wear. I found the wardrobe full of clothing and pulled a deep blue robe out that glided against my skin like silk. It took a moment to figure out the strange multitude of fastenings. The robe smelled like a spring morning, and I sniffed it and let it fall back in place. There were soft little slippers of some kind of leather. They also went on like silk and fit like a glove. I was confused. How did anyone know my size?

I hurried down to Megan's room, assuming she would just be getting out of the bath the same as me. I knocked. The door was hard, wooden, and heavy, and it hurt my knuckles. I shrugged, assuming that made for good security. I couldn't hear her, so I tried the handle. I hadn't really examined my door for a lock, and apparently neither had Megan, because I walked through without a problem.

"Megan?" I said in a normal voice.

There was a shriek from behind a closed door.

"It's just me!" I yelled louder.

"I'm in the bathroom; give me a minute."

I looked around her room, which was almost exactly the same as mine. The only difference was that instead of dark green, the bedding and furniture were in shades of dark purple.

I sat on the bed and waited a few minutes. "Do you have clean clothes, or do you want me to hand you some?" I asked when I grew bored.

"I'm good," she answered. A few seconds later, she entered the bedroom.

"You have good taste," I remarked when she walked out in the identical robe to the one I was wearing. She looked at me, then we both burst into laughter.

"They must buy guest clothing in bulk," Megan said.

"Let's see!" I stood and opened her wardrobe. Sure enough, they both had the same garments within.

"I wonder how sizes work here?" I said.

"Magic?" she quipped. After a moment, she continued, "Hmmm, I think they're all just a 'one size fits all' thing." She pulled another robe out of the wardrobe. "See, these ties and things are adjustable."

I shrugged. I hadn't paid much attention when I'd put mine on, but it made sense and explained the multitude of ties and fasteners on each garment.

"Smart."

She nodded.

"When do you think they're sending up that food? I'm starving."

"Yeah, me too," I agreed.

"Should we go look or wait?" She stood and looked around the room. "Think there's one of those rope pull thingies around?"

There wasn't, or at least not one we could see.

"I think we should check on Mr. Mittens first. He's spent time here; he might know how things work. Plus, I'm sure I'll never find my way back if we go further than our three rooms."

She nodded, and we headed to his door. I wasn't sure what we'd see if we walked in, so I knocked again. There wasn't an answer. Did he go back to his natural form or was he in the bath? Did magical shapeshifting cats bathe when they weren't in cat form? Huh.

"Do you think he's having a bath?" Megan echoed my thought.

"I really don't know."

Come in, your conversation is draining, a tired voice said in my mind.

We looked at each other and entered the room. It was another room identical to ours, only in shades of blue. Mr. Mittens was in his Splintercat form, sprawled in the middle of the bed. At least that was a normal sight. His huge round head with his long killer teeth swung towards us.

Are you not tired? he asked.

"Yeah, exhausted, but we're starved. How do you get food brought up?" Megan asked.

He gave his usual exasperated cat sigh. *You pull the cord. It notifies the serving quarters, and someone will come.*

"Where is it? We looked all over," I asked.

He pulled himself up into a standing position and stepped off the bed. He walked over to the wardrobe and glanced behind it. *It is there, close to the wardrobe corner, out of sight. Now, shouldn't you go eat and rest? I have a feeling tomorrow will be even more draining.*

Concerned, I asked. "Did you eat, Mr. Mittens?"

No.

"Do you want to eat with us?" I asked.

I wish to rest. He hopped back up on the bed, found a spot, and plopped down.

We looked at each other, both of us frowning thoughtfully.

"Come on," I said to Megan, "we better go so we can all rest."

We proceeded back to Megan's room. "Stay with me?" she asked.

I shrugged. I was feeling odd here, too. I wished my cat was with me, but here he could be more of a what?...entity? person? than he could on Earth. Plus, he didn't have to protect me in my grandfather's house. I guess he deserved to be off duty for a time.

I didn't want to be alone. So, I walked in. Megan pulled the silken rope we located just where Mr. Mittens had indicated.

When the food came, it was beautifully exotic to look at—colorful and fanciful shapes and interesting arrangements. I wasn't sure what was animal, vegetable, or mineral. Megan and I looked at each other.

"Is it safe for us to eat?" she said, voicing what I was thinking.

"I guess, I mean people have talked about going to Faerie before, and they always say the food is great." I frowned at the beautiful dishes and the food items upon them.

"Yeah, but then they tell you not to partake of any food or drink, or you're trapped here forever."

"Are you sure that's for Faerie or Hades?" I asked, not sure.

"I'm sure it's for both," she said, a sarcastic twist to her words. That meant she didn't have a clue.

"Really? Because you have degrees in mythology and folklore?" I threw out.

"Yup! So, we should send this back. People can go weeks without food." She frowned. "I think."

I picked up a flower. That's the only way I could describe it. It was purple and gold. It was obviously something edible, but it was in the shape of a delicate flower. I wasn't sure how to hold it, it looked too dainty to just pick up, but it held together as I examined it. Megan was pacing, still debating if she should eat the food. My head swam, and I didn't think that my grandfather would do anything to put me at risk. Gruff as he was, he seemed dutiful or at least concerned. I mean the Fae had to care for their own children just as well we cared for ours, right? Otherwise, their civilization would collapse.

I took a bite. It crunched at first, but then sent a shiver of delight through me. The taste was simultaneously sweet and savory, if that was possible. And I mean beyond the usual salt and sugar delight of a good dessert. I moaned.

Megan whipped around, still talking about whether or not we should eat.

"What are you doing?" she screeched then slapped the rest out of my hand. It shattered on the stone floor.

"Why did you do that?" I asked, staring at the broken flower.

"We decided we couldn't eat or drink while we're here."

"*We* did not decide that. *You did.* I'm hungry, and it's good. Like really good," I said and picked up another exotic looking food item.

I took a bite before she could grab it away from me. Another culinary delight. Sunshine exploded in my mouth; I tasted summer and happiness. I figured this was a fruit of some kind. It vaguely reminded me of a peach. Sort of a firm but gentle flesh that gave away to my teeth and filled my mouth with juicy delight. Yet, it was so much more than a peach from my world. I'd never be the same again. Like the saturation of color and the richness of the air, even the food was superior to Earth. I was beginning to understand why people were cautioned not to eat when in Faerie. Not because the food was bad, but because you would never be satisfied with Earth food again.

I finished the fruit—whatever it was—and looked at Megan. She glared at me.

"Just eat. You'll never be satisfied with food again, but it's wonderful, and we need to keep our strength up."

She gave a disgusted snort at me and picked up another fruit similar to what I'd just eaten. I watched her as she bit into it. Ecstasy spread across her face when the flavors hit her.

"Damn," was all she said when she finished. She stared at the other food. "That was better than sex. No, better than chocolate." She grabbed another flower. Only this one was red and orange. She bit into it and groaned. She offered me half, and I ate it as well. It was similar to the last one but sweeter.

We both looked at the next unidentifiable food design. It looked more solid than the flowers, or even the delicate fruits. Maybe it was meat of some kind. I sniffed it. It smelled spicy and savory. I took an experimental bite. It had the mouth feel of meat, but the flavor was again unique. It was spicy smoky, and a tiny bit sweet, with an almost imperceptible gaminess that on earth you could find revolting but with the other flavors only accentuated the deliciousness. Plus, it melted in your mouth like good barbecue ribs. We ate everything. I even tasted the plates, just in case. They were not edible, unfortunately, because I'm sure they'd taste divine as well.

"OK, food is fabulous here," Megan said with a satisfied sigh.

"Yes, oh yes, better than anything I've ever had!" I licked my fingers.

"Even Gabe?" Megan said slyly.

"I don't know, I haven't had him yet," I said snippily. Talking about him immediately put me in a bad mood. I felt horribly guilty that I'd left him alone and unconscious in the woods with a coven of evil witches.

"Sorry, I shouldn't have brought him up," Megan replied. "That was dumb."

I shook my head. "I feel helpless. All I can do is hope the were-wolves retrieved him, and he's safe. But I don't know. He must think I abandoned him."

"He'd never think that. You fought so hard."

"Yeah, but he didn't see it. All he saw when he woke up was that I wasn't there."

"Well, at least Sofia wasn't either," she said.

"Yeah, that's one consolation. I hope something in Faerie ate her."

Megan giggled. "Yes, that would be awesome."

"Most likely she's rediscovered her magic, refilled on all the free stuff floating around here, found allies, and is now back on earth destroying all that I own," I said, the weight of everything bowing my shoulders and dragging my mood all the way to the basement.

"Let's see if your grandpa can send us home in the morning. I'm sure he can," Megan tried to cheer me up.

"Yeah, maybe. I'm going to go to my room. I'm exhausted. Do you mind?" I asked, knowing she'd wanted me to stay.

"No, I'll be OK. The food helped," she replied.

"Night, Megan. Sorry I dragged you into all of this."

"You know I'd have found a way to be here with you no matter what. Don't worry about me."

That was why it was good to have a best friend.

THREE

I woke up with a familiar warmth in the small of my back. I reached behind me to stroke Mr. Mittens's Ragdoll, cottony soft fur. I did that for a minute, before I sat up with a start. I was in a strange room with dark forest green curtains surrounding the bed. I blinked a few times before it all came back to me.

"Mr. Mittens! What are you doing in here?" I asked. I remembered he'd been set up in his own room.

I felt him stretch, and then he walked over my legs and sat down, facing me. I scratched his ears.

I am your protector. I came to watch over you while you slept, he said with a yawn, his teeth white and sharp.

"You can say you missed me. I missed you, too," I said.

Hmpf.

But he followed up his dismissive sound with a head butt and a demand for belly rubs and scritches.

I smiled. My cat made me happy. He was still the best companion I'd ever had. Definitely better than my ex, Evan—the man whore.

"What do you think will happen today? Do you think my grandfather will send us back?" I asked, hopefully.

It's more complicated than that. If we could have made it to your grandfather's home without running into any issues, he could have sent us back directly. Since we were captured by the king himself, we are at the mercy of the court. There is no easy way out of our dilemma. He leaned against me to groom a back leg.

"Well, shit. We can't stay here very long. I don't know what happened to the witches, or Gabe, or even the rest of our allies." My heart started to pound. I really didn't know what had happened, and now that I wasn't worried about my immediate safety, I was terrified that one of them was hurt, or worse, dead.

I'm sorry that my presence got us captured, he said.

"Is that why you were out of sorts yesterday?" I asked him, while scratching behind his ears.

He didn't answer, but his purr grew louder. I took that as a "Yes, I'm sorry."

"It wasn't your fault. I'm the one that dumped us here, I don't blame you."

There was a sharp knock on my door. Since Megan would just waltz in. I jumped, and my heart hammered. I knew it wasn't her. Mr. Mittens jumped down, and I leapt out of bed and grabbed the robe I'd discarded on the chair the night before. I hurriedly ran my fingers through my hair and wrapped the robe tightly around myself. I opened the door.

A servant stood there, dressed in what I was starting to recognize as my grandfather's livery—dark blue velvety tunic, tight leggings in black, and a stylized dragon emblazoned in silver on the breast.

I blinked.

"You are requested in the dining hall," he said with an imperious air.

Since I'd just awakened, I nodded and asked, "When?"

He looked me up and down. "After you are properly attired."

That didn't really give me a time limit, but I nodded and shut the door.

"Can you interpret that for me, please, Mr. Mittens?" I asked, as I hurriedly went into the bathroom to wash my face and do something with my hair.

They want you to wear something fit for court, would be my interpretation. I'll look inside your closet. Something should be waiting there for you.

I dried my face and smoothed the wild hairs that were shooting off in all directions. I had no straightener here, and no product, but the brush that was left behind did wonders to smooth my hair. I checked the wardrobe. Last night, it had been full of those one-size fits all robes. True, the material was dreamy, but they were more dressing gowns than something to wear at court. I didn't know how I'd missed anything else, but nonetheless I opened the closet door in hope.

"What?" I gasped in surprise. The closet was full of lovely garments—all things I'd consider fit for court. They looked fancy enough.

I picked out a gown—the perfect shade of blue for my eyes—and put it on. Like the magical closet, the second I pulled it over my head and the folds fell, the magical gown fastened itself, and fit itself to me perfectly. I glanced in the mirror. It was perfect in every way.

"This is amazing!" I crooned to my cat, who looked bored. I bet clothing wasn't anything he'd ever worried about. When he shifted, his spectacular spotted coat turned into a spotted robe in the Fae style.

After I'd looked at my reflection and maybe did a twirl, I told Mr. Mittens I was ready, and we headed to pick up Megan.

She too was excited about the magical clothing. She had to show me her closet before we left and exclaim over the ruby gown she had chosen. It was the perfect color for her skin tone and dark hair.

Together, we followed Mr. Mittens down corridor after twisting corridor and several stair cases until we were finally ushered into the dining hall. The room was large and pretty, a whole wall was replaced by floor-to-ceiling windows. The rest was covered in rich wood with plants hanging everywhere. It was almost garden-like. The room was dominated by a long intricately carved table and chairs.

I expected a room full of people since we'd dressed up and the castle and dining room were so large, but it was just the three of us, my grandfather, and Dana, his mistress of magic. She frowned at me with her dead, shark eyes, and horsey face. The smile I planned to greet her with melted off my face. When my eyes flicked to my grandfather, I realized something was extremely wrong.

"What's wrong?" I asked. My voice breathy with distress.

My grandfather waved away my question with a hand. "We will discuss it after we eat. No sense being worried on an empty stomach."

That might work for him, but now my stomach was roiling with upset. What was so bad that everyone looked so glum? Had the king made a decision about me? Was there news from home? No, I dismissed that one. No one knew where we were or how to contact my grandfather. Was there a team of female centaurs outside to drag us to prison? Had Sofia regained her magic and brought a team of sorcerers against us? I shivered.

Food was brought out, and servants began piling items on our plates. I didn't have the energy to watch, or choose between selections, I just nodded when something was presented until there wasn't room left on my plate. The food was still beautiful and exotic, the flower things, fruit, and meat that I'd noticed before had been replaced by different versions of those items. Knowing I had to keep my strength up, I ate without tasting or thinking until I was full and pushed my plate away. I noticed Megan was basically doing the same. Mr. Mittens had transformed and was eating in his Fae form. He handled the eating utensils with graceful movements, so he must have spent significant time in this form at some point.

Maybe someday, he'd tell me his story. How had he ended up exiled and under a geas for my protection? He must have done something horrifying to the Fae. I couldn't imagine what. Then again, I had zero understanding of the local culture or customs. It could be easy to get myself exiled as well.

Once finished, Megan and I waited patiently for the dishes to be cleared and my grandfather to fill us in. When he could stall no longer, he stood and paced the large room, hands clasped behind his back. He was dressed in a beautifully embroidered blue tunic and dark trousers, his feet and legs encased in supple leather boots.

I watched each step, too nervous to look at his face and the worry etched on it.

"The king has sent a request this morning," his voice rumbled forth.

I looked up to view his face briefly. He was looking out the long windows that framed one side of the dining hall. I only caught his profile. His jaw was clenched, and his eyes appeared pinched.

Not good.

I was going to ask, but before I got it out of my mouth, he continued, "He has requested your presence, officially, at court." He turned and faced me.

I met his eyes. "What does that mean exactly?"

He shook his head and sighed. "It is as your people would say, a mixed bag. It could just be a polite way of welcoming you as my granddaughter."

I felt a wave of relief.

But he wasn't done. "However, there are sinister implications that are more likely true."

My elation dimmed, and my stomach fell. This wasn't a good sign.

"In truth, we have been in the midst of a minor power struggle. He believes he can call on me for every minor fray." His voice rose, and his face reddened with fury. "I'm his Pendragon—the supreme commander. He can send his minor Drakes for that." He looked at our confused faces.

"Right." He shook his head, and his voice softened again. "That is not your concern. What is your concern is that he's found a way to control me—through you." He looked right at me.

My heart stopped, and then started and fluttered in my chest. Pure fear gripped me, and the blood drained from my head. I felt faint. "What do you m-mean?" I stuttered.

"If I'm right, he's going to propose one of two things. An alliance or..." He trailed off. "Something I don't want to do." He smiled at me.

"What does alliance mean?" I asked, my blood cold.

"Connecting our houses and political ties through marriage."

"Marriage?" For the life of me, I couldn't imagine how that concerned me. I was thinking that he wanted my single grandfather to marry his daughter or something and life flickered back into my soul. But then the implications finally hit me. If it was my grandfather whose marriage was imminent, my arrival wouldn't have changed anything. What made the difference was now my grandfather had a family member to bargain with. And that family member was me.

"You mean me?" my voice was a little shrill, and I cleared my throat.

"The king has been looking for a worthy consort. He requires a certain blood line, a strength in magic, and a political tie that would be worthy of a queen. I'm afraid you showed up in the middle of that search."

Damn my luck. I had enough problems on my own world, and I didn't give a *shit* about the High King's.

"No." I emphasized that by shaking my head. I might have stood up and even stepped back to escape.

My grandfather stiffened. He wasn't used to being disobeyed. I lowered my face so I wouldn't have to look at him. I sat back in my chair and scooted back up to the table. I could see Megan out of the corner of my eye. Her eyes were wide and fixed on my grandfather. Mr. Mittens melted from Fae into his Ragdoll form and jumped lightly into my lap. He was attempting to comfort me. I buried my fingers in his fur.

I put up my hands as though to deflect a blow. "I don't live here, and I don't intend to stay. Not to mention, I'm not for sale. I'm forty-two, infertile, and I have no intention of marrying anyone again." *Except I'd think about it if it were Gabe. Let him be alive.*

"We may not be given a choice." He started to pace again. "You don't know the history of this land or our culture."

I knew that. I didn't, but they were also about to oppose me on mine. I just wanted out.

434

"What does it matter? I'm not from here, and I intend to leave as soon as I can," I said stubbornly.

He stopped and shook his head. Then he turned to appeal to me. "Not too long ago, we were ruled not by one High King, but by four different courts. We divided ourselves into Summer, Winter, Spring, and Autumn Courts, and all the Fae aligned themselves with one or the other based upon their natures."

He started to pace again, agitated.

"But we fought for millennia over land and titles and who could claim which of the strongest of us. We were tearing our planet apart—both literally and figuratively. There was a final war shortly before I reached maturity, and the courts of old fell. We decided we should be one people under one ruler. We couldn't fight if we were one? Right? So, the strongest magic user took the throne. Someone who all would tremble before and not oppose."

"So, you're saying you cannot cross him in this?"

"I am not strong enough." He hung his head.

Dana had been silent through everything. I never thought of her as a friend, I knew she only helped me learn magic because my grandfather willed it, but she looked as though she wished to say something.

"What do you know, Dana?" I asked her. My grandfather's head whipped up, and he stared at her.

"You *could* oppose him, master," she replied not to me, but to him.

"Don't speak of this again; you know the consequences," he barked at her.

Her black shark eyes widened, but her lips thinned. Dutifully, she bowed her head. She didn't want to shut up. She knew something. "Yes, master."

My hands clenched. "Your High King didn't even like me. He acted as though he found me abhorrent," I said. It was true. He acted as though the fact I was from Earth made me lower than a bug in his eyes. "But today he wants me to marry him? Is he all there?"

"This has nothing to do with you, my granddaughter. This isn't personal past the parameters he requires of a bride. This is because of me." His eyes flitted to Dana, who remained demure, her eyes cast down. "What Dana was trying to tell you is I'm the only other person that could oppose him and stand a chance at deposing him. I know it, he knows it, and most of the court knows it. If I agree to marry you to him, it would unite us and give him peace of mind that I will not attempt to overthrow him. If I do not, I must be ready to fight and plunge the kingdom back into civil war."

CHAPTER

FOUR

"Civil war?" I was back to a breath away from a full-blown panic attack. "Over me?"

I guess that wasn't fair, it was over politics, damn them all, but it felt personal. "So, somehow, I've thrown myself, and my friends from the frying pan into the fire? Figures." I stood up, displacing Mr. Mittens, and paced around the dining room.

My grandfather sighed. "This could just be a ploy at some long game the king is playing. He may only be inviting us to be polite and welcome you. We won't know until he tells us. But I thought that you should be prepared and a little more knowledgeable."

I threw up my hands, but that made me lightheaded, so I placed them on my waist, then bent over and took deep breaths. Once my head stopped swimming, I said, "Yeah, the politics seem simple enough, but how am I going to keep from offending anyone at court? I'm completely ignorant of the rules and traditions." I was amping up again and stopped to take some more deep breaths. "I don't even know what Mr. Mittens did that offended someone enough that he was banished." I waved at my cat, who hung his head. "If this is just a polite thing, the king could be watching me for the chance to use me against you. Did you think of that?" I said, my tone a little snappish. It wasn't his fault I'd landed in his lap and created a whole bunch of new problems.

"Yes, I've thought of that." He turned back to Dana who was still sitting with eyes downcast in her chair. "Did you bring it?"

"Yes, master." She stood and walked over to me. She presented me with a metallic bronze colored ball.

"What is it?" I asked her.

"A spell. Concentrated magic. You must swallow it."

"Why would I do that?"

Her eyes flicked to my grandfather.

He sighed dramatically. It had obviously been a while since he'd been around children, and I was feeling childish. I rolled my eyes.

"It is a spell to give you the knowledge of customs and traditions, so you won't cause any incidents."

I eyed the ball. It looked for all the world like a metal marble made of bronze.

"How long does it last?" I asked, assuming it was like a pill. You got four to six hours out of it.

"It is knowledge. It doesn't fade. You will understand, and for at least two days you will be unable to offend. A bonus from the magic. Everyone will find you—delightful."

I sensed a tiny bit of sarcasm. "Do I want the king to find me delightful?" I asked, seriously.

"Yes. The alternative would be catastrophic."

"But I don't want to marry him!" I whined. Now I sounded as childish as I felt.

"That is out of our hands. But whatever he plans, if you don't offend him, we are much better off."

I nodded. I plucked the offered ball from Dana's spidery fingers. I studied it. It didn't feel metallic despite its appearance. It was pliable and warm to the touch. Megan watched me with a frown.

"Should you eat that thing? You don't know what it will do to you. You know, you aren't really Fae," she said.

That was solid logic. I lowered my hand with the ball. "She's right. How do I know it's safe?"

Dana's eyes flicked to Mr. Mittens, he nodded and jumped up on the table to observe us all. His floofy fur was even fluffier and more alive in Faerie than on earth. His glow here was visible even in the light.

You have ingested a magic ball before. It did you no harm, he said.

"No, I haven't. I'd remember something like that."

It was the first time you came back to the house since you were a child. We had a painful encounter with your husband's mistress. She nearly killed you. Dana saved you and in return, you chose to have your memory erased. You swallowed a golden memory ball and forgot about magic for a time.

"No, that can't be!" Could it? I knew I'd purchased the house, looked at it and engaged the services of the Whelan's on a trip last year while my divorce was ongoing. But that time was fuzzy and murky in my memory. Was it because my memory had been messed with?

I trusted Mr. Mittens. If he said it was true, it must be. I could see myself doing it, too. I was overwhelmed at the time. My divorce settlement was being debated. Evan was yanking my chain, going back and forth from begging me to come back, then telling me horrible, hateful things. He and his she-devil mistress, now new wife, had just had a baby. I bought the house with no guarantee I'd be able to pay for it, and I was alone for literally the first time in my life. Magic would have just thrown me for a loop. It rang true.

What about Vanessa? I suddenly realized he'd said something about my husband's mistress being magical.

"My ex-husband's mistress is magical?" I blurted out.

She is a siren. A bird-like shapeshifter that lures men into marriages and slowly sucks them dry of desire, money, and life... Mr. Mittens said.

Seemed fitting. I wanted to smirk and be secretly gleeful, but I couldn't. Now I had to wrestle with my conscience over if I should tell him. Dammit. Well, I couldn't do a thing at the moment.

"Oh, she came to the house before I owned it fully?" I asked.

That is correct. She attempted to kill you. We prevailed. She was forced to take one of Dana's magic balls to forget her obsession with you. That is why she no longer troubles you, he replied.

Great, I owed Dana a favor. Vanessa had been the bane of my existence for a long time until I'd moved to my family's old house. I'd assumed it was only because of distance, not because she'd been bespelled. I'd take it though. If I never saw her homely face again, it would be too soon. Maybe she'd trip and fall off a cliff and I wouldn't have to tell Evan about her sucking him dry slowly. That made me smile.

Oh well. Thinking about this was a delay. I didn't want to eat the bronze ball. I didn't want magic giving me knowledge I wasn't sure I trusted. I trusted Mr. Mittens. I mostly trusted my grandfather, but only because I was sure he cared for me in his own way if only because he was obligated. But Dana? She was a wild card. She'd never been friendly; she was rude and harsh. I couldn't believe anyone with her fierce nature would bow and scrape to a master, so I didn't believe the show she put on for my grandfather.

On the other hand, I had little choice. If I didn't do it, I could get myself, my friends, and my grandfather hurt or killed, or *bonus!* start a civil war in Faerie. I was seriously screwed. I looked at Megan. Her eyes were wild and open, but she couldn't help me or make the decision. I popped it into my mouth before I could overthink it anymore and swallowed.

Megan gasped, then put her hands over her mouth.

I closed my eyes and wondered how long magic took to hit you. Was it like ibuprofen, thirty to forty-five minutes? Was it like…

Nope. It was pretty instant. One moment I was ignorant, and the next, a hot flash and I was full of knowledge on how to navigate the courts. In fact, I was being told to bow to my grandfather. How deep, how long, and how often. The compulsion was strong. I started to bend my neck but stopped myself.

"Will it be like this? A compulsion?" I asked through gritted teeth.

"For about two days, then it should wear off," Dana replied.

I felt the need to acknowledge her and heard myself say, "Your gift was well made and thoughtful." When my human mind wanted to thank her, the new knowledge forbade it. I remember my grandmother telling me as a small child that you never thank the Fae.

I fought off the desire to bow and asked my grandfather, "Do you have one for Mr. Mittens and Megan as well?"

He frowned at Megan. He hadn't wanted to acknowledge her at all. I remembered the sneer the king had given to Megan when he knew she was human, the scathing look at me until he realized I'd smelled Fae, and the disdain Dana had towards humans.

I sighed.

"Xrsrphn knows the customs and how to avoid trouble and notice. He is on very thin ice here. I had not thought to include your *human* friend in a trip to court."

"She goes where I go," I said, and Megan's jaw clenched. She was going.

He looked into my face, and his shoulders drooped slightly. "Dana, please prepare another knowledge ball for the human."

Dana turned and walked out after one of her "Yes, master" responses and a nasty look at Megan.

"Are you sure?" Megan hissed. "She's probably going to poison me."

"No. But I don't want us to be the cause of a civil war on another planet," I whispered back. "And she isn't going to go against my grandfather's wishes."

She shrugged but looked miserable. "Fair enough. Did it do anything to you? Make you sick or anything?" she asked.

"No, just a slight hot flash and the knowledge popped in my head, along with a sort of compulsion to obey that knowledge. I feel fine, if a bit weird."

She looked down. "Are you sure you want me to go with you? It sounds like I'm just a liability. The people here seem to hate humans." Her bottom lip trembled a little. She had to be scared and lonely.

I hadn't thought how Megan would feel. I was a terrible friend. I just assumed that she'd want to be with me because I wanted her around. In a terrifying situation, it was a solid and comforting feeling having your best friend. "I'm so sorry, Meg. I shouldn't have assumed. I want you with me, but do you want to go?"

She looked thoughtful. "I guess I want to go. At least, I don't want to be alone. If we piss off the wrong people, I want us to go out together. Blaze of glory, right?"

I laughed and looped my arm through hers. "That's right; we'll go out in a blaze of glory. Thelma and Louise style." The only problem was we didn't have a convertible to drive off the cliff.

Megan must have been thinking something similar because she said, "We might have to go over that cliff in a chariot or wagon or something else, but sure, why not?"

CHAPTER

FIVE

Dana brought back the bronze ball within an hour. She plopped it into Megan's open hand, her lips twisted in disgust. At least she was consistently nasty. Megan's eyes slid to mine, asking silently for reassurance that it would work, not be poisoned, and she'd be OK. I didn't think I'd trust anything the Kelpie would give me if she wasn't working under my grandfather's orders. But she was, and for whatever reason, she seemed currently devoted to him, so I nodded.

Megan popped the ball in her mouth, and I watched her throat swallow reflexively. After a few moments, she gasped, "Oh my!" I grinned. The knowledge had hit her. She gave a little curtsy to me and Dana. "Oops, that is hard to resist," she said. "I guess that's good when we're at court."

"Yes, remember to listen to it, and obey. If you cause the master danger or embarrassment, I'll slit your throats and throw you to the dogs," Dana said encouragingly.

I shuddered.

Megan's eyes grew darker, and I knew her temper was flaring hot. I reached out a hand before she did something stupid. Luckily, the knowledge ball overrode her natural response, and she inclined her

443

head, although her cheeks were flaming red, and her hands were clenched into fists.

My grandfather had left the room shortly after Dana, and he chose that moment to come back in.

"It is time." He gestured for us to follow, and we dutifully fell in behind him, eyes downcast as the compulsion commanded. Mr. Mittens trailed behind us. I had the feeling my cat was reluctant to go. We traipsed back to the room we'd used before to transfer between places. It was a cold, plain room with nothing but an inlaid, embossed, silver circle that filled the space between four walls. Once the door shut behind us and we'd taken our positions, my grandfather did whatever he needed to, and we were in a different if similar room.

"How does that work?" I asked in wonder. I'd been too tired and terrified the last time to ask.

He looked at me. "It is a simple transfer spell. It is worked into the circle and renewed often by technicians. You simply give it your pre-arranged word for the location you wish to travel to. The High Keep has thousands of pre-arranged locations loaded into it." He looked thoughtful. "If you ever need to travel to my fortress without me, the word is, Niamh."

I started. Niamh was his wife, my great-grandmother. He wasn't as unfeeling as Mr. Mittens made out. He had treasured her in his thoughts for many years if that's what he'd named his home. I smiled. Even Mr. Mittens seemed surprised, although it was harder to tell in his Ragdoll form.

"Can you go between the...uh...splinters?" That's what Mr. Mittens referred to as the realms—splinters of reality—when he talked about realm walking, anyway.

Grandfather frowned. "Yes, but those aren't pre-loaded, you would need a very clear picture of where you wanted to arrive, and a strong magic *push*, for a better word, to make it happen. It is easier to use the pre-arranged locations."

I nodded. The information seemed important and could probably get us all home when my magic came back. I filed the fact away in my brain for later thought.

As we left the room and started down the marble corridor to wherever we were headed, Mr. Mittens pressed against my leg until I was afraid I'd trip over him. I didn't want to say anything because he'd seemed so out of sorts, so I walked a little slower than normal and more carefully. By the time my grandfather approached a closed door, we were several steps behind him and Megan.

They waited for us to catch up, then my grandfather opened the door. Unlike the grand court scene we'd been thrust in the other day, this was more like a private reception hall. There was still the throne on its dais at the far end of the hall, but there were far fewer people and courtiers hanging around. The king was seated on his throne, and he had two of his centaur guards behind and to the sides of the throne. A richly attired man in robes that looked like fire in stripes of red, orange, and yellow was organizing people. Another man that appeared to be an important courtier—dressed in dark, somber colors—stood next to the king, and a line of people waited to address the king. We joined the line.

When I peeked over at the king, he appeared bored, or he was talking and offering judgements on a variety of things, mostly disputes it sounded like. I tuned it out. I didn't even know enough to understand what people were arguing about. At one point, I caught the king's gaze upon us, and I shivered. He gestured to a servant, said something I couldn't hear, and pointed at us. The servant then hurried over to us.

"Come with me, please," he said as soon as he was close enough for us to hear. Then he scuttled over to a door next to the throne that I hadn't noticed before. It was the same color as the walls, and the only thing that distinguished it was a door handle.

He opened the door and gestured that we should enter. He closed it behind us. The room was small, like the size of an average bedroom on Earth, maybe ten by ten. It was painted a rich, mellow blue with comfortable seating and small tables spread around the space. A waiting room. I guess that meant we'd be here a while. I sank gratefully into a chair, lifted up my feet and rotated them around. Yesterday had been exhausting, and I still hadn't recovered. My legs were sore and felt like gelatin. My feet were bruised, and the little slippers weren't protecting them from the hard floors.

We quietly sat in the room, reluctant to speak. My stomach was an acid factory as we waited for whatever horrible fate awaited us at the hands of the High King of Faerie. Still, part of me was annoyed he'd called us here and made us wait for hours. But that was a common power play on earth as well. Mr. Mittens had initially sat at my feet, leaning against me, but as time went on, he jumped in my lap to get comforting pets and scratches. I think I caught my grandfather rolling his eyes at the antics of my cat. You could tell that my grandfather had spent time with earthlings. Eye rolling didn't seem to be a Fae thing.

When the door finally opened, I was almost relieved that my fate would be decided soon, because I was weary of waiting. I'd forgotten how it was to not be constantly entertained by an electronic device, but my phone was worthless here. I couldn't charge it, there was no inter-net, and I'd left it back at my grandfather's castle, anyway. I was almost disappointed when it was only a servant with refreshments, but by then we were pretty hungry, and even the state of my anxious stomach was grateful for something to eat besides itself.

We ate more colorful and unrecognizable Faerie food. When we'd finished, it was hurried away by yet another servant. The logistics of this place must be incredible. Finally, after what seemed like several hours and might have been, the head servant from the other room opened the door and beckoned us out. By then, I was sure I was seri-ously wilted, my clothing wrinkled, and my breath foul. Maybe that was good, and the king would take one look at me and decide that marriage was out.

Megan looked fairly good, and of course, my grandfather looked the same. We followed the servant back into the room we'd started in, only now it was empty of all but us, the fancy courtier, the servant, and the High King. He either was giving us a great honor, or he was making sure there weren't any witnesses. I wasn't sure. I shivered involuntarily.

This time, the king seemed more informal, less imperious. He addressed my grandfather, this time calling him Lugh rather than

Pendragon. I watched carefully, listening to what the magic was telling me to do so I wouldn't offend anyone.

It compelled Megan and I to curtsy and look down. I did lower my eyes initially, but eventually I glanced up and looked around because I was dying of curiosity, and keeping my eyes on my toes was never my forte—unless a great pedicure was involved. Megan was also scanning the room, head still bowed. We caught each other's eyes and grinned.

We appeared to be inconsequential, though, merely chattel. The king and my grandfather were only focused on each other. This was an old struggle between two powerful Fae lords. Now that I knew the stakes, I concentrated intently on their conversation.

"I'm grateful that you came, Lugh," the king said. It sounded sincere to me, but then again, I didn't know him.

My grandfather dipped his head in acknowledgement.

"May we speak plainly?"

"Yes, my liege," my grandfather replied.

"I did not know you had another Fae child."

Even I felt that lie. He did know. This was the opening gamut of all the politicking and maneuvering I knew I was going to hate. Plus, I'd probably only understand a fraction of the underlying game, and that also pissed me off.

"As you know, my wife and my only child were from Earth." He gestured at me. "As is my great-granddaughter."

His eyes flicked to me, and I looked down.

"That is interesting. Does she take after her Fae heritage or her earthly one?"

Even though I didn't get the game, it made me sick to listen to it as though they were discussing my heritage like I was a prize horse.

"Though she is untrained, she has strong Fae magic," my grandfather replied.

I was growing angrier and angrier. Why was he answering and giving away all of my secrets? I didn't want to be stuck here in the Fae realm as someone's property, regardless if that made me a queen or not. I had a house I was turning into a bed-and-breakfast, a boyfriend to save, and a witch coven to defeat. I didn't have time for this.

"Would you consider her a worthy consort to someone like me, old friend?"

My grandfather looked miserable, but he answered with a simple, "Yes, my liege."

I wanted to slap him. I could feel the color rise in my cheeks and rage burn in my bosom.

I waited for my grandfather to offer up that I was not planning to stay, but he was silent.

The king turned to me. "Come forward, child."

Child? I was forty-two. I looked around in case I missed someone else that had snuck in while I'd been concentrating. There wasn't anyone but us.

I stepped forward, the magic inside of me compelling me before I could think. I walked forward, stopped, and curtsied. "My lord."

He studied me for a moment.

"How are you called?" he asked.

"Brigid, my lord."

"Brigid. He said my name slowly, testing it on his tongue. Show me your magic."

I looked at him confused. What did he want me to do, throw a lightning bolt at him?

"My lord?" I asked.

"Show me your best spell."

"My lord, that would be a lightning bolt, I don't think I should do that in here," I replied, uncomfortably.

He stared at me for a moment and guffawed. "Fair enough, child. Show me something small and controlled instead."

I'd forgotten that my magic had been stripped away, I reached for it, to show him a fire flower, but nothing happened. "I'm sorry my lord. When I accidentally realm walked us to this plane, I stripped away my magic. It has yet to regenerate."

His face was steely, waiting. I kept talking.

"I've just begun to learn, my lord, but I have lightning, fire, water, shadow, mind, reality, earth, aether, spirit, time, and light. Ice was stolen from me, and I'm missing air—at least I haven't found or re-integrated it yet," I said all of that so fast, I had to gulp a breath.

The king looked at me for a moment, then at my grandfather. "That is an impressive list. I didn't know that your family line consisted of thirteen elements, Lugh."

My grandfather gave a head bow but said nothing. The king seemed a little annoyed. Had my grandfather deliberately held out on him? That wasn't going to help our cause. Dammit. Why hadn't he warned me?

"I've other possibilities for a wife. I have another candidate who also claims her magic was stripped by an unintentional realm walk. Maybe I'll wait and see who's magic appears first," the king said sullenly.

My throat closed off, and I gasped for air. He had to mean Sofia. How did she get in a position to proposition the king? What was happening? Why hadn't something eaten her? Megan jabbed me in the ribs, I looked at her. Her face showed she was thinking the exact same thing I was.

The king took one look at my grandfather's face, which when I glanced over was suffused with rage. This was a political jab, and they both knew it. I wish I understood all the undercurrents to this meeting. It was frustrating. Plus, now I had to worry about Sofia coming into a place of power if he chose her instead.

The king waved a hand. "No matter." He sniffed as though he smelled something bad. "The other choice is unsuitable. She is also from Earth, as your great-granddaughter is, but she is human."

Well thank God for small favors. Maybe the Fae penchant for unsubtle bigotry was a good thing.

"We will talk further," the king finished, and I wondered if he was going to make the offer for my not interested hand. But he dismissed us. I nearly fainted with relief, and Megan's quick squeeze of my hand let me know she thought we were off the hook, too. There must be better Fae candidates out there that weren't from Earth.

Boy, were we wrong.

CHAPTER

SIX

The official proposal was sent the next day by a court official. I was *officially* screwed. I couldn't see a way out of it, neither could Megan, Mr. Mittens, or my grandfather. I was going to have to marry the king. I could never go home again. I felt gutted. I didn't even have the strength to cry over my loss. If it didn't mean I'd destroy the kingdom and plunge it into civil war, I would try to go home the moment my magic came back, but it hadn't yet.

Mr. Mittens said maybe two weeks. It'd been three days. Two weeks was a long time to wait on a foreign world with no chance of escaping your fate, a bunch of murderous witches running loose on your property, and a missing Gabe. This was crazy. I couldn't help anyone, least of all myself. Plus, I'd gotten Megan stuck. Mr. Mittens could go back, although without me, there was no point. He was my protector, and I was the last of the line.

Hopefully, I could arrange to send Megan home soon. I'm sure my grandfather or Dana could send her, if she'd go. She could run the B&B herself; I could transfer the property over in her name. It was only fitting. I plunged into a deeper depression.

One of the things I was required to do before the wedding was attend classes on how to be a queen. Who knew there were queen classes? I would never in a million years guess that such a thing was a well, a *thing*.

The first day of classes, I had to leave Megan, while one of the king's Scáthanna centaurs picked me up.

"I'm so sorry, Meg. I wish you could go with me," I said once I was summoned to my grandfather's transporter room, as I called the place in my head. At least Star Trek had never let me down.

"It's cool," she replied, although she looked scared and afraid.

"It's not, but they won't let you or Mr. Mittens come."

She shrugged. "We'll find something to do. We'll put our heads together and come up with a plan to get us all out of here."

"OK." I couldn't think of a single way to accomplish that, but maybe they could find out about Sofia and her plans. "Can you two find out about Sofia?" I asked.

"That's an even better idea," she replied.

Finally, I turned to leave and follow the servant to the transporter room. It wasn't ideal, but at least we could work on our problems from different angles.

The centaur waited impatiently for me. She had a front hoof cocked and was leaning against the transporter room wall. She straightened up tall and fierce when I neared, and I wasn't sure if I was being escorted under guard or under arrest. As she followed me into the transporter room, I tried to get her to talk to me.

"Hi, what's your name?" I asked friendly like, although I felt like sobbing.

Silence.

"I'm Brigid. I've never met a centaur before you guys dragged us to court."

One scathing look.

"So, are there a lot of centaurs in Faerie?"

Exasperated sigh.

I wanted to ask even more personal questions like if there were male centaurs, if their hair was like a true mane, but those seemed intrusive.

"How fast can you run?"

If I kept up the endless questions, she might decide to answer one.

The centaur activated the transport.

Something occurred to me suddenly. "I'm so sorry, I didn't even ask if you can understand me or if you can speak."

"I can speak, but I'm on duty."

Yes, a win.

"Oh, that's wonderful. What's your name?"

I didn't know if eye rolling was a thing for the Fae outside of my grandfather, who learned it on earth, but I had that definite feeling she would—if that was done here.

"I'm called Sorcha."

Yes. "Nice to meet you Sorcha. How long have you been one of the royal guards?"

Another sigh, but she'd finally given in.

"This will be my second year as one of the king's Shadows."

"Shadows? Is that what Scáthanna means? Interesting."

"Yes."

We walked down the corridor, her hooves clopping on the hard surface, and her tail twitching with irritation, I assumed.

I noticed, now that I wasn't being death marched, and because she wasn't wearing armor today, that the centaur woman didn't have breasts on her human torso. They must be more horsey than human, and her mammary glands would be located where a horse's were. I didn't look or ask though. Must be easier to shoot a bow without breasts in the way, I surmised.

"How many weapons are you proficient in?"

"All of them."

"All?" I doubted she'd ever fired a gun. I might have laughed a little because she gave me a sharp look.

"Do you have to do a lot of training to make the elite guard?" I asked.

"Yes, it is quite vigorous and extensive."

"Are only centaurs in it?"

"We are *not* centaurs."

"You aren't? That's a term for half human half horse on earth. I didn't mean to offend. What are you called?"

"We are *Baincapall*."

I tried to pronounce it, and she corrected me until I got it right.

"I appreciate that you took the time to correct me. I don't wish to offend." I felt the compulsion of Dana's magic ball push me.

She inclined her head in a short acknowledgement and pointed me to a door. "Your class is inside. I will wait and escort you back."

I almost thanked her, but my magic manner pill was still working. "I'm grateful for our conversation."

She opened the door, and I walked through.

Inside was a team of people. I shivered. I was so far out of my element I wished I could flee. Apparently, it wasn't just lessons on manners and court rules.

I had to learn what to wear, how to do my hair, how to look, and who each courtier was and how to speak to them. I wished Dana had a magical pill for those too, but apparently, the pills were limited or no one thought about making one for this, hmmm.

At the first station, for lack of a better word, I was stripped and measured. My protests were completely ignored, and once the measurements were finished, I was bathed—although I'd done that before I came to court. I was scrubbed, oiled, and perfumed. I wanted to scream. The Fae must have a big thing with smells. I remembered the king sniffing us. Did humans really smell bad to them? I hadn't noticed any strange smell difference between our two races, but I hadn't been that up close and personal to any of them yet.

Once I was "clean," I was redressed in the Fae version of silken robes of a rich and beautiful color that reminded me of Megan's alexandrite pendant. The color changed in the light, and all the shades of purple, blue, and green shimmered around me. It was magnificent.

Then my hair was done. Apparently, curls weren't something the Fae had interest in, because time was spent straightening and smoothing my hair into a silky mass. My hair color wasn't common here either. My grandfather had dark red hair, but most Fae seemed to either have blonde or dark hair, and none had my mix of brown and red. At least the Lord of the Rings movies got that right. The hairdressers seemed to like to touch it.

This was the straightest I'd ever seen it, and it was longer than I thought, brushing over my waist. Their hair styles were simple, long straight hair, with a few elaborate braids on the sides and top to form fanciful shapes. Although for today, mine was simply swept back in a knot of four braids on top. It shone like a burnished dark copper when they were finished and contrasted with the soft robes I wore.

Next, how to stand, walk, and sit? I couldn't even remember all the things they wanted me to learn, and I was positive that I wouldn't tomorrow. I sighed. I couldn't do this, and I didn't want to either. There had to be a way out of it I was missing.

One interesting side effect of having so many people working on me and ordering me around was the amount of court gossip I got to hear. Most of it was just noise, since I didn't know anyone but my grandfather and the king, but when the gossip switched to the king, my ears were like radio antennas.

"He's having an affair with one of his Shadows," a whispered voice said somewhere behind me. My ears perked up.

I didn't want to think how that even happened with a creature who was only a step away from a horse, but who was I to judge?

"Really? I thought that was just vitriol," someone added from the other side of me.

"No, she's been bragging to the others and lording it over them."

"So, why did he choose this one?" someone whispered, thinking I couldn't hear.

"She's a powerful magic user."

"What about that Earth creature from the other day? You know, the one with the Swamp Lord?"

Could they be talking about Sofia? Who was the "Swamp Lord?" That sounded shady as hell. Talk about someone needing a bath and perfume.

"No, he turned that one away. The Swamp Lord was furious."

"I heard that he's trying to keep his Pendragon from overthrowing him," another said.

I was having a hard time keeping track of all the speakers, and I was starting to think they just didn't care if I could hear, or they knew it didn't matter because I was helpless to change my position.

"There's a rumor that…" Her whisper grew quieter, and I had to strain to hear. "…the Pendragon has more magic than the king."

There was a hush after that revelation. I shouldn't have answered the king on that one. I sealed my fate and my grandfather's with that.

"Yeah, someone said she has thirteen!"

"Thirteen? Is that the most in the kingdom?"

I lost the thread as my heart began to pound, and my mind went a million miles an hour wondering what that meant for us. If it was true, no wonder the king was intimidated and looking for a way to control my grandfather and me. Part of me wanted to say I only had eleven, but it wasn't really true. I was born with thirteen, and I planned to get them back. Part of me wanted to say I had none because I currently didn't have any. But I held my tongue. Once I came out of my state of despair, the conversation had moved on.

"There was another attempt last night."

An attempt at what, I didn't know.

"Really? Who caught it?"

"I don't know, one of the Shadows I assume, probably the king's mistress."

There was another discussion about if the rumors of a horsey mistress were true. I tuned out for a minute.

"The assassin actually made it into the king's chambers this time?"

My ears perked back up.

"He's dead now. That's one good reason to keep a deadly mistress," another said glibly. There were several titters of amusement.

My mind caught up with my ears. My heart raced, the king was dead? I wanted to cheer for a moment before I realized they meant the assassin.

"Nah, that can't be true, we'd have heard about it widely."

"You are wrong. He can't let anyone know that an assassin came that close to him; it would weaken his position and cause more to come after him." This came from an authoritative voice, and it took all my will not to look back for the speaker.

Seemed like logical reasoning. These servants probably understood court intrigue a million times better than I did. They needed to know to survive.

Before I could hear more gossip, the door opened, and an official came to retrieve me.

"If she is presentable, the king is ready for his audience."

It didn't sound like a request, and the team doing my "instruction" didn't think so either.

They scrambled with last-minute adjustments and hustled me out the door in two minutes.

I didn't even have time to work up a good head of terror before I was being escorted down a new hallway towards the king. However, by the time I made it to him, my hands were sweating, I was shaking, and it was all I could do to not burst into tears. What would he expect of me? Was this a private audience? Was I expected to perform "wifely" duties before the wedding? I was one suggestion away from a complete meltdown, and a shorter amount of time away from just choosing a direction and running. I wished fervently I had my cat and my bestie with me.

Before I cut and run, I was escorted into a chamber. I nearly collapsed with relief to see that I was not alone with the king. The room was full of courtiers and other important and officious looking people. The king sat on his throne, elevated in the middle of the room as usual.

I entered with the official and my *Baincapall* guard, Sorcha. I sure hoped she wasn't the king's secret or not so secret mistress. That would be awkward. I was announced, and I stepped forward and gave a deep curtsy. My knees almost collapsed at the bottom of it, my legs were still sore from the march two days ago, and I was weak and shaky from fear.

The king gestured, and the court official waved me forward to the throne. They had me positioned a step down. I turned to face the crowd.

The court official stood in front of the dais where the king's throne was and made a sweeping motion with his arm.

"Lords and ladies of the court! I present to you, Brigid of the line of Lugh, Pendragon to the king. She who will be queen!"

The crowd cheered and clapped. I'd expected them to bow or something, but apparently that wasn't appropriate for me, a nobody. Maybe they were really excited or faking it. Probably faking it. Although a wedding was probably a great big celebration with lots of free food. My stomach grumbled at that thought.

I smiled and waved, as the magic urged me to do, although inside I was screaming.

Once the announcement and subsequent waving, bowing, and scraping were done, the court official waved Sorcha over, and she escorted me back out and to the transporter room. She ushered me inside after checking that the room was empty, and I stepped into the circle. She said, "Niamh."

I felt the twist that indicated the magic had activated, and when I opened the door, my grandfather's walls greeted me, along with Mr. Mittens. He looked concerned. I squatted down and scratched his ears.

I should be allowed to accompany you, my pet, he said, his grumpy Ragdoll face even grumpier than usual.

"I agree. I could have used your company. It was awful. All dressing and having my hair done, and people telling me how to act. I much prefer you." I stood, and he walked me back to my room.

It sounds absolutely dreadful, he said.

I grinned. I'm sure Megan would also commiserate with me, so I had him drop me off at her room.

She squealed when she saw my dress and hair, so that made me feel good for a minute.

"How was it?" she asked and bounced a little on her bed where she'd been sitting when I came in.

"Just awful." I sat down next to her. "Not only did they re-bathe me —talk about humiliating—they talked over me like I wasn't there. I was pulled and pushed and ordered around. When I was done, I had to go to court and be admired and paraded about like a prize horse. I did, however, get a lot of court gossip."

"Do tell!"

"Most of the gossip was about people I don't know and I can't really remember, but the really juicy stuff was about the king. You know, the guy I'm being forced to marry? Apparently, his side piece is one of his horsey guards."

"I'm not sure what to think about that," Megan said, wrinkling her nose. "The horse thing is a bit cringe worthy. Also, are you ready to take on another cheating spouse?"

"Absolutely not. But you already know I want out of this and back home as quickly as possible. I find everything about being forced into this distasteful."

She put her arm around me and gave me a side hug. I rested my head on her shoulder for a moment. "Thanks, Meg. The only thing that makes this bearable is you and Mr. Mittens. I should probably make it possible for you to take over the B&B, and all of my other possessions so you can go back and enjoy your life."

"What? No! I'll go later, maybe we can both go back and forth! The king is gonna want time with his sidepiece, and you are only part of this for your ability to keep your grandfather loyal. Surely, he can't begrudge you time on Earth?"

I thought about it. Why would he? I was a political alliance, not some great love of his, or even a wife that could bear him children. As long as I was around for whatever queenly appearances I had to make, why couldn't I have a normal life back on Earth? I could learn to realm walk safely. I'd have to ask a boon of my soon to be husband. A tiny bit of hope and relief blossomed in my gut. I smiled.

"Yeah, why not?" I replied.

She smiled, and deftly changed the subject before I worked myself into another pit of despair. "So, tell me about your centaur guard? She looked terrifying."

"She is. Her name is Sorcha, and they call themselves, *Baincapall*, not centaurs. She was *offended* I called her a centaur." Then when it looked like Megan was going to pour on questions, I finished. "I don't know why."

"Ok, anything else we need to know about them?" she asked. I thought the same thing. If we ever had to make a quick escape, you should know your enemy.

"Yeah, they are badass. Sorcha said she was proficient with all the weapons. *All* of them. Their training is extensive. I'm thinking they are like special forces or something."

"All the weapons? What does that mean?"

I shrugged. "No idea. But remembering what we witnessed from them, and what I've seen my grandfather use, I'm thinking any medieval weapon is suspect. They already had crossbows, spears, probably swords and axes, maces. I don't know, that's about the extent of my medieval weapons knowledge, outside of like catapults and trebuchets. What does it matter? I'm only proficient at clunking someone over the head with a board."

"Have you done that a lot?" she asked.

I thought about it. Why had I said that? When was the last time I'd clunked someone over the head? I shook my own head. "I don't know where that came from. I do think I could do it, although a cast iron frying pan might be more satisfying."

She laughed. "Definitely, and it's cold iron—don't forget that."

"Next time I accidentally transport us to Faerie, I'll remember to pack one."

She snorted. "When we get back, we'll stock up!"

"Oh, another big thing. Sofia has hooked up with a dude they call the 'Swamp Lord.'" She has already petitioned the king for marriage," I said flippantly, as though it were an afterthought, rather than the most important information I had.

"Petitioned to marry the king or the swamp thing?" she asked, and I chuckled.

"King."

"Well, that sounds better than ole swampy."

I laughed. "Yeah. Much better." I sighed. "The king turned her down flat. He hates humans." I waved my hand around. "They all do, it seems."

"Yeah," she said.

We both flopped back on the bed. "I don't know about you, but I'm already tired of being here," I said.

"Yup. The food is good, but I'm giving it two stars for service," she said.

I shrugged. "I'm only giving it one star on Yelp.

CHAPTER

SEVEN

I felt like I was in the movie *Groundhog Day*, since I had to wake up and go to "Queen" lessons every day, over and over. I was beginning to miss my magic lessons with Dana; they were less intrusive if you could believe it. Only, no magic, no magic lessons. Sad, since it would be much more convenient for her to instruct me here.

I hadn't been called into court again, so that was a relief, but I had to do whatever the equivalent of deportment was here. I had to learn to walk and talk correctly. The magic pill was still helping, but knowing why the pill told me what to do while I was doing it was helpful. I figured they only let me in court last time because they had to announce me, but it was too scary to set me free in court to screw up and embarrass the king and my grandfather.

Megan and Mr. Mittens had something up their sleeves, but they refused to talk about it to me, and I'd been too tired to push. The only thing they'd told me was they were looking into the "Sofia angle." Since I hadn't had time to do anything about that, I was glad someone was working on it.

The court gossip was along the same lines as the previous days. More dish on the king's mistress and more supposition about the assassin. Any mention of Sofia and Swampy had been abandoned. They really did dislike humans here. It sounded like the king had several assassination attempts a month. Why wasn't the Swamp Lord a suspect? He'd already tried to place someone in the king's bed. Seemed like a logical follow through to me. Would the assassination attempts affect me once we were married? Would I be on an assassin's list? The idea made my mouth dry, and my fight and flight response go into overdrive. I started checking the exits halfway through my sessions.

I did receive other pretty gowns. I figured the king or my grandfather were fronting the beautiful clothes. I had no idea how money or payments worked here.

The newest gown was just as colorful and unique as the last few. The difference was that instead of the cool colors, it was warm—a deep ruby red with shimmering orange and yellow iridescence, depending on the light. It made my hair look like dark fire. This time, they created an elaborate braided basket on top of my head, and no matter what they did to show me how, there was no way I'd ever be able to duplicate it. I assumed as a queen I wouldn't have to.

Sorcha continued to be my escort, which was cool since it had taken me so long to encourage her to speak and took a lot less effort now that we'd been at it for a while.

"Do you like being one of the king's Shadows?" I asked first thing.

She sighed. Probably annoyed that I never stopped asking questions, but how was I going to learn anything if I didn't?

"Yes, it is the most elite unit in the realm."

"Who leads your group, after the king, of course?"

"Diamin is our leader. She is the best of us."

"Are you high up in the…" I didn't know the term. I didn't have any military experience outside of movies. "Group?" I added lamely.

"I am a leader of my…*group*," she said sarcastically.

"Sorry, I don't know the proper term."

"Together, we are called Scáthanna. We are grouped in tens. Those are called Deicheanna.

"Oh. How many of those do you have?" I didn't even try to

pronounce the word which sounded surprisingly like Irish to me. I guessed the Irish and the Fae had ancient ties.

"Ten."

"So, there are a hundred of you all together?"

"Yes, are you curious, or do you intend to raise an army against us?" she asked. I bet she was worried. I had come out of nowhere, and the king was already worried about my grandfather, although surely the king's Pendragon already knew this info.

"Uh, no. You are completely safe from me. I couldn't fight my way out of a paper bag." I snort laughed.

Her brow wrinkled. "Paper bag? What is this thing?"

"It's just a dumb earth saying. It just means I'm a horrible fighter, sorry."

"Hmm. They are saying you're a powerful magic user."

"I don't know about that. I just found out I had magic, I've already had one piece stolen from me, I haven't found the last piece, and currently I have none because I realm walked without the proper preparation." I shrugged.

She looked at me sharply. "They are saying that your line contains thirteen elements. This is unheard of."

"Why, how many do most Fae have?"

She frowned. "I think the king has seven. That is a high number. Most magic users have four or five. The weakest, one."

"Do all Fae have magic?"

"No."

"Do, *Baincapall* have magic?" I hoped I pronounced it correctly.

"We are made of magic."

"What do you mean, 'made'?"

She stopped and stared at me. "You are ignorant for the daughter of the Pendragon."

"I'm his great-granddaughter, and he only found out about me a short time ago."

"The *Baincapall* were created long ago by a powerful magic only a true Draoi can wield."

"Draoi?"

"Magic master."

"Like Dana? My grandfather's mistress of magic?"

"Yes, but she is not known for creating magical creatures such as the *Baincapall*."

"What is she known for?" I asked, curious now.

"Portable spells."

"Like her magic balls," I said, but it wasn't a question.

Sorcha acknowledged that with a horsey sound in her throat. By then, we had returned to the transporter room. I grinned to myself. "Beam me up, Scotty," I whispered. The door was shut, so we had to wait for the transport that was currently happening.

Her sharp ears caught my comment. "Who is this Scotty?" she inquired.

"A great earth magician who could send people from ships to new planets with a tiny spell," I answered, no idea how to explain television or science.

Her brow wrinkled in confusion. "Between realms? He is a great magician indeed. Few Fae are realm walkers, and fewer still can transport others."

I stopped. I'd taken me and three others on our trip to Faerie. Did everyone know that? Was I giving away something I should keep quiet? "How rare?"

She tilted her head in thought. "I've only ever known of three in all of Faerie."

I choked out, "Three?"

"Yes, why?"

I couldn't talk about it, so I mumbled something like, "just curious." I shut up. I'd definitely screwed my grandfather over by telling the king about my magic. He must have been keeping it all on the downlow for a long time. I doubted he was one of the three she knew of. I started to tremble. What had I done? I'd never get free now. I opened my mouth to ask another question.

Bam! I was thrown into the transporter room door, and Sorcha was knocked off her four hooves. Dust and rubble fell around us, and my ears rang. I was stunned. I looked around. Sorcha took a minute to get her legs under her. People were running and shouting. I heard Sorcha's name called faintly as though through water. I opened my mouth and moved my jaw to make my ears pop.

"Wait here," she commanded and galloped down the hall toward the rubble.

I didn't know what to do. I wanted more than ever to go home, but I didn't know what was safe, or correct in this situation. I didn't even know the situation, and my court knowledge magic didn't know either. I slid myself back up the door to my feet, leaned my back against it, and watched things unfold. More *Baincapall* galloped past me, with other normal foot soldiers running alongside.

I was still stunned, and there was so much noise and confusion I couldn't figure out what was going on. My first thought was that Sofia had found me and brought an army to attack. That would explain the explosion, but that was stupid. It'd been less than two weeks, if my magic wasn't back neither was hers. Also, I doubted she could find more allies this quickly unless Swampy was continuing to help her—if she was even still alive after the king's rejection. I took a deep breath and tried to let that idea go. It wasn't her. This had nothing to do with me.

I don't know how long I waited, frozen and fearful. The next thing I saw surprised the hell out of me. The commotion moved until I could only hear muffled noise in the distance. I continued to watch down the hall towards the billowing smoke and rubble, when I caught a large figure striding down the corridor.

I blinked, confused. It was my grandfather. I didn't know he'd been at court today. He hadn't mentioned it earlier, and I hadn't seen him here at all. Not that anyone told me their plans.

"Grandfather!" I said in surprise. He was covered in dust, and blood trickled down his forehead. He just grabbed my arm and shoved me into the transport room. I stumbled in, hurt and shocked. I'd assumed the room was still in use, but it was empty.

"What's going on? What happened?"

"We'll talk when we get back home." He maneuvered us into the circle, took a deep breath, and said, "Niamh."

The room shifted, and we were in his home. He pulled me out of the transport room and shut the door. Then, he wilted like a huge weight had been lifted, and he could relax. He kept his hand firmly on my elbow, leading me to the room I thought of as his den.

I'm sure he could feel the questions burning through me with the force of my stare.

"Grandfather." Nothing. "Grandfather!" I repeated louder. Nothing. "Lugh!"

He shook his head and looked at me. He collapsed into his favorite chair, and I sat opposite, waiting. He leaned forward, elbows on knees, and scrubbed his hands over his face.

"You're bleeding," I said.

He lifted a hand to his forehead and looked at the blood on his fingers. He shrugged.

"I'm fine. There was an assassination attempt on the king tonight."

"What? Another one?"

He looked up at me sharply. "How do you know there have been others?"

"Court gossip. All the servants in my queen classes do nothing but talk to each other while they try to mold me into a Fae princess."

"Hmpf."

That startled me like the first time I'd heard Grandfather make that sound. So, like Mr. Mittens.

"Is that why you were there?" Part of me wondered if he had been the one to make the attempt. Was my grandfather interested in taking over the kingdom? He hadn't seemed to be. But he was there at the same time. What did it mean?

He considered me. "Do you think I would attempt to kill my king —without success?"

That question didn't help my doubt. "No?"

"I had a suspicion. I went to investigate it and discovered I was correct. I had nothing to do with the attempt. However, I think I might know how to stop a future one."

"Oh. Was it Sofia and the S-Swamp Lord?" I asked, terrified that my worst fear would come true.

"Who is Sofia?" he asked, alarmed.

"The witch who stole my power. Remember, I told you she was also accidentally brought here when I realm walked. She also petitioned the king for marriage."

I'd told him this the day after I learned about it when we were all at breakfast. He had brushed it away then, and he did it again. Being human really was dismissed here. Foolish. If any of them knew of human ingenuity and human weapons, they'd change their minds quickly. Their dependence and reverence for magic really made them blind to other things.

He waved the conversation away with a hand. "She has no magic then, and the Swamp Lord is only a minor threat. His magic is limited."

I thought that maybe he should look into them. Even without tons of magic, they could still gather an army or pay an assassin. I opened my mouth to say that, but he glared at me.

"Go, I must think." He waved me away after that. A clear dismissal. It angered me, but I wasn't going to get anywhere with him in this mood, so I stood and walked out and down the hall to Megan's room.

CHAPTER

EIGHT

I let myself in and plopped on her bed. She was in the bathroom. I waited a few minutes, but when she didn't come out, I pulled the cord and ordered food when the servant came to answer the summons. Megan must be in the bath. I finally knocked on the door.

"Megan, it's me."

"I'll be out in a minute," she replied.

"OK, I ordered food."

"Thank heavens, I'm starved."

I could hear the tub drain. A while later, she opened the door, wearing a silky robe, her hair in a towel.

"How was queen class today?" she asked.

"Umm, it was fine, but afterwards was more exciting."

She eased herself into a chair with a groan and scrubbed at her hair with the towel.

"What happened? What's wrong with you?" I asked, concerned.

"Nothing. Just stiff from...uh, sleeping wrong," she responded.

I frowned, that was more than sleeping wrong. But I forgot it quickly in light of my news. "There was another assassination attempt on the king."

471

She stood up suddenly. "Oh no, were you there? Were you in danger?"

"No, I was waiting for the transporter room when it happened. It was chaos." I took a breath. "Then my grandfather showed up."

"No way, why was he there? Was he the one trying to kill the king?" she asked.

"No, but I thought that, too. Have you seen my cat?"

"Yeah, earlier." Her eyes shifted, and I knew she was lying about something, but I couldn't fathom why. "He came by to check on me. I think he hates not being with you when you're gone."

"He takes protecting me extra seriously."

"You don't get to change the subject. How do you know it wasn't your grandfather?" she asked, redirecting me back to the important information.

"He told me. He said he thinks he knows who's behind it though, and then he kicked me out of his den."

"Very odd."

"Either my grandfather is plotting against the king, or he is a loyal servant. I'm just not sure, but he doesn't seem like he's the kind that wants to rule the world. He seems more like me, mostly wants to be left alone to do his own thing."

She shrugged. "I guess. We can go get Mr. Mittens and have him weigh in."

"Is he in his room?"

"I don't know, but do you think he'd be hanging out with Dana?" She laughed, and we both shook our heads. "He's a cat. He's probably napping."

"True."

Before we went to check on him, I asked her, "Did you have a good day?"

She gave me the so-so sign. "I'm a bit sore."

"From sleeping funny?" I asked deadpan.

She looked away. "Yeah, something like that. Let's go check on your cat."

We both walked to his room, and I knocked.

There was a grumpy, *Come in,* in my mind. I cracked open the door.

"Mr. Mittens?"

Yes.

"Do you want to come eat in Megan's room with us?"

He looked up from his spot on the bed. He was in his natural form —four hundred pounds of exotic looking killer. Spotted like a leopard, sloped from his shoulders to hips like a hyena, with curved teeth that hooked below his jaw like a saber-toothed tiger, and a bobbed tail like a bobcat, Mr. Mittens was terrifying. However, when he saw me his eyes lit up. Maybe he was missing me, still feeling guilty, or missing his purpose. He hopped down and shifted into his Ragdoll form in the same motion.

I held the door for him, and he followed us to Megan's room.

Once the door was shut, I told him all that had happened on my way back. Then we started with our interrogation. "Do you think that my grandfather would plot against the king or try to kill him?" I asked point blank.

He did give me a few minutes of a thoughtful pause before he answered. *I have known your grandfather for a long time. I do not believe he has any ambition to rule a kingdom. I would be greatly surprised if he would do so. He's very loyal to his king.*

I breathed out a sigh of relief. That was what I thought as well. My grandfather wasn't lying to me. He really wanted to catch the culprit. "Thanks, Mr. Mittens."

Hmpf, was his reply.

And since I'd just recently thought of it, and had no other current distractions, I asked him, "Who started that first, you or my grandfather?"

Started what, pet?

"The hmpf sound when you are annoyed or thinking?"

He cocked his head. *I believe your grandfather picked it up from me.*

That's what I thought. That small mystery solved, I brought up something else that was on my mind.

"Mr. Mittens. If I am stuck here forever, would you go home?"

He looked at me, his blue eyes wide and luminous. *Home, to Earth? No, while you are here there is nothing for me there.*

"No, home to your planet. The Splinter realm."

Splinter Realm? He chuckled into my mind. *There is no such place.*

"Well, what do you call your home?" I asked. Before he could answer, the servant arrived with our food. We set it up on a table and sat down to eat. My cat joined us at a plate and shifted into his Fae form to make it easier to eat with us at the table.

Mr. Mittens took a few dainty bites of finger food, and in between told us about his home planet.

"My home is called Xstlebdmnrdhgpl. I realize that is difficult for the human and the Fae tongue to pronounce. It means 'the true place.'" He ate another careful bite, as though it took concentration for him to eat in a humanoid form. "There is a legend among my people. There used to be only one realm. All that exists in the many realms existed once as only one people and one place. There was a great cataclysm. What caused it is argued about by our scholars. It might have been natural, or accidental, or a master plan, but the one realm splintered into millions of pieces. Each piece was a new realm and the people that had existed as one became another and spread among the realms to create new cultures, new creatures, and new people."

He grabbed another nibble. Megan and I were hanging on every word.

"We call ourselves the Xstlerphnm, it means those that walk the splinters. Many of our race and others from the other realms are able to realm walk. We can roam the splinters of reality."

Megan raised her hand. I reached out to pull it down, but Mr. Mittens raised one tawny eyebrow. "Yes?"

"Umm, you said not all of you could walk the splinters. Is it common though?"

"It is well known, so I'd say yes. It is a common skill among my people."

He grabbed a few more bites and continued.

"Brigid has this gift as does her grandfather. That is how he and I met. I was a young Splintercat, looking for adventures in the splinters as those of my kind often do. I wandered a few realms and found this one. It was very different and exciting compared to what I'd known. Its people balanced on two legs and were bare skinned rather than furred. I was fascinated. Since the people here relied on various items to barter with, I took a job as a type of bounty hunter so that I could provide for myself here. I'd hunt down dangerous creatures and bring them back for justice, or I'd kill them and bring back their heads for payment."

"How do the Fae pay you?" I blurted out. I'd been thinking about it earlier but had no idea how currency worked here.

He gave me an annoyed glance. "They pay in bars of silver."

"Oh. Thanks." I looked down. I hadn't expected that. I thought it would be something more exotic, that was almost Earth-like.

"May I continue?"

I nodded.

"Your grandfather hired me a few times for the court. I became a top hunter for them. The last hunt I went on was for a unicorn."

"Unicorn? Like the one that tried to kill us?" I asked.

"Much like. Only this unicorn was hunting young, innocent Fae girls. Young innocent girls are the unicorns' favored prey. They have a common tactic. They graze in a field, acting like a regular pony. Most of them are silvery white when they aren't aflame, and their horns are crystalline and beautiful. So, they'll lure in a girl, act timid and shy, and make their way carefully to the unsuspecting maiden. Then when their prey is close, they strike."

I shivered and wiped my sweaty palms down my gown. "I'm not sure I want to know, but what do they do with the girls?"

"Unicorns don't eat grass," he answered, and the goose bumps raised on my arms.

I remembered the one we fought. They looked like handsome, stout ponies, but their manes, tails and legs were black flames. Their feet were clawed like a cat's, and their teeth were fanged. They were nightmares when they were trying to kill you.

"So, what happened when you hunted it?"

"There was a girl it was trying to lure in."

We leaned forward.

"I didn't know that at first; I was focused on the beast." He took a few more bites and launched into the story. "The unicorn made a horsey snort, and I froze, one paw suspended in the air. It was just blowing a piece of grass from its nose. Then it went back to fake grazing. I moved forward. Just before I could leap on it, a young girl—caught somewhere between childhood and adulthood—came into view. She squealed with joy, and the unicorn's head shot up. Its eyes lit with avarice. Times up, I thought and took the last few steps I needed."

He paused, and I wanted to smack him. Who knew my cat had a flair for story telling?

"I leapt; my powerful hind legs and my own magic carrying me forward." He lifted his hands, twisting them into claws as he spoke.

"To someone watching, it would appear I flew a short distance. I landed neatly on the unicorn's back. Unfortunately, unicorns are real bastards, as you've discovered. Not only did the unicorn's black flames light up, but it began to buck and throw its head around to dislodge me. Remember, it was my first time hunting one."

We both nodded, enthralled.

"I dug firmly into the unicorn's hide with my claws and tried to grasp its neck with my fearsome teeth, but before I could take the killing bite, the unicorn launched me into the air with a powerful jolt of its body. I twisted around to land on my feet. The unicorn barreled towards me, its head lowered, its wicked horn poised to skewer me."

I grasped my throat, my heart pounding with dread—which was stupid, he'd survived.

"I leapt away, and as the unicorn slid to a stop further down the field, I turned and raced towards it. By this time, the girl saw what was happening and started screaming for *me* to stop. Me! I scoffed, the silly thing didn't know that young girls were the unicorn's favorite prey. She just saw a pretty pony with a crystalline horn and went nuts. I was *saving* her from certain death! The unicorn turned, and we lunged at each other."

Megan grasped my hand, her eyes intent on my cat in his Fae form.

"To add insult to injury, the unicorn's flames had set the field on fire. The girl was in danger from that, too. If she was smart, she'd have run away. I wasn't flameproof either, although I was resistant in the realm because magic abounded, but my fur was getting singed.

"The girl finally ran away, right before me and the unicorn clashed. The horn slashed a burning path down my side. I yowled in pain, but the unicorn got the worst of it." Mr. Mittens lips curled up at the satisfying memory.

"My claws gouged a furrow down the unicorn's side, and it screamed its fury. I heal quickly, but the unicorn didn't have that ability. It also let rage rather than thought guide it. All I needed to do was wait for the beast to make a mistake."

He paused and took a long drink from a bowl of cream. Megan tapped her fingers on the table. "What happened?" she finally asked after he'd stalled longer than her patience would allow.

My cat continued, "For all its reign of terror, the unicorn was young. Its rage caused it to make its very last error. It whirled and charged me again, and that's when I broke its neck with a careful swat of my paw. I left the body lying in the field. Before the fire in the field consumed it, I snapped off the horn with my teeth as proof of death and *walked* back to my employer, your grandfather." He inclined his head at me.

"Something happened here. It must have or you wouldn't have ended up in the human realm," I chided him.

He looked at me with a tilt of his head, but he continued.

"Since I couldn't realm *walk* within the same realm, I stepped to my home realm, Xstlebdmnrdhgpl, and back to the Fae realm outside the door of the home of my employer, a certain Fae lord. I didn't know the lord's name then because that wasn't done here—I didn't know why at the time. I thought that maybe their names were hard to pronounce since I'd noticed that people from other realms struggled with my name." He shook his head at his own ignorance.

"Since it was polite, I shifted into my new Fae form." He gestured to his current shape. "Splintercats like me aren't fond of two-legged forms. They are ungainly, and you two-leggeds tip over easily even if you are a perfect specimen of feline grace like me."

Megan and I tittered. He was definitely a cat. He was so full of himself.

He glared at us for a moment, then continued, "I took a moment to make sure I was centered and called the servant to announce me. I was new to the culture, but I'd figured out that was what you did here. I had a firm grasp on the horn in my hand. The servant escorted me to your grandfather's sitting room."

He pointed down towards the room I'd dubbed my grandfather's den.

"Your grandfather had me join him by the roaring fire."

I looked at Megan. She grinned. Cats liked nothing more than a warm spot.

"Before I sat, I handed the horn to my employer. He examined it, the light from the fire dancing over its crystalline beauty and sending prisms of light shooting over the room. I itched to bat at the light, but I gripped my hands together." He took another drink.

"Your grandfather recognized it was a young unicorn but believed it was the one he'd sent me after. He sent a servant to retrieve my payment and deposit it in my accounts. While we waited, he asked me for a favor. The thing that was to become my downfall."

We waited for him to continue, but before he could there was a knock on the door.

Damn cat and his dramatic pauses, I huffed to myself as I reached out to open the door. I expected a servant since that was all that had ever knocked on our door or come to see us at all.

I jerked it open with an imperious "Yes?" on my lips.

It wasn't a servant. It was my grandfather in the flesh and flanking him was a bored looking Dana. I invited them in, a questioning eyebrow raised.

Once the door was shut, Dana did something magical. I felt it ping against my ears like a pressure drop.

"We needed to meet in secret." My grandfather looked around. "Whatever I say here cannot be revealed to anyone, do you understand?"

We looked at each other and agreed.

"You are aware there have been several assassination attempts against the king?"

We mumbled, "yes," waiting.

"I've uncovered those involved in the plot, and I'm going to need your help to bring them down."

For some reason, that caused my throat to go dry and my hands to sweat. "How?"

"First, we are going to need your magic."

I looked at him, my brows scrunched and my eyes narrowed. "How? It was stripped away."

"I've had Dana working on a renewal spell. It has never been done successfully, but we might have found a work around."

"So, I have to take one of Dana's untested spell balls?"

"Precisely."

"Even with my magic, I'm worthless. Just ask Dana!" I protested.

"She believes you are competent in the area we need."

My eyes drifted over to her. She didn't acknowledge me or agree with him. She just stood there, staring, her poker face utterly blank.

I sighed and paced around the room. "What is it you think I can do?"

"I need a lightning bolt."

CHAPTER
NINE

"A lightning bolt? Are you nuts? I can't control those things! I could kill you, the king, or a lot of other people, slinging around lightning!" I protested. "Can't you do one?"

He stared at me stonily. "I can, but it can't come from me. We may only have one chance at this, and we might need it. Besides, we have yet to see if Dana's spell can renew your power or not."

He waved her over. She held out her hand, a shiny blue ball in it.

I sighed. "If it doesn't work, what will happen?" I looked directly into her eyes.

"The worst-case scenario...you will vomit." She looked thoughtful. "Perhaps pass out. Maybe die." She looked a little too happy at that prospect.

"Die? Do I have to sign a release?"

"What is that?" she asked.

"Nothing. An Earth thing," I answered, my sarcasm going over her head.

I looked at Megan. She was staring at the ball and shaking her head. "You shouldn't do this, Brigid. Even a slim chance of death is too much!"

I looked at my grim-faced grandfather and Dana with her horsey smirk and grabbed the ball. I didn't want to think about it. But if it renewed my magic, maybe I could realm walk us home if I had to— you know, in an emergency. Being without my magic was too risky. I could die anytime I was at court. Who was to say an assassin wasn't going to be waiting for me next time?

I tossed it to the back of my throat, grabbed the fruity beverage I'd been drinking, and swallowed. I felt sick. I wasn't sure if it was from the magic ball or the anticipation of death. I burped up a little acid. So, maybe it was the ball. All I could do now was sit and wait. Megan and Mr. Mittens looked on with something akin to horror on their faces. Would Dana be happy or relieved if I died? Would my grandfather?

We were all silent for approximately ten minutes, waiting, when Dana broke the silence. "It was only a very slim chance of death. Whatever is going to happen has. Try something, Brigid."

I didn't feel anything different. No rush of power, no hot flashes or sprays of mist, nothing. I held out my palm, concentrated through my ring, and attempted to pull up a flame. I probably should have started with water, but flame seemed more appropriate.

It was like flicking a lighter. My flame sputtered to life a few times then died. I looked at Dana.

"Continue."

I took a deep breath and concentrated. Finally, a steady flame appeared. It was weak and took a lot of effort.

"Good," she said.

"That was weak. I can barely do it. I doubt I'll be able to summon a lightning bolt."

"Your magic is restarted, it will grow now. You should be restored by morning."

"So, it's like a battery?" Megan asked. "You just jump start her and if she keeps the car running, it will return to full strength?"

The two Fae looked at her, confusion on their faces. My grandfather had to have had some experience with cars, but he might never have known how they worked or what the battery did. The analogy worked for me though. I nodded.

I only knew very generally how a combustion engine worked, but

I tried to explain. "A battery provides an electric spark—like a small jolt of lightning—which ignites a flammable liquid in a car engine, and that drives pistons up and down that then turn all the rods and things in that engine to make it go forward." The blank looks continued. "When the battery goes dead, another battery can charge it, so it'll spark again. If the engine runs for a while, it will recharge the battery fully." I didn't want to explain an alternator, so I left it at that.

They didn't get what I was talking about, so I dropped it. It didn't matter; my magic was back. And all I had to do was wait, and my magic would be recharged.

"I appreciate the effort it took to make that ball, Dana," I said to her. My courtly magic pill still suggesting the appropriate responses.

Her mouth might have twitched briefly into a smile, but I wasn't positive.

"Do you feel sick at all?" Megan asked.

I thought I was fine, and the twinge of nausea I had after I took it seemed to have passed. "I think I'm good."

She looked relieved, and we sat at the table to discuss plans to stop the assassin.

"Who is the assassin?" I asked. I figured we might as well get the ball rolling—no pun intended.

"I believe it is his Phoenix."

"Phoenix? A magical bird that dies and resurrects from fire?" I asked.

"What? No, the king's most trusted advisor," Grandfather said.

"So, Phoenix is a title," Megan mumbled. My cat continued to eat, not interested.

"Have we met the Phoenix?" I asked.

"You have seen him at court. He was the one announcing everyone and directing the supplicants."

"The guy in the fire robes?" I asked, remembering back.

"Yes, those are the robes of his office."

"Why would he want to kill the king?" I asked. "Is he next in line for the throne?"

"He is a contender, although killing the king would be only the first step in a series of challenging tasks to replace him," Dana added.

"So, how do we prove it's him and stop him?" Which really was the most important thing.

"Cautiously. If I'm found around him and something goes wrong, I will be blamed. If we fail to stop him, and I get caught, I will be blamed. If for any reason we cannot prove it is him and stop him I'll…"

"Yeah, you'll be blamed." I finished for him. A small wave of fear for my only relative flashed through me.

"Correct."

We looked at each other.

"What about Sofia and the Swamp Thing?" Megan asked.

My grandfather wrinkled his brow. "The Swamp Lord?"

She nodded, with a twinkle in her eye.

"They do not have the power or the fortune required to hire elite assassins," he said dismissively.

"Alright. I guess that could be true." Megan sighed. "If this were earth, we'd just put up some cameras or hide a microphone or something."

That was true, but it reminded me of something. The witch's bug. When we'd been spying on the witch coven, Megan had snuck in to break the ward on the building they were in. She was successful, but when she came back, we'd found that the ward had implanted a tiny insect looking tracking device on her. Compared to what Dana did with her magic balls, it was primitive at best. Unable to record or take images, it could only report where someone was, and probably didn't have a huge range.

"I think I might have an idea," I said. "Meg, do you remember the bug?"

"Bug?" she asked, thinking, then her eyes lit up, "Yes! At the witches' warehouse."

I turned to Dana. "The witches had a small magical device." I held up my fingers to indicate the size. "It looked like an earth insect." I shook my head; she might not know what an insect was. "Do you have insects on Faerie?" I asked. It was a stupid question, I remembered brushing some away when we'd been marching to the king's palace.

"We do," my grandfather answered. "Please continue. This sounds intriguing."

"So, we were trying to spy on the witches." I looked at my grandfather. "You know, the bad ones that stole my magic."

He inclined his head in acknowledgement.

"So, we couldn't get into the place they were in because it was warded against magic users."

Both he and Dana appeared confused with the word warded, and I remembered that Fae didn't have wards in their repertoire.

"Uh, a ward is like a magic bubble that keeps out whatever you have warded against. In this particular case, magic users."

"So, we sent Megan in because she isn't a magic user, and she broke the ward so we could enter. But when she did, she came back with a bug on her. It was made to keep track of where she was, but that was all. We found it and removed it. This is the part that is exciting. It was crude and limited, but since Dana's specialty is portable magic, perhaps she could design a bug that could record sound or images."

We all looked at Dana expectantly. She looked perplexed. "I do not understand images or record."

I looked at Megan, and she at me. "Does your phone still have a charge?" I asked.

She shrugged. "I don't know. I turned it off when we arrived here."

"Me too. We can see. That would be the best way to explain it to her. Where's yours?" I asked.

"In the bathroom, under my clean earth clothes," she said.

"I'm going to go get mine. Hopefully one still has enough of a charge for this to work."

I left and hurried down to my room, retrieved it, and returned to Megan's room. She already had hers. "Ready?" I asked. We both hit the power buttons and waited for the phones to turn on. The moment of truth. Mine had been fairly full when we'd gone up against the witches, and I'd turned it off before that. We'd been dumped in Faerie several days ago. I'd never turned mine off for longer than a few hours, and I didn't have a clue if they retained a charge when they were off. I held my breath.

The tone sounded, and both phones lit up. My grandfather had looked at mine before when I'd shown him a picture, and he had remained curious because he leaned in to see the device. Mine was slightly more than half full. I looked at Megan's. It was more than three quarters full. We bumped fists.

"Ok, I'm going to show you what record means, Dana." I flipped to my camera feature and hit video. "Dana, walk over to the closet and come towards me and say something while you do it, please." I tacked the courtesy on at the end because her frown was angry and terrifying.

She dutifully stood up and walked over to the wardrobe. As she started towards me, I hit record.

"This is a pointless and ridiculous exercise," she muttered as she walked. Once she was by the table, I ended the recording, and then turned the phone so both Dana and my grandfather could watch. I hit play.

I could hear the tinnier version of Dana's voice through the small speaker, but Dana and my grandfather's reactions were violent and priceless. They reeled back, my grandfather jumped to his feet, and the chair crashed behind him. Dana lifted her hands, probably to blast the device with magic, but I stopped her.

"This is a recording with sound and images. This device is made with human knowledge of machines like cars, Dana." I'd taken Dana for a ride in a vehicle, and it had scared her. It'd gone too fast, and she couldn't handle it. But, before we'd gone on our ride, I'd told her it was a machine made by people without magic. "It isn't magic. Do you think you could replicate what it does *with* magic?"

Dana took the phone from my hand and looked it all over. She tried to peer inside the charging hole, but that was useless. She handed it back. "I do not know. I didn't know such a thing was possible. I will have to think."

"What do you think, Grandfather?" I asked.

He shook his head. "It is a marvel. If anyone can figure it out, it would be my Dana."

Dana had remained frozen in a state of thought. Suddenly, she looked up and announced. "I must go to my lab."

My grandfather excused her, and she left.

"I guess she had an idea," I said.

Everyone agreed.

"If this works, we have a way to prove your Phoenix is dirty," I said. "We will record him and give the recording to the king. Then we will be free to help him bring the traitor to justice."

My grandfather looked as though a weight had been lifted. The entire plan was weak, but it was a start. If we could stop this, maybe the king's trust in my grandfather would be renewed. Who knew? Maybe he'd be willing to let me go home once in a while.

TEN

D ana came through. It took her three days of tinkering, and no one was allowed to disturb her. I continued with my queen classes; grateful no assassination attempt was made on me. I tried to listen harder to the gossip, desperate to see if anyone suspected the Phoenix or for more news about Sofia and the Swamp Lord. But the gossip was hard to focus on, there were too many people in the space working, too many voices to try to separate. I considered just asking, but I didn't want any suspicions getting out before we were prepared.

Sorcha continued to be assigned to me. I was becoming more and more comfortable with her, and I thought she was more comfortable with me. I wondered if it would be appropriate to ask if she could help us, but I figured I'd run that by my grandfather first. It was his neck most at risk unless he fled the kingdom with us. That wasn't a long-term solution for him though, he couldn't stay on earth for longer than a week or two without deleterious effects. The magic there was weak, and the atmosphere was thinner than on Faerie.

Dana called us into my grandfather's den. Her long horsey face and shark black eyes were alight with anticipation. She must have pulled it off to look so pleased and excited to show us. Her horsey ears twitched constantly with her poorly concealed anticipation to unveil her toy.

When we were gathered, she pulled out a thing about the size of an average earth beetle. About three-quarters of an inch long, it had a dark carapace that shimmered with iridescence like many of the things here in the Fae realm. The Fae seemed to have a love of multiple colors that changed in different types of light. It reminded me of corvid feathers. They appeared black until the light caught them, then they glowed in purples, blues, and greens. She moved the beetle thing back and forth so we could see the color change then launched it into the air. Its wings parted, and it flew like a beetle did as well.

"Is this a common insect here in Faerie?" I asked.

"Yes," my grandfather said, watching it with curiosity.

Dana watched us watch the beetle; her eyes lit up with delight. She let it fly around the room, then opened her hand. It came back to her and alighted, wings folding back under the hard shell.

"Is that all it does?" Megan asked. I swatted at her hand next to her side to get her to shut up before Dana annihilated us with a twitch of her power.

Her eyes went from excited to pissed off in an instant. "No, that is not all it does, insolent human."

"Sorry," Megan muttered. "I thought that was pretty impressive."

Dana then stood and approached my grandfather. She placed the beetle right between his eyes, he froze and gasped a little. Once she let go, the beetle's inner wings spread to form delicate spectacles that covered his eyes. His body twitched with shock, and then wonder. After several moments, the wings furled back into the beetle's body. She plucked it off the bridge of his nose and looked at me.

"OK," I said before she could ask. My curiosity overwhelming the ick factor.

She approached me, and my eyes crossed, watching her place the beetle on the bridge of my nose. I closed my eyes and fought off the urge to swat it off my face. Its magic hummed. I opened my eyes as the wings unfurled and was presented with the beetle's view of the room as it buzzed around watching. It replayed our conversation. It was miraculous that she could create something like this without microchips or the knowledge of video players. The replay stopped, and the wings furled. She plucked it from my face. She looked at Megan to see if she wished to experience it, but she shook her head and put up her hand. She'd been wary of insects since the Soul Spider incident. Dana even offered it to my cat, who also declined. He seemed bored.

"It's brilliant!" I exclaimed after Dana folded it back into her hand.

She almost cracked a smile.

My grandfather was strangely silent, but he must have been thinking.

"That beetle." He gestured at her closed fist. "How long can it fly and re-re-cord?" he stuttered over the strange word.

Dana frowned for a moment. "I'll have to perform further tests, but my crew is producing five more of these delightful *bugs*." She emphasized the word, since it was one we had introduced to her. "So, we will have better specifications soon. We will need to destroy one to see what their capabilities are to the fullest."

"Crash test dummies," Megan mumbled, and I suppressed a laugh.

"How soon before we can use them?" he continued.

Dana gave a slight frown. "Another day, maybe two."

We could tell he wasn't happy that it would be so long, but he gave her a weak smile. "Perfect, make it so." The dismissal was cruel and obvious to all of us. My shoulders stiffened as I saw the light in Dana's eyes go out. She went from cherished team member to servant in an instant. Rage lit up my heart. He'd just treated her like Evan used to treat me.

Her shoulders hunched, but she turned and left. I watched her shut the door behind her carefully.

I couldn't stand for that. I had my issues with Dana, but I had more with abuse. "Grandfather, I know this is not my place or my business, but you just destroyed her with that dismissal. She created something impossible in a very short amount of time. I know that this is time sensitive, but she is more than a servant, and you've made it clear she is less than your equal with that one statement. I don't know if you

491

want to turn her against you. She is deeply loyal to you, and my experience has shown that praise and care go further than what you just did."

He frowned at me, and I was sure he would strike me or reprimand me. But he looked at the door and sighed. Then he turned and looked at me with a little fire in his eyes.

I took a step back.

He shook his head. "You are correct. It is not your business. However, I'm not unfair. I will make it right."

He gave us a curt nod and left to follow Dana.

We did not need her to join our enemies. We had to keep her firmly on our side. Plus, I couldn't tolerate any type of emotional abuse. Although what he'd done was small, it still hurt, and I understood that better than anyone.

"Well," I said to Megan and Mr. Mittens. "I guess we should eat and go to bed. There's nothing else to do until Dana has the finished products ready."

* * *

ALTHOUGH EVERY DAY THAT PASSED, THE DESIRE TO RETURN HOME AND check on Gabe and my house only intensified, but we couldn't do anything except wait for Dana's "bugs" to be ready. We had to stop the plot against the king. At least she'd been right about my magic, and it seemed fully restored—at least the eleven pieces I had. Now, in between tedious queen lessons, I added in magic lessons with Dana. In the few short hours we had, she needed to teach me how to better control lightning—the scariest and least manageable of my powers. I guess grandfather wanted to keep his plan on the back burner in case the new plan failed.

Dana wanted me to learn the smaller applications like shocking someone and creating a throwable ball of electricity. The only time I'd used my lightning to shock someone was because it was being repressed by witches. If I tried it now, I'd turn someone to ashes. To say I was scared to experiment was an understatement.

I explained that to Dana. She laughed in my face.

"Look around, child," she said. "This room is shielded from all magic. You will be able to wield your power safely, and no harm will come to either of us."

"Then how will you know if I'm doing it right?" I asked, confused.

"You will see. Now, aim your power at that spot." She pointed to what amounted to a target on the other side of the empty room. I didn't see how this room would suppress anything; it looked just like a basic room, nothing special. The only thing in it was the target on the wall, and us.

I gathered my will, focused it through my ring, held up my hand, and aimed at the target. I let a lightning bolt fly. It was odd, to say the least, the room did suppress my magic in a way, but not the way I was expecting. The bolt blasted from me as strong as always, but it wasn't lightning. The room changed it into light. So, it seared our eyes, but no killing force blasted into the wall, missing the target by ten feet. That was what I was afraid of. I couldn't aim the bolt like I wished; the lightning arced the way it wanted.

"That is pathetic," Dana, the best teacher in the world, encouraged. Even said directly into my head it sounded sarcastic.

"I know," I breathed out in a disappointed sigh.

"Again. This time try throwing it, not aiming it with your hand. Can you throw straight?"

In other words, "you throw like a girl."

"No."

She huffed at me.

"Try anyway."

One thing about Dana's method of teaching. She was harsh, but she didn't play games. She called it as she saw it.

She was just going to call me inadequate which I was, so I gathered a ball of electricity into my hand, as she'd shown me, and threw it at the target. It went from my hand, arcing down, and hit the ground well short of the target. I'd warned her.

An exasperated snort came from her horsey face. I rolled my eyes. "You are correct. I would have to teach you to throw properly before that is worthwhile, but we'll continue to practice building it up in your hand, you could just smash it into someone's face. Try the bolt again."

It was pretty sad when one form of defense was off the table because you grew up being bookish rather than tomboyish. I built the magic in my mind, aimed my hand, and fired. I did that until I could barely lift my arm anymore, and although my aim improved, I never once hit the target.

"We'll continue tomorrow," she said finally. Her sigh and the shake of her head let me know how completely disappointed in me she was.

I didn't have the motivation to even respond. I just stumbled out the door, wondering if I could even help my grandfather at all.

ELEVEN

The next day, I remembered to talk to my grandfather about Sorcha before queen classes and torture with Dana. I called the servant and had her contact him since I didn't know how to find him or where he was in the castle.

It was early by Fae terms, but he was already up and working in his den. Plans of the high king's keep were spread over the table near the bookshelves, and he was poring over them.

"Grandfather," I addressed him to get his attention.

His eyes drifted up to me. "Yes, child?"

I hemmed and hawed a bit, not sure how to bring this up. "I've sort of made friends with one of the king's Shadows, and I was wondering if you want to bring her in on this. Maybe she could help get close to the Phoenix, where you and I would struggle?"

He stared at me, but I could see the wheels turning.

"That could be a great risk," he said.

"I know. I think we can trust her. She is loyal to the king and would want to see him protected."

He nodded, unfocused as he continued to think.

"She knows I'm not a threat, although I don't know what she thinks about you."

"That is a problem." He looked down at his plans for a moment. "Do you think she would be willing to come speak with me? I might be able to convince her. Show her the bug and the plans?"

"Yes, but what if she won't agree after you speak?"

"Then, we'll have Dana give her a forget ball."

"She's a highly trained weapon, how would we do that?"

"We have ways; Dana can accomplish it."

I looked at his face, it was firm, but his eyes twinkled a bit. He had a lot of faith in Dana's abilities, and it showed in his subtle expressions. He even looked forward to Sorcha failing and having to turn her into Dana, huh?

Still, I knew Dana was his Mistress of Magic, but I didn't think she was some badass weapon like Sorcha, so a little trickle of fear ran through me. She was scary. Maybe Dana liked me more than I thought, because she was free to do anything to me when I was with her. But now? I was terrified to be alone with her. I'd always shuddered a little to be near water when we worked at my waterfall since she was a Kelpie, but now I could never work there with her again, if I ever got to go home. Even if I could hold my breath for forty-five minutes or more.

"OK, I'll ask her if she'll come, invite her for tea or something."

"It has to be today; we launch the plan tomorrow."

"Yes." I looked at him and glanced at the plans on the table, they just looked like drawings and useless words to me. "Thanks, Grandfather, I've got to go to queen class now."

He looked back down at his plans, dismissing me.

I hurried to the transporter room since I was a little later than usual. I loved saying that. I'd always loved Star Trek growing up.

Sorcha was waiting at the door to pick me up. My loyal guard. Only she was there for two reasons, to protect me and to keep me from doing anything I wasn't allowed. A double-edged sword.

She wasn't very talkative, and I was curious, so I asked her what was wrong.

"There has been another attempt on the king. We've been on high alert today, not much sleep in my past or future," she said.

"That's terrible! I'm so sorry, my friend." This looked to be the perfect opening to invite her, give her a bite, and let her be a hero. "What if I told you I could help with that?" I asked.

She stopped and whirled on me. "What do you know? Is your grandfather part of this?" she hissed.

"What? No! But we have an idea on how to catch the culprit. I was going to ask you today if you wanted in. If you could help us."

Her eyes narrowed.

"What would be involved?" she asked, still suspicious.

"Come for tea? We can talk with my grandfather, and he can show you what we plan to do."

"Tea?" What is that?

"It's a drink made from leaves, it's an Earth thing. You can drink whatever you want, or not drink, it's just a saying. I'm inviting you over for light refreshments and the chance to save the king."

"Why would you want to save him?" she asked. It was a great question. The truth was I'd be out of the marriage and on my way home if he died. She knew I didn't want to do this and that I wanted to go back to my realm.

I thought a moment more, planning the best way to answer. "Because if that happens, this realm will be thrust into a huge civil war. My grandfather would be fighting, and I could lose him. I just found the one family member I have left in all the realms, and I'll do anything to keep him as safe as possible. He is loyal to your King, even if I couldn't care less about the problems of the kingdom. That's why."

She looked at me, a frown deepening on her face. "I will come."

"I think you'll be pleasantly surprised at what we're going to do."

That arranged, my heart lifted, and I strolled happily to my gossiping session with the courtiers. After a little makeup, hair, and dressing by my gossipy pack of servants, I was ready to get the dirt on our target. Boy was this place a hotbed of intrigue. I was going to pay close attention, and not let them distract me from finding out about the assassin, the king's Phoenix.

Sorcha dropped me off at my session and wandered off to do whatever she did when she wasn't with me. I sighed and opened the door for my torture session to make myself court presentable.

The servants were all a titter today, their tongues wagging about the new assassination attempt. One thing was sure, it was hard to keep a secret from the servants. They saw everything because they were everywhere.

The one doing my hair was deep in the description of what happened to the king with the lady doing my face. "He leapt out from behind the wall hanging in the king's chambers. No one knows how he got there!" she exclaimed. The hair lady paused, her fingers deep into my curls, attempting to smooth them.

"Oh my, what was the weapon this time?" face lady asked, swiping color on my cheeks.

"Magic, no physical weapon. He tried to burn the king to a cinder."

"What did the king do?"

Hair lady started tugging on my scalp, braiding my hair into some elaborate net. "Well, the king is apparently a fire elemental as well along with his other powers. So, he extinguished the flame and called his Shadows in. The chambermaid said she'll be cleaning blood off the ceiling and walls for days!"

I swallowed hard. They were vicious, the king's Shadows, and I wouldn't want them angry at me. At least that assassin was done for. How many could be hired before the pool ran low? I shook my head. The serving lady tugged hard. "Hold still, please, milady," she asked politely, although I could feel the desire to rip strands of hair out through her hold.

"Forgive me, that news was disturbing."

"Of course, milady."

You'd think my comment would quiet them down, but that only lasted a few instants before they were deep in conversation again. I figured, what the hell, I'll just ask what I really wanted to know.

"Does anyone know who is behind these attempts?" I asked, trying to slip it in organically.

They both stopped and stared. I don't think they thought I cared or that I was listening to their constant chatter.

"No, milady," hair lady replied. Of course, why would they give me anything, my grandfather was probably high on the list. And now I alerted them so they would quit talking.

"You know, I've been coming for days, and I don't know what you're called?" I switched topics, trying to disarm them.

"Oh, I'm Tessa," the hair lady said.

"I'm Sencha," the make-up lady said.

"I'm Brigid," I added, so they didn't think I was stealing their names. They were only giving me the names they "went by" not their real ones, so my gift should be better received.

"That's my given name." I added so they would understand the trust I was giving them.

"That is very kind, Lady Brigid," they both said in unison. They knew not to thank anyone, which was something that even with the magic ball's power running through me I had a hard time remembering.

I inclined my head gently to them, since Tessa still had a firm grip on my hair.

"I know that people believe my grandfather is involved, but his loyalty is true. Who else do people suspect?" I asked.

They both took in a breath, shocked that I would address their unspoken beliefs so blatantly.

"Ummm, there are several possibilities, milady."

"I'm sure. My prime suspect is the Phoenix. Is he on anyone's list?" I asked point blank.

There were surprised gasps from both of the serving ladies.

"Yes, milady," Sencha answered. Then, she closed her mouth and wouldn't say anything more. Were they afraid of the Phoenix? I couldn't see Tessa's face, but Sencha looked frightened and her hand trembled when she went to smooth on my eye shadow.

I backed off. This talk could get them in trouble. Especially if they suspected I was a spy in their midst. I was an idiot. Now they wouldn't speak any court gossip around me at all. I sighed in despair, but I had other stations, and hopefully they wouldn't alert the others, slim chance, but I hoped.

I was surprised, when near the end of the hair session—Sencha had left earlier, since my makeup was done long before the elaborate hair dressing was—Tessa leaned in close and whispered conspiratorially, "The Phoenix is everyone's top choice for the assassin, but he is so dangerous, no one dares speak it. Be careful, Lady Brigid."

I gulped. That made sense. I needed to be sneakier about this. He was the most dangerous man in the court besides the king and my grandfather.

How was I going to get my info then? "Is there a code word people use to speak of him?" I asked quietly.

Her hands stilled for a moment.

"When we wish to speak of him, we use the word bird. It's silly, but it makes us feel safer."

"You are very kind to share that, Tessa," I acknowledged, and her hands returned to twisting and tugging.

"He has spies everywhere. Be careful, we are fond of you."

I felt tears well up. I had no reason to have anyone fond of me, and it touched me deeply. I felt the need to thank her, and although the magic screamed at me not too, I said quietly. "Thank you, Tessa. You have touched me."

Her hands stilled again, and I could sense her surprise behind me. "Why would you place yourself in my debt?" she asked, her voice uneven. She might have even believed I was setting a trap.

"Because I'm in your debt for that information. It might save your king."

"I accept," she said. A zing ran through me, and I realized that those thank yous I'd been warned about were real. I now owed her a debt. I had no idea how that would play out, but it was real, and that zing was a geas upon me.

She went back to my hair, and we finished in silence.

I proceeded to my next station, being dressed, but Sencha must have warned them as they were unnaturally silent. They kept the gossip to other servants who I didn't know rather than about the king. It was fine, the meaty thing I needed to know, I was clutching to my breast with all my will.

After my lessons with the courtiers on how to address everyone and how to recognize them by rank, I transported back to my grandfather's to change and practice with Dana—the worst part of my day. The only thing that cheered me was maybe I'd be better when the final conflict with the witches happened, if I could ever go home. That sent me down the rabbit hole of worry for Gabe and what was happening back home. We'd essentially disappeared for a couple of weeks now, and everyone must be frantic or think we were dead. What was going to happen to my friends, to my house?

Dana slapped those creepy long hands at me when I drifted away in a funk. My eyes snapped back to hers, and she crisply demanded I throw the ball of electricity again. My throwing was still disappointing, and the look in her eyes let me know that was one trick unavailable in my repertoire, and thus out of hers.

"Is it true not everyone here has magic?" I asked her. Mainly to distract her from making me do it again and again. My arm felt like it wanted to fall off.

She ignored me. "Use the other arm. You use that one constantly, and it isn't working. Aim a bolt with your left arm."

It felt awkward, but when I aimed at the target, the bolt struck true. At least it hit the target, if only barely.

We both froze in surprise.

"Hmmm, it seems you are better when you don't think too hard about it," she remarked.

It was true, I'd basically shot from the hip.

"Finally," I grumped.

"Again." she commanded. Not that I wasn't expecting that.

Each bolt erupted on the target closer and closer to the center, and the excitement in my chest grew. I could do it; I could aim lightning without killing anyone near me.

Of course, that excitement ended with a flash, when she said we were moving out of the safe room to the practice field where others would be. My knees began to shake.

"What if it doesn't work when I know it's not safe for everyone?" I asked, my voice quivering.

"Then they will die."

Like that helped.

We stood in the practice yard. I swallowed down the urge to yell, "Incoming." Mostly because Dana would probably smack me upside the head. She wanted me tense and focused.

The targets here were further away, and the archers practicing were closer than I wished they were.

"Now, Brigid, I have work to do." Her annoyed tone stabbed through me.

I flinched, but I raised my left hand and let a bolt fly. It barely hit the edge of the target, but no one was struck, and the static in the air increased.

My anxiety was buzzing when she made me do it again. This time, the bolt went off target, and someone practicing with their bow went flying. I gasped and ran over to check on them. "Sorry, so sorry!" I kept saying. But the person was only stunned and wobbled back to a bench to get their wits back.

Now, I was terrified of killing someone, but Dana wouldn't let me back down.

She commanded me again and again, until I was frazzled, but the bolts hit true. She finally gave me one terse nod and announced that we were finished. I sighed with relief and headed to the transporter room minutes before Sorcha arrived for "tea."

She'd had to wait until her shift ended, although she only had a four-hour reprieve before she was back on duty. She exited the transporter room, and I froze to see that she was only on two legs not four.

"What?" I gasped.

She sighed. "Yes, we have two forms. It's easier to do some things this way like dine with two-leggeds. Although we don't like to change since we feel more vulnerable."

She was dressed in Fae casual—basically fitted robes—still tall, built like a warrior, but now she had small breasts, and a more regular female shape. I also noticed she had bags under eyes, and her eyes were bleary with exhaustion. I was taking her from her one chance to rest. I felt bad, but this was important. More important than sleep.

Grandfather spent some time talking to her privately in his den, before Dana, Megan, Mr. Mittens, and I were invited in. Dana brought her newest, perfected prototype to demonstrate, and those of us that had experienced it watched with high interest when the bug spread its wings over Sorcha's eyes, and she experienced the wonder of a recorded video for the first time.

She gasped and flung her arm back for her weapon but stopped herself. I was impressed that her first response was to fight, rather than to run. She was well-trained.

Once Dana plucked it from her nose, we all looked on with antic-ipation.

"That, that was…" She had no words.

Her eyes were alight with something. Excitement? Terror? I had no idea.

"I think that could make the difference," she finally said.

"We would need your help to deploy the bugs," my grandfather added. "We need to get them into places where it would be odd for us to be seen. However, they would be places you can go easily."

"Like where?" she asked.

"Places that the Phoenix is commonly found or where he's known to meet people privately."

"I normally only see him in the public places with the king," she responded.

"Yes, but off those rooms are the private chambers. You'd only need to crack open a door and let the bug in," Grandfather said.

She looked thoughtful. "Yes, I think that can be done. How many do you have?"

We all looked at Dana.

"There are eight working prototypes."

Eight? I thought she'd only had four. I guess she was fast at this— fast and capable.

Sorcha reached her hand out for the bug that had recorded us, and Dana plunked it into her hand. She examined it up close, weighing it, measuring it with her eyes. "I believe I can smuggle in eight of these without any trouble. When?"

"Tomorrow. I can bring you the other bugs now," Dana answered.

"How do I make them work?" Sorcha asked.

"The magic is already there; they just need the command word that will start them and another to end the recording. You will need to retrieve them within a day, if you do not, the magic will cease to work, and the bugs will fall to the ground and the recordings will be lost."

"That is reasonable," Sorcha replied. For the first time in a few days, she seemed to perk up. Hope was a powerful drug.

Dana took Sorcha to her lab for the rest of the bugs, and we retired to our rooms, anxious that all would go smoothly.

Now, it was a matter of waiting. I sucked at that. Waiting made me worry, gave me time to think of everything that could go wrong, and made me dwell on Sofia, Gabe, the house, the werewolves, Brightfeather and Goch, and me. Was I going to be trapped here forever in another horrible marriage, more of a slave now than ever? I couldn't face it. I had to find a way home—a way to end this ridiculous situation. I buried my face in the pillow that wasn't mine on a bed that wasn't my glorious king-sized memory foam. Mr. Mittens was consulting with my grandfather, and Megan was resting. I had this grand Fae power, and it was nothing without my home and my friends.

After this, if it worked, I was going to throw myself on the king's mercy and get my life back. That was the only thing that kept me going. I even wondered about Sofia. What if she made it back before me? That got my heart beating fast as I wondered if Gabe would ever escape her enslavement. I fell asleep sobbing those thoughts into the foreign pillow.

* * *

THE NEXT DAY WAS THE DAY THAT SORCHA WAS GOING TO DEPLOY THE bugs. Dana had gifted me with another, just in case. She'd told me to activate it with Mr. Mittens's true name, Xrsrphn. I could deactivate it with Splintercat. Since I rarely said either of those words, they were good ones for me to use. I practiced with Mr. Mittens to make sure I pronounced his name correctly.

I've also given the spymaster Sofia's name, so he can search for any mention of her, Mr. Mittens announced to me.

"There's a spymaster?" I choked out.

Of course, your grandfather is a high Fae lord, and must look out for his own interests. The spymaster requires an image as well, when you have time, stop by and give him your last mental picture.

"Didn't you give him one?"

Hmpf. He said that mine was inadequate.

I could see that. I doubted cats saw the same as us two-leggeds. I smiled at him. "I will stop by, if you show me where."

Then, we all went about our usual tasks, our minds distracted with the worry that the bugs wouldn't work, or maybe worse, would. How would we convince the king without suspicion? Without letting the scary Phoenix know? Those were worries that distracted me through queen class. I watched but had zero opportunity or need to launch my bug.

I was surprised at the end of my day—I expected to return to my grandfather's—when I was instead brought to the king and into a large dining chamber. There was a long table and seated at it were many courtiers. My lungs seized for a moment when I realized I had to perform without embarrassing anyone and without getting myself or my grandfather imprisoned—or worse—for treason.

I was announced and seated at the opposite end of the table from the king. That was a relief until I realized all eyes could watch me. Then I nearly melted the makeup off my face with flop sweat.

The only thing keeping my hair from following in a river of salt-water was its elaborate braids and all the pins. The sweat ran freely down my back, however, to make everything more comfortable. I made it through the serving of the first course without error. I kept up inane and meaningless small talk to those next to me. Finally, the nervous sweat stopped, and I made the mistake of thinking that I could handle it.

That's when the fun began.

The grand doors into the chamber opened as they had to allow me to enter earlier, and my grandfather was escorted in and seated to the king's left. He was followed shortly by the man I now knew as the Phoenix.

I gasped quietly and hid it with a delicate cough. I didn't know why my grandfather was here, and judging from his ruddy complexion, he wasn't happy about it. The Phoenix had on his court face—one that said he was pleasant and slightly amused. He took his seat on the king's right. I blinked.

My heart sped up, and my mouth went dry. What was going on? Not knowing what else to do, I pretended to reach down and grab something I'd dropped. When I did so, I took the bug from my shoe, whispered, "Xrsrphn," and let it go. It rose out of my hand and disappeared from view without anyone noticing. It should now buzz around the ceiling and record until I called it back.

I fervently wished that Mr. Mittens and Megan were with me. I couldn't see this situation ending well. There were some courtly shenanigans or machinations going on behind the scenes that I didn't understand, but the level of tension in the room doubled with every course. I tried to eat, so I didn't appear rude or ungrateful, but all I could do was nibble and push things around on my plate. I couldn't hear the discussion at the other end of the table; I could only hope that the bug did.

Finally, the last course was cleared away, and we were free to exit the table to the adjoining grand throne room to mingle. My grandfather caught my eye and gestured for me to hold back and stay unnoticed.

I tried. But everywhere I went, courtiers were vying for my favor, and I had to keep up the chatter and empty compliments as I was passed from group to group. Still, I managed to keep a look out for my grandfather and the bug, which had dutifully followed us and was now lazily buzzing the ceiling of the throne room, no one the wiser. My grandfather, the king, and the Phoenix were near the throne. The Phoenix had his back to the crowd, the king facing him; my grandfather stood off to the side.

They looked to be discussing something serious. They were focused intently on each other and not paying attention to anything else. I was still being shuffled from group to group, so I couldn't keep a constant eye on them.

A scream rang out, my breath caught, my heart beat hard, and I twisted to see what was happening. The king was being hurried away by his Shadows who, until then, had been lining the walls. Others were dragging my grandfather and the phoenix away. I ran towards them. Before I'd gone more than a few steps, I was also being grabbed and wrenched back. I reached out my hand, whispered, "Splintercat," and the bug dropped into my hand. Then I was being shoved to and fro. I fell at one point and used the motion to put the bug back in my shoe. A rough hand finally hauled me up, and two of the Shadows I'd never met escorted me out—under arrest.

CHAPTER

TWELVE

y heart was in my throat, and I begged them to tell me
what had happened. After they'd bound my hands with
magic dampening cuffs, one smacked me across the face
and said, "That's because the Pendragon tried to kill the king." She
bent down closer and hissed into my ear, "You'll never replace me in
his bed." I recoiled in shock and hurt.

Realization hit me with a blast. This was the leader of the
Scáthanna—the king's mistress. What had Sorcha called her? I racked
my brain, but nothing came to me. I was too worried about my fate.
Didn't matter that I didn't want to replace her in his bed, she would
have it out for me. I would be replacing her in a way. I doubted they'd
end their affair over something so trite as a political marriage, but
maybe he was the loyal type. I muffled a laugh in my shoulder. I was
growing punchy as I was dragged and poked and prodded down a hall,
out a door, and down several staircases.

We walked forever. It made sense to me in a way. Why would you
want your dungeon to be under your palace? They appeared to be
linked, but it felt like we walked miles, and as big as it was, the palace
wasn't *this* large. We finally entered the part where the cells were kept.
They weren't what I expected, no iron bars, no dirt floors or filthy

people weeping and wailing. The cells were separated by clear sheets of something I'd say looked like acrylic. I knew that wasn't true, because this was a different planet with different resources.

A door opened into an empty cell. The floor was stone, and there was a cot and a wooden bucket for waste. They removed my cuffs and the king's mistress shoved me roughly inside with a sneer. I rubbed my wrists. The sensation of having my magic shut down was like having a nerve block in a way. I could feel heat, cold, and sensation, but at the same time I felt numb. It was hard to describe.

Once the door shut, I realized the numbness was gone, but when I tried to reach for my magic, it was faint and far away. Whatever the thick clear walls were, they continued to block magic. I pressed a hand against the clear door, and a shock drove me back. I rubbed my hand against the smooth fabric of the elaborate gown I wore. I looked around. Because the walls were transparent, I could see several other inmates in the dungeon. I scanned for my grandfather. Would he be brought here? Would they execute him? What was going to happen?

I hoped we had a chance to show our evidence, if we had some. The bug. I needed to see what it saw. I looked around, but the inmates were focused on their own misery, and no one was watching me. I dug the bug from my shoe, and like Dana had shown me, I placed it on the bridge of my nose. It activated its replay mode. I had to watch it in real time because it didn't have a fast forward or reverse. But it looked like time wasn't a problem for me.

Most of what I watched was cringe worthy. I looked ridiculous trying to be a courtier. I could pull off a gown, but not as daily wear. I usually relied on jeans and t-shirts, especially since I was out of the corporate world. I pulled my attention back from me and focused on the king. There was a lot of background noise, so I couldn't tell what they were saying in the dining room. I hoped it would clear up when we switched back to the throne room.

There we went. The king led the way, followed by my grandfather and the Phoenix. I was in the last group since I'd been at the far end of the table. We were all gathered in various groups in the throne room, and the bug circled, getting video of different parts of the room. How I wished that instead of a limited magical bug, we'd had a drone to focus on what I wanted to see and hear. Again, an occasional snippet of conversation I could understand wafted through, but most was a hum of noise with only random words peering out.

There. They were in position and the bug was headed in that direction. Maybe it saw what had happened. I continued to watch, my breath ragged and my hands clenched in anticipation.

It was subtle. My grandfather turned slightly to look at something that the Phoenix was gesturing towards. When he did, his shoulders blocked the king's view, and the Phoenix used the opportunity to stab forward with a stiletto, hiding his intent and making it hard to distinguish which of the men did it.

The knife flashed towards the king and was eaten up in the king's voluminous robes. I gasped. The king lurched back, igniting a flare of magic that whited out the bug for an instant. When the flash ended, I saw my grandfather's eyes flick to the knife and reach towards the Phoenix to grab it from him. Then I couldn't see anymore because the centaurs leapt forward, and it was too chaotic. Plus, the bug had moved away. We had it. We had the proof.

I closed the bug carefully and stuck it back in my shoe. Now, how did I get it into the right hands? How did I get free long enough to save my grandfather and myself? Would any of my magic reach through these walls? Could I call Mr. Mittens?

I sat on the cot, and gingerly felt my cheek. It was a little swollen and now that the sting of the slap had diminished and left it throbbing. I set my mind to ignore it, and closed my eyes, intent on sending one call to my cat, my one protector in this realm now that my grandfather was arrested. I didn't know if I could depend on Sorcha, or if she would risk her neck to get us out, but I knew Mr. Mittens would do anything for me. I concentrated and yelled with all my will and intent over and over at him until I was interrupted by a jailer bringing in food. After that, I continued until I must have fallen asleep.

* * *

THE NEXT DAY WAS MORE OF THE SAME. THEY FED US TWO MEALS, AND I spent the rest of the time calling to my cat. It was mentally exhausting, especially when I spent that energy on something I wasn't sure would even work. I don't know how many days I tried until I decided I had to try something else. If Mr. Mittens had heard me, he'd be here. I had to conclude that he couldn't hear me. I needed to break through the walls to give my call a chance. I tried each aspect of my magic. Water wasn't an option since I had none but what little they gave me to drink. I tried using earth to fling stones against the clear panes of the prison walls. The stones from the floor barely wobbled. I did manage between my fingers and my magic to pry one up and use it to bang against the walls. It did nothing.

Fire didn't scorch the material either. My strongest, messiest, magic was lightning, but I kept it as a last resort. It wouldn't do anyone any good if I ended up taking myself out with it. After everything else failed, I attempted to gather it in my hand. A few sparks flicked between my fingers. I'd never build significant power by going quickly. This was the last resort, if I didn't pull this together, free myself, and show the evidence, we were doomed. I'd never get home, Gabe would be enslaved forever, and my house would go back to a state of rot. I wanted to sob, only crying did nothing. I was a strong woman. I had a goal; I just had to work.

I waited until the second meal was delivered and I knew I'd have a span of uninterrupted time. The sparks were so small, I almost despaired, but I continued to layer sparks a little at a time. The sweat poured off me, but I had time—all night until the morning meal was brought—and no interruptions.

Sparks layered on top of sparks and started to stick. A tiny electric ball the size of a BB grew in my palm. I figured I had to increase it to at least the size of a softball to have any chance of it being useful against the magic walls of my cell. I kept my concentration on it for hours. I don't know how I did it, except for the fact I had to. No one else could save me. When I heard the breakfast servants coming down the stairs, I knew it was time. My electric ball wasn't quite to softball size, but it was somewhere in between a baseball and a softball, and I was out of time. If I didn't try now, I'd have to release it and try again after the evening meal when I had enough time to build it back up, and I didn't know if I could concentrate that long without sleep two nights in a row.

I stood and walked carefully to the door, keeping my concentration up and the ball crackling in my hand. I checked for the guards or for the servants bringing breakfast, but my portion of the dungeon was clear. I probably had other inmates watching me, or they continued to ignore each other as they sat in their own world of misery. I didn't have the energy to notice. I said a short prayer, applied the concentrated lightning to the mechanism in the door, and sent my will outward to push through the door to the other side. For a moment, the lightning ball sat there between my palm and the material of the door, and nothing happened. I pushed with all my might, the effort causing my arm to shake. I placed my other hand over the one with the lightning, and using my back foot continued the pressure. The lightning bucked and wiggled in my hand, trying to take off in another direction, since the wall material was resistant. I curled my fingers around it slightly. I imagined my hand sizzling under the concentrated electricity, but I set my will and kept pressing. Finally, to my relief, the ball began to melt its way through the door material, magic and all.

I'd hoped it would be an instant process. But it took several minutes. When the door finally cracked open, the magic broken, I could hear the guards approaching on their rounds. There was some commotion in my cell block, and I looked around. The other inmates had been watching me. The closest beckoned for me to come close and let them out.

I shook my head, and mouthed, "Sorry." Their plight touched me, but I couldn't help, I didn't have time. The noise of trays being scraped over floors was growing louder, and I knew the guards would turn the corner and see me at any moment. I'd done nothing but study how to get out of the dungeon in the days I'd spent trying to contact Mr. Mittens—staring at the halls and where guards and servants turned and disappeared to. I chose a corridor that seemed empty and bolted out.

Once free of the cell, my magic rushed back. I felt revived and tingling with energy, which I needed after my all-night vigil. I wrapped myself in shadow and looked around to find an exit or a good place to hide. The corridors were narrow, and I'd have to avoid guards running into me as I made my way out. It wouldn't be long until someone noticed my cell was empty, my door open, and the cell magic broken.

I didn't give myself much of a chance if they recaptured me. They'd keep me in magic dampening cuffs forever if I was caught. I tried to control my breathing, since it seemed loud and rasping to me, but the adrenaline was hard to fight when I was so afraid of getting caught. I slipped down an empty corridor and ran to the end. A dead end. This part only dropped a level to more cells. I retraced my steps. We had come down to this level, I needed to find a staircase that went up if I wanted out.

I tried another corridor. More cells, no exit. The next corridor had many guards running about. The alarm had been sounded, at least I could hear guards yelling that there was an escape. Now, they were actively looking for me. This had to be the one that led to the exit. Even though they couldn't see me, I could easily bump into someone if I wasn't careful and give myself away. The gown I still wore wasn't helping. It was voluminous and would get in the way. I stripped down to my underwear. For a gown like this, they had me in a type of shift. It had support for my breasts and hugged my form to mid-thigh where it flared into a short skirt. I reminded myself no one could see me as I kicked the gown as far as possible into a corner. I renewed my shadow camouflage, checked the busy corridor, and rushed in between the masses of people, avoiding touching anyone as best as I could.

I only bumped into one person, but they blamed a guard next to them. I cleared the last corner, and the exit to the prison became visible. My heart thumped in my throat, and my breath was ragged. I raced to the exit.

"Mr. Mittens!" I yelled mentally.

I could feel his surprise. *Brigid? Where are you? What happened?* his mental voice rang between my ears, filling me with happiness.

I looked around, the coast was still clear, and I bolted to the door.

"I've been in the dungeon, locked up. I'm escaping now." I hoped, anyway.

I'm coming.

I nearly sobbed in relief. I ripped the door open. There were more guards outside the door, and I almost backpedaled, but I knew they couldn't see me, although the door opening on its own had to be suspicious. I hoped Faerie had ghosts, and the guards were superstitious.

They weren't, dammit. The door opening alerted them, and they branched out, completely aware that someone masked from their view was here. I stopped suddenly when one of the guards told everyone to be quiet and listen for the intruder. I was wearing soft court shoes, but all the marble-like flooring made even a soft shoe loud.

We were at an impasse. All of us were still and listening. I just hoped my panicked breathing didn't give me away, so I worked at taking small shallow breaths and tried to calm my racing heart.

Where was my cat? How long would it take him to find me? Did I need to call him to me and hope my inherent magic would bring him, or would it hurt him to be hurtled through space at me? I didn't dare. I had to wait. I also had to remember he was in trouble with the court and had been banished to Earth. I didn't want him hurt or killed either. But, he could realm walk, and I hoped if he were in trouble, he'd escape.

There was a loud clatter behind the guards, their heads turned, and I used the noise to skitter forward. More rattles and clanks—it sounded like armor. Were more guards on their way? I had to use the noise to flee, so I scurried forward a few more steps and waited for more noise. It came, I fled to the doorway and through—expecting to see rows of soldiers on the other side. Nothing.

THIRTEEN

T looked around. Up ahead, Mr. Mittens in his Splintercat form turned a corner dragging a long chain. He stopped briefly and rattled it. I wanted to scream his name and gather him in my arms and squeeze the stuffing out of him.

Instead, I sent him a mental, "I'm in front of you."

We should run, pet, he replied.

I ran. I skidded around the corner with Mr. Mittens. He could easily outpace me, but he heard me just fine and stayed by me. I wrapped him in shadow as we went, although the passage of the air kept wearing our camouflage away, and I had to concentrate to keep us hidden.

I didn't know where to go or how to get my evidence to the king. The only person I could think of was Sorcha. I wondered if being my escort had resulted in her also being imprisoned. I hadn't spent time looking in the cells during my desperate escape from the dungeon. Although, I'd like to think I'd have noticed her if she were there.

"Mr. Mittens," I gasped as I ran, "We need to find Sorcha. Any ideas?"

I'm a cat making a jail break. That's the extent of my plans, he mumbled.

Fair enough. "Where are the *Baincapall*? You must have seen some on your way in," I insisted.

I did see some heading into the palace, but I don't know where they went.

Nope, that made sense, they must have been called in to guard the king. I had to think. Where would the king be? It was daylight, shouldn't he be holding court in the throne room? My thoughts raced even as my legs faltered. I was worn down and exhausted. I couldn't keep up this pace. "Stop for a minute," I begged my cat.

My shadow magic was thin, so I watched as he looked around and found an alcove. We ducked in, breathing hard, and I renewed the shadow magic hiding us. "I think we're going to have to find the throne room and get the bug to Sorcha. I only hope she's there."

All the guards are searching for you. Do you think that is a good idea? Mr. Mittens's sarcastic voice rang through my head.

"No, but I have to prove our innocence, and to do that, the king has to see the recording on this bug."

Hmpf.

His weight slumped against me, and I staggered as my hand reached out on its own to stroke his silky fur. A different sensation from his Ragdoll floof.

We have to retrace some of our path, pet. I can already hear guards coming this way. Are you sure? He shifted and the weight against my leg went away.

I nodded, then remembered he couldn't see me. Truth was I wasn't sure, but I saw no other way out of the mess if the king didn't get the evidence. "Yes."

Fine. The coast is clear, let's go. His mental voice was resigned.

I slipped out of the alcove and looked both ways; it was clear. We retraced our steps. I knew I was close to him because his fur brushed my hand. I was grateful for the small comfort it brought me. If Mr. Mittens were here, I was safe. He would kill anything that threatened me. I was sure of it. We slunk down the corridor and passed several courtiers, servants, and guards. The guards grew thicker the closer we moved to the throne room.

As we drew nearer, it was clear why we hadn't seen any *Baincapall*; they were all here ready to protect the king from me. Stupid. I wasn't a threat. The room was tightly watched, and no one was moving in or out of it. That was a problem. I searched the centaur-like guards for Sorcha, but I didn't spot her. She must be inside.

We watched for several minutes, and in that time, the doors did not open. All we could do was watch and wait.

It seemed like forever before the door opened, and when it did, it was to disgorge several courtiers. We rushed in before the door shut completely. Mr. Mittens staying close to my side.

There is your Baincapall friend, he announced before we were all the way in, and I scanned for her. His senses were more advanced than mine, and I was grateful for the reassurance she was here. I spotted her, and we made our way carefully through courtiers and servants until we were close enough she could hear me.

The constant hum and drone of voices and people moving about filled my ears, and I hoped it was enough to cover my voice this close to the warrior.

"Sorcha, don't react," I said.

She jumped slightly, but her face stayed neutral, and when I looked around, it appeared that no one noticed. Even being startled, her discipline was topnotch.

"It's Brigid. I'm cloaked. I have evidence that proves my grandfather did not try to kill the king."

Her eyes moved from side to side, trying to gauge whether or not her fellow *Baincapall* noticed the disembodied voice or not.

"What do you have?" she hissed quietly.

"A bug of the event," I answered.

"Hmmm." Her eyes continued to move side to side as she scanned the room. "This is going to be tricky. My captain hates you and will do anything to block this. I don't know how to give this evidence to the king without going through her. How good is it?" she whispered.

"It shows the event and proves that the Phoenix was the one with the knife."

"The king was injured, and the only people that have been to see him are my captain and his personal physician."

I looked over at the dais, I hadn't noticed before because of the crowds, but the throne was empty. My heart sped up further, which I didn't think was possible in the situation. I could feel panic licking the edges of my senses, as my vision narrowed, and my brain began to go haywire.

"It's got to be possible for him to see this, doesn't she want him to be safe? He's keeping the viper and blocking the mongoose."

She looked confused. Right, earth metaphors. "A viper is a venomous, oh never mind."

"I understand. Give me the bug. I'll figure it out."

I bent over to retrieve it from my shoe, when there was a bunch of rustling, and the crowd stirred. A richly dressed servant entered and walked up to the dais. He turned and stood in front of the empty throne. I stood up straight, bug forgotten for a moment.

He cleared his throat and tapped three times on the floor with a staff to get our attention. Once he had it, the background noise died, and Mr. Mittens and I slipped behind Sorcha, since people began to move and readjust to hear the announcement.

"Hear ye, my fine courtiers." He paused for affect, making sure all eyes were on him. "Welcome back to court the Conqueror of Winter, the Subjugator of Summer, the Annihilator of Autumn, and the Vanquisher of Spring." He swept his arms around and finished. "I present to you, the High King of All Faerie!"

I could hear gasps, and the courtiers and servants all started to whisper their gossip and suppositions around the room.

"Sorcha," I whispered. "This is our chance. Do you think you can approach the king?"

She shook her head quickly, the movement slight.

"I can maybe keep my fellow Scáthanna away for a few moments if you can get near him."

I shook, and my knees went weak. Could I do this? Could I approach the king, put the bug on his nose, and get him to watch long enough that I could save my grandfather and myself? Could I do it fast enough that a *Baincapall* Scáthanna wouldn't slip a spear between my ribs?

"Mr. Mittens. Can we do this?"

He pressed against my leg, and I wobbled slightly from the force.

I will help your Baincapall friend to keep the rest at bay. Drop the shadows on my command, he replied simply.

I took a deep breath, and with my hand in his fur, we began to wend our way slowly to the dais.

The king was being escorted in by my rival, Sorcha's boss. There was a group of six other two-legged soldiers with her. They kept the king surrounded and waited until he was seated on his throne. Then the guards backed up to a position behind the throne where his guards usually waited.

We bumped into a few people, but luckily it was crowded enough that they would throw their nasty glances at someone near them and didn't suspect that invisible creatures walked among them.

It seemed like miles to reach the king. Every step felt like it was in deep sand. I panted and sweated through every step. It was a wonder the people in the room couldn't smell me. Luckily, the penchant for heavy robes meant mine wasn't the only sweaty body in the room. My trepidation and doubt grew with every step. If I failed, it could mean death for me, my cat, and my grandfather. Every footfall dragged us closer to that possible end. The room was large, but it wasn't that large, and my concentration was all about winding through the crowd, until suddenly, we were in front of the king. I halted, and Mr. Mittens did as well.

What is your plan, pet? he asked.

I didn't have one beyond "get to the king," and here we were. I thought back to him, *"Umm, go up there, plunk the bug on his nose, and hope for the best."*

That's what I was afraid of. His kitty sigh echoed between my ears. *Follow my lead and drop your shadow concealment when I tell you, come, we are going up to the throne.*

I was partly relieved he would take the lead, and of course, terrified not to be in control of the situation. But I knew this was it. We'd either succeed or die. I took a firm grip of his fur and let him lead me up the dais and into the position he wanted me.

When we were close, he spoke to the king, mind to mind. I assumed he kept his mental voice to a tight band, including only me and the king because no one else reacted to his words.

You have been greatly deceived, sire. I bring you proof of a great wrong and evidence of the true assassin that keeps attempting to end your life.

"How dare you try to tempt your king, show yourself!" the king roared.

That got everyone's attention, and the guards began to move towards us.

Now, Brigid, let the shadows fall.

I said a quick prayer to any god that could hear me and let our concealment fall. We stood before the court—me in my Fae underwear, my prison dishevelment, and stink and Mr. Mittens in all his Splintercat glory. He was poised behind the throne, his massive body between the guards and the king and a paw with knife-like claws near the king's throat. My heart leaped in my chest. This was his plan?

Brigid, his voice was calm and controlled. *Bring the bug.* I leaned down to pluck it from my shoe.

Meanwhile, his mental voice was broadcast to all in the room. *If one person takes a single step towards us, the king will die. If you wait until we are done, we will leave, and the king will be unharmed.*

I took the bug and moved towards the king. "Sire, we wish only to present this evidence. This wondrous device will show you the truth." I placed it on the bridge of his nose, and the inner wings of the beetle opened over his eyes. I knew when the recording began, because his body jerked back in his chair, and then the wonder spread over his face as the moving pictures started.

"This is miraculous," he murmured.

The guard's faces around us were murderous, and I knew that we would be harshly punished or killed on the spot if the king did not react how we wished him to. Poor Mr. Mittens was going to be banished forever from Faerie for his stunt. I guess if things didn't go our way, our best bet was to kill the king and try to flee.

The recording lasted several minutes, and the entire court seemed to hold its breath as the impasse between us and the king's guards continued.

Finally, as I watched the king's face, I saw his realization about the deception. His face flushed, and anger radiated from him. I knew the recording was near its end, and I reached over to pluck the bug from his face. Once I did, its wings closed, and I slipped the thing back into my shoe.

The king was silent. Then his head turned to gaze at Mr. Mittens. "We will have words, cat. Remove your paw from my throat."

Mr. Mittens lowered his claws and shifted back to Ragdoll form. The guards leapt forward, weapons leveled on us.

I closed my eyes and waited to feel a spear thrust between my ribs. When it didn't happen, I opened my eyes.

The king held up a hand to tell them to hold. The breath I'd been holding escaped me, and my knees finally gave way. I sank to the dais. Mr. Mittens joined me, and we sat below the king awaiting his judgment.

He called the Scáthanna leader to him. She was his mistress, and I was sure that was the end of our lives. She bent to his mouth, and he said something we couldn't hear. She jerked up sharply, pointed to a few of her soldiers, and they exited the room.

The king stood and paced back and forth for a moment, probably gathering his wits about him over the surprise we'd gifted him.

"Brigid."

I jumped, surprised he'd used my name, but then again we were engaged. Sort of. Probably not anymore. I didn't know what had happened while I was in the dungeon, but there had to be some sort of announcement.

"What was that wondrous device?"

I stood awkwardly and curtsied, Mr. Mittens small form solid next to me.

"It is a magical device that records what is happening and replays it. What you saw was exactly what happened that day, sire."

His head dipped, and his chin rested on his chest for several moments. I was still shaking and weak from the aftereffects of adrenaline. If Mr. Mittens hadn't been pressed against my leg, I'd probably sink back down to the dais.

It felt like forever, and the king stayed in that position. I could almost feel the wheels turning in his mind as he considered all that had been presented.

Finally, the main doors opened, and the guards came through, dragging the Phoenix in his court splendor, and my grandfather, who was filthy in chains and rags. His body was covered in wounds, and it was clear he'd been tortured. He stumbled and dragged one leg. My heart cried out to see him like this—a proud warrior reduced to a shadow of himself.

Warm tears ran down my cheeks. I wiped them away angrily.

The guards roughly stood both men before the king, who looked up and stared at both of them for a moment. Then he stood.

"Lugh, come forward," he ordered.

The guards dragged him to the dais and dropped him there. The chains jangled, and I could see the wounds they left on his flesh. They had to be iron. Luckily, I could see the fight was still in his eyes, as he lifted himself by sheer willpower and stood, swaying, before the king.

"Sire." A single word, but proof that he was the king's man always.

The king wasted no time. "Describe what happened the day I was stabbed."

My grandfather stared at the king, and his gaze flicked quickly to me and back.

"The Phoenix and I were engaged in conversation with you, sire. While I turned away to look for the noise that had bothered you, the Phoenix stabbed you in such a way that both of our views were blocked, and it appeared as if the knife was wielded by me. It was not true, sire."

The king called the Phoenix forward. "How would you describe the event?" he asked, all formality gone.

The Phoenix bowed elaborately. "The Pendragon speaks true for part of it." He gestured grandly to my grandfather, a smirk on his perfect face. "He was the one that stabbed you and used his movements to make it hard to distinguish between us. You arrested the right Fae." His smug demeanor made me wish *I* had a knife.

The king appeared to consider both men. I felt nervous. Would he accept the evidence we'd given him? Would he continue to harass and imprison my grandfather, or worse? My mouth was dry, but my palms were sweaty. I wiped them down my soiled shift.

The king addressed the court. "Friends and courtiers. It appears we have two conflicting accounts of the violent act upon my body. Which is the truth? You have all seen the wondrous device that the grand-daughter of my Pendragon has placed upon my face, but you did not see what I have seen. The device r-records..." He looked at me when he stumbled over the foreign words.

I nodded in encouragement that he'd used the correct word.

"...Events as they occur. It paints tiny, moving pictures as they happen and lets you view them again. I have watched such a thing of the day when I was violated before you. I know the truth."

For the first time, the Phoenix looked worried. At least the smirk was gone, and a tiny line appeared between his eyes.

My grandfather only stood still and waited.

"Who, you may ask, is a loyal servant, and who is a traitor in our midst?" He looked over both of the men, and a delicious shiver ran through me. Anticipation.

"The Fae lord that stabbed me, I thought of as a true servant of the crown, even a friend, but he was ambitious and wanted my crown for himself." He faced the Phoenix. "I hereby strip you of all of your lands and titles and condemn you to death. Guards." He pointed at the Phoenix, and the guards leapt to grab him. There was a scuffle, and the Phoenix pulled another fearsome looking dagger from his robes. Before they could stop him, he threw it at the king.

The entire court held its breath, the drama unfolding in a way they never thought they'd be allowed to see. The dagger spun through the air like the tight spiral on a football. I had no idea how you threw one to get a motion like that. I assumed they would tumble end over end. Must be a magic that the Phoenix wielded. The king stumbled back but couldn't get out of the way. The dagger flew at his heart, and the king knew it.

My grandfather, wounded, exhausted, and betrayed as he was, exploded into motion. He threw himself in the path of the dagger, and it struck him in the back somewhere by his right shoulder blade. I cried out, and the court let out its collective breath. I raced to my grandfather. The king had fallen back on the dais, and I saw him reaching for his chest where the knife was headed before he realized what had happened.

His personal servants raced over but were beaten back by the guards who quickly surrounded him and protected him with their bodies. The remainder grabbed the ex-Phoenix roughly and dragged him away. He protested loudly, repeating, "I'm the rightful King, kill the traitor!" But no one listened, and finally as the door shut behind him, I heard sobbing and pleading.

I sat by my grandfather and cradled his head in my hands. Mr. Mittens stared at him as though the power of his gaze would heal him. No one was paying attention to us, so I whispered, "Get Dana, please!"

Mr. Mittens blinked; his gaze caught by the sight of my grandfather bleeding on the floor. But then he took one step and disappeared before my eyes. I felt the pulse of power and realized he'd realm walked. I didn't know how that worked, but as long as it did, I was thrilled.

CHAPTER

FOURTEEN

My grandfather and I were ignored as the king was hurried away to safety. From what, when the danger was gone, I didn't know, probably just a part of the court protocol.

It felt like hours but couldn't have been more than minutes before Mr. Mittens reappeared, running with Dana through the doors into the room. I'd been keeping pressure on the wound as best I could with the knife still stuck in his back. The tension in my body eased some at seeing Dana. I didn't trust her fully, but for this I did. I didn't know her agenda, but I was sure she was loyal to my grandfather. Tears started to fall as she rushed to us.

Her face, strange as it was, had a perfect human expression of despair on it. She loved him, I realized. That was the source of her loyalty. She knelt down by me and held her hand over the knife and the wound. She pulled something from a bag slung over her head and shoulder, and with her other hand, removed the knife quickly. My grandfather gasped and bright blood burbled and foamed out of the wound. Blood poured from his mouth and nose. It must have hit his lung.

Dana used the knife to cut his clothes away and pressed whatever she'd taken from her bag to the wound. My grandfather coughed, and more blood sprayed from his mouth. I sobbed silently.

She muttered something and pulled something else from the bag, one of her magical balls. This one was mottled and ugly. She handed it to me.

"Get him to swallow this."

I wasn't able to say anything back, but I turned his head and slid my fingers between his lips, "You have to swallow this, grandfather, to get better." I wasn't sure if he heard me, but his mouth was slack, and I pushed it to the back of his tongue. Nothing happened. "Swallow," I commanded louder and pressed his mouth closed. His eyes flickered open and then closed, but he swallowed. I used the hem of my ruined shift to wipe his mouth and nose clear of blood. He was limp, and there was so much blood. Dana continued to work on the wound, and finally, I saw it start to close.

My grandfather's breathing seemed to ease some, and the blood stopped. I breathed a sigh of relief. Dana sat back on her haunches, and the tension left her shoulders. She also looked relieved. I looked into her face.

"He's going to be fine," she said without my asking.

"Thank you," I said. I didn't care about the debt that would incur. I truly owed her.

She gave me a brief nod. Really, just a short bob of her head.

Now that I wasn't focused on just my grandfather, I realized Mr. Mittens had been by my side the whole time, I reached out a hand and stroked his head. "Thank you, too. He wouldn't have made it without your quick actions." No debt was incurred thanking my non-Fae cat, but I owed him one, too. He leaned against me, and his purr soaked through and eased the rest of the tension.

"Is it safe to take him home?" I asked Dana.

"He should be able to walk in a few minutes, then it would be best if he rested."

"Can he walk all the way to the transporter room?"

"With help, we'll get him there."

"OK."

We waited until he indicated he wanted to try to stand. Just before we attempted to get him into standing position, a group of people came through the doors and hurried towards us. They looked like servants or courtiers. At least they were well dressed and officious looking.

They stopped before us at the bottom of the dais. A pompous looking Fae in rich, voluminous robes addressed us. "I'm here at the king's behest. I'm the king's personal physician and at your service." He looked as though butter wouldn't melt in his mouth, and although he was below us, I had the impression he was looking down his nose at us.

If it hadn't been for Dana, my grandfather would be dead. I wasn't that impressed with the king's physician. He'd taken his sweet time getting here, I was positive, and I had a hard time keeping the disdain from my voice. "You're a little late. We're good. Scurry off to your master."

Mr. Mittens's purr stuttered, and Dana gave a soft gasp. I'd probably pissed off the wrong dude again, but I refused to care. We helped my grandfather to his feet, and between the two of us, supported him so he could stumble to the transporter room. Once we were at the bottom of the dais, the physician's group simply moved out of the way. The court, who had stayed to watch the drama, watched us although no one ran over to help. Even bent over, supporting half of my grandfather's weight, I kept my gaze up, eyes glaring their way. Most averted their eyes from the accusation and disdain in mine. The physician's face was red with fury, but he too shifted out of our way. Mr. Mittens galloped in front of us, transforming from Ragdoll to Splintercat form, and people scurried away faster.

Mr. Mittens used his hard head to shove the doors open, and we followed all the way to the transporter room—people backing away from the fierce cat, us, and the wounded general.

* * *

MY GRANDFATHER HAD BEEN VERY NEAR DEATH, AND EVEN WITH Dana's magical healing ability and medicines, he still needed a few days rest in bed to recover fully. I kept expecting soldiers or *Baincapall* to show up at the gates and haul us all back to prison, but nothing of the sort happened. On the third day, Grandfather was back in his den, although slow and not completely himself. He sat by the fire, fully dressed, and summoned us in.

The three of us entered and sat with him by the fire.

He was silent for several long moments, then he simply said, "Thank you."

Since that was not normal for the Fae and would incur a debt, I accepted his thanks, but rose and threw my arms around his neck. "I couldn't bear to lose you, too," I said simply, and was surprised when his arms wrapped around me as he returned the hug.

After a while, I released him, and he let me go.

"I've had word from the king. He's coming here."

My head swam. What new hell was this? I must have blanched, because my grandfather smiled gently. "Don't worry."

"Don't worry?" I heard Megan repeat. "They've already thrown both of you in prison, and you almost died!" She paced a circle and came back to continue her tirade. "They kept us locked in this castle, and I couldn't..." she looked at me and trailed off. "Do anything." She finished eyes down, shoulders slumped.

Since Megan had covered it all, I huffed out a lame, "Yeah, that."

My grandfather chuckled, obviously not worried. "I believe this will be a pleasant visit. The king is in our debt."

I narrowed my eyes at him, attempting to read his body language. He appeared relaxed. "You're sure?"

He gave me that Fae single bob of the head that was more an acknowledgement than a yes. He looked us over. "You should go dress to welcome the king."

We were dressed in Fae casual—robes made of the iridescent silky material that on earth would be formal, our hair down in the everyday style here.

"I'm done impressing him. I'm not changing."

Megan simply stood next to me, arms crossed. Mr. Mittens stayed splooting in front of the fire, his eyes drifting between the three of us.

"As you desire," Grandfather said, but his eyes narrowed, and he looked uncomfortable.

Too bad. I was done with all the nonsense. If that kept the king from wanting to marry me, or offended him, screw 'im. My hand dropped to my side, and Megan grasped it. I squeezed hers and went to sit down and await whatever new nonsense the king brought with him.

As we waited in silence, servants entered and left, turning the den into a welcoming room with refreshments. Finally, the king was announced, and he and two Scáthanna entered the room, flanking him on both sides—the mistress, I still couldn't remember her title, and Sorcha. I smiled at my friend, and although she fought it, her lips lifted a tiny bit at the corners.

They checked the room and then retreated to the doors to make sure no one could enter without being checked by them. The king was offered a seat facing my grandfather, and the rest of us stood behind my grandfather's chair.

We waited for the king to speak. He took his sweet time, probably hunting for words.

"Lugh, I must apologize for treating you the way I did," the king began.

I almost fell over from shock. This was a lot more straightforward than I thought he would be.

"I've ever been loyal to you, sire," Lugh replied.

The king looked at the fire. He looked for all the world as though he was ashamed—as he should, in my opinion.

"I shouldn't have doubted that. You have proven your loyalty again and again, but I allowed the worm of suspicion to crawl in my ear on the voice of my Phoenix."

There wasn't an answer to that, so we all remained silent.

"I can't make up for what I did to you and your great-granddaughter, but I can offer something as a token of my faith in you." I blinked, and my grandfather folded his hands in his lap, looking down.

"My loyalty isn't something that can be bought. It lies in the faith I have in you as a ruler," my grandfather said.

"This isn't to buy your loyalty, but to show that I know of it, and am grateful for it," the king replied.

There was some political game going on. I didn't get it or want anything to do with it. However, my grandfather seemed to know how to play. So, I continued to watch and didn't interfere or storm out. Megan and Mr. Mittens watched me to see what I would do, and when I didn't react, they relaxed.

"I'm raising you from Pendragon to Phoenix," the king continued.

My grandfather stiffened. "I wish you wouldn't. I'm much better at leading armies than politics."

The king smiled. I thought he'd be angry, but he appeared to expect that response. "I think you've always been good at politics, you are just terrible at kowtowing."

Grandfather laughed. "True."

"This is temporary." The king waved away my grandfather's concerns. "I want you to find your replacement. We both know you are much better at leading my armies and fighting my wars than you are at court. But it's time to scare the rest of the traitors into the light once and for all. Would you do this for me?" he asked.

My grandfather tilted his head and looked at the king. "I will."

"Good, it's settled." He stood and brushed his hands down his thighs as though to wipe away sweat. The king worried, huh?

"Before we partake of those lovely refreshments, there's one more thing." He looked at me. "Brigid."

I jumped.

"Yes, sire." My voice squeaked a little, and I cleared my throat.

"I owe you a boon."

"A boon, sire?" I repeated, confused.

"Ask me for anything within my power, and I will grant it."

I looked at my friends and my grandfather, but their faces gave me nothing. I cleared my throat again, nervously. "There is only one thing I want, sire."

"Ask," he repeated.

"I want to go home to Earth. I'd like to be able to visit my grandfather, and he me without issue." I attempted to read his face and his posture, but it gave me nothing. "There's one more thing. I do not wish to marry you. I have someone back on Earth." I fidgeted, nervous I would offend him. "I don't wish to offend, sire, you seem lovely, but I have a life I want to go back to, and that life isn't here."

The king was quiet, contemplative. "Granted."

I nearly dropped to the floor in relief. "If I may be so bold, sire."

"Yes." This time he frowned. I probably was starting to piss him off.

"The *Baincapall* captain loves you. If you must marry, choose the one that makes you happy."

He sighed, and his eyes flicked to her standing at the door. He inclined his head at me but didn't say anything else. He went to the table, chose some refreshments, and ate. We followed. Not much conversation passed, all of us deep in our own minds, but near the end the mood changed, and soon we were all chatting meaninglessly. Soon enough, the king and his entourage left.

"We can go home!" I said to Megan and Mr. Mittens.

"Finally!" Megan crowed happily, and even Mr. Mittens's face was less grumpy for a while.

My grandfather was happy for us, but he seemed sad. Since I was on a roll, before we left the room and went to our rooms for the night, I left him with this thought.

"Dana is in love with you."

He looked like a man that had been hit upside the head with a two by four.

"What?"

I grinned and followed Megan and Mr. Mittens out and left him to figure it out by himself.

CHAPTER

FIFTEEN

D ana thought she could teach me how to realm walk back home—without stripping my magic away again—quickly. If she wasn't able to, we'd have to wait for my grandfather to take us, and he was tied up with his new court business, without a timeline. Dana couldn't take a passenger, and neither could Mr. Mittens, so it was me or an indefinite waiting period for my grandfather. Now that I knew I could go back and everything here was fixed, I was desperate to do so.

There was one more issue. I needed to know about Sofia. With all the other things going on, like prison, I hadn't been free to investigate her or see if she'd survived after her failed marriage proposal to the king. I'd never visited the spymaster to give my description, since I ended up in the dungeon before I could.

Communication and news sources weren't the same here as on earth. There wasn't a widespread network that didn't involve spies and magic.

I finally went in and gave a detailed description of what she looked like and her capabilities to the spy network. They were already keeping her on their watch list, so my input had been minor to zero on the help scale. After it was done, I did have to fight my desire to check every three minutes, even though that was ridiculous.

Then, because I needed something to do in the meantime, I continued with my magic lessons. I'd been declared "adequate" in water, fire, earth, shadow, and light. I considered Dana's "adequate" to be high praise, considering the source. I felt adept at those magics. She thought I was "fair" at lightning but wasn't willing to practice it now that my grandfather didn't require it for his failed plan that we'd never had a chance to put into action. I didn't blame her. It scared me, too.

I had realm walking to figure out, and I was finally going to learn what aether was and how to use my time magic.

Mind was telepathy, and since I was using that already with the non-speaking creatures in my midst, Dana wasn't motivated to teach me more. Since the other thing it did was give me the ability to exert mind control over others, she wasn't willing to participate as my guinea pig. Because that particular power made me feel icky, I didn't push it. Spirit did have to do with ghosts, but it was a passive power, only giving me the ability to see and hear them, which did not require training.

I was anxious to begin. I wanted to finish and take us all home as soon as possible. Dana gave me one of her patented dark looks when the first thing out of my mouth was, "What is Aether?" That question had been eating at me for a while. I mean, I knew that it was once considered the stuff that made up the heavens, but that meant *nothing* to me in terms of my magic.

She gave me a look that lasted longer than was comfortable before she answered, "Aether is the ability to connect to the spiritual and the power of intuition." That meant nothing to me.

"I don't know what that means," I said, bluntly.

She sighed. Her look was one that showed how hard it was to work with someone as ignorant as me. "Once trained, you should be able to foresee certain happenings."

"Like tell the future?"

She inclined her head. "More or less."

"How much training does it require?" I continued to badger her.

"Much, and you'll need another teacher, it is not a skill of mine."

I shrugged. I didn't want to know the future. I barely had the mental fortitude to deal with the present. "No worries."

She started with the problems of realm walking, namely the one I discovered on my own—stripping my magic away accidentally.

"How do you protect yourself from that?" I asked.

She frowned since I'd interrupted her. "You create a mental shield. It is difficult at first, but it will become automatic the more you practice."

The next issue was not *walking* into a solid structure. I shuddered at that one. When I'd *walked* us that first time, I hadn't known any of this, in fact I hadn't even intended to bring us anywhere else, it was blind luck I hadn't implanted us all in a tree. We'd ended up in a forest after all.

Before she'd let me explore any realm walking, I had to practice a mental shield. It had the added benefit of keeping me safe from others with mind magic. Once I had it down, no one weaker than me would be able to enter my mind, read my thoughts, or control me. She had me visualize a rock wall around my thoughts. I tried, but each time she launched an attack at me, my wall fell. After the fifth attempt, I was growing tired, and she was becoming more irritated.

"Children learn this quicker," she snapped at me.

I didn't know why I wasn't getting it. The concept was easy, I could build the wall in my thoughts, I just couldn't maintain the necessary concentration. The second she sent any level of mental assault, the wall disappeared.

This had to be from my years as Evan's emotional whipping post. I was used to crumbling and giving up just to keep the peace. I had to get over this. I'd gotten over him—I'd stood up to him, left him, divorced him. This should be easy, I'd already conquered it, even though it wasn't a mental attack such as Dana was using. In the past, I'd learned how to bend, not block, Evan's attacks. Maybe that was my issue. I had to let the mental attacks bend around me, rather than blocking them.

I had her try again, and I imagined the attack was one of Evan's verbal assaults about how I looked. "Are you going to lose weight? Why did you do your hair like that? Are you wearing that to the party?" Then, I did my usual thing of letting them wash over me so I could avoid the hurt, the underlying insults, and the pure nastiness he'd thrown in every statement or question.

I could feel Dana's mental assaults bend around me. They didn't bounce off or stop at a wall as she'd described. Instead, they just bent and went on by. After several moments, she stopped and stared at me.

"That should not work," Dana said, a deep frown on her horsey face.

I looked at her. "Why not?"

"That is not how it is done."

"It's how I do it," I countered.

"Hmm. Let's try again."

I could feel her attack increase in intensity, and again, I imagined myself as a stone in the river and the attack the water. I let it warp around me rather than batter me.

"I don't know how that will protect you from depleting your magic when you *walk*," she said. I realized it wasn't a frown, since it was hard to read her non-human face, but confusion.

I wasn't worried. I knew nothing would get through my defense. I'd used this for years, and now that I knew it was a shield, I realized I was well practiced.

"It'll work," I said simply.

"Well, we will know as soon as we practice," she stated haughtily.

"Yeah, I guess so. Are we doing that soon?"

She stared at me, her shark eyes unblinking. "Yes."

A mixture of excitement and terror filled me, and I felt nauseous. "OK."

"What does this, 'OK' mean? You speak it often," she asked.

I thought. I knew what it meant, but I had no idea where it had come from. It was an old expression. "It means that everything is alright. It's good."

"I see."

"So, are we going to go home, to Earth I mean?" My stomach rolled over, and I thought I'd throw up.

"We are not ready for that. I will take you to the place all realm walkers from Faerie go to practice. There won't be a spot to walk into terrain, dangerous animals, creatures, or people. It is as safe a place as we can go."

I was disappointed and a little relieved, but I nodded. I had to learn how to avoid landing myself or my friends in something solid, so that made sense.

"O…um, alright. I'm ready."

She gave me a sidelong glance. It mainly said, "You are an idiot." I knew I wasn't actually ready, I just wanted to try and master this as soon as possible.

"How do I activate the magic and tell it where to go?" I asked.

"You are ready, but you don't know?" she asked sarcastically.

I sighed. "I know I was a bit premature. I'm ready to learn and practice."

"That's better." She handed me one of her magic balls. I didn't know what it was for, so I just stood there, my hand outstretched, the purplish ball lying in my palm.

"This is a precaution. As long as it stays in your hand, if we encounter any issues, it will snap you back to this spot. Among other things."

I stared at it; glad I didn't have to swallow it. It was bigger than the marble sized ones I was familiar with. More of a golf ball, and if I had to swallow it, I was doomed. I'd choke and die for sure.

"Now, I'm going to give you a mental picture, so don't block me. This is the training site."

I was careful to let her in, so I knew where we were going. It felt strange, having someone in my mind, forcing an image there, like cold fingers grabbing my brain. I struggled with not pushing her out. I knew I was successful when the image appeared. It was a grassy field, with what looked like a fence in the distance as well as some low outbuildings. I nodded once I had the image firmly in my mind.

"Before you ask your magic to transport you, don't forget to bring up your shield. I'll follow, so don't try to come back until I am there. Hold that ball tightly."

I clasped my fingers around it until I knew it was secure. I concentrated on my shield and let everything pass by. Once I had that firm, I pictured the place she had shown me, felt the connection to my magic, and stepped forward.

CHAPTER

SIXTEEN

I must have closed my eyes because when I opened them, I was in the grassy field. It was so earth-like, that for a moment, I thought I had traveled to Earth, and joy filled me. Dana arrived a second after, and her nod let me know I'd done well.

Moments later, I knew this was not earth. The air smelled odd. Not bad, just not like home. It wasn't as rich as Faerie either, so I knew we were on a different world. I wanted to jump up and down, but Dana wanted to test my magic to make sure my shield had worked.

She had me call light, and soon a small ball of glittering diamond sat in the palm opposite the one with the purplish ball. I did a little victory dance.

"It worked! I did it!"

"Hmmm." She looked serious, then she smiled a little. "Now, go back. I'll see if you can remember all the steps."

I frowned. A dark shadow fell over me. Since it had been a bright sunny day on whatever world this was, I looked up in curiosity. Something was flying over us. Not a vehicle that I knew of, but something large like Goch. It wasn't a dragon though. I looked at Dana. She glanced up as well, and then lunged at me, and we fell to the ground. The magic ball flew out of my hand.

A blast of wind flung my hair around and tugged at my clothing. "What's going on?" I yelled at Dana over the rush of air.

"It's a hunter," she explained.

I didn't know what that meant to her. I knew what a hunter did, they hunted and killed. So, I caught her meaning and her fear. "I thought you said this planet is safe."

"It is for realm walking. We don't ever stay here, and we rarely run into the natural predators."

"Great, just great. What now?"

"Go back. You do remember how?" she sneered.

I did. But I needed the magic ball to ensure I did it safely. I looked forward for it. The grass kept its secrets. I scrambled forward and skimmed my hands through the base of the grass stalks, searching and feeling for the ball.

"What are you doing?" Dana hissed. "It'll be back soon!"

"I dropped the ball!" I hissed back.

"Incompetent!"

But she scooted forward and started feeling through the grass as well. We both sent furtive glances at the flying thing. It continued to be silhouetted against the bright sky, a dark shadow.

"It's coming!"

I looked up. This time, we were already on the ground, it would get us for sure. I swept my hands through the grass in desperation.

"Got it!" I yelled and thrust my hand into the grass. I yanked up the ball, grass and all.

"Go!" she yelled.

I looked at the skies. I had maybe two seconds before whatever the huge flying creature was swooped down and grabbed me. I took a deep breath, grasped the magic ball harder, gathered my shield, and thought of the room we'd just left. I lurched forward. There was a bright flash, and I opened my eyes. I was back in Dana's training room. I felt a sense of elation until I looked down. I was standing inside her big wooden table where she created her magic balls.

I almost screamed, but instead I froze. Luckily Dana was only a fraction of a second behind me, and she reappeared in the open spot we'd abandoned when we first *walked* out. I was panting with terror, while she smirked at me.

"You are an accomplished realm walker, I see." Her snark was warranted. I had been a little haughty about my skills earlier.

"What do I do?" My voice came out in a squeak.

"Did you drop the ball, again?" she asked.

I would have laughed at the saying if I wasn't sure I was going to die embedded in a table.

I opened my hand. The ball was there in a wad of grass.

"The ball is your protection. You can simply walk out of the table. You aren't injured." She crossed her arms and waited.

I clasped the ball hard and closed my eyes. I took a step forward, two steps. I was holding my breath, afraid to do more than move slowly through the table. I could feel the odd nauseating sensation of having a table slide through my guts and then disappear. I opened my eyes, and looked around, astonished. My hands grasped my abdomen. I was out and unharmed as she'd promised.

I sagged with relief, almost falling to my knees.

"That is why you need to practice with a teacher. You won't always be lucky like you were that first time."

"I didn't mean to, the first time."

"Hmmm, now, make a light ball, let's check your magic."

"Why aren't you coming down off an adrenaline rush like me?" I asked her. Refusing to comply.

"I didn't realm walk into a table."

"I'm talking about the hunter thing. You were just as terrified as I was."

She smirked, and I wanted to rip her horsey face off.

Realization hit me like a Mack truck. "That was fake!" I yelled at her.

She guffawed, sounding for all the world like a braying donkey.

"Why?" The anger vanished and I felt hurt. Betrayed. I must like and trust Dana more than I knew, or I wouldn't feel this way.

She shrugged—nonplussed about my reaction. "It is a training exercise. If you pass it, you can face anything on a realm walk."

"Did I pass?" I asked hopefully, trying to push the hurt away.

Her deadpan stare answered me. Right. I walked back into a table. I nodded at her and prepared to do it again.

We went back and forth to the training area several times—scary flying hunter, no longer needed—until Dana felt I wouldn't make any more mistakes on that run, anyway. She dismissed me.

Poor Megan and Mr. Mittens. I was sure they thought we'd return home immediately but knowing we were so close, yet so far away, had to be equally disappointing for them, even more so, since they needed me to go home—Megan because I had to take her, and Mr. Mittens since there was no point in him going home without me.

So, when I returned from lessons, I made it a point to gather us together and spend time planning what we would do when we returned. We thought of different scenarios, and what we'd do for each. But without knowing what was happening back home, they were all nothing but supposition. Still, it was something to do.

At the end of the week, my grandfather's spymaster brought news. Megan, Mr. Mittens, and I gathered in his office to hear what he'd learned recently about Sofia. The spymaster, whose name was Elegurd, was a strange little Fae. He was grizzled and stooped. His face looked like a dried apple, and he was barely as tall as my navel.

I didn't ask because I wasn't sure if it was rude, but he had to be a gnome or a dwarf or something. He didn't seem infirm, so he had to be just an example of his kind, whatever that was. The room was large and sort of stuffy. It was overly warm and crowded with furniture, books, and papers. I looked for somewhere to sit, but I was afraid to move anything off the chairs. He sat behind a desk that dwarfed him and was even large for us, but it needed to be because it was covered with different magical paraphernalia that I couldn't identify.

We stood impatiently, shifting from foot to foot, looking around, and waiting for him to talk. It took a while for him to look up, as he was intent on something that looked like a crystal ball. He wore coke-bottle glasses, and when he finally looked up at us, his eyes looked as large as an owl's. He blinked at us a couple of times, then laughed and took off the glasses.

"Sorry, I didn't see you there."

I couldn't imagine how he didn't see us, but maybe the glasses were just for looking into crystal balls.

"The human that you are looking for has been located. She is hiding in the court of an ousted Summer Lord. This is very bad. Very bad indeed."

He must be talking about the Swamp Lord. We sort of already knew that, I thought.

Megan and I looked at each other, confused. "Why is that bad?" Megan asked.

"Oh, they are plotting, plotting!" he continued, the repetition seemed to be how he spoke.

"If the Summer Lord has been ousted, what kind of trouble can they get into?" I asked, and Megan nodded.

"He has been looking for magical support to rise against the King! Against the King!"

This must have started after their bid to marry Sofia to the king. Idiots. His repetition was growing annoying, but this was the best info we'd had so far. Proof she was deeply involved with the swamp thing as Megan liked to call him. How had she stumbled on the one person that would put up with her nonsense, even desire it? This was terrible luck.

"Are they close to doing that?" Megan asked as I thought.

"They have an army, an army!"

Shit. Would she bring that army to earth or against the king? It seemed foolish to bring an army against the king. Was she that nuts? Did her ambition have no limits?

"I must inform my lord immediately, immediately!" The little man said and scurried away.

We watched him leave.

"I've got to go to Dana, we have to go home now. If that army is headed to Earth, we won't be able to stand against them. If they are going against the king here, there isn't anything we can do to help. I need to warn everyone."

Megan looked at me, defeat showing in her eyes. "Yeah, we do. If she is bringing an army against us, we're screwed."

I felt the same, but all I could do was try to fight. "I've got to try."

Regardless of what she did here, I knew she'd bring someone back to try and defeat us. Even one trained Fae warrior, or magic user was enough to defeat us. It was demoralizing and defeating, but I had to try. I left Megan to go back to her chambers alone and headed to Dana's lab.

"Dana, we have to go back, now," I said as I opened the door. She and my grandfather turned to face me. I didn't know he was there. They both had serious looks on their faces. I guess the spymaster, for all he looked old and infirm, had imparted the bad news.

My grandfather nodded and stood up. He straightened his clothing, gave Dana a stiff courtly bow, and left the room. I'm sure he had plenty to do as the king's Commander.

"I'm going to have to use my meager skills to take us home. Do you think I can do it?"

She looked me up and down, her usual grim expression on her alien face. "Yes, but we still haven't used the element of time."

"Time? Why is that important?" I was really confused.

"Time doesn't flow the same between here and your realm. It can be a very short time, or several years could have passed."

"Years?" I gulped and sank to the floor in defeat.

"Get up, you fool. You have time magic, you can return to any time you wish."

I looked up at her. "Really?"

She just gave a disgusted horsey snort.

"How do I use it? The time magic?"

"You have to be able to clearly recall the time you want."

"So, if I can picture where I was when I brought us here, I can return us to the same moment?"

"More or less."

I should have been worried about that statement, but all I could think of was being there in time to help Gabe and defeat the witches for good. We'd had them on the run, then bam! I'd flashed us to Faerie and this mess. At least we'd fixed the disaster here in Faerie before we left.

"How much practice do you think I need to be able to do it?" I asked.

"How would I know until we try?"

Fair enough. She had me take her to the training realm. Then I pictured a day I remembered clearly in the past and took us back to my grandfather's castle at that instant.

I did what she said and pictured the first time we'd used the transporter room. I could see it clearly, exiting after my grandfather had picked us up that first day from the throne room. We'd been dirty, ragged, tired, and bloody in patches. It was my grandfather with his weapon and armor, Megan, Mr. Mittens in his Ragdoll form, and me.

I pictured it clearly, all of us stumbling out of the room, and I stepped forward, flash.

We appeared in the hallway in time to observe us step from the transporter. Grandfather saw us and frowned, but Dana shook her head and gestured for him to be silent. She ushered me back out of sight, but our earlier selves were too tired to look around and were dragged out of the room and into the hall.

Dana had me return us to the practice realm.

Once we were there, she said, "We are in the same time as your past self. You'll need to picture the time we left to return us."

I looked at her. I couldn't remember specifics because I hadn't been paying attention. "Umm, do I picture ourselves in the room?" I asked.

"Did you see us pop in as we were leaving?" she asked sarcastically.

"No."

"Then don't use us as a reference."

"What if I get a detail wrong?"

"Then we won't end up in the right time, will we?"

I let out a frustrated breath. Dana was a good teacher, but you couldn't expect a lot of praise or "atta boys" from her.

I took a deep breath, let it out to center myself, and hoped my visualization was correct. I took a step. Flash.

We were in the lab. There were subtle differences to what I'd pictured. I'd been wrong.

"This is not the correct time," Dana announced, just as I realized it as well.

Just then, the door opened, and Dana walked through. The two Danas stared at each other. Then the new Dana looked at me and addressed herself.

"You are in the wrong time."

The old Dana gave a curt nod and grabbed my arm. She had me open my mind to her for the correct image. Then we walked one step, and we were briefly in the practice field. And then another step and we were back in the lab, but I knew that now, we were in the right time. I breathed a sigh of relief. I think part of me wondered how I'd make it back to the correct Mr. Mittens and Megan.

"Did you learn the importance of making a mental picture?" she asked.

I nodded. Dana's lab was easy to overlook. It wasn't my space, it was often cluttered with various equipment and items, and without studying it and fixing it in my mind, I'd never get back here at a specific time. I'd do better the next time we practiced.

"Do not practice without me or Xrsrphn with you. You could be lost in time, and we'd never know where or when to find you."

That sent a chill down my spine. If I realm walked, I had to be sure. It would also be a good idea to take a seasoned companion. The idea of doing this on my own was terrifying.

I stuttered out an "OK" and fled the room. Dana was going to meet with my grandfather to help him plan for the coming war or offensive thing.

Mr. Mittens must have picked up on my disquiet because he met me a few steps outside of the lab.

"I blew it," I said to him.

He brushed up against my legs, and I bent to pet him.

What is the matter? he asked.

"I'm practicing my realm walking, but knowing where I am in time is another matter. I don't know if I'm going to be able to get us back in time to save Gabe and stop Sofia."

He purred. *I will help you.*

"Do your people use time when you realm walk as well?"

It is common.

He hadn't really answered the question, which could mean that *he* couldn't. However, he seemed so sure, and I trusted he'd keep me safe.

I brushed my hand down his fur and up his tail before I followed him back to my room.

We will go back soon, he added.

I was losing hope, but it was time to go back, passed time, so I just nodded and smiled down at him.

CHAPTER

SEVENTEEN

I had one more lesson with Dana. One more before I took us all back. She was about to be too busy to deal with me, so I had to be ready to be on my own. She took me to the past on the practice world again and wanted me to return us to the right time in her lab. I knew it was coming, so I scanned the room to memorize specifics. The other part was to know how to avoid obstacles.

So far, I'd used her safety ball, but I wouldn't have that when I returned the three of us to earth. Dana wasn't going to give it to me, it stayed with the training facilities, and she didn't have one for each of us.

I was sure Mr. Mittens would be fine, but I was terrified of hurting my best friend. Unfortunately, the only way to avoid obstacles was a knowledge of your landing zone. There was also a split second—the moment before you stepped from one place to another—where an adept realm walker could sense anything near them and adjust their trajectory. My grandfather had taken that skill to another level and had used a concussive blast the first time I'd called him. I realized that was a safety response to the fact he didn't know who had summoned him. It could also be used to clear the area to avoid embedding yourself into a solid unforgiving surface. Its use was limited though. If it was some-thing dense or heavy, the blast wouldn't move it out of the way.

Plus, I didn't know how to make a concussive blast. I didn't even know what piece of my elemental magic could do it. With my luck it was air, which was still lost.

Since I wasn't an adept realm walker, I had to be precise, choose an empty space like the parking area behind my house or the space around the altar. I did remember the night I'd *walked* us here. In fact, I couldn't get it out of my mind. I was pretty sure I could take us back close to when we'd left. I wasn't supremely confident, but that was more nervousness and anxiety than anything.

I held the purplish colored ball in my hand, set my shield, and pictured the lab the moment we left. Dana kept her cold eyes on me, narrowed, judging. The butterflies of anticipation built in my stomach, and with her hand on my shoulder, I took a step. Flash.

I must have had my eyes closed, because I opened them in the lab. It looked like what I'd pictured, and it felt right. I looked at Dana for confirmation. She gave a terse nod. I almost did a little dance but held it back in front of Dana. She'd definitely judge me. In my head, I did a fist pump. Yay, I was a verified realm walker. It terrified me, but for the first time, I was confident I'd get us home.

Now, if I could find out what Sofia's plans were, we'd be ahead of the game for once. It would be nice to finally be prepared, be a step ahead.

I might have skipped back to Megan and Mr. Mittens.

They looked at me expectantly as I bopped into Megan's room where they waited.

"Why are you so happy?" Megan asked. She was sitting in the one comfortable chair in the room, Mr. Mittens was sprawled on her bed. But his ears perked up when I walked in.

I couldn't keep the grin off my face. "I did it!"

They both gave me bored looks.

"Did what?" Megan yawned.

"I realm walked."

"Haven't you been doing that for days?" she said.

"Yeah, but this time, I did it through time. I can return us to the moment we left." This time I did a little dance and a fist pump.

Megan jumped out of the chair and did her own little dance. "Yes!"

Mr. Mittens stretched and jumped down. *When do you wish to leave?*

I looked at Megan. "What do you think? Tomorrow?"

She gave another twirl and a few more dance moves. "Yes! This vacation blows. I give Faerie two stars."

"It hasn't gone down from the last time?" I laughed.

She shrugged.

"Well, for me, the food brought it up, lodgings weren't bad, but everything trying to kill you? Half a star. Too bad. I don't think they're too worried about their Yelp scores," I said.

"They should be. My review will be *scathing*." Megan emphasized that with a sweeping hand gesture.

I laughed. "I'm sure they will be devastated and will change their entire society."

"And that's the power I wield in these." She spread her fingers and waved them in classic jazz fingers. She danced a minute more, then went to the wardrobe and threw it open. "I'm taking a couple of these home as well. I've never had anything so soft and silky."

"Well, get a different color from me, I'm taking the blue."

"Fine. Whatevs."

We laughed some more and flopped on her bed like teenagers at a sleepover. "I know I said I loved the food, but the thing I'm looking forward to most is an old-fashioned, greasy, cheesy pizza covered in all the meats," she said.

I looked over at her. "That sounds divine."

"Then, I want to take a shower. Not a bath, a long, hot shower with all the good smelly stuff. Then I want to go to the movies."

"No more magical bug vision?"

"Hell, no!"

I laughed at her. "Me either, I loved spending time with my grandfather, but I don't ever want to come back here. No matter how much magic there is, or how good the air makes me feel."

She held out her fist for me to bump. "Sista."

We laid on the bed for several minutes more until I started to drift off. I shook it off and gave Megan a nudge. "Let's go down and eat with my grandfather and say our goodbyes." We both struggled up. Mr. Mittens was already waiting, his kitty stomach ready.

We were almost to the door when the servant brought the summons to dinner. "Perfect timing," I mumbled.

"Let's hope your timing is this good tomorrow," Megan added.

I nodded and even Mr. Mittens gave a soft, *Hmph,* in agreement.

* * *

BEFORE WE LEFT, WE HAD TO CHECK ON SOFIA. ELEGURD THE spymaster was back at his desk, his glasses on and a crystal ball in front of him.

"Yes, yes I have news, news," he said after I asked about Sofia. Megan looked at me, having noticed the repetitions seemed worse today.

"What the hell?" she mouthed to me.

I shrugged. I didn't know.

We waited for him to remove his glasses and focus on us.

"The witch is planning to bring the army against the king in support of her Summer Lord. This is disturbing, very disturbing."

"Have you found out if she has plans to return to Earth?" I asked.

His focus seemed to be all over the place, which to be honest, seemed to be the opposite of what you wanted in a spymaster, but he probably had other skills that I didn't know about.

"Yes, yes." He nodded fiercely and searched his desk. He found something and pulled it out. He read it over and handed it to me. "This, this is what you need to know!"

I thanked him, and having been clearly dismissed, the three of us left to gather in my room.

Once the door shut behind us, Megan said, "Well, don't keep us waiting, what does it say?"

I looked at the paper. It was covered with pictures, and tiny words were randomly placed over the page, but as I stared at it, everything seemed to slip into a pattern. I realized it was spelled. If I hadn't been who I was, the page would have continued to look like someone had doodled all over their notes. Finally, it settled, and I could see the content clearly.

"Look at this," I said to Megan, who leaned over to see what I was indicating.

"What is it?" she asked.

"You don't see the diagram?"

She shook her head. "It looks like some middle school kid's notes."

I chuckled. "This is so cool. Only I can see the correct information. This rocks."

"So, what does it say about Sofia?" She redirected me.

"Yeah, sorry. Umm, according to the diagram, she is two villages over from the High King's palace." I squinted at some tiny script. "She is still with the same Summer Lord whose unfortunate title is 'The Lord of Swamps.'"

"I'm sure he's a pleasant sort," she remarked with a half-smile.

I moved my finger along to some more interesting information. "Here, Sofia is mentioned. Apparently, she has her magic back, and being in Faerie, she's apparently super charged. Joy."

"Just what we need." Megan sighed.

"We could bail, our fight is back home," I added.

"Yeah, but she's our problem. We can't leave that for your grandfather." Megan was being the voice of reason. I was still hoping someone here would kill Sofia. She'd involved herself in local politics after all.

The wind was seriously going out of my sails with this one. "Yeah." I sighed. "She's Earth's problem and our problem. The Fae can deal with the swamp lord. We have to take her back with us, or she'll end up in charge and ruin any future dealings with Faerie. Damn. At least on Earth, she only has one piece of Fae magic, here she's drowning in it."

"Are you suggesting what I think you're suggesting?" Megan asked.

"Do you disagree?"

"No, but I was hoping something would eat her."

I was not. If anything is going to eat her, it will be me, Mr. Mittens weighed in.

Right. He'd promised. She'd probably give him heartburn, though.

"She's yours, Mr. Mittens," I reassured him.

"OK. We go home, make our plans, come back at this moment, and take her back to Earth. Then, it's up to Mr. Mittens." I grinned down at him.

As you wish, pet.

CHAPTER
EIGHTEEN

We *walked* back to earth just in time to see ourselves
disappear from the clearing in the left-over flash. It was
still the night we'd battled the witches. We hadn't seen
ourselves arriving at the time, being too involved in the fight. I
wanted to cheer and give a little fist bump to Megan upon our safe
arrival, but we were still in the middle of a witch war. Sofia was gone,
having just been whisked to Faerie with us. Thinking about the time
differences made my head hurt, so instead, I rushed back to the altar to
check on Gabe.

The werewolves, Goch, and Brightfeather had routed the witches
during my magic battle with Sofia, and several witches lay dead in the
clearing. We could see the mounds of black clad bodies in the light of
the bonfire and the moon. The Whelans were gathered around the few
that were left standing, but the witches looked completely defeated.
The giant wolves had them cowering near the altar. The wolves looked
at us strangely, since Megan and I wore Faerie robes rather than the
jeans, t-shirts, and jackets we'd been in moments ago.

Gabe was still lying on the ground where he'd been dumped for
what seemed like forever ago. I rushed over to him. He was still unconscious but breathing. Megan helped me pull him up and prop him

against the altar. He stirred. I hoped that was a good sign he'd wake up soon.

A wolf peeled off from the group and shifted, pulling a black robe from a dead witch and wrapping it around him.

"What is going on?" Luke asked, staring at us or Megan, anyway.

She skipped over and threw her arms around his neck. He hugged her back with one arm, the other occupied holding on to the robe.

"We've been in Faerie!" she announced with a little flourish of her arms.

Luke choked and covered it with a cough. "What?"

"Faerie, you know." She put her fingers next to her head to pantomime pointed ears.

It looked more like devil horns, but I wasn't going to ruin her fun.

"You were just here a few seconds ago," Luke said, in an attempt to understand.

"Yeah, but we were in Faerie for months, luckily Brigid figured out her magic, and poofed us back here at the same time we left!"

He blinked a couple of times, the wheels in his head catching up with her announcements. "OK. That explains the clothes."

Megan looked down at herself. "Yes! You have to lurve this fabric, here, feel." She twisted and jutted out a hip for Luke to pet her.

He smiled and swept a hand slowly from her shoulder, down her side to her waist, and over her backside. She waggled her eyebrows at him. He pulled her in and kissed her.

I waited a moment or two. When the other wolves began rolling their eyes, I cleared my throat. "Um, hate to interrupt, but we have witches."

Luke and Megan pulled apart reluctantly. He mumbled, "Witches." Then his eyes sharpened. "Witches, where's Sofia? You two and the cat ran after her."

"Yup," Megan said. "Plot twist. She's in Faerie."

The tension in Luke's shoulders relaxed, and they dropped an inch.

I hated to ruin Megan's fun, but I had to. "Let's take this group to the house, we have to talk." I cast a light ball and raised it up to illuminate our trek back.

There were only five witches that remained alive or were caught before they'd fled. Luke and Noah, who were both on two legs and now clad in witch robes, picked Gabe up under the armpits, slung his arms around their necks, and began the long walk back. The remaining Whelans in wolf form nipped at the heels of the captured witches until they started to move. After greeting us, Goch and Brightfeather flew back to the house to meet our captives, Megan and I trailing behind. Mr. Mittens brought up the rear to watch for any of the escaped witches who might try to take advantage of the situation. We were a motley crew.

We broke through the woods, finally. The little Fae slippers Megan and I wore were barely better than being barefoot, and we stumbled and complained the whole way back. My house never looked so good. I wanted to run up and give it a hug, but I held myself back. I'd look like an idiot if I did that. Mr. Mittens did run ahead and jump up on the railing of the back porch. He loved to sit there; it gave him a vantage point.

Since everyone was faster than us, the witches were in a group in the yard, Goch and Brightfeather keeping their eyes on them. I lifted my light ball into the air until it lit up the back area like a streetlight. The Whelans had shifted back and dressed. Luke and Noah had deposited Gabe in the house on his bed upstairs to recover from the spell and had dressed in their regular clothes as well. I considered going in and putting on jeans and a sweater. But there wasn't any point in any more delay.

I had to decide what to do with the witches, so I had Mr. Mittens, Megan, and the Whelans gather in the kitchen to decide what to do with the ones that were left.

"Kill them," Noah said, coldly. The Whelans were still rightly upset about their father's death.

Mr. Mittens's vote was the same, not that I expected anything different from him. He had a strict "kill first, ask questions later" belief system.

"We should find out all they know before we do anything," Megan added.

Everyone agreed that was a definite point.

"I just want to bring up this point and discuss the pros and cons, so don't get upset." I took a deep breath. "What would happen if we just let them go?"

I expected some arguing from the wolves, but they took a moment to consider before they answered.

"Cons," Noah started. "They gather up their evil buddies and come back, or they involve other supernatural races and start a war against us."

"Pros," Madison added, "They all move out of town and no more witches will bother us."

"Not likely," Noah snorted.

"Look, they are beaten, if we kill them at this point, then we are the murderers. I say let them go. We can make them swear an oath or something," Izzy said.

"Will they keep it if we do?" Megan asked, hopefully.

"If it's on their magic, they won't have a choice," Izzy added.

"That's a thing?" I asked because if it was, that was the best solution in my book.

Izzy shrugged. "I've heard about it. Anyone else know for sure?" She looked around at her family.

Anna, who had remained quiet, finally chimed in. "Yes, and that is the best solution."

Noah started to protest, but a flash of her green eyes shut him up. He might be the new alpha, but his mama was still in charge of the family.

"Agreed?" she asked.

The vote wasn't unanimous, Mr. Mittens still thought we should kill them all.

We walked out and faced the witches who were sobbing and clinging to each other. It could have been the dragon looming over them, but they didn't know he was a sweet kid at heart.

I can eat them, Lady Brigid. I'd be happy to! Goch said, and I knew that everyone heard when the witches reacted by cowering further.

"Thanks, Goch, we decided to let them go."

He looked dejected at that, and I felt bad. "You did such a great job, you are welcome to eat any witches we left behind in the clearing."

He brightened. *Thank you so much!* he said and launched himself in the air, his wing beats blasting us and sending dust and leaves swirling around. At least I wouldn't have to sink those bodies into the ground. Plus, it added a layer of intimidation for the living ones.

I stood before the five witches. "We've come to an understanding." I looked at my companions and they all nodded. "We will release you to your lives if you are willing to take a magical oath."

A few witches stood a little taller, hope shining on their faces. A brave woman stepped forward. "What oath?"

"It's a simple thing. You swear on your magic to never come against us again in any way."

The speaker frowned, but she turned to the others, and they spoke quietly to each other. I guess she had made herself the speaker because she turned back. "If we don't?"

Death, Mr. Mittens answered for me, morphing into his Splintercat form before them and snarling.

They cringed back, but the spokeswitch just closed her eyes briefly, tension in her form.

I nodded. I didn't need to say anything more.

"We accept. Under one condition."

I looked at my companions and mouthed, "condition?" I turned back to the witches. "What is it?"

They looked at each other. "You protect us from Sofia. She will kill us if we don't obey her."

That seemed fair, and I didn't doubt for a minute that once she learned of their perceived betrayal, she would kill them.

"Agreed. We have plans for her, anyway."

She's mine, my cat broadcast, with an image of him leaping on her and crushing her to the ground.

The witches each took the oath, and we allowed them to leave. They wandered back in the direction of the altar. I wanted to remind them there was a dragon feasting back there, but I let it go. They'd figure it out.

I thanked Brightfeather, and she flew off. That left the wolves, me, Megan, and Mr. Mittens. We gathered in my kitchen to hear about our adventures on another world and my plans to defeat Sofia.

CHAPTER
NINETEEN

After everyone left, and Megan was taking her "glorious" hot shower, I went up to Gabe's room to check on him. He was still asleep. But when I shook him, he stirred, and his eyes opened briefly. It seemed that whatever spell had been laid on him was wearing off. I figured I'd give him another hour before I really got worried and attempted to remove the spell. I didn't know if the spell I had used on him before would work for this, but I'd try if he hadn't awakened by then.

Megan was in the kitchen dressed in flannel PJ bottoms and a soft cotton top. She had her phone and was scrolling through it.

"I'm ordering pizza. What do you want?" she said.

"The usual, but get double, Gabe will be starving when he wakes up, I'm sure."

"Got it." She called the number and placed the order for delivery.

"Thanks, I'm gonna take a shower."

I went into my marvelous bathroom, took a shower of my own, and changed into my own clothes. No matter how lovely the fabrics we'd worn in Faerie were, they just couldn't beat my broken-in jeans and long-sleeved t-shirt for comfort.

After, I wandered back to the kitchen, filled a glass of water, and drank it down. For whatever reason, realm walking was thirsty work. "I'm gonna go check on Gabe," I said to Megan.

She waved me away, still scrolling through her phone.

"I thought you'd be hanging out with Luke?" I said as I passed her.

"I told him tomorrow, I'm tired, and so was he." I bet she was. I was exhausted with the feeling of *extra* jet lag. The last time I'd realm walked extra people with me, I'd been too exhausted from the marching to notice the extra fatigue. Since I'd already been tired from practicing almost non-stop with Dana, dragging a non-magical person with me was even more fatiguing.

I dragged myself up the stairs to the second floor, anxiety increasing with every step. I knocked on Gabe's door softly, but he didn't respond. My heart fell. I was so sure he'd be awake by now. I opened the door and walked in. He wasn't on the bed, but the shower was running. I smiled.

I debated waiting, but I wanted him to know I was here, so I knocked on the partially closed bathroom door.

"Gabe?"

"I'll be out in a second," he answered.

"OK, I'll wait by the bed." I walked over and sat on his bed.

Soon enough, I heard the water shut off and the sound of the glass door opening and shutting. A minute later, he came out, damp hair tousled, a towel wrapped around his hips. My mouth fell open. He was beautiful. All firm flesh and defined muscles. Did he work out? Or was this just the way he was made?

He chuckled, a deep rumbling sound that I felt in my bones.

I closed my mouth. "Are you feeling alright?" I asked, my voice squeaky. I cleared my throat and tried to get a hold of myself.

"Yes, why?" he asked. Was it possible he was unaware of Sofia's latest ploy? Surely, he remembered being kidnapped at the clinic. I did, and it had been months for me.

"Because you were kidnapped and held captive by the witch bitch Sofia," I stated.

He frowned. "That really happened? It seems like a bad dream. How long ago?"

I had to think back. How long had she had him after she'd captured him at the clinic?

"Just the day, I think?"

He looked confused.

"Sorry, I forgot you were asleep when we told the others about our little adventure. We've been in Faerie for almost two months. I realm walked us back to the moment when I accidentally realm walked."

"Us?" he asked confused.

"Oh, yeah, umm, me, Megan, Mr. Mittens, and Sofia…" I trailed off.

He sat on the bed and pulled me into a hug. His shower hot skin blazed against me. I laid my head on his chest and smelled the scent of his soap and beneath it, him.

"That's wild. You'll have to fill me in on what happened there. What was it like?"

"Um, mostly terrifying." My hand was unconsciously exploring the firm muscles of his back. And my mind was not on the conversation. His voice grew huskier.

"I'm sorry, Bridge."

I kissed his neck and mumbled into his skin, "It's OK."

He groaned and reached down to tilt my head up to meet his lips.

I buried my hands in his hair and kissed him back. He tasted like toothpaste. I smiled against his lips, before I was sucked back under by the heat of his kiss, the warmth of his tongue, and the hardness of his body. He eased me down on the bed, and I pulled him to me, my heart beating hard and fast. His weight pressed me into the mattress, and I moaned into his mouth.

Before things went too far, the doorbell rang. I almost ignored it, since Megan was downstairs, but it was probably the pizza, and she'd just come up here looking for us. I kissed him one last time.

"We gotta go. That's the pizza," I said with a smile.

His eyes were dark and half lidded. He rolled off me onto his back, his towel barely covering him. "I'm gonna need a minute," he said. "I'll see you down there."

I grinned. Looking at his towel, I could see he would need a minute. "OK, see you in a minute. I leaned down and kissed him again.

"Stop doing that, or I'll be up here a lot longer," he remarked.

I dragged myself away and shut his door behind me.

I smiled all the way down the stairs. I'd missed him so much. And he was here, he remembered me, and he wanted me as much as I wanted him. Life, for the moment, was good.

When I entered the kitchen, Megan took one look at me, and said, "Spill. You couldn't have gotten too far in the few minutes you've been up there, but that is a serious loved up look."

I nodded. "We just kissed, but *what* a kiss." I sighed. "Now, he's getting dressed, so quit with the questions. I'll get the plates."

She laughed. "He's getting dressed? What did you do to him in…" She looked at her wrist like she wore a watch. "Three point five minutes?"

I scoffed. "He was just getting out of the shower. Stop."

"So, he was nakey?" She waggled her eyebrows.

I rolled my eyes. "There might have been a towel."

"Did it stay on?"

"Unfortunately."

She giggled, and then we had to shut up, because we could hear him coming down the stairs.

I set the table, and Megan tossed the salad she'd started and placed the bowl on the table.

When Gabe entered the kitchen, we were the picture of non-gossipy domesticity.

We started to eat. Megan was in her element, dipping her pizza in ranch dressing and declaring it better than Faerie food, when Mr. Mittens walked into the kitchen. At first, I assumed he was just ready for his supper, but I turned to look at him, and I saw fear in his eyes.

I jumped up, rocking the chair back slightly. "What's wrong?"

She's here.

My stomach fell. My face flushed with heat. I didn't need to ask, but I did. "Who is here?"

Sofia. She's brought an army.

Shit.

Megan and Gabe leapt up. Megan grabbed her phone, and so did Gabe, they were calling the werewolves. I put out a mental call to Goch and Brightfeather.

Even with our few allies, how could we stand against an army?

"What do we do?" I asked, but it was mainly to myself. My mind raced. What options did we have?

We are already fighting, Goch's mental voice was faint, and I was worried about my two charges, creatures who came to *me* for safety. If Sofia brought an army, that meant she had more than one magic user with her. How could she transport more than a few people at a time from Faerie? How had she known when and where to bring them? This couldn't be!

My mind flicked to a conversation about the transporter rooms. You only needed a clear picture to any place to use them. I was sure Sofia's memory of my clearing and the altar was as clear in her mind as it was in mine. My fists clenched.

"How many?" I asked my cat.

They were still arriving when I walked here, he said. *Dozens?*

Dozens. That meant they weren't quite ready, more were probably still arriving. I had time. Time. I had time magic! I could do something. I hoped I could beat her.

"I have an idea. Please trust me. Stay away from her, stay safe. I'll be right back."

I took a step, and there was a bright flash.

CHAPTER

TWENTY

I stepped into my grandfather's study. He looked up at me in surprise.

"Didn't you just leave?" he asked.

My Earth clothes were a big hint that I had indeed.

"Yes. I need your help," I said.

He must have heard the desperation because his eyes sharpened, and he became more alert. "What's the matter?"

"Sofia, my witch nemesis…" I took a deep breath and tried to slow my heart rate. I was sweating and breathing like I'd run a race. "She's brought an army from Faerie to my house. I need help, there are so few of us, and I'm the only magic user. She faked us out, Grandfather. She decided to hit us first, not the king. Can you help me?"

He stood. "Yes, I owe you a favor, if this is how you wish it repaid, I'm honored."

I'd forgotten about the thanks I'd given him. I felt a tug in my chest, demanding a response. "Yes, this will follow your obligation."

There was a snap, and a wave of rightness zinged through me.

Grandfather gave me a Fae nod, "How many did she have with her?"

"Mr. Mittens said dozens."

"I believe we can borrow some of the king's Scáthanna. He owes us. But the only magic users will be you, myself, and Dana."

"I don't know how many magic users she has with her, but that'll have to do."

He tilted his head and folded his arms over his massive chest. "It might only be herself, the swamp lord and one other from what my spymaster has been telling me."

I nodded. This could work. The panic was starting to die down. The pizza I'd eaten had decided maybe it would stay in my stomach.

"Do you have thirteen elements, too, Grandfather?" I asked him. I hadn't dared before.

He looked at me strangely. "Yes, how else do you think it came to you?" he asked, simply.

"OK." I took another deep breath. "What about Dana?" I remembered the court gossip, and how the king only had seven. Could Dana have more? Was she also his equal? Had my grandfather been keeping more than one secret from the king?

He smiled. "Don't worry about Dana. She's got a few tricks up her sleeves."

Right, not his secret to share. I wondered if being half-Kelpie gave her gifts the rest of the Fae didn't have. I'd have to watch her in the fight if I could.

He closed his eyes, and I realized he was sending out telepathic messages. That was handy. Maybe someday, I'd be a strong enough telepath I could do that. I could usually contact people on my land, but I hadn't tried anyone off my land. I guess my magic was strongest there and here.

"Grandfather, I've got to go back, can I give you the mental picture you need to arrive at the right place and time?"

He gave me the Fae head bob, and I reconstructed the exact place and time in my mind and pushed it to him.

"She's gonna arrive about an hour from the time I just gave you. It should give you a little time to prepare an ambush. Just remember, wait until the griffin and the dragon have engaged, otherwise we'll screw up the timeline I'm building. OK?"

"Yes, child. I've been in a few battles and realm walked a couple of times in my day."

I laughed nervously. "Yeah. I'm counting on that. Hope your swamp lord is an idiot."

"Appears to be. He's picked a fight with the wrong Fae family, hasn't he?"

"Hope so." I gave him a wan smile, fixed my destination and my shield in place, and

walked back in a flash of light.

I stepped back into my kitchen, pizza boxes strewn about, my friends standing where I'd

left them less than a second ago.

"That was fast," Gabe said.

I smiled at him and waggled my fingers. "Time magic."

He pulled me into him, and I wrapped my arms around him.

Megan reached forward and grabbed my arm. "What did he say?"

"If all went well, he's been here for an hour preparing a trap. Gabe, Mr. Mittens and I are heading out. You should stay, lock yourself in the attic. I think I left it open forever ago."

She scoffed. "Hell, no." She pulled two of Dana's magic balls from her pocket. "While you were getting pampered at queen class, and then languishing in prison, Mr. Mittens has been helping your grandfather's master at arms train me to be a badass." She activated one of the balls, and a seven-foot-long spear appeared in her hands.

"No way you could keep that from me," I said, incredulously. I pulled away from Gabe and put my hands on my hips. I stared at my cat, pointing an accusatory finger at him. "You either."

"There were hints; you just didn't pick up on it. I was gonna surprise you." She paused, held out her arm without the spear, waved a jazz hand, and said, "Surprise…"

I sighed and looked at my cat.

I'm a cat. If I wish to keep a secret, no one will ever know it, Mr. Mittens remarked smugly.

I rolled my eyes. "How much of a badass are you?" I asked Megan.

"Well, I had almost two months of training, so…I know where the pointy end goes," she said with a shrug. "I also have this." She whispered something and activated the other ball, and a shield appeared in her hand. "This one is handy because it protects me all the way around. Magical shield, baby!"

I squinted at her. "What were your activation words?"

"Why? You gonna take my magic balls away?" she asked with an edge of suspicion.

"No, because I swear you just said, 'It's just a flesh wound?'" I said.

She smirked. "You got it in one."

I rolled my eyes. "What was the one for the shield? Still from the Holy Grail?"

"Maybe…" She looked away.

I sighed again and waved my hand, letting her keep her secrets. I wasn't keeping her out of the fight. Frankly, she now had a lot more fighting experience than I did, and I'd never be able to convince her to hang back.

"Gabe, do you have a weapon?" I asked.

He looked at me funny. "No, I am a weapon."

I remembered he'd told me the other side to being a magical healer, but I didn't know how it worked. He could give life force and fill a well of power, but he could take it away as well. I hoped he didn't have to touch anyone to do that, or he would be vulnerable.

I was scared—terrified even—that I would be sending my friends to their deaths, but I couldn't stop them. How did my life end up like this? Why did I drag those I loved the most into this mess? I twisted my focus ring on my finger—a nervous habit I'd developed when I was married to Evan. I dropped my hands. This wasn't the same. Unlike Evan's bullshit, this was real and had hard and lasting consequences to others besides me. I took a deep breath and centered myself. Game face.

"Fine. I'm gonna wrap us all in shadow for camouflage, and we're heading to the field where Mr. Mittens said they were fighting. Meg, it's the field by the dairy. Remember how to get there in case we get separated?"

"Yup."

I'll transform outside, then wrap me in shadow, Mr. Mittens said.

"Ok, here we go." We walked out so Mr. Mittens could shift. Once he was in his Splintercat form, I reached my hand out for Gabe, since he wouldn't see me once we were camouflaged. Megan, whose hands were full, was partnering with Mr. Mittens. He would stay close so he could touch and guide her. He always knew where *I* was. Gabe grasped my hand. I wrapped the four of us in shadow, and we headed out to stop the evil witch.

I was a little premature with the camouflage because I had to renew it right before we arrived at the field. But in my defense, I was super nervous and terrified.

Gabe kept tight hold of my hand, and Mr. Mittens made sure he rubbed against me. He always seemed to forget his size while in Splintercat form, and I rocked against Gabe's side. He steadied me, physically, so I didn't fall over, and emotionally as his presence centered me. We were finally together. I wouldn't let a witch or something else separate us again.

The field had been brush-hogged. So, the grass was short, and the weeds and blackberry bushes were gone. In the spring, I'd have it tilled, fertilized, and planted with a hay mix of grasses for my herbivore clients—if we survived. And for those that weren't, the grass would feed the stock I'd use for their eating pleasure. There were several fields that the fences had recently been removed from, and that's where Sofia had placed her army to prepare them for the attack on my house. I hoped she was surprised we found her out before she reached it.

Goch and Brightfeather were busy harassing the troops. Goch's fire was keeping them held down, which was good, and I hoped he wasn't getting injured from the spears and arrows being shot at him. Brightfeather was cannier about her attacks, and being naturally camouflaged under the color of the usually grey sky helped her avoid being wounded.

I so wanted to send them off to keep them from getting hurt. But I knew they wouldn't stop. They took their gratitude to me and their friendship to the limits. My heart swelled with love for them, and my eyes filled with tears. The best thing I could do was send in help to relieve them.

I sent the pre-arranged signal to my grandfather telepathically, hoping he was really here and ready with his ambush. There was one terrifying second while I waited for a reply. If he wasn't here, we were screwed and everyone I loved would die. My heart fluttered in my chest, and I held my breath.

It didn't come in my mind as I expected, but suddenly, I heard the pounding of hooves, and from the copse of trees to our left, a group of about twenty *Baincapall* warriors burst out and gallop toward Sofia and her army.

I wanted to cheer, but that would defeat the purpose of being cloaked. Grandfather, Dana, Gabe, and I were the magical backup. We needed to keep that element of surprise.

A shout went up from Sofia's army, and I saw her swamp lord barking out orders. I knew it was him because he shot a magical blast of fire at my dragon. Foolish, dragons were most definitely fireproof. Goch responded with a massive blast of dragon fire, and swamp lord ducked down and cowered. Sofia threw up a shield of ice. It melted in the wake of the dragon fire, and I wanted to laugh.

That's the moment they noticed the king's Scáthanna, their troops turning and rushing to meet them. I sent a mental call to Goch and Brightfeather to move to the opposite side and try to drive the enemy towards the first wave of our attackers.

We were close enough now that a stray magical attack almost hit us, and I figured it was time to do our part.

"Ready, Gabe?" I whispered.

"Ready."

"Mr. Mittens and Megan are you ready?"

"Yup."

Yes.

I sent my grandfather a telepathic, "*We're in position.*"

This was better than walkie talkies.

When I give the signal, hit them with lightning, was the reply.

"Ok, Gabe," I whispered. "We're about to be up."

He squeezed my hand in acknowledgement.

The signal came, and using my left hand, I sent a lightning bolt into the mass of the enemy. Our shadow camouflage fell, and we were in the battle.

Mr. Mittens charged in and started annihilating Fae warriors. His claws and teeth were a blur, and soon he was surrounded in a mist of red as heads rolled and bodies stacked up around him. He reminded me a little of the Tasmanian Devil in the Bugs Bunny cartoons—only the R-rated version. A whirling dervish of death.

Megan made herself our protector as we used our magic to fight. I engaged a soldier close to me. I smacked him with a blast a fire, and he fell, screaming to the ground, roasting in his silvery armor. Megan skewered another I hadn't seen to my left.

Gabe had to be close—at least two feet—it appeared, but once he was near, soldiers left and right dropped courtesy of his death gift. It took a few seconds for each non-magical soldier to succumb. Probably because his gift worked by draining the well of life force. Since he was the most vulnerable, Megan and I stayed close and tried to keep him protected. I watched as Megan blocked with her shield or cut soldiers down with her spear. She *was* a badass.

Soon, I couldn't tell what was happening or who was winning the day. It was a mess of troops, *Baincapall*, magic, and magical creatures. I threw out fire and lightning at anyone I didn't recognize and tried to keep Gabe protected on one side, while Megan took the other. Luckily, he could heal himself and Megan if the wounds weren't grievous, and they both picked up many of those.

I caught a glimpse of my grandfather once, being taller than most and savage. He hacked with his ax and threw magic with his off hand. It was amazing to see him in action. I had no doubt why he was the king's Pendragon. I hadn't seen Dana yet, but my attention had to remain focused.

I don't know how long the battle went on, but eventually, I caught a glimpse of Sofia. In the murky darkness, lit only by magic and torches, she looked harder than she had before Faerie and fiercer. Her hair was braided back, and she was dressed in armor and held a spear not unlike Megan's. Our eyes met.

She saw me. She pointed the spear at me and screamed, "You!" She ran towards me. Or tried to. We both fought through the crowds to meet. I threw spells right and left. I caught Sofia from the corner of my eye flinging her spear at a *Baincapall*; the warrior snatched it from the air and used it against another foe. Sofia screamed her rage.

Her real spear gone; Sofia formed an ice spear as she drew within throwing range of me. I reached into the earth and drew up a barrier just as she flung it. The earth caught it, and I yanked it down deep under the ground. She screeched and launched her ice darts at me. I met them with fire. She was stronger. Much stronger. Faerie had been good to her magic. But she forgot one thing, it had also been good to mine.

My fire melted them easily, and she frowned. She formed another ice spear and jabbed it at me. I melted it away.

"How are you doing this!" she bellowed at me.

"I'm no longer the beginner you've been taking advantage of. I'm Fae." I sent the lightning at her. She jumped back and stumbled. But she pulled up an ice shield in time. I blasted it over and over until it disintegrated, and for the first time, I saw fear in her eyes. She called a name, and the swamp lord joined her.

He was a Fae lord, so he had to be strong in magic. However, I had it from the entire gossipy court of the high king's servants, that no one was stronger in magic than my grandfather and by extension, me. Since my grandfather was busy kicking the swamp lord's army into dust, I figured I could take down the bastard myself. Sofia scrambled behind him, probably to take a breather.

He smiled like I was foolish to stand before him. He let his fire loose.

It was a lot. The fire streamed at me, the heat flushing my skin and singing my hair. I gasped, the air almost too hot to breathe. I had fire, too. Fire, water, earth, and lightning, and I'd trained myself to hold two ready in my mind. I blocked his fire with earth and slammed a lightning bolt at him.

It crackled and flashed as it struck him. He flew back ten feet and skidded on the churned ground. Now, he looked the part of swamp lord —mud covered and slimy. His armor must have protected him from the bolt because he sprang up quickly. Sofia and Swampy fired attack after attack at me. Gabe had disappeared from my side, and I couldn't stop long enough to check on him. I hoped he was alright.

I did catch Megan out of the corner of my eye. If we'd had armor for her to wear, she'd have looked as fierce as a Valkyrie. She lunged, thrust, and blocked with her spear. When she needed to, she manifested her shield and blocked. She was truly a badass. Her weeks of training coupled with years of rage from working for Evan was doing her well. She screamed at another opponent, and I almost turned to see if she was hurt, when I heard her yell, "I fart in your general direction."

I turned to block another ice spear and saw Megan smack down a sword attack with her shield. I grinned. Monty Python to the rescue.

Fire, ice, block, attack, lightning, water, fire—exchange after magical exchange until my arms were so tired from casting that they ached, and my blows started to miss in random directions. Since there were two of them, they were still relatively fresh, and I realized I was in trouble. The returning blows were coming faster and striking closer. I backpedaled.

The next blast of fire nearly singed my eyebrows off, and I almost sobbed in fear. I could barely lift my arms to respond. That's when I saw Gabe reach out to Sofia.

She stumbled, and I whirled to him.

"Watch out!" I yelled.

Gabe's face was grim, but he didn't move; he didn't stop. I wasn't going to be in time for her next blast of magic. I gritted my teeth, reached down deep and threw the strongest lightning bolt I could muster at the swamp lord. He collapsed, twitching. I gathered up all of my strength and ran at Sofia.

Her face was distorted with hate and rage. She was hideous, her black heart and soul finally showing on her usually perfectly made-up face now streaked with mud and blood.

Gabe was attempting to empty her well, but it must have been deep and filled to the brim, because he was struggling. He had to stop her before she finished him, and I didn't think he was going to make it. She raised her hands, and I could feel the air temperature drop as she reached for the ice magic. She moved them forward. I wasn't going to get there in time. I sobbed, and threw fire at her, Nothing. The magic she built shielded her. I tried lightning. It arced away. I screamed in frustration and threw myself at her.

I'd never been sporty in my youth, but I'd watched plenty of football in high school, so I knew what a tackle looked like. She launched her ice attack at Gabe just as I struck her legs, knocking them out from under her. She fell on me, and I grabbed her arm to hold her down. I couldn't see Gabe, so I didn't know if she'd hit him with her spell.

Sofia was thin. All those unhappy food choices made for one skinny bitch. I wasn't that large, but I ate, and I had all that carb energy from the pizza. Even though I wanted to vomit it up now, I rolled over her and held her arms in the mud—pinning her torso under my thighs. I could feel my own ice magic building up in her as she attempted to use it against me. But, she made one tiny mistake. It *wasn't* hers.

With the skin to skin contact of my hands on her bare arms, the power called to me, just like the pieces of jewelry. I opened myself to it, and in a flash, it left her and sank into my skin. Her face sunk slightly, giving her gaunt look, and fine lines appeared where she'd had none before. I bared my teeth at her.

She screamed in rage, "Die you Fae bitch!"

This time, she blasted me off with a witch spell. I landed on my back next to Gabe. I reached out a hand to touch him. He was cold.

"No, no, no!" I scrambled over to him and looked into his face. His eyes flicked to mine.

"I'm OK, Bridge, she stunned me, but I'm good." He struggled to sit up, and I gave a sob of relief.

He shivered. "She hit me with a glancing blow."

"Your skin is cold, I was afraid..."

We didn't have time to talk; swamp boy was back up and angry. He sent another blast of fire at us. This time, I was tired, and I did something I didn't think to do before. I had the ground swallow him. I had no idea if he had a defense against that, but I figured if he did it would give us a minute at least.

Sofia threw one more spell our way and took off running towards her army and the relative safety of her allies.

I had to end this. I had to end it now. I couldn't go through life looking over my shoulder. I couldn't let her escape to Faerie to worry my family there. She was done.

I stood, wobbly, and unsteady. Gabe reached out and steadied me. I could feel the magic all around me and in me, but I was nearing the end of my endurance. I focused all my will through my focus ring and wished Sofia back here. My cat had told me once that my inherent magic could call things to me. I just had to be careful that no one saw, and that the thing existed. Frankly, I didn't care if anyone saw. Sofia flew off her feet and sailed through the air. She splashed down at my feet.

I debated having the earth swallow her as well, but that wasn't her fate.

"Mr. Mittens!" I bellowed.

Sofia's eyes flew open wide. With her well partially drained and her Fae magic gone, she had nothing to fight with. She tried to scramble away. I heard the rumble of my cat's growl and caught him galloping towards us out of the corner of my eye. He was drenched in blood, although I couldn't see any visible wounds. He looked fierce and terrifying, and I shivered. Unlike his Ragdoll grumpy face, he almost looked happy. It was probably his huge fangs hanging below his jaw. Mud and blood were blocking his spots and usual glow, but his large body rippled with muscles as he trotted up to my side.

You rang? he said, his eyes alight with glee.

I might have let a little nervous giggle escape. My cat loved a battle.

Brigid, a mental call reached me from my grandfather.

Before I answered him, I addressed my cat. "I saved you a little something."

Sofia finally got her feet under her and started to run.

Thank you, pet. I love a good snack after a battle.

His bobbed tail twitched once, and he crouched down. Then he launched himself in a huge Splintercat flying leap. His front feet hit her in the back, and she splayed forward in the mud. I turned away just as his teeth grasped the back of her neck, and he picked her up like a doll and shook her. The crunch of her bones echoed in my mind. I shivered and felt ill.

I couldn't bear to watch my cat eat a person, even one as deserving as Sofia. I turned around and reached for Gabe's hand. *Yes, grandfather?* I replied.

"You have won the day." He strolled out of the woods on my other side, and I smiled at him. Dana and the *Baincapall* wandered through the remains of Sofia's army, those still alive were bowed in submission and being cuffed for transport back to Faerie.

My grandfather, like my cat, was covered in blood and gore. But he looked happy, refreshed even.

"I appreciate the help," I said to him.

He threw back his head and guffawed. "You saved me the trouble of mopping up this pathetic rebellion back on Faerie. I should be thanking you. I'll make sure the king knows you took care of his problem as well."

"Is everyone OK?" I asked, afraid that I'd been the cause of casualties on his side.

"An acceptable amount for a battle this size. Don't worry. It would have been worse on Faerie with the extra magic available there."

I obviously didn't have the same values, but if he wasn't angry about it, I'd let him deal with the fallout. I had to deal with the same here.

"We've already started *transporting* the prisoners back. We should be off your world in a few hours." He took a deep breath and looked around. "The magic is thicker here. It is almost bearable." He smiled at me.

"Do you have to go? You could come clean up back at the house and see what I've done to the place." He looked towards the house, although it couldn't be seen from here. "I will, soon. I promise you."

I understood, he was in charge and had his people to take care of.

"OK, I'll hold you to it," I said.

He reached out and hugged me. Both of us were filthy, but it didn't matter.

"I'm grateful for you, Grandfather."

"You are my child. I'll always be here for you," he said and then turned and walked off, barking out orders and directing his troops.

I looked for Megan and Gabe. They joined me as did Mr. Mittens. The wolves hadn't even made it to the final battle. I was sure they'd be disappointed. I smiled at my friends, and we shared muddy, bloody hugs. "It's over," I said.

It was glorious, pet, Mr. Mittens added.

TWENTY-ONE

I stood in the grand entry and gazed up at the tree. I'd bought the largest one I could find at the lot. I guess I could have cut one down from my own property, but that would have required a whole different crew than having the people from the tree lot bring it in and set it up for me. The ceiling in this part of the house was twenty feet tall. The tree was sixteen.

I didn't know what I was thinking. How was I going to decorate this beast? I didn't own a ladder this tall. Well, I had magic. I'm sure it would make a difference when we had to put the star on top.

I had a small scar now on the top of my left arm, and I rubbed it through my shirt thoughtfully as I admired the tree. After the battle, Gabe had healed our cuts and scrapes. My grandfather had returned to Faerie with his prisoners. The wolves showed up when we were cleaning up, disappointed they hadn't been in the battle. I hadn't wanted to kill anyone, except Sofia, but after the battle ended, I realized that Swampy hadn't clawed his way out of the ground. I'd felt bad about that for a while. I'd seriously thought he'd pop back up in a minute or two, but I guess he wasn't that strong of a magic user.

No one else felt bad about me ending him; he had tried to kill me and had planned to kill the king as well. I didn't think he needed to die for being delusional, but he did try to kill me and my friends, which was rude. We didn't even know him.

It didn't matter anymore. Sofia was gone, and the witches were handled. I turned away from the tree, the thrill of seeing it up zinged through me one more time. I smiled. Megan was practically vibrating with excitement, and even Mr. Mittens looked less grumpy. I looked down at him, sitting by my side as he gazed at the glorious noble fir.

We were going to have a party this weekend. Sort of a combination Christmas party and opening of the bed-and-breakfast. The house was finished, and everything was ready for visitors. The only scary thing was the type of guests we'd get...if we got any. We'd been working on subtly advertising to the supernatural community, and it wasn't easy.

"Did you buy enough ornaments?" Megan asked, eyeing the height and breadth of the enormously full tree.

"Umm, I'm not sure, now," I sighed. "We can do the visible parts and leave the back bare, then we'll be OK," I finished weakly.

"Yeah, that'll work. Did you finish that light spell?"

"I think so. It should work. I'll just have to renew it weekly."

She looked at me.

I looked behind me. "What?"

"Well, do it," she demanded.

I snorted. "Fine." I used my focusing ring and concentrated on creating little bits of light to cover the tree with. *Magical* twinkle lights. I figured they'd be easier than wrapping the entire behemoth in wire. I finished the creation and cast the light into the tree. It flashed brightly for a second, and all of us looked away. It subsided until the tree was afire with a multitude of tiny white lights. It was stunning.

"Whoa," Megan commented.

I nodded. It worked better than I'd hoped.

What is the purpose of the tree in the house, again? Mr. Mittens's surly mental voice interrupted my moment.

"It's traditional. A symbol of the season."

Hmpf. It is strange. There are trees outside. If you want to enjoy them, you simply can glance out the window or walk outside. He sat heavily and looked at me. His head cocked slightly as though he really were trying to figure it out. *Humans are strange*.

"I know you've seen Christmas trees before," I answered.

Hmpf. He picked up a large paw and groomed it, dismissing me. I rolled my eyes at him.

I looked back at the tree. The ornaments were supposed to be delivered tomorrow. That would give us two days to get the tree and the house decorated for the party. I sighed. I had a lot of work ahead of me. Too bad magic couldn't do everything.

I checked my phone for the time. Gabe would be here soon. My stomach fluttered, and I gave a little gasp of air. He was picking me up for a date. A real one. Now that we didn't have Sofia and her witch coven machinations hanging over us, this would feel *real*—a brand new start.

Megan threw me a knowing look. "Go do your finishing touches, I'll feed the cat."

Mr. Mittens's face grew grumpier. *Human, don't forget my food is in the second drawer of the refrigerator. The halibut will be adequate.*

Megan glared at him. "If I don't strangle him first."

Hmpf. He strolled towards the kitchen, his floofy tail erect, a little sway to the tip of his tail and a slight glow to his fur.

I gave a flourish and bow to Megan. "Go serve your cat master with the proper deference he demands," I said in a bad English accent.

She groaned, threw her head back, raised her hands to the heavens in a fake plea of supplication, and then followed him.

"Cats," I muttered as I turned and headed to my bathroom for the final touches, as Megan had called them, to my hair and makeup and to pull on my date clothes. I was happy. My date wouldn't care that my new style consisted of jeans and long-sleeved t-shirts. That in itself was a breath of fresh air. So, I pulled on my best fitted jeans and the nicest t-shirt I owned. It was blue to bring out my eyes, and I paired it with puffy warm vest since it was cold outside.

I brushed my hair with one of those Fae brushes that smoothed the frizz. Then, I freshened up my mascara. I looked...happy. I hadn't seen this side of myself for a long time. It brightened my face, made me look younger than my forty-two years, and filled my heart with contentment.

Things were good. The Inn would open after the beginning of the year. My people were safe. My grandfather promised to come visit, and Gabe was back in my life after a twenty-four-year absence—my first love. Plus, Christmas was in a few days, and I was excited to give gifts to my friends and family. Something I hadn't put my heart into for years.

The doorbell rang. I grinned at the formality. Gabe was welcome to walk in at any time, and he knew it. Hell, he'd just moved back out less than a month ago. Once the threat Sofia had represented was gone, he thought it would be best for our very new relationship if he went back home to his house.

I grabbed my coat and opened the door. "Ready," I said and smiled up at him.

He held out his arm, and I grabbed his elbow. He opened the car door for me, and I climbed in.

"Where to, oh gallant one?" I asked once he sat down and pulled on his seatbelt.

He smiled and winked at me. "It's a small town, Bridge, it's not like we have a lot of choices, but for you, nothing but the best."

"Pirate's Cove, then?"

"Right as usual!"

"Yay! I was in the mood for some dungies!" I said.

"I felt that," he laughed.

I narrowed my eyes and looked at his body language. "You played me!" I said. "You didn't plan anything."

"Not true, I planned on eating *somewhere* with you."

I slapped him lightly on the shoulder. "I guess it beats the 'Where should we go?' game."

"True. Just hint around that you are prepared, and let the lady accidentally choose. Works for me." His mischievous grin lit up the car or maybe just my heart.

We drove the twenty minutes or so to Garibaldi and actually found parking in the tiny lot next to the waterside restaurant. I loved it here.

Gabe got us a table next to the windows, and although it was getting dark quickly, we enjoyed the last of the sun over Tillamook Bay. Dinner was nice, and the conversation and laughter was lovely, too.

When we returned to the house, I found that making out in the car like a teenager was even better. Either I had to go in or invite him in, but we'd decided we wanted to take this slow. We'd both been burned by our exes and needed to do this right—*know* it was right.

So, I let him open the door for me and then kissed him some more against the car. Eventually, I made it through the door of my house after I waved goodbye to him.

Mr. Mittens greeted me at the door, meowed like a normal house cat, and rubbed against my legs.

"How was your evening, Mr. Mittens?" I asked as I bent to pet him. *Dull, at first, until there was an incursion.*

"I thought we were done with those?" I asked, curiously.

You are still missing a piece of magic. They won't slow down until you have incorporated your last piece, he said. I vaguely remember him telling me something like this before. I guess I should pay more attention to the tidbits of info he deigned to throw me.

The house was dark, so Megan must have gone to bed. The only lights were the ones I'd covered the tree with. It was beautiful and peaceful. I'd placed a bench in the entryway for taking off and putting on shoes. I sat down on it and stared up at the glorious tree. Mr. Mittens jumped up and climbed in my lap, flopping over so I could scratch his belly.

His eyes closed, and his purr filled the space. This was peace and contentment.

"Tell me about the incursion?" I asked.

He continued to purr. *Nasty creature.* He paused. *Do you want the highlights, or the whole story?*

I looked down. I usually only wanted the highlights, which wasn't always fair. I'd discovered my cat had a flair for storytelling. Since I was comfortable and in a good mood I said, "The full story, please."

One periwinkle eye opened and gazed at me. *As you wish.*

I was doing my rounds. Checking out the boundary. Before you bought the original land back, I was pretty cramped here on just two hundred acres. I sometimes roam it all if I'm not needed here.

I scratched his head. "Sorry, my friend. I didn't know."

Hmpf. He gave his usual sound that meant a whole range of things and covered a bunch of emotions. He rolled to his side so I could scratch his ear.

I heard an owl call and flicked an ear at it. Was it the Lechuza I'd been hunting? It often took the shape of an owl.

I interrupted him again, and he sighed. "What's a Lechuza?"

I got an annoyed single eye look again, and another "hmpf."

If you listen, I will explain in the narrative, he said somewhat imperiously.

"OK, carry on."

I hid under some brush and watched. The owl glided silently past me, searching the ground. No, it was a regular old barn owl. I came out and started my patrol again.

He gave me a blue-eyed gaze to check if I were going to interrupt. I smiled and made the zip lips throw away key gesture.

A passing scent caught my attention. I sniffed; mouth open to catch more. Yes. The Lechuza was near. I drifted into the shadows, everything hidden but one eye. A massive owl, dark feathered and red eyed, fluttered down to the ground. It picked something up. I couldn't tell what she'd taken. I waited. The owl shifted into a woman, old and dressed all in dark clothing with long, dark, snarled hair. She put the object into a pocket and started to shift back. I leaped out and landed on the woman just as she completed her owl form.

"What happened to speak before you kill?" I interrupted him.

He huffed. *Some creatures are too dangerous. Now listen.*

"Ok, sorry, continue."

I crunched the bird's neck bones with my teeth, killing it, then to make sure it couldn't regenerate, I continued through until the head was severed. I picked up the head, carried it several yards away, dug a hole, and buried it. The Lechuza could not regenerate from that. I brought you back the body. I figured you might like to try owl.

He threw me a questioning glance. I had to suppress a shudder. It wasn't an owl; it was a shapeshifter! I'd attempt to cook an actual owl. I'd have to fake it and throw it out, so I didn't hurt his feelings. "Sure, thanks," I mumbled. "Uh, where is it?"

The usual spot, he said smugly.

So, back door. I always waited until he wasn't around to dispose of his "gifts."

"What did she put in her pocket? Did you check?" I asked.

I do not know. What use do I have for things I can't eat? he asked.

Well, that made sense. I mean he did have use for his bowls and apparently my bed. But he didn't have anywhere to put things or carry things about. I guess I could get him a fancy collar if he wished for something of his own.

"Do you want something of your own?" I asked. "I can find a space for you that would be just yours if you want something. I could get you a fancy collar or a special toy?"

Hmpf. I have the entire house to store items. I just have no need of things.

He was a cat; it only stood to reason he considered the house his. In a way, that made sense. He'd lived in it for close to a hundred and fifty years; it was more his than mine by that old tenant "possession is nine-tenths of the law."

"This is so gonna ruin your Christmas surprise," I said.

You got me a gift? he asked. His cranked his head back to look at me, and his eyes wide with surprise.

"Of course I did. You are my best friend. I love you, Mr. Mittens." I stroked his fur, and he purred louder.

Suddenly, he jumped up and ran towards the kitchen. I sighed. He probably sensed another incursion, and my peaceful night was over.

I stood up slowly and wandered to the tree. I should take the gifts I'd wrapped and throw them under it to give it more of a Christmas feel. I went to my closet and started pulling out gifts and placing them under the tree. It took a few trips, but eventually, I stood back to admire the bright packages and shiny bows. Even though the tree was undecorated, the gifts made the whole scene more festive. I sat back on the bench to admire it.

I heard Mr. Mittens making cat sounds as he trotted back in. He had something glinting in his mouth. He jumped up on the bench and dropped something in my lap.

This is for you—the Lechuza's item from her pocket. It's shiny; you might like it. His eyes glowed with excitement as he looked up at me. I had no idea where an owl hid its pockets, and I didn't ask. He probably shredded the whole thing, and I'd be sweeping up feathers for a week. I shook out the negative thoughts and determined I would love whatever shiny dirt covered item it was. I looked down at my lap and gasped.

It was dirty, but it was also a silver chain with little swirly charms hanging at regular intervals around it. It *had* to be!

I looked at my beloved cat. "Thank you Mr. Mittens, this is the best gift ever."

I picked up the chain and slipped it over my head. I let it drop down inside my shirt, so it touched my skin. There was a little zing, a flash, and the necklace disappeared into my body.

Mr. Mittens sat down hard. *I didn't know what it was*, he said, surprised.

A cold breeze ran past me, and my hair whipped around my face for a few moments before it stopped. I felt complete. "You found it! The last splinter of my magic." I jumped up and gave a twirl. Then I picked him up and draped his limp body over my shoulder. We danced a few steps together. "You are the best cat that ever lived," I gushed.

I put him down when he started to wriggle. "Don't move, I want you to have your gift, too, even if you don't really need it."

I knelt under the tree and dug around for the large package I'd wrapped for him. I pulled it free and sat it down beside him.

What do I do with that? he asked.

"You open it."

He walked around, looking at the package. *I don't know how the item opens,* he said, confused.

I laughed. "You rip off the paper, it'll be fun."

He wiggled his butt and leapt into the middle, ripping and tearing into the paper with gusto. Frankly, that looked like more fun than the gift would be.

When he'd destroyed all the paper, I pulled the remainder off the gift.

What is it? he asked.

I picked it up and gave it a shake. "Come with me."

I walked into my bedroom and stood in the middle of the room next to the bed. "It's your very own, premium, memory foam bed."

I watched his reaction.

Really? Just for me?

"Yes, now choose where you want it to go," I said.

I should have guessed where that would be. I should have just chosen a spot on the floor. But it was Christmas, and it was his gift.

He jumped up. *Right here*, he said, his eyes glowing with excitement and happiness.

That's the whole story of how my lovely, king-sized bed gained a custom, memory foam, periwinkle blue, cat bed smack dab in the middle of it.

I sighed a little and looked indulgently at him as he rolled around in the new bed, relaxed, all four feet in the air.

Cats.

The end.

PLEASE REVIEW SPLINTERED MAGIC OMNIBUS

Wow!

You finished the book. Thanks for reading it. I appreciate it! Please, please, please consider leaving an honest review. Love it or hate it, authors can only sell books if they get reviews. If I don't sell books, I can't afford cat food. If I can't buy cat food, the little bastards will scavenge my sad, broken body. Then there will be no more books. Look at their terrifying, savage, little faces. They have sunken cheeks and swollen tummies and can't wait to eat me.

Please help by leaving that review!

PLEASE REVIEW SPLINTERED MAGIC OMNIBUS

* * *

SPLINTERED HAVEN

SPLINTERED MAGIC SERIES BOOK FOUR

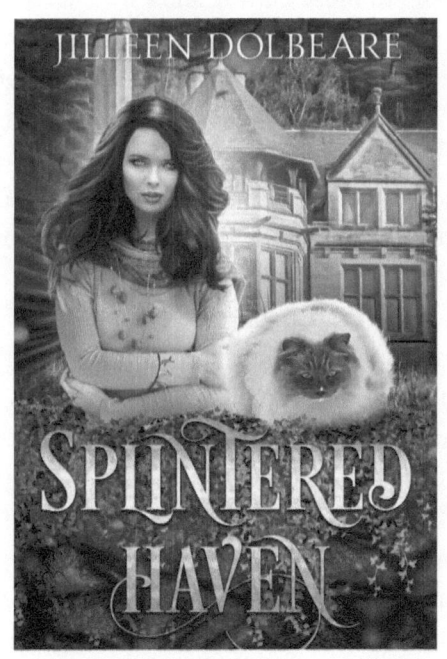

NOTE: This is an unproofed sample.

CHAPTER 1

"Megan, can't you get them to move faster?" I yelled. The rain had soaked through my hair, my jeans, and was running down my back.

"Maybe if you got me a horse, I'd be a proper cowgirl," she replied. Waving her hands and running back to stop a cow from veering away from the gate.

"Have you ever ridden a horse?" I asked, huffing and puffing. I knew full well she hadn't.

"No, but you could teach me."

I was on the opposite side of our chosen five steers, trying to get them into the enclosure.

"I ride dressage. I don't know many dressage people who herd cattle on their off days."

"You loved going to those cutting shows," she replied.

"That doesn't mean I know how to herd cows, now push them this way." I waved my arms like a dumbass, yelling weird sounds at the small herd.

I looked back at Megan just in time to see her feet fly up and land flat on her back in the mud and shit. I'm a terrible friend, because instead of running over to help her up, I burst out laughing. The double-up kind.

Once she got her breath back, she let out a string of curses that even a sailor would blush at. I pushed the last cow through the gate, closed it, and went to help her up.

"I'm just gonna die here. If I move, I'll be too grossed out to walk back to the house, just leave me to my cold, disgusting death," she muttered.

"No, you'll just have to gut it up. I still need help holding them while I shave them," I answered.

"Just shoot me." She gave a very dramatic moan. "I'm ready to go."

I laughed and offered her a hand. "No, you aren't. I'll hose you off when we get back, you'll live, cowgirl."

She reached out a hand. "Why are we doing this again? Don't we have people that can do this?"

"Uh, no. Jim is off tonight. We're doing this because our client doesn't like fur in his fangs." I pulled. We both slipped this time. I let go to catch my balance, and this time she fell forward into the muck.

"I'm getting a new best friend," she said after she picked herself up. She tried to wipe some of the muck off of her, but it made little difference.

I couldn't stop laughing. She threw a handful of mud at me.

"Hey, I can't fight back, I have to keep this hand clean to use the clippers." I held out my right hand. It was only sort of muddy. I wiped it down my pants and held it out again.

"Fine. Let's get this over with. I need time to pack up and move to Australia."

I opened the gate and closed it behind us.

"Which one do you want to shave first?" I asked Megan. I figured her sacrifice earned her first choice.

"That one. How do I hold it still?" she asked.

I hadn't thought that through. I wondered if I should have invested in cow halters, but it was too late now. "Um, just stand there so it won't veer away."

"Fine." She stood on the cow's left shoulder, and I pulled out the clippers and shaved a foot wide spot near its large vein.

"That was easy," I said.

"Yeah, this won't be too bad," she agreed.

We went to the next one. It was also placid and let us shave it without any issue. I relaxed.

The third cow wanted nothing to do with us. It bellowed and charged Megan. She jumped out of the way. It ran to the corner of the enclosure.

"How many do we need to shave?" she asked. "I'm thinking two is great."

"I told him we'd have five cows ready," I said.

"What about the sheep? Sheep seem easier, and smaller. Lots smaller."

I sighed. "He said wool was the worst thing to get caught in your fangs. It takes forever to get out, and he wouldn't even hear of it even if I shaved them."

"Argh!" She threw up her hands. "Fine, let's go to the next one."

It took us three hours. Three. I was thinking of charging extra, but it was my fault for trying to be all inclusive and not asking up front for species or magical type. Now, I had to create a completely blacked out room, and supply blood. Hopefully, he could chase his own cows down now that they were shaved and returned to the pasture. I wasn't doing one more thing with cows—ever again.

When we got back to the house, we both needed to be hosed down. Megan was the worst, since she'd rolled in the muck, but I was barely better. While we'd chased cows in the corral, they managed to splash us with everything. I mean everything. I was covered in stuff I didn't want to think about. I hosed Megan off first, then she took pleasure in the repeat. It was ice cold, but we were already cold and wet. It was January in the temperate rainforest, and forty degrees Fahrenheit with rain was a typical winter. We stripped to our underwear on the porch, and I took our clothes directly to the laundry room and tossed them in the washer. Then we both headed to our respective showers.

Tomorrow was the grand opening of my B&B. So, this was our last night of privacy. I was scared and excited. I was inviting strange magical beings into my house. I already knew I had a vampire, since he had special requirements. I didn't know what the others were. I was already regretting that choice and considering changing it. Unfortunately, I was stuck with this group. I set my alarm for bright and early.

*

I'd set up a reception desk in the front foyer. We'd taken down the tree a few days before, and the house felt empty. The desk had a computer, and a machine for key cards, along with the main phone line. The first guest was checking in at noon, so I had time to go through the rooms for last minute inspections. My cleaning crew had done a great job, and everything looked amazing.

I'd even hired a cook for meals, and I could smell breakfast cooking. He'd started today. Megan had found him on one of the supernatural only sites she'd found and started advertising on. Megan said he was a shifter, but we didn't know what kind. That seemed invasive since he hadn't offered to tell us.

I rechecked the room we'd blacked out for the vampire. He'd been very specific in his needs, as I would be too if I were severely allergic to sunlight. At least on the Oregon coast, sunlight was a rare happening this time of year.

We had three other guest rooms that were being rented at the same time, three days for two of them and five days for the other two. I was nervous, excited, and scared to see how everything would go. I didn't need the money, but it would be glorious if the new business could support itself and pay my new staff.

After this week, I also had a couple of supernatural creatures coming to stay in the stables and hunt in my woods. We'd stocked cattle, sheep, and goats for easy access to food, and would allow a deer and an elk to be hunted in the woods. Mr. Mittens would supervise those hunts.

Since I had a dragon to feed, we needed to keep the prey levels up and at healthy numbers, although Mr. Mittens was currently teaching him to realm walk so, he could hunt for himself on other worlds.

When I came down the stairs from checking on the rooms, Megan was on the phone.

"Yes, that is completely fine. We do allow small pets as long as they are in a carrier or on a leash when they aren't in your room. That's for their safety. We do not guarantee the safety of pets." There was a pause while she listened. "This is a private bed and breakfast, not a large chain, those are the rules." Another pause, I was close enough now to hear a tinny voice over Megan's headset. "That's fine. Have a good day."

"What's up?" I asked, curious.

"I think that was a human. I hope I discouraged her from making a reservation."

"If she calls back just say no vacancy."

She wrote something on her message pad. "Yeah, good idea," she answered, distracted.

"Was there something else?"

She looked up. "Huh? Uh, no. I was writing down some notes and ideas on what we can add to figure out guest species and requirements. If we just do a generic, 'dietary needs' that would cover things like blood." She snorted. "I'm not chasing cows again."

"Me either, but if I'd had earlier notice, we could have had Jim do it," I remarked.

"Yeah, that is why we are making this new checklist."

"Is Madison watching the desk tonight?" I asked.

Madison Whelan was one of the Whelan werewolves. They were friends and owned a local restoration and construction business. The Whelan's had begun the restoration and transformation on my old Victorian house. They'd quit after their father had been killed by witches. Madison hadn't been into the family business and was still searching for her dream career. She filled in for them when they needed a receptionist on occasion and had applied to work as a receptionist here when I was looking for one. She said she was interested in hospitality, and since she was a friend, and was Megan's boyfriend's sister, it had been a great fit for all of us.

Plus, it wasn't easy searching for supernatural workers for a supernatural B&B. It wasn't like we could put an ad on the general internet or in the local paper. We were in the process of advertising across the splinters, as Mr. Mittens called them. Mr. Mittens was a Splintercat. A cat-like creature from another world that could shapeshift, and realm walk. When he was here with me, he was a fluffy blue-mitted Ragdoll that was more than a little ridiculous, liked to sleep in the middle of my bed, and kept my woods clear of evil, dangerous creatures who were attracted to the power that a link to the Fae realm provided my land.

Since I'd finally re-integrated all of my magic, the loose power was less, but it hadn't stopped all of the incursions. Mr. Mittens had a little more time for me, but he still made his patrols, and discouraged or killed marauders.

"Brigid!" Megan yelled.

"What?"

"Where did you go? I've been talking to you." She waved her hand in front of my face.

"Rude, I was just lost in thought, what did you say?" I asked.

"I said that Madison was on for the next three nights, then she'll do days for the next two."

"Oh, yeah, right. I forgot." I looked at my phone. We'd be having guests soon. I'd set check in at three in the afternoon, but since this was our first group of people, and everything was ready and set up, I'd allowed the first group ever to have early check in. People would be arriving at any moment. I'd had our cook make up sandwiches for lunch just in case anyone was hungry, and he was going to do a celebratory supper. I wasn't going to offer three meals in general, but I thought I would for this first day. Then, he was on call for room service, or purchased meals for lunch or dinner. Breakfast was included. I heard a car coming up the newly paved drive. My palms started to sweat. This was it!

"Here comes someone," I said to Megan, she nodded. She also looked excited and nervous. She stepped behind the desk. She was going to play receptionist, and I was playing hostess.

A couple stumbled through the door with their baggage. They looked like normal humans. He was dark haired and dark skinned; she had blonde hair with warm brown skin. I greeted them and directed them to the desk. Megan took their information and gave them their keys. We'd put them on the third floor.

"If you'll follow me, I'll show you the dining room and the elevator," I said and waved a hand for them to follow me. I stopped at the elevator on the other side of the massive staircase. "The dining room is here; I swept my hand to the door. "Or you can choose to eat in your room, just phone the kitchen with your order." This is the elevator. Turn left on your floor, thank you for staying at the Secret Haven Inn." After they entered the elevator and the door closed, I leaned against the wall and exhaled a sigh of relief.

Megan came around the staircase. We gave each other a fist bump.

"We rocked that," she said. They'll never know they were the first guests ever!"

We welcomed our two other guest groups; the vampire would be arriving after dark. The Secret Haven Inn was officially in business.

Order Splintered Haven Now!

ABOUT THE AUTHOR

 Jilleen Dolbeare is the author of the Shadow Winged Chronicles, an urban fantasy series about a shape-shifting bush pilot in Alaska. And the Splintered Magic Series, about a woman rebuilding her life and learning about magic with the help of her cat.

She loves riding horses, warm ocean beaches, and long walks in the mountains, none of which she can do in the Arctic, so she writes. Her activities are riding her four-wheeler on cold ocean beaches (often frozen or covered with ice), and long walks to and from work when it's 40 below—in the dark. She does keep her stakes sharp for those vamps that show up during the 67 days of night.

Jilleen lives with her husband and two hungry cats in Alaska where she also discovered her love and admiration of the Inupiaq people and their folklore.

Piper's Logbook

ALSO BY JILLEEN DOLBEARE

Shadow Winged Chronicles:

Shadow Lair: Book .5

Shadow Winged: Book 1

Shadow Wolf: Book 1.5

Shadow Strife: Book 2

Shadow Witch: Book 2.5

Shadow War: Book 3

Splintered Magic Series:

Splinter Cat: Book .5

Splintered Magic: Book 1

Splintered Veil: Book 2

Splintered Fate: Book 3

Splintered Haven: Book 4*

*Forthcoming

* * *

www.ingramcontent.com/pod-product-compliance
Lightning Source LLC
Chambersburg PA
CBHW031020030726
47497CB00004B/932